SOME OF MY BEST FRIENDS ARE MURDERERS

SOME OF MY BEST FRIENDS ARE MURDERERS

Critiquing *the* *Columbo* Killers

CHRIS CHAN

As usual, to my parents, Drs. Carlyle and Patricia Chan.
And to Fr. Patrick Ohl, one of the best mystery reviewers around and a fellow Columbo fan.
And also to Richard Levinson, William Link, and Peter Falk for all of the happiness they've brought me over the years.

Contents

Introduction

There's a Little Niceness in Every Murderer

> *"Even with some of the murderers I meet, I even like them, too. Sometimes. Like them and even respect them. Not for what they did. Certainly not for that. But for that part of them which is intelligent or funny or just nice. Because there's niceness in everyone. A little bit, anyhow. You can take a cop's word for it."*
> *–Lieutenant Columbo, "Try and Catch Me"*

Columbo is more than a show about murder. It's a show about relationships. Specifically, it's about the relationships that Peter Falk's immortal Lieutenant Columbo forms with the killers he investigates and nearly invariably arrests.

The series swiftly became a hit during the 1970s, was successfully revived from the late 1980s through the early 2000s, and is now a classic of crime television. Its popularity endures to the present day, especially with the show experiencing a strong resurgence in public attention during the pandemic. While the series continues to gain fans, critical analysis of the show has largely minimized the issues of character connections.

The hallmark of the *Columbo* series was the use of the inverted detective format. The identity of the killer was generally known from the outset, though a little over ten percent of the episodes shook up the pattern and actually left a level of mystery regarding the identity of the culprit.

Every episode (with one prominent exception that will be discussed at the appropriate time) was centered around Columbo's investigation of a homicide. The show followed a standard template, though there were exceptions to the rules. Most episodes introduced a character, a future victim, and explained the soon-to-be killer's motive. Usually, the villains of the story would have a clever alibi planned, or some other strategy to protect themselves from suspicion or arrest. It was Columbo's duty to keep digging, challenging the murderer's statements with perceptive questions and observations, leading to an eventual revelation of the truth and (with three prominent exceptions) the arrest of the suspect.

The heart of every episode was the interaction between Columbo and the killer (or killers). Initially, the relationship between the detective and the culprit would usually be fairly cordial, with the villain acting very helpful. Columbo would catch little holes in the perpetrator's story, often through logical observation, though sometimes seemingly through a sixth sense. He would then pepper the murderer with repeated visits and a constant barrage of questions, slowly and steadily making it clear that he believed that person to be guilty, though rarely making an explicit accusation until close to the ending.

The rapport between Columbo and the killer varied widely. Sometimes the murderer would seek to crush Columbo through influence or social position. In other cases, the criminal and the detective would actually establish a friendly bond, and the eventual arrest was accepted with grace or even relief. Some of the killers felt contempt by Columbo, while others reluctantly found themselves being charmed by the detective. Annoyance, amusement, and anxiety were also common reactions to meeting Columbo. In most cases, the killers developed varying levels of respect for the lieutenant.

This book is meant for multiple audiences. *Columbo* fans will hopefully find a great deal to interest them in these analyses of the show's villains. This study is also meant as a guide for aspiring writers, who will hopefully find the analysis of these murderers an edifying experience. One of the most difficult aspects of crafting quality crime fiction is characterization, especially the relationship between the detective and the antagonist. Hopefully, fans of *Columbo* and mysteries, in general, will find both their viewing experiences of *Columbo* and their watching and reading other mysteries enhanced by these explorations, studying why people with so much going for them would risk everything to commit a murder and how their personal flaws and mistakes would lead to their eventual downfall. As these analyses focus on the characterization of the killers and the interplay with Columbo, certain extraneous plot points will be overlooked for the sake of brevity and focus.

Whether readers of this book are longtime fans of the series who have seen every episode, or casual fans with just a passing acquaintance with the show, it is my hope that these essays help bring a deeper appreciation of the characterization that helped to elevate *Columbo* into one of the greatest crime shows–indeed, one of the greatest television series–of all time.

A Note on Sources

The central sources for this book were the actual episodes of *Columbo*, with the Internet Movie Database (www.imdb.com) providing additional information on the actors and crew. To double-check some plot points, I checked the Columbophile blog (www.columbophile.com), The Ultimate Columbo Site (www.columbo-site.freeuk.com, and The Columbo Wiki (www.columbo.fandom.com/wiki/The_Columbo_Wiki). I also consulted William Link's *The Columbo Collection*, William Link and Richard Levinson's *Shooting Script and Other Stories*, and their play *Prescription: Murder*. The excellent YouTube series "Analyzing Evil" by The Vile Eye (https://www.youtube.com/channel/UCxNlX8AUIh2nlLf4IL1DWzg) was also an inspiration for me.

I

SEASON ONE

Chapter One: Prescription: Murder

Dr. Ray Flemming (Gene Barry) and Joan Hudson (Katherine Justice)

In the first *Columbo* pilot, the detective's character is still being developed. His suit is a bit neater, his haircut is a bit sleeker, his personality edges are a bit sharper, and he allows himself to vent angrily, but he still embodies most of his classic mannerisms. "Prescription: Murder" introduces most of the show's series' hallmarks fully formed. This pilot episode begins the series' tradition of focusing on the killer's seemingly flawless plan for getting away with murder. Columbo does not appear until more than half an hour into the movie. The initial third of "Prescription: Murder" is all about Dr. Ray Flemming.[1]

When the viewer is first introduced to Dr. Flemming, he's charming his peers while playing party games. It soon becomes evident that there's one person who isn't swept off her feet by Flemming's charisma: his wife, Carol. Flemming is having an affair with one of his patients, an actress named Joan Hudson. Carol threatens her husband with an economically and socially shattering divorce, but he coaxes her, assuring her that he's committed to the marriage and then telling her that he's arranged for a romantic getaway. Carol is thrilled, and her suspicions towards her husband are totally alleviated, right up until the moment when Flemming wraps his hands around her throat and strangles her.

Flemming stages a robbery, tucking some valuables into his luggage.

When Joan arrives, his plan for the perfect alibi becomes clear: Joan is made up to look exactly like Carol, and the pair make sure to be seen at the airport together. Before the plane takes off, the pair fake a very public argument, and the disguised Joan storms away, leaving Fleming to spend the weekend alone, disposing of the supposedly stolen valuables on his fishing trip.

When Flemming returns home, he finds Lieutenant Columbo at his apartment and is flabbergasted to learn that Carol is still alive, though she is unconscious and clinging to life. When the pair arrive at the hospital, they are informed that Carol has just died, managing only to say her husband's name before expiring.

Over the course of the episode, Columbo's suspicions of Flemming grow steadily stronger as he notices countless little inconsistencies in Flemming's stories and repeatedly questions him about them. Flemming quickly realizes that Columbo suspects him and takes pleasure in avoiding Columbo's traps, obliquely, asserting that any attempts to prove his guilt will prove futile. Initially amused by Columbo, Flemming grows steadily annoyed by the detective and tries to use his influential connections to have him taken off the case and disciplined for harassment.

Columbo's not deterred, however, and he eventually determines Joan's role in the crime and tries to break her down into confessing. She withstands an initial round of harsh questioning, but the next day, Columbo calls Flemming to Joan's house, telling him that she had died from an overdose of sleeping medication. Columbo calls upon Flemming to show some decency and confess, but Flemming shows no emotion whatsoever over Joan's death save smugness and subtly implies that he arranged her death by overdosing on one of her sleeping pills. His self-satisfaction is crushed, however, when Joan appears, revealing that the scene was staged. Realizing that Flemming never loved her and intended to murder her, Joan makes a full confession, leaving Flemming to reflect upon the destruction of all his plans.

The relationship between Columbo and Flemming became the template for most of the best detective/killer relationships for the remainder of the series. When Columbo meets Flemming at the apartment, after the dying Carol has been taken to the hospital, Columbo exudes concern and sensitivity, explaining the situation in a manner that exudes compassion. For Flemming's part, he handles the confrontation well, exuding concern and refraining from overacting maudlin expressions of grief, unlike many future *Columbo* murderers. The one time when his composure cracks is when he learns his wife is still alive (one would think that a medical doctor would make certain his victim was absolutely dead before leaving!). Flemming regains his self-control fairly quickly, but Columbo does an equally skillful job of hiding the workings of his mind, disguising the fact that he suspected the doctor seconds before he ever spoke to him.

Flemming made a critical error as he entered his apartment, though it would have done him no harm had Columbo not been there. Fleming did not say a word as he came inside, and Columbo knows that a husband should have immediately called out, "Honey, I'm home!" or some variant of that phrase. This illustrates a critical flaw in Flemming's behavior—he can wear a mask of normalcy in public, but he lacks the dedication to play his role (a man who couldn't possibly have known anything was wrong with his wife) even when he thinks nobody's watching.

Columbo commits to playing his role, in contrast, offering emotional support to Flemming even while he's scrutinizing him, realizing that the emotions most people would interpret as concern for his wife are actually fears that she'll recover and accuse him of attacking her. After Carol dies, Columbo investigates the homicide, disguising his suspicions and picking up on the little inconsistencies in the case, noting a significant difference in the weight of Flemming's luggage (caused by the "stolen" valuables he would toss in the water during his vacation), the missing dress and gloves worn by "Carol" on the plane, and so forth. Flemming recognizes Columbo's tenacity and, instead of trying to dismiss the detective's questions, admits that "he'll only be satisfied if all the loose ends are in place." Throughout these early scenes in Columbo's investigation, he's careful not to show his suspicions towards the doctor.

Flemming proves himself to be a clever and shrewd antagonist when

Columbo brings him in to witness the confession of a man who claims to have committed the robbery and the murder. Flemming refuses to embrace the possibility of the man being responsible, pointing out some serious discrepancies in the story. One might think that a guilty man would have leapt at the chance to find a patsy, but Flemming smelled a trap and for the first time, shows temper, angrily complaining that Columbo suspects him. Flemming commits a tactical error by turning to an influential friend to get Columbo kicked off the case. Such an action is a power play that Flemming might think would secure his position, but, in fact, only serves to make him look guilty in the eyes of the police.

This leads to the richest and most complex conversation between the two characters. Columbo meets Flemming at his office, claiming to have been taken off the case (it will later be revealed that Columbo's superior has his back). Columbo asks to be taken on as a patient, saying, "I seem to bother people. I seem to make them nervous." After a civilly-spoken threat to talk to Columbo's superiors, Flemming laughs, declaring, "Columbo, you are magnificent." "You are the most persistent creature I've ever met, but likable… You're droll." There's a level of amusement and even respect on Flemming's part towards Columbo, but no anxiety. Flemming realizes that Columbo is a dedicated investigator, but at this point, he's convinced himself that the detective is no threat to him.

At Flemming's invitation, the pair have a drink together, and Columbo tries to use the doctor to provide a psychological profile of his wife's killer. Flemming fails to describe his wife's murder as the act of an impulsive burglar and instead paints a flattering self-portrait of a man who is "above" traditional morality and who is far too clever to ever be caught. Flemming tries to end their relationship, suggesting, "Why don't we just part as friends?" and implies they'll never see each other again.

It is not until their last confrontation that the pair have a final argument, with Columbo pressuring Flemming to accept responsibility, if not for his wife's murder, then at least for Joan's death. This does not happen, and Flemming relaxes, content in the belief that his plan has worked perfectly and he faces no possibility of retribution. Just as he thinks he's won, Columbo's last desperate throw pulls the rug out from under him, and the doctor is left to smoke a cigarette stoically , forced to confront the fact that he is not the invulnerable criminal genius he thought he was.

Columbo's relationship with Joan receives far less screen time. After a brief meeting at Flemming's office, Columbo and Joan's primary scene together comes at a film studio, where she is immediately hostile, and Columbo questions her with a ferocity that he rarely displays again over the course of the series. Joan's composure is weak, and she makes multiple mistakes when answering Columbo's questions, demonstrating she knows more about his investigation than she should. She even slips by referring to the doctor as "Ray." Columbo engages in a tactic he almost never will use again– relentless badgering, yelling, and pressure. Joan is one of a very small number of *Columbo* villains that the titular detective never tries to befriend and disarm. Joan clearly is not cut out for withstanding a long-term third-degree, and she quickly retreats into the one defensive posture that can save her—refusing to answer more questions. Columbo stops his interrogation, admitting she was too strong for him that day, but inquires whether she'll be able to maintain her resolve in the face of a continued barrage of daily questioning over the foreseeable future. It is an excellent point, and from the expression on Joan's face, it is clear that she is also worried about her fortitude as well.

In order for the reveal of Joan's survival at the end of the episode to work, the viewers are denied a potentially fascinating scene. Between his attempt to browbeat her and the final trap that exposes Flemming, Columbo must have come to visit Joan one more time and convinced her to go along with his plan. Did he plant doubts in her mind over Flemming's love for her and provide her with an opportunity to prove his feelings? Did Columbo make a bargain with her, telling her if she went through with this one deception, that he would never bother her again? The details will never be known, but it must have required a massive change in tactics on Columbo's part in order to earn her acquiescence.

By the end, Joan is a shattered shell, realizing the man she became an accessory to murder for never truly cared for her and even plotted her death. Her final action shows that she no longer cares what happens to her and she wants revenge (or perhaps more charitably, justice), against Flemming. She could have simply walked away and gone on with her life without the doctor, but instead, she chose to bring Flemming down with her. It is an ironic twist of fate that the man who tried to crush her resolve less than twenty-four hours earlier is now her ally in destroying her faithless lover.

It is further notable that this was the fourth version of this story, and each one saw the not-so-good doctor get caught in a different way. Levinson and Link started the tale as a short story titled "Dear Corpus Delecti," which is essentially the first third of *Prescription: Murder*. The story covers the murder plan and ends with the doctor returning home after his alibi trip. In the Columbo prototype, Lieutenant Fisher meets the doctor outside his locked apartment and informs the doctor that his wife is dead. In this initial version, the girlfriend was killed in a car crash on the way back from the airport, though as she was carrying the wife's purse as part of her impersonation, the contents of the purse caused the body to be wrongly identified as that of the wife! Lieutenant Fisher asks to be let inside, where the true wife's body is yet to be discovered. The story ends there, but it is implied that with the discovery of the second body, the doctor's plans will unravel, and he will be brought to justice.

Levinson and Link thought the story had enough potential to become an hour-long episode of the television crime series *The Chevy Mystery Show*, which was a short-lived anthology drama featuring a different story from a different author each week, starring a different cast. On July 31, 1960, the episode was released with Richard Carlson as the doctor (*Roy* Flemming here) and Bert Freed as Columbo. The episode is a condensed version of the Falk version's narrative, with two main differences. The first is the portrayal of the doctor's wife, who is a shrill and overdramatic character in "Enough Rope" as opposed to the more dignified and restrained version that would come later. The second is the ending. In "Enough Rope," Columbo presents the doctor with a collection of valuables that he claims are the stolen items from the robbery, found at the bottom of the lake where the doctor vacationed. The doctor is not fooled, as he knows at once that the cheap silverware and other items are not his possessions. The situation changes when the girlfriend arrives, and when she sees the phony valuables, she immediately blurts out an incriminating statement, proving she was aware of the doctor's plan, leading to a double arrest.

The stage play *Prescription: Murder* premiered at San Francisco's Curran Theatre on January 20, 1962. This adaptation follows the general narrative, aside from the limitations imposed by stagecraft. The play uses yet another different ending, as Columbo informs the doctor that his girlfriend is dead, implying suicide. After an emotional confrontation, the doctor breaks, and he is willing to confess, as without his lover, the whole affair has all been for nothing. Columbo takes him down to the station, where it is implied that he will make a full confession. Soon after they leave, the girlfriend appears onstage alive, purring over a gift from the doctor. Without being explicitly stated, it is implied that after the doctor confesses, Columbo will arrest her as well.

The 1968 television movie is the fourth and final adaptation of the story, where Columbo's gambit of staging the girlfriend's overdose leads to the doctor revealing his true, nasty colors and lack of any real affection for his paramour. The implication that he placed a lethal dose in one of Joan's sleeping pills illustrates that the unconsumed pill is an additional bit of evidence against Flemming beyond Joan's confession.

It is important to realize that each of these four endings produces a very different take on the doctor's and Joan's characters. In the first story, neither Flemming nor his girlfriend makes any mistakes or cracks. It is simply a one-in-a-million twist of fate that destroys them both in different ways. In contrast, in "Enough Rope," it is the girlfriend who ruins everything through an unguarded comment in the wake of a simple trick. The stage version is the only one to put the doctor's downfall solely upon his own shoulders, as he proves to have an emotional Achilles' heel in the wake of Columbo's strategic lies and psychological pressure.

Ultimately, it's the full-length television movie "Prescription: Murder" that has the most emotionally and intellectually skillful ending. Flemming's downfall comes from more than just a simple deception, but by the brutal reveal of how cold and calculating he really is. Flemming is not foiled by a lie Columbo told, but by the lies he told, the lies professing his love for Joan. Joan does not give him away because she was fooled by a simplistic ploy, she turns him and herself in because she realizes their whole relationship was a sham. Had Flemming feigned grief or even stormed out, Joan might have stayed silent. Instead, he chose that moment to gloat about the triumph of his plans, and it was his choice to revel in how clever he had been that ultimately doomed him.

What sort of man was Dr. Ray Flemming, and what led him to become a murderer? He was a highly intelligent psychiatrist, well-liked and respected in his social circle, and attractive to women. He chose a wife whose personal wealth could advance his career and social position, and once he was certain he had a foolproof way to inherit her money without risk to himself or his reputation, he decided to commit not just one murder, but a second, that of a woman who loved him so much she was willing to become his accomplice in homicide in order to become his next wife. He was cautious and a thorough planner, yet despite his careful attention to detail, he still missed some critical points that ultimately fractured the narrative he tried to create.

Ultimately, his greatest failing was that he considered himself to be a kind of Nietzschean *übermensch*, a man whose innate superiority gives him the right to set himself apart and above other human beings. Dr. Flemming believed himself to be sufficiently brilliant to plan and carry out the perfect murder and that his own career, comfort, and reputation were more important than the lives of two women who loved him. It was his belief that he was far smarter than any police detective that led him to underestimate Columbo. Because, for all of Dr. Flemming's knowledge of human psychology, he never realized that a homicide investigator might be so determined to pursue the case that he would never give up until a killer was brought to justice.

In contrast, Joan was not a naturally hardened criminal. She bore Carol no hatred, but she was passionately in love with a man who neither returned nor deserved her affections, and so she was prepared to let an innocent woman die so she could have what she thought would be a happy relationship. The fact that she was Flemming's patient indicates that she may have had long-term psychological instabilities or vulnerabilities that the doctor manipulated for his own nefarious purposes. Had she gone to a different psychiatrist, it is highly unlikely that she would ever have been involved in a murder. Flemming tried to mold her into being the perfect accomplice, but she retained enough of her morality to know that if his love for her was fake, then she would see justice done, whatever the cost to herself.

Columbo solved this case by realizing that the only way to bring down Flemming was to destroy his accomplice's trust in him. He would use similar tactics in the future.

[1] * Stylistic Note: As Columbo's first name is never revealed, for the sake of consistency, most characters will be referred to by their last names, except when there are major characters who are spouses or family members sharing a surname, in which instances first names will be used.

Chapter Two: Ransom for a Dead Man

Leslie Williams (Lee Grant)

In the second pilot for *Columbo*, an ambitious lawyer seeks to kill her husband, make it look like a kidnapping, and profit by keeping the ransom money. As the episode opens, Leslie Williams is clipping letters out of publications in order to make a ransom note, and splicing a recording to set up an ersatz ransom call. Moments after her husband returns home, she shoots him. After hiding the body, she calls the authorities and puts her plan into motion. She plays the part of a concerned wife, winning over the FBI agents and investigators sent to secure her husband's safe return.

But there's one detective she fails to fool. Twelve and a half minutes into the episode, Columbo makes his first appearance, stumbling around Williams' front porch looking for the pen he dropped. This is before he knows who will open the door and prior to developing any suspicions towards Williams, so this is not just a disarming tactic. It's a genuine moment of awkwardness, and it shows that Columbo's sometimes-bumbling demeanor is not just an assumed schtick. The lieutenant is treated with disdain by the other law enforcement professionals and incredulous amusement by Williams. Yet when the ransom call comes in, courtesy of a tape placed in a machine that is programmed to dial Williams' house at a prearranged time, Columbo's the only one who notices something odd–Williams neglected to ask if her husband was O.K. Williams overhears this remark, and realizes that he suspects her.

Williams' scheme goes as planned. She raises hundreds of thousands of dollars for the ransom by cashing out investments and stuffs the money into a bag. At the self-appointed time, she flies her private plane over the desert and throws an empty bag out the window, having switched the bag with the money with a decoy before flying. The FBI, following the plane in a car, finds the empty bag and assumes the kidnappers took the money. A suspicious Columbo snoops around the airport, but can find nothing against Williams.

Williams has left her husband's body in a place where it will soon be found, and when it is discovered, she's informed of the grisly revelation shortly after a successful court appearance. She makes a great show of swooning in front of witnesses, and she soon has the sympathy of those around her, save for Columbo and her stepdaughter Margaret (Patricia Mattick), who has come back from boarding school to mourn her father and hates and distrusts her stepmother. Columbo notes that Williams failed to ask any questions about her husband's death, and when another officer in charge of handling the kidnapping threatens him with consequences if he "harasses" the widow, Columbo politely but devastatingly reminds the officer that this is now a homicide and he's in charge of the case now.

Columbo begins his investigation, picking apart the facets of Williams' plan one by one and raising a lot of unanswered questions about the case. Their relationship is fairly cordial until about two-thirds of the way through the episode when she snaps and refers to his observations as "absurd hypotheses." At one point, she declares she'll only answer his questions if he flies in her plane with her. She correctly deduces that Columbo is not comfortable in airplanes, and she successfully throws the detective off his game, but once they're safely back on the ground, Columbo recovers his acuity.

When Margaret tries to point Columbo towards her stepmother, Columbo hides his own suspicions and subtly conveys to Margaret that a missing set of car keys might prove crucial to the case. Soon afterwards, Margaret claims she found the keys to the car where her father was found, stating they were hidden amongst her stepmother's possessions. Williams knows she didn't leave them there, and surprisingly, Columbo comes to her rescue, saying that he's kept watch over Margaret and knows she had a set of keys copied, and she's framing her stepmother. Margaret's furious, and Williams is grateful, though Columbo makes it clear that he still believes she's guilty without openly admitting his beliefs, saying, "I just couldn't have you accused of murder on the wrong evidence."

The tension heats up between Columbo and Williams as she starts to taunt him in the hopes of undermining his confidence and even threatens his position. Columbo eventually informs her he was taken off the case, but of course, he's still investigating. Williams, who has been enduring occasional attacks of nerves when she has flashbacks to the murder, is confronted in the house by Margaret, who chases her with a blank-filled gun. Frazzled, Williams wants to know what it'll take to get her stepdaughter to go away, and Margaret declares that she wants her trust-fund money that Williams withdrew for the supposed ransom. Soon afterwards, Williams presents Margaret with a case full of money and puts her on a plane with a one-way ticket.

Believing she's in the clear, Williams sees Columbo at the airport and offers to buy him a consolation drink. Her mood quickly sours when Columbo reveals he and Margaret were working together and that Margaret would never have accepted money to ignore her father's murder. Now that Margaret has turned the money over to him, he can match the serial numbers and has the evidence he needs to arrest Williams for murder. He offers to let her finish her drink, but she coolly declines and is led away, leaving Columbo to pay the bill for the beverages, but he doesn't have enough money with him, and he can't dip into the suitcase stuffed with cash in front of him.

The relationship between Columbo and Williams sets the stage for the rest of the series, adjusting the template that began with "Prescription: Murder," softening the lieutenant's rough edges while playing up his eccentricities and stressing his tenacity. Williams' first reaction towards him is amusement, even incredulity that a man so patently ridiculous could find his way into the police force, though she soon picks up on his observational skills and realizes that he's probably an effective investigator, though importantly, she never treats him as a serious threat. Less intelligent criminals might probably feel his handcuffs around their wrists, but Williams is always convinced of her own superiority until the final minute of the episode.

When Columbo questions her after her husband's body is discovered, she's politely dismissive of him, though his continued gentle pressure brings back flashbacks of the crime, a reaction that isn't mirrored in the experiences of later killers. At times, she practically swoons as she remembers committing murder, but though Williams is shaken by recalling what she is capable of, she never expresses actual guilt for what she did. At best, she simply treats this as an unpleasant memory of something she did, but doesn't regret.

Towards the end of the episode, while Williams is convinced that she is untouchable, she tells Columbo what she really thinks of him. She declares that "you're almost likable in a shabby sort of way," deliberately adding the qualifier "almost." She remarks that some of his affectations, like "the humility, the seeming absent-mindedness, the homey anecdotes about your family," all might be charming to varying extents, but notes that he's always after "the jugular." As Columbo reveals he knows how she crafted her deceptions, she dismisses this, sneering that he can't prove she faked it, trying to tear him down by saying his attempts to get under her skin are "vaudeville." It's a supercilious attack, but Columbo is immune to these thrusts at his ego.

Columbo accurately sums up Williams' central character flaw at the end when he informs her that "Mrs. Williams, you have no conscience. And that's your weakness." Not only does she not have a moral compass, she can't conceive of other people being more humane than she is. She was sure that a hefty payment would silence her stepdaughter, and the idea that love was more powerful than money was so alien to her that this extremely savvy woman walked directly into the trap that would reveal her to the world as a killer.

At times, her amoral persona cracks. After her triumph in court, where she discredits a man charging her clients with negligence, she's angry at her clients, but not really because of their lack of regard for their tenants, but for how clumsily obvious they were about their failure to maintain their property. For Williams, criminality is forgivable, especially in her own case. It's stupidity that's contemptable. As it stands, Williams is well-respected professionally and personally. Her male subordinates seem to worship her, her female friends admire her, and law enforcement outside of Columbo defers to her.

There is only one other person who sees through her: her stepdaughter Margaret. This is reminiscent of the Father Brown story "The Actor and the Alibi" by G.K. Chesterton. In the denouement, Father Brown declares, "If you want to know what a lady is really like, don't look at her, for she may be too clever for you. Don't look at the men around her, for they may be too silly for her. But look at some other woman who is always near to her, and especially one who is under her. You will see her real face in that mirror." Prior to Columbo's entry on the scene, only Margaret saw through her stepmother. Williams had poisoned her acquaintances' minds against Margaret, as her circle of friends is full of indignation at how awful they believe Margaret to be, and the only way they could have heard these stories is by Williams herself. Acting as a skilled manipulator, Williams leaked negative stories about Margaret without seeming to complain and afterwards, played the martyr, sighing about how impossible her stepdaughter was.

In many reviews of "Ransom for a Dead Man," the character of Margaret has been singled out for criticism due to her fits of pique and mercurial temper, but this may be unfair. When one considers that Margaret has been the victim of extensive emotional abuse by her stepmother and her continual frustration at the adults in her life for failing to believe her, coupled with the grief and rage she feels at losing her beloved father, Margaret's characterization may be more psychologically realistic than it is commonly given credit for being. Margaret is a teenager with a teenager's emotions and volatility, stuck in a world that neither respects nor protects her, and it is no wonder why she decides to flout society's rules in order to get revenge against the stepmother she hates and why she is so desperate to have Columbo believe her. He is the one adult in her circle of acquaintances who is willing to listen to her without unfairly dismissing her as a neurotic spoiled brat.

Margaret tells Columbo that Williams convinced her husband to abandon his life's ambition of a judgeship in order to pursue a more lucrative law career, and he acquiesced to please her. Linking herself to him helped Williams rise to the top of her profession, and once she had achieved her career goals, she demanded a separation from her husband. Margaret reveals that her father was emotionally devastated, but he was willing to fight to protect his assets and dignity, and this is why Williams killed him. While Margaret is biased, it's most likely that her account is accurate. While it must be acknowledged that during the 1970s, women had much fewer opportunities to succeed in the law and other professional fields, the cruelty and exploitative nature with which she treated her husband after she had risen to the top is not morally justified. For Williams, her entire marriage was a means to an end, and when she shot her husband, she saw him not as a human being who deserved respect, but as a hindrance to her goals of success, wealth, and prestige.

While Williams probably credited her career triumphs to her own perspicacity, intelligence, and talent, it's unknown if she ever realized just how she sowed the seeds of her own destruction through her ill-treatment of her stepdaughter, her inability to understand the sincerity of her husband's feelings for her, and how Margaret felt a desire for justice that was completely alien to Williams. Williams believed that she was clever enough to have everything she wanted, but due to her conviction that others were both inferior to her and similarly venal, Columbo was able to unravel her murder plot.

Chapter Three: Murder by the Book

Ken Franklin (Jack Cassidy)

Ken Franklin is a lover of the high life, a skilled self-promoter, and a ladies' man. Unfortunately for him, he's not very skilled at his supposed profession of mystery writing, which leads to him becoming a murderer. In the first of Jack Cassidy's trilogy of *Columbo* villains, "Murder by the Book" tells the story of the partnership behind the "Mrs. Melville" book series. Jim Ferris (Martin Milner) is the one who does all the plotting and writing. Ken Franklin can't string together two sentences on paper, but he's very skilled at telegenic interviews and drumming up attention on book tours. With Ferris providing the quality literary product and Franklin knowing how to get those novels on the bestseller charts, the Mrs. Melville mysteries are a profitable franchise.

But all is not well in this collaboration. Ferris is tired of writing these crime stories and wants to move on to something else. This won't do for Franklin, who has spent his half of the profits on luxuries, and doesn't intend to switch to clipping coupons to stay within his budget. As he can no longer look forward to a steady stream of royalties from new Mrs. Melville books, he decides to kill Ferris and collect a million-dollar life insurance policy. Such a policy is standard in comparable partnerships, so its existence in itself isn't enough to raise suspicions. The two previously argued over Ferris's plans, so Franklin decided to return to their shared office with an ersatz reconciliation attempt. After pointing a gun that can't fire at his partner—a fact that Ferris observes after a moment's observation—Franklin laughs and mocks his own skills as a murderer. This is, of course, a gambit to place Ferris at ease, and after assuring Ferris that all is now well between them, Franklin convinces Ferris to take a break from writing and hang out with him at his cabin in the woods. Once the pair reach Franklin's car, Franklin claims to have forgotten something and rushes back to the office, trashing the room to make it look like a struggle occurred, and plants a list of underworld figures amongst Ferris's notes, which he had previously had Ferris handle so as to leave fingerprints.

After a couple of hours' drive, Franklin stops at the small general store near his cabin While Ferris waits in the car. It's run by Lilly La Sanka (Barbara Colby), who has an unrequited attraction to Franklin. Franklin maintains a friendly relationship with her and gives her an autographed copy of the latest Mrs. Melville. Franklin uses La Sanka's phone to make a call to Ferris's wife Joanna (Rosemary Forsyth), telling her that Ferris is still working in the office, he's at his cabin, and the two have patched up everything.

His alibi set up, Franklin drives Ferris the rest of the way to the cabin and suggests he make a call to his wife to tell her he'll be late getting home. After making sure Ferris calls in a way that can't be traced back to his cabin, soon after Ferris starts talking to Joanna, Franklin shoots him, and Joanna's shocked when she hears the gunshot. Soon after Franklin hangs up his phone, Joanna calls him, tells him what happened, and Franklin reassuringly lies and tells her everything will be all right.

Columbo appears eighteen minutes into the episode, trying to reassure the distraught Joanna. It's not clear if he suspects her of complicity at first or not, but after a little conversation with her and making her an omelet, Columbo decides that her anxiety is genuine, and she also tells him the truth about the pair's writing partnership. After returning back to Los Angeles with Ferris's body in the trunk of his car, Franklin plays the role of the caring friend. He goes with Columbo to the office, where he produces the list of organized crime figures and attempts to convince Columbo that underworld goons kidnapped Ferris in retaliation for his research into powerful mob bosses. Columbo pretends to act convinced, and Franklin gifts Columbo a stack of Mrs. Melville mysteries and sends him on his way, but not before Columbo can ask why he drove back, instead of taking a much faster plane.

Later that night, Franklin dumps his partner's body on his lawn and calls the authorities, pushing the story that the mob had Ferris murdered. Columbo coaxes his way into the house, observing the expensive artwork and the fact that Franklin has opened that day's mail. Franklin continues to try to direct Columbo's investigation, and Columbo continues to poke holes in Franklin's story.

By their next meeting, Franklin's geniality is wearing thin, and he starts showing temper at Columbo's continued friendly questions. But the most pressing threat to Franklin turns out to be La Sanka, who saw Ferris in Franklin's car while Franklin made his phone call. She blackmails him in the most apologetic way possible, and he hides his homicidal plans behind an ingratiating smile and invites her to a romantic dinner at her place. That night, he spends the evening charming her, plying her with sparkling wine, and putting her at ease… right up to the moment when he strikes her on the head with a champagne bottle. He then takes her out onto the lake, tosses her into the water, upsets the rowboat, and swims back to shore, convinced that he's made it look like an accident– she got tipsy, went out for a late-night boat ride, capsized and drowned.

Columbo arrives at Franklin's cabin the next day, having heard about La Sanka's death. Franklin makes precious little effort to wear the mask of cordiality and claims he was at his cabin all night. Columbo finds that odd, as he tried to call Franklin at his cabin, but he wasn't home. Throughout the episode, Franklin grimaces or growls the second Columbo leaves, and this meeting proves to be no exception.

Convinced that Franklin is guilty, Columbo questions Joanna for any details about her husband and Franklin that might be used as evidence against Franklin. The discovery that Ferris used to scribble notes for mystery plots on random scraps of paper and leave them everywhere inspires Columbo. After an extended search, he discovers a slip of paper describing the alibi method Franklin used in the murder. Realizing that this note in Ferris's writing is damning evidence, Franklin surrenders with a laugh, but as he's led away, he reveals that he came up with that alibi plan himself, but after he told Ferris, he never dreamed his partner would write down the idea.

Ken Franklin is a classic example of a murderer who thought that he could manipulate Columbo, only to realize that the detective wasn't easily fooled. From the outset, Franklin's attitude towards Columbo was patronizing. He repeatedly compared Columbo's detection skills negatively to the fictional Mrs. Melville's, a recurring slur that Columbo absorbed without a trace of pique. Franklin repeatedly attempts to push Mrs. Melville's intellectual dominance, saying she'd solve the crime fast. This is a highly questionable stratagem on Franklin's part, as such denigration could only serve to antagonize most people, and there's no point in making an enemy of a homicide detective. Franklin repeatedly demonstrates he has no subtlety, as his approach to pushing a version of events is consistently ham-fisted. It's also proof he has no skills as a writer, for if Franklin plotted books the way he tries to misdirect Columbo, his readers wouldn't be fooled by the clumsy red herrings. Not only that, but the characters would be unconvincing, as Franklin has little understanding of psychology.

For his part, Columbo gives a great performance as a gullible man, looking like he's lapping up Franklin's story about the kidnapping being the work of organized crime. Franklin is so convinced of his own persuasive powers that he's certain Columbo's been fooled and beams at the lieutenant with a self-satisfied crocodile smile. When Columbo wonders why the list of names has been folded up, Franklin laughs, saying, "I'm beginning to like you… Because you're finally beginning to think like Mrs. Melville." By acting like he knows detection better than an actual police officer, Franklin gives a back-handed compliment drenched in patronizing arrogance. Close-eyed viewers will pick up another clue connected to Franklin's carelessness, as the stack of books he presents Columbo with contains multiple copies of the same novels.

Franklin seems to be frustrated by any challenges to the narrative he's advancing, as every one of Columbo's questions, whether it's about his own personal finances or insurance, is met with irritation. When Columbo claims to be uncertain as to why Ferris's body was left on Franklin's lawn, Franklin acts dismayed and says, "Lieutenant, you disappoint me." Franklin takes on the role of guide and mentor, and Columbo always acts very deferential, even when he's pointing out psychological inconsistencies in Franklin's actions, such as tearing open his mail after "discovering" the body. Franklin's first show of temper and annoyance comes when Columbo interrupts his interview with an attractive reporter, illustrating Franklin's penchant for pursuing women and his inability to tolerate any distraction from his preferred pursuits. Later, Franklin refuses to hold the door for Columbo as he leaves and snaps, denigrating the importance of his questions. The rudeness reaches its apogee when Columbo asks if it's possible for him to rent a cabin like his. Franklin plays the class card and bluntly states that these cabins are out of a policeman's price range.

For his part, Columbo relishes his final confrontation with Franklin as he seizes the opportunity to pay back some of the condescension Franklin's leveled in his direction the entire episode. Once he's armed with the crucial evidence, Columbo drops the pretense of deference and is far more confident, even triumphant. When Franklin arrives at the office, Columbo's comfortably seated at the desk, reading a Mrs. Melville and smoking a cigar. Still amicably, he says, "Why dontcha make a statement and save us both a lot of trouble?" Columbo walks through all the mistakes Franklin made, with a special focus on how he failed to get the psychological profile of an innocent man's reactions correct. Franklin was so eager to direct the investigation that he forgot to show any real grief for a man he'd worked with for a decade. When Franklin is still defiant and confident, Columbo lands a punch against his ego by declaring the first murder was "brilliant," but the second crime was "sloppy," giving as strongly as he got earlier in the episode. He reminds Franklin, "You're not a writer," and he has "no talent for mysteries." As he couldn't plot his own murder, he had to have taken his idea for the perfect crime for someone else. After Columbo reveals the incriminating notes for the unbreakable alibi idea, it would have been wise for Franklin to stay silent and launch a full-bodied defense at trial. Instead, Franklin can't help but protect his own pride by taking credit for the alibi and chuckling about how he gave Columbo a run for his money. It's not an unequivocal confession, but he still incriminated himself out of a desire to defend himself.

Franklin's ultimate downfall came from a variety of personal flaws. He was addicted to a comfortable life of pleasure, and he had created a role for himself where he was able to earn his bread and cheese by traveling, schmoozing with members of the press, and self-advertising. Still, he was always the less important member of the partnership, as there were many publicity agents who could do his job, but the actual writing was more specialized work. He was expendable, and he knew it.

When Ferris wanted to break up the partnership, Franklin had options. He could have turned his promotional skills to trying to get Hollywood interested in adapting the Mrs. Melville books, which would have brought him a substantial sum of money. Not only that, but he could have sought out some other talented writer who had proven his literary skills but still hadn't met with public success. After identifying a suitable new partner, Franklin could have proposed an alliance along the lines of the one he had with Ferris and then used his talent for publicity, along with his own brand name, to build up the new franchise. Perhaps he could even have gotten Ferris to agree to let someone else take over writing the Mrs. Melville mysteries. This time, he could have drawn up a contract preventing the dissolution of the partnership. With some luck and a lot of effort, he could have been just as successful, even more so with the new writing partner. But apparently, murder was easier.

It's worth wondering how long that million dollars would have lasted, given Franklin's talent for spending lavishly, gambling, and enjoying life. Had he run through the money, he'd need to find another source of income quickly.

Franklin is a bit like a cat playing with a mouse, as he spent over two hours with Ferris before killing him. He seems to revel in the role of deceiver, genuinely appearing to enjoy his last conversations, as he convincingly acts as if nothing is wrong before killing his victims. His dinner with La Sanka was necessary, as it was critical for him to get her pretty drunk in order to make the "accident" more convincing, but once again, he forgot to step back and consider how the crime would look to an outside party. He failed to retrieve a popped champagne cork, which was a clumsy oversight, and he never stopped to realize how suspicious it would look to withdraw a large sum of money from his bank account only to deposit it again soon afterwards. As Columbo rightly explained, his second murder was particularly sloppy, and sloppiness was the weakness that continually undermined Franklin. He overlooked little details and rarely took the time to think about the consequences of certain actions, the necessity for certain reactions, or how to behave around the police so as to remain in their good graces. Ken Franklin was not a meticulous man, and his lack of attention to detail doomed his attempts to get away with murder.

Chapter Four: Death Lends a Hand

Carl Brimmer (Robert Culp)

Of all the Columbo killers, Carl Brimmer is the only one to not be a murderer. Though he is responsible for taking a life, this is the first unpremeditated killing in the series. It may be considered an accident, but at the very worst, it is only manslaughter. While other killers in the series may initially commit manslaughter or even self-defense, the rest commit a second, premeditated killing later on that makes them incontrovertible murderers.

Carl Brimmer is the head of a private detection and security agency. As the episode opens, he assures the wealthy magnate Arthur Kennicutt (Ray Milland) that his wife Lenore (Pat Crowley) isn't cheating on him. After a relieved Arthur leaves, Lenore, who has watched the conversation from another room, confronts Brimmer, revealing she has indeed had a romantic relationship outside her marriage (though she has ended it), and asks him why he covered for her. Brimmer suggests he wanted to see the two of them get a fresh start, and she can repay him by feeding him information about her husband's business dealings, which he can use to improve his business.

Soon afterwards, Lenore visits Brimmer at his home and tells him that she won't submit to his blackmail and that she plans to tell her husband the whole truth, including Brimmer's proposed extortion. They argue and struggle, and Brimmer angrily shoves Lenore, accidentally sending her falling upon his coffee table, where she hits her head and dies. In a famous series of video clips superimposed on Brimmer's glasses, Brimmer moves the body far away and cleans up the crime scene.

When the body's discovered soon afterwards, Columbo enters just shy of sixteen minutes into the episode and begins to investigate. Based on his questioning, Columbo initially zeroes in on the husband as the most likely suspect, but after getting the sense that Arthur is an okay guy, the lieutenant starts looking elsewhere for a killer. He finds his target in Brimmer over twenty-five minutes into the episode. Arthur Kennicutt hired Brimmer to assist in the case after Brimmer offered his services. This was a risky move on Brimmer's part. It might have been wiser to try to stay off of the official police's radar for as long as possible, but by introducing himself into the investigation, he could keep an eye on the case's progress. Brimmer probably made the wrong decision, as Columbo starts suspecting him at their first meeting, as evidenced by the lieutenant's talk of palmistry, which is simply a ruse to scrutinize the ring on Brimmer's hand. Columbo had previously noticed a small wound on the dead woman's face, indicating that she had been struck by someone wearing a ring on the left hand. It is unclear what awakens Columbo's suspicions—perhaps it was something in Brimmer's attitude.

Columbo starts following up on the people in the victim's light and eventually tracks down her golf instructor. The instructor denies close knowledge of Lenore Kennicutt, but Columbo makes it clear he doesn't believe him, declaring, "You get so you develop a nose for things." Perhaps this statement explains how he became suspicious of Brimmer. Later, the instructor admits to the affair, but says she ended it and denies involvement in the crime. Columbo believes him, as the tan on his hands means he doesn't wear a ring and, therefore, wouldn't have left the abrasion on the late woman's face.

Now that Columbo knows that Lenore Kennicutt did indeed cheat on her husband, he knows that the "clean bill of health" Brimmer gave her was wrong. Brimmer's too good an operative to make such a mistake, which means that he must have deliberately misled her husband. So why would he lie, and what did he hope to gain from this deception? This strengthens Columbo's suspicions.

When Columbo visits Brimmer's office to bring over some files, he compliments him on the beautiful building (illustrating how prosperous Brimmer is). When Columbo brings up the ring mark, Brimmer draws attention to his own ring, which is just about the only action he can take, as it's too late to remove his jewelry. Columbo reconstructs the crime, and Brimmer himself notes that the wound indicates a left-handed killer. Columbo notes that it might have been an accident, but that the punch means that the killer has a terrible temper. When Brimmer is asked to sign a form, Columbo notes that he's left-handed. Brimmer claims to be ambidextrous. As Columbo makes his exit, he makes it clear he's aware that Brimmer's beach house is quite close to the Kennicutts' and as soon as Columbo leaves, Brimmer sags in his chair. Unlike many other *Columbo* killers, Brimmer can't threaten to complain about the detective's so-called "harassment." He invited himself onto the case.

At Columbo's next visit, Brimmer reveals his fiery temper when an underling starts babbling about a confidential case. As the two sit down to a fancy fish lunch, Columbo explains how he knows about the deceased's affair, though he breaks up the narrative to keep Brimmer anxious to learn more. Columbo proposes a theory where the victim was being followed and blackmailed, which he dubs a "crazy theory." Despite the lieutenant admitting there's no proof, Brimmer encourages this line of thought, saying "Lieutenant, you have a marvelously convoluted mind…I like it."

But Brimmer knows that Columbo's on his trail, so he tries a new tactic to distract him. Brimmer offers Columbo a job with triple his current annual income. It's a bribe, for he knows that Columbo is suspicious, and hopes that a hefty paycheck will be enough to blunt the lieutenant's determination. After Columbo asks if he'd still be on the Kennicutt case, Brimmer informs him he'd be working elsewhere, and Columbo gives him a knowing glance over a toast. Columbo also learns the agent who trailed Lenore Kennicutt has been sent overseas on a case, where he can't be questioned.

As the endgame begins, Columbo sets his trap. He notes that a contact lens may have been lost, and asks for an exhumation. Brimmer tries to shoot down the theory, but Arthur Kennicutt agrees. After the exhumation, Columbo informs them that a contact lens is indeed missing, and it's likely at the scene of the crime. Brimmer's voice is steady but clearly agitated, as he tries to minimize Columbo's theories. Columbo skillfully works Brimmer up until the private detective is desperate to find the lost lens. Columbo stops by Brimmer's home after Brimmer's driven himself nuts trying to find the contact lens. Columbo officially declines the job offer, saying he can't stop until he finds a solution.

Brimmer realizes the contact lens may be in the trunk of his car, where he placed the body for transport. Unfortunately for him, his car is in a garage being serviced after it malfunctioned. Brimmer sneaks into the garage, opens the trunk, and locates a contact lens, but he's caught by Columbo, Arthur Kennicutt, and some other detectives. Brimmer shows signs of temper and calls the situation a farce, but when the lens is found on him, he confesses immediately, but insists it was an accident. He's a tough man and could have bluffed his way out of the situation, and it's possible his conscience needed unburdening. After Columbo explains how he started suspecting him, Brimmer tells him "you should have taken that job."

In a final reveal, Columbo explains to Arthur Kennicutt that this was all a sham to trap Brimmer. No contact lens was missing, and the lens in the trunk was planted. As for the car breaking down, Columbo recounts how as a child, a favorite prank was to stick a potato in a car's exhaust pipe, causing it to malfunction. As the episode closes, Arthur Kennicutt starts to check the car's exhaust pipe for a potato but thinks better of it.

The relationship between Columbo and Brimmer is one of the most genuinely respectful in the series. Brimmer is a former police officer himself, and he appreciates strong detective work. Brimmer genuinely seems to appreciate Columbo's tenacity, intelligence, and perception, and it's possible that if they'd met under different circumstances, he would have offered Columbo a job anyway. He might have enjoyed working with Columbo rather than against him. While Brimmer's opinion of Columbo is clearly positive, it's much more difficult to tell what Columbo thinks of Brimmer. Columbo doesn't demonstrate the same level of actual fondness that he feels for some of the nicer murderers, and he may have the veteran police officer's disdain for someone who leaves the force for a more lucrative career, and when he realizes that Brimmer is guilty, he may also have the more intense disapproval honest detectives famously have for cops gone wrong. The profitable job Brimmer offers as a bribe may also be a point that sours Columbo against him. By the end, though the two may have a high opinion of each other's talents, there is very little warmth between them.

Brimmer is a smart man and a talented investigator, but his downfall began when he believed that some quiet blackmail to strengthen his client list was a wise business move. His knowledge of psychology is seriously flawed, as he failed to realize that many people can't live with a secret hanging over their heads, and they can't be happy in an atmosphere of secrets and lies. Brimmer also left himself wide open with his blackmail attempt, as Lenore Kennicutt rightly saw that she could destroy him by revealing his corruption. If Brimmer couldn't have been more ethical, he should have at least been more prudent by doing his blackmail more obliquely.

Brimmer's collaboration was always a risky gambit with an unclear endgame. The investigation always ran a risk of leading back to him, as indeed it did. The investigation could wind up going nowhere, and this failure would reflect badly on the reputations of himself and his company. If he wanted to close the case, he might have to try to blame an innocent man, which could backfire if the target could wind up clearing himself. The only way Brimmer could manipulate the situation to his advantage would be to frame a person with a history of violence, possibly someone who died of natural causes or an accident not long after the murder and couldn't defend himself. Brimmer's "lending a hand" was a high-risk and low-reward plan, but Brimmer's inability to sit on the sidelines drove him to ignore prudence.

Brimmer was not a murderer. He was indeed a killer, and a man whose ethics had been warped to the point where he was willing to lie to a client in the hopes of landing more profitable cases down the line. Due to his anger and lack of self-control, he committed manslaughter. Notably, he never expresses much guilt or remorse, but he does appear upset at himself every time he makes a mistake. Brimmer had a successful business, but it's not clear how many corners he cut to become so successful. It's possible that Lenore Kennicutt was not the first person he tried to blackmail, though there is no direct evidence of this. Furthermore, viewers know nothing about his reasons for leaving the police force. Perhaps the same dishonesty that he displayed as a private investigator was already present when he was an officer of the law, and this may or may not have precipitated his career change. Given the limited information available to the viewer, it cannot be known when Brimmer started his moral slide, nor is it clear just how deep his corruption ran. The only point that can be said for certain in his favor is that he had not yet devolved to the point where he was capable of cold-bloodedly taking another human life. He was, however, still determined to protect himself from the consequences of his actions, but his desire to control the situation, rather than avoid the limelight, wound up leading to his exposure as a killer.

Chapter Five: Dead Weight

Martin Hollister (Eddie Albert)

Major General Martin J. Hollister made a serious mistake when he committed an impromptu murder. A witness saw him committing the crime. In order to protect himself, he decided to take some unusual steps to combat the witness's testimony. In order to cover up his career-shattering secrets, he became both a killer and a lover.

Thanks to his heroism in wartime, Major General Hollister has a legendary reputation as a soldier. But Hollister also has a fondness for creature comforts, and to live the good life, one must have plenty of money. As a military pension isn't enough to support his wants, Hollister supported his income with a bit of embezzlement from the armed forces. Colonel Roger Dutton (John Kerr) was his accomplice, and Dutton panics when he hears that the authorities are looking into their finances. Dutton's planning to go on the run, but Hollister isn't about to let Dutton potentially implicate him. When Dutton visits Hollister at his home with large windows overlooking the ocean, Hollister shoots him. If only he had taken a moment to close the curtains...

Helen Stewart (Suzanne Pleshette), a divorced woman on a boat with her mother, Mrs. Walters (Kate Reid), looks up at just the right moment to see Hollister firing his gun. Mrs. Walters doubts her daughter, but Stewart insists on filing a report to the police, and Columbo just happens to catch the case. He enters eleven minutes into the episode and, after hearing

Stewart's story, questions Hollister. Hollister is quite polite to Columbo when they first meet, even offering him a drink, which is declined. For his part, Columbo is apologetic about his questioning. But a quick look around produces no evidence of homicide, and Hollister civilly produces a plausible albeit clumsy excuse about how the witness misinterpreted some packing and rearranging he was doing. As Hollister spins a yarn about how he was holding a pistol, reenacting what he was supposedly doing and how it might have looked like a shooting from a distance, the major general seems to be overdoing it a bit, which raises Columbo's suspicions, as there's a glint in his eye as he responds to Hollister. Perhaps Columbo fears for Stewart's safety as he protects her anonymity despite Hollister's pressure.

As it turns out, Hollister isn't a bad investigator himself. Correctly deducing that the witness saw what happened from a boat, he inquires into recent rentals and eventually tracks down Stewart and her mother. He confronts Stewart about her story, but doesn't threaten her. On the contrary, the pair soon start seeing each other socially, and while he charms her, he convinces her that she was mistaken in what she saw. Soon, Stewart's smitten and it's possible that Hollister is genuinely attracted to her as well.

Meanwhile, Columbo keeps investigating and learns from a news report that Hollister is famous for his trademark pearl-handled gun. It's revealed that Hollister hid the body behind a panel in his home, and he ties the corpse to a pair of fireplace andirons, loads the remains onto his boat, and gives his former colleague an unceremonious burial at sea. Columbo meets him back on shore, and Hollister's previous geniality is mostly gone as he responds curtly to the lieutenant's questions and is clearly annoyed when Columbo starts asking about the pearl-handled gun. Hollister declares that the firearm was lost a while ago, and he delivers a veiled threat to Columbo as he leaves.

The situation changes when Dutton's body is discovered. Apparently, Hollister is not particularly skilled with knots because the corpse came loose from the andirons and floated to the water's surface. If only he'd done a better job of securing the body, he might have escaped all punishment. Now that he has an unquestionable homicide to investigate, Columbo comes back with a new barrage of questions and a bit of subterfuge. The lieutenant joins Hollister on his boat and observes that Hollister is now a person of interest. Columbo makes a big show of how he thinks it's ridiculous that Hollister could be involved, but it's "the people downtown" who think the major general might have knowledge of the shooting. Columbo plays up the role of the unsuspecting, amiable "good guy" while revealing he knows the motive for the crime. For his part, Hollister makes it clear he knows Columbo suspects him and successfully makes Columbo seasick through fast, swerving maneuvering of the boat, a tactic similar to the one used in "Ransom for a Dead Man."

When Columbo returns to shore, seriously discombobulated from his boat ride, he sees Stewart, who is now infatuated with Hollister and convinced that she was mistaken in what she thought she saw. Columbo's stunned by her recanting, but he continues his investigation.

The climax of the episode comes at a military history museum, where a special exhibit devoted to Hollister's career has just opened. Hollister has donated a lot of memorabilia from his exploits, including uniforms, souvenirs, and weapons. The pearl-handled gun in a case is supposedly a replica of the lost original, but Columbo realizes that Hollister is the sort of man who saves everything, especially anything that might burnish his legend. He knows that the Major General hadn't lost his signature firearm, that he would only have used that gun to shoot Dutton, and that he couldn't destroy it. The gun in the glass case at the museum is the murder weapon, and Columbo knows that a ballistics test will prove it. Hollister quietly accepts defeat, and Stewart is devastated, having just lost not only what she thinks might be her last chance at love, but her self-respect for being so easily manipulated and fooled by a murderer. Columbo comforts her, assuring her that she still has a chance at a happy ending.

The relationship between Columbo and Hollister is the shallowest of the series so far. Their screen time together is comparatively limited; there is no real connection between them, and the interplay between them is more of a checkers game than a chess match. There is no sincere friendship or respect on Hollister's part towards Columbo, and the major general seems to see the lieutenant more as an annoyance to be pushed away rather than a threat to his freedom. At the end, there's no real recognition of Columbo's skillfulness from Hollister, and Columbo seems to have no particular liking or respect for the military man. Hollister's attempts to thwart Columbo through clumsy threats and a bit of reckless boating aren't intelligent long-term solutions. By the end, Columbo treats Hollister as little more than a bully who's gotten his comeuppance. Their interactions are the slightest of the first season and amongst the least memorable of *Columbo's* early episodes.

Hollister's murder plan is one of the simplest in the series. Commit a murder on the spur of the moment, toss the body in the water, and make the only witness fall in love with you so she revokes her testimony. There's none of the imaginative alibi-making of the cleverest crimes (though this murder is unpremeditated), but the psychological manipulation of a witness is Hollister's chief triumph. Other *Columbo* murderers would see killing as the only way to eliminate such a threat, but Hollister's plan is much safer, far more challenging, and ultimately, quite effective.

Major General Martin J. Hollister was a man of action, but he was not a skilled tactician. His murder was committed on the spur of the moment, and he made three critical errors that doomed him. First, he failed to take even the most basic step to protect himself when committing the murder by shooting Dutton in front of an uncovered window. Second, he allowed the body to be discovered by his shoddy knot-tying when he disposed of the body in the ocean. Thirdly, he ought to have tossed the murder weapon into the ocean as well, and he would have been wise not to have used a weapon that was closely connected to him. Had he avoided any two of these mistakes, perhaps even any one of them, he would had a much better shot at getting away with his crime.

Then again, it's made clear right before the murder that the financial mismanagement was already being investigated, so Hollister may have already been under scrutiny for his theft. He was very likely a man under suspicion, and it proves that his embezzlement may not have been particularly subtle or clever, much like his murder. This reflects the mentality of the man. He was a blunt individual who pursued his objectives but failed to consider the consequences and barriers to his goals. As evidenced by his courtship of Stewart, he correctly believed himself to be a charming and charismatic man with a talent for persuasion, and judging by the implication that he began to develop real feelings for Stewart, he was not purely cold-hearted.

He was a man who had come to believe in his own legend, that of a dashing war hero whose bravery and calculated nature left him nearly invulnerable. He was, of course, wrong. Hollister was careless and put sentiment over self-preservation, acting as if everything would work out in his favor anyway, so he didn't have to put any effort into looking out for himself. Hollister consistently acted rashly and thoughtlessly, proving himself to be his own worst enemy.

Chapter Six: Suitable for Framing

Dale Kingston (Ross Martin) and Tracy O'Connor (Rosanna Huffman)

It's often said that a picture is worth a thousand words, but is a collection of priceless pictures worth two lives and the imprisonment of an innocent woman? Dale Kingston, an art critic with his own television show, seems to think so. In the opening moments of the episode, Kingston shoots his uncle point-blank, fakes a struggle by disrupting the room, and takes some artwork off the walls. Tracy O'Connor, Dale's girlfriend, arrives, gathers up the pictures, and waits for the right moment. After Kingston leaves, he establishes an alibi at a busy party, and O'Connor waits until the neighborhood security guard comes by and makes sure he sees her (but only from behind) running away holding some pictures.

Columbo arrives just shy of fourteen minutes into the episode and is immediately suspicious about the robbery, noting that the thief didn't grab the most expensive pictures first, and as the door was picked rather than the window, it's clearly not a professional job. Kingston is a bit testy as he tries to control the situation by chiding Columbo's behavior and questions, but part of this is due to the lieutenant's catching some holes in his narrative. Columbo's polite but clearly suspicious of Kingston, and Kingston repays this with superciliousness.

O'Connor thought she was going to live happily ever after with her boyfriend, but Kingston had other plans, striking and killing her in an out-of-the-way spot. As he leaves the crime scene, he retrieves the paintings O'Connor took, carrying them in a bag. When he returns home, he finds Columbo dozing in a chair. Kingston had previously lent Columbo a key so the lieutenant could search it, proving the artwork wasn't hidden there. Understandably anxious to see Columbo there while he's holding incriminating evidence, Kingston tries to shoo Columbo away, but Columbo reaches into the bag, asking to see the artwork he's carrying. He's met with a sharp rebuff from Kingston.

At the reading of the will, Columbo is stunned to discover that Kingston's uncle had changed his last testament and that Kingston only gets a pittance. It's the uncle's ex-wife, Edna Matthews (Kim Hunter), who inherits the art collection, and a triumphant Kingston produces a letter proving he knew he'd been disinherited.

Kingston acts caring and protective towards his aunt, but it's all a sham. He plants the murder weapon near her home, and Columbo states that she's under suspicion, but he's not going to arrest her until he finds the stolen art. Thus prodded, Kingston slips into her house and hides the paintings there. He then encourages his aunt's lawyer to demand a search of the house to prove her innocence.

The police find the stolen art right away, and Kingston is practically purring, confident he's won. But Columbo isn't the least bit fooled, and he accuses Kingston of the crimes. If he framed his Aunt Edna, she'd go to jail, and he'd inherit the art. Kingston is indignant, but Columbo explains that they're looking for fingerprints on the stolen pictures. Kingston declares they won't find his prints, but Columbo explains they're looking for *his* prints, left there when he reached into the bag Kingston had carried earlier. A deflated Kingston babbles and claims it's a trap, and that he saw Columbo touch the pictures just minutes earlier. In one of the most legendary moments of the series, Columbo wordlessly pulls his hands out of his coat pockets, where he's kept them the entire time he's been at Edna Matthews' house, and reveals that he's wearing gloves.

Tracy O'Connor is one of a very small number of *Columbo* killers who the detective never meets. Though she doesn't commit the murder herself, she knew it would happen and was a full and willing accessory. Her motive lay both in her feelings for Kingston (which she wrongly believed he reciprocated) and in her belief that he could advance her art career. Foolishly, she failed to see that she was nothing more than a loose end to him, and she paid for her crime with her life. It's not clear if Columbo is ever able to prove Kingston was responsible for her death, and O'Connor becomes a forgotten footnote to the case by the episode's end.

It's the relationship between Kingston and Columbo that's the backbone of the episode. Columbo is his usual self, masking keen suspicion with aw-shucks politeness, and Kingston is all oily disdain. It wouldn't have hurt Kingston at all to have been friendlier to Columbo, but it wasn't in his nature. Kingston was, at heart, a snob, and he couldn't find it in his cold, supercilious heart to be kind to this shabby little man. Though he acted like a comfortable member of the glitterati, as his modest accommodations prove, as an art critic with a niche educational television show, Kingston was only *wealth adjacent* rather than wealthy himself. Though he dressed well and conducted himself like a princeling, he was neither rich nor powerful. He was simply a minor celebrity with connections to famous art lovers.

Kingston was rude to Columbo from the beginning, treating him like a lackey who couldn't appreciate the great art around him. The art critic grudgingly concedes that Columbo's sharper than he thought, especially when the lieutenant suggests a phone tap in case of an art ransom, a suggestion Kingston hadn't considered but has to agree to in order to avoid suspicion. Kingston quickly realizes that Columbo is a dangerous opponent, but his arrogance convinces him that he's much too clever to be caught.

In their next meetings, Kingston peppers his conversation with snide remarks, sneering, "My, how observant you are," responding in a hostile manner to all of the lieutenant's suggestions and snapping that Columbo's wasting his time. It's bad psychology, as Kingston is also trying to manipulate Columbo, but he does nothing to make the lieutenant like or trust him. He switches from snotty art snob to a caring nephew so quickly it's not convincing. A man so obviously self-obsessed hasn't got a filial bone in his body.

He deliberately drew suspicion to himself simply to discount the theories against him, and his making a great show of having someone search his car for a supposedly lost cuff link right after the murder didn't fool Columbo for a second—he knew it was just a feint to prove he didn't have the art in his trunk. Once the will seemingly evaporates his motive, Kingston is smug and derisive, calling Columbo a "compulsively suspicious bureaucrat" and telling him, "Stop pestering me…find the real killer." Later, Columbo knowingly turns this back on him, saying he's going to be careful with the aunt, as "I sure don't wanna make the same mistake I made with you."

This is a classic example of the supposed manipulator not realizing how transparent he is. The whole time, Kingston believes he's come up with a foolproof plan, but Columbo knows at once that he's trying to frame his aunt (technically, his ex-aunt). Like many killers, Kingston believed that the police would take the illusion he created at face value. Furthermore, he had the common shortcoming of believing himself to be a much better actor than he really was. Kingston's failure to maintain a psychologically consistent approach to his own characterization helped defeat him.

Dale Kingston wanted to become the owner of a massive art collection, and he didn't care that he'd have to destroy a trio of lives to do it. He was a haughty man with pretensions of grandeur, and his inflated self-opinion, mixed with his unjustified self-confidence in his own crime-planning skills, led him to believe that he was invincible. He thought that he'd created a masterpiece of murder, but in a supreme irony, the art critic's work couldn't stand up to close scrutiny.

Chapter Seven: Lady in Waiting

Beth Chadwick (Susan Clark)

Traditionally, critics and viewers view Beth Chadwick as an oppressed, smothered young woman of spirit and intelligence who was forced into a quiet and mousy role by her overbearing family. While there is certainly some validity to this interpretation, there is another, possibly more convincing, way of looking at her character. She can also be viewed as a mentally unstable bad seed whose family members tried to reform and protect but failed.

Beth Chadwick is a young woman whose life is controlled by her older brother, Bryce (Richard Anderson). She dresses in a quiet manner, and when she's around her brother, she acts submissive, but in private, she plots her escape from his influence. She's wealthy, but her brother controls her inheritance, and he also has the power to wreck her relationship with Peter Hamilton (Leslie Nielsen), an up-and-coming employee at the Chadwick family advertising firm. Bryce Chadwick is convinced that Hamilton is only interested in his sister's money and announces his plan to fire Hamilton and break up their romance.

Not willing to let this happen, Beth plans her brother's murder. The servants are out that evening, so when he returns from his trip, no one will be there to let him inside the mansion they share. She removes her brother's house key from the ring and anticipates that when he comes home, he'll be unable to get inside. She won't answer the doorbell, and expects that he'll try to come in through the door of her ground-floor bedroom. When he comes inside, she plans to take her handgun and shoot him, claiming she thought he was a burglar.

But her plan goes awry when her brother returns home, and not finding his key on the ring, picks up the spare key he hid in a flowerpot without her knowledge. He enters the mansion, leaves his newspaper and attaché case in the foyer, and goes to his sister's room to ask why she didn't answer the bell. Impulsively, she shoots him as he stands in her inner doorway, triggers the burglar alarm, drags his body to the door leading outside, and makes a couple more adjustments to set the scene.

Though Columbo's voice is heard in her imagination as she predicts how the police will believe it was all an understandable accident, Columbo first appears nearly twenty-one minutes into the episode, though oddly enough, his voice is heard in Beth's mind as she imagines how smoothly her plan will work out for her, even though she hasn't met Columbo yet. He's immediately suspicious, noting that the newspaper and attaché case's locations prove he came in through the main door. Hamilton, who was on the edge of the grounds at the time of the shooting, planning to confront Bryce Chadwick, is immediately able to comfort his fiancée. Later, when Mrs. Chadwick (Jessie Royce Landis), Beth, and Bryce's mother arrives, she slaps her daughter and chastises her. Columbo starts asking questions, but Mrs. Chadwick's attitude turns on a dime, and she protectively defends Beth.

Beth is cleared at the inquest, and immediately, her attitude becomes upbeat and ambitious. She goes to the beauty parlor and gets a makeover, and updates her wardrobe to flashier 1970s styles. A fancy car is delivered to her house, and when she notes how she needed a change in the wake of everything that's happened, Columbo points out that the car would have to be ordered weeks in advance, long before she shot her brother. This proves that she was planning the crime prior to when her brother vowed to end her relationship with Hamilton.

Columbo questions Beth at her home, pointing out the discrepancies in her story, such as the imprint of a spare key in a flower pot. She claims she left the key there and removed it when she realized it was a security risk, and she soon gets angry and impatient with him. Soon afterwards, she announces her plans to take over the family business, along with an aggressive new management plan. Columbo questions her some more at the office, noting more discrepancies in her story, and she orders him to leave and never come back. Hamilton becomes wary of her radically changed personality, and she suggests that perhaps their relationship shouldn't continue.

A dejected Hamilton sees Columbo at a bar, and Columbo informs him that he's sure it was premeditated murder and asks Hamilton to help him by telling him everything he can remember. Hamilton becomes the key witness, as he remembers that the gun was fired *before* the alarm was activated. Had Bryce opened his sister's door as she claimed, the sound of shooting would have happened *after* the alarm started blaring.

Armed with this proof, Columbo comes to the mansion to confront Beth that night, setting a trap to set the scene beforehand. When she hears a noise, she immediately believes it's Columbo and invites him in without seeing him, grabbing her gun as she does so. Is she planning to shoot him as well? Surely, killing two men would raise suspicions. In any case, Columbo appears at the inner door and walks her through his evidence, proving that he knows it was first-degree murder. She tries to dismiss his conclusions as "a bit of nonsense," but Columbo presents a solid case. Rage flashing across her face, she points the gun at him, and when he tells her that other officers are outside and know what's going on, she doesn't waver. It's not until Columbo tells her she's "too classy a woman" to fire the gun that she lowers it and surrenders peacefully.

The relationship between Columbo and Beth Chadwick is antagonistic from the beginning, partly because Columbo notices the holes in her story right away. Based on the location of her brother's attaché case and newspaper, he knows that the late Bryce didn't come in from his sister's outer door. Beth doesn't show her hostility immediately, but once she starts voicing her displeasure, she can barely hide it. Based on a close-up of Beth when they first meet, she clearly gets the sense that Columbo suspects something. The three people closest to Beth: her brother, her mother, and her fiancé– all want to protect her. Hamilton shields her out of love and chivalry, Bryce sees her as an easily manipulated woman who needs to be protected, and Mrs. Chadwick is furious with her daughter yet still wants her to avoid the scrutiny of the law. When Columbo first meets her after the murder, Beth Chadwick acts scared, shaken, and shy. Given how quickly she sheds her vulnerable persona, it's almost certainly an act, but it's an extremely effective one. By adopting the timid attitude, everybody close to her underestimates her, and they each position themselves as her defenders. She doesn't need it, but it's possible she likes this treatment as long as she still gets what she wants when she wants it. But Columbo doesn't buy what she's selling, and that is a threat to her.

Mrs. Chadwick declares that her son, who was several years older than his sister, "looked after her all of her life." This means that he was protective of her ever since she was a child. Was this evidence of a controlling nature, or did she really *need* that sort of oversight? Was she always unbalanced, or at least impulsive and prone to getting into trouble? Did her big brother get into the habit of rescuing her and cleaning up her messes early on and never tried to wean himself from this role? Or has she always acted weak and vulnerable? Based on some snippets of dialogue from Mrs. Chadwick, her daughter hasn't been a mousy wallflower her whole life. On the contrary, she's gotten into some serious trouble in the past, and if this depiction of her is accurate, it proves that her initial persona is not the result of repression and that she quickly grows out of it once she gets some freedom, but that it's a mask she wears because it helps her endure the strictures placed upon her, possibly because of very real mistakes she made in the past. Whether her mother and brother have overreacted and treated her as a child for too long, whether they recognized signs of dangerous instability and did their best to counteract this, or whether their motives lie somewhere in-between is entirely up to conjecture. It is clear that Bryce Chadwick is totally wrong about Hamilton, who genuinely cares about her and is unconcerned about his fiancée's money. If he misjudged Hamilton, could he have made other mistakes in his treatment of his sister? Or could he be so used to her poor choices that he unfairly jumped to the conclusion that any decision she made was wrong?

But for the first time, Beth has to deal with someone who sees through her persona. Columbo runs through the many "points bothering me," but Mrs. Chadwick races to her daughter's rescue. Columbo notices the rapid change in Beth Chadwick's demeanor, and at first, she's amiable when he makes her "a captive audience" at the hairdresser's. But when he finds evidence that shatters her story, her attitude sours quickly. Columbo observes that had Bryce Chadwick walked through the lawn to get to his sister's room, there would have been grass clippings from the freshly cut lawn on his shoes, and there weren't. Having no answer to this, she barks, "I think you've finally overstayed your welcome," insisting the inquest's verdict should satisfy him. She snaps with hardly any provocation, illustrating what a volatile temper she has.

This quickness to anger is even more pronounced when he visits her at the office, pointing out that the lightbulb by the front door was tampered with, as it's much too clean, handing her the pristine blub. She snaps, "I don't ever want to see you again," and tells him that he's to be barred from her home and workplace. Columbo maintains his friendly and self-deprecating demeanor, even when she threatens his job. Her reaction isn't proportionate to his questioning, and Hamilton can tell that something's very wrong with his fiancée, especially when she smashes the lightbulb and throws a fit. Hamilton notes that she's acting like a completely different woman, and it seems he's wondering if she's changed or if he's just seeing the real version of her for the first time. (Clearly, he's not a golddigger, for if he were, he'd simply say whatever was necessary to keep her happy.) Beth Chadwick isn't happy about her fiancé questioning her decisions, and her last words to him leave the status of their relationship in doubt. Certainly, Hamilton isn't sure if he's engaged or not afterwards.

Was Beth Chadwick a downtrodden woman who sought empowerment? Or was she an impulsive person with genuine mental disorders who was being cared for, albeit a bit too strictly, by her family, and eventually, her destructive and negative personality broke through in the form of homicide? The verdict probably depends on the viewer's point of view. Whether Beth Chadwick is seen as an initially sympathetic character or as an always dangerous and manipulative character is a point that is up to the individual analyzing her behavior. From a psychological perspective, Beth Chadwick might be diagnosed with any number of conditions due to her quick and violent temper and her lack of empathy for anybody else.

In the scene where she announces her plans to run the family business, she declares her goal of expansion and threatens the jobs of anybody who is content with the status quo. A policy of growth can be an intelligent move, but it needs to be backed up with a sensible business strategy. All Beth Chadwick is doing is ordering her staff to drum up more business. For an advertising agency, that means more clients, more meetings, and more work. Advertising isn't just selling an existing quantity of a product, it means creativity, thought, and research put into campaigns, artwork, and maintaining customer relations. Notably, she offers no rewards for success, such as promotions or raises, only punishments of unemployment if people balk. Essentially, she's telling them to "work a lot harder and make me richer." A wise executive seeking to expand a business would first hire more talent to make the acquisition of additional clients possible without spreading the existing staff too thinly. Beth Chadwick's management style is to demand a result without actually putting in the effort and resources to make it possible.

The final scene between Columbo and Beth Chadwick illustrates his measure of her character. He tells her straightaway that he's going to arrest her and wants to see the look on her face when he comes in the way her brother did. He punctures her ego by telling her he knew she was lying from the moment he met her, illustrating that her acting skills weren't enough to sway him. The revelation that Hamilton knew the facts that would prove her guilt, though he didn't recognize their significance, is another blow to her self-esteem. It's questionable what Columbo's strategy is, as he's riling up an armed woman with a history of anger management problems. As is shown several times throughout the series, Columbo can take pleasure in taking the powerful and arrogant down a peg. When he realizes that he's in real danger, a warning regarding her own safety doesn't help, but an appeal to her vanity does. In any event, Columbo almost certainly realizes at the end that he came very close to being shot, for even though he showed no fear to Beth Chadwick, he lit a cigar as soon as she left to get dressed to go down to the police station, and from his body language, he desperately desired the tobacco in order to steady his nerves.

When evaluating Beth Chadwick's character, it is critical to consider the plan she plotted. In order to convince everybody that she shot her brother by accident, she had to convince the authorities and the inquest jury that she acted out of fear and panic, and to create that impression; she had to create the persona of a timid, anxious young woman who people would feel the urge to protect. If she projected strength and confidence, her story would be far less convincing. Given the evidence of her ordering a flashy new car long before the murder, she had been planning the crime for some time. Her mousy persona, it follows, was not a genuine attitude brought about by her overbearing relatives. It was, more bluntly, a long con cultivated for the purposes of deception.

In his final meeting with Columbo, Hamilton told him, "I like you, I really do, but you are devious." Beth Chadwick was also devious, but Columbo succeeded in catching her because he paid close attention to details, whereas Beth was so focused on attaining her goals that she neglected to take the necessary precautions to allow her to protect and preserve her victories, and she was so blinded by her objectives that she forgot to address the discrepancies in the narrative she created.

Chapter Eight: Short Fuse

Roger Stanford (Roddy McDowall)

Roger Stanford is a young man with great ambitions, but emotionally, he is stuck in a state of arrested development. The term "man-child" might be applied to him, but this would be unfair to children, who overwhelmingly don't turn to homicide to achieve their goals.

Stanford is a prankster, dealing in juvenile jokes that only he finds funny. As the episode opens, he hands out exploding cigars and sprays the secretarial pool with silly string. He's the scion of a family-owned company, but he's currently stuck in a lower-level position with no power. It's debatable whether Stanford is caught in this position due to his unserious nature, or because his controlling uncle by marriage, David L. Buckner (James Gregory), who runs the company, is deliberately keeping him down for selfish reasons.

Buckner wants his nephew out of the company and tasks his investigator/chauffeur, Quincy (Lawrence Cook), with proving that Stanford is guilty of financial mismanagement, and orders Stanford either to leave the company or face criminal prosecution. Stanford goes with the third option: murder. He's clearly been planning this long before the confrontation. Using his scientific knowledge, he rigs a box of expensive cigars with a bomb and places it in his uncle's car. Later that night, when Buckner and Quincy are driving along a cliffside road, the bomb explodes, sending the unfortunate pair over the edge to their deaths.

Columbo enters nearly twenty minutes into the episode, though at the time it's a missing persons case. Columbo starts questioning Stanford, who acts flippant, but underneath his levity are pointed attempts to get Columbo searching in the direction he wants. When the car is discovered, Columbo soon suspects that the two men were killed by a bomb, and soon deduces the only place where such an object could have been hidden is in the cigar box. Stanford bobs and weaves to both attract and deflect suspicion, making it obvious he's keeping secrets.

Stanford's plan involves framing two innocent people. Everett Logan (William Windom), an uptight vice president who wants to avoid a scandal, is targeted to take the fall for Stanford's financial malfeasance. Betty Bishop (Anne Francis) is Buckner's secretary, who Stanford is quietly dating. Stanford takes intimate photos of Bishop and uses these images to create suggestive pictures of his uncle with his secretary.

Stanford later waits at Quincy's hideaway, where the late investigator kept his files. When the police arrive, Stanford makes a big show of running away and getting caught. He insists on being brought to his Aunt Doris (Ida Lupino), and urges Columbo to let him talk to him alone. After a bit of manipulation, the content of the files Stanford was caught taking is revealed. The faked dossiers implicate Bishop and Logan, the former for an affair with her late boss, the latter for financial impropriety. Quietly enraged, Aunt Doris takes steps to have the pair forced out of the company and touched by Stanford's determination to protect her feelings, places him in charge of the company.

Unfortunately for Stanford, he's not on top of the world for long. Columbo invites Logan and Stanford to watch him uncover the truth, saying he now believes that this was an accident and there was no bomb. As the trio ride up a funicular towards Aunt Doris's house, Columbo produces a scorched cigar box, saying it was just found near the scene of the crime. Stanford's stunned, now believing that his bomb never did go off after all and that his uncle and his chauffeur simply fell victim to a genuine inadvertent car crash. Columbo opens and closes the box, which activate the timer and denotes the bomb within a short time. Columbo and Logan chat as Columbo explains the charges of fraud Logan faces while Logan protests his innocence. Meanwhile, Stanford slowly freaks out, hoping that they can reach the top of the cliff before the bomb goes off. When he realizes that there isn't enough time, he panics, grabs the box, and attempts to throw it out the door, though the box opens and cigars spill everywhere. Columbo reveals that the cigar box he was holding was never in the car and that he burnt it himself. It was all a trap to get Stanford to reveal he knew about the bomb and the box. Caught, Stanford bursts into peals of laughter.

Is Stanford's laughter simply his appreciation of a joke at his own expense, or is the frenzied cackling a sign that he has had some sort of mental break? It's an unanswered question. Looking back, is his frequent practical joking and lack of seriousness a sign of mental illness? There is no definite answer to that question.

What is not in doubt is that he has no qualms about destroying other people and ruining the lives of those who have never done him any harm. He developed his plan to kill his uncle before he knew that Quincy had compiled a dossier against him, which means that his murder plot had already called for Quincy's death before he even knew for certain that Quincy knew incriminating secrets about him. Quincy's death would have just been collateral damage, but he was targeted for death before Stanford had an actual motive to kill him, and no remorse or regret on Stanford's part is ever shown.

Stanford's immature behavior reflects both his desires and his character flaws. He resents how people treat him as a joke, but Bishop observes that he "plays the fool." He doesn't like being called "Junior," but until late in the episode, when he commands respect as the new company head, he does nothing to encourage people to treat him seriously. He's clearly a highly intelligent person, perhaps even with a genius-level intellect. He has a doctorate in chemistry, an MBA, and a law degree as well. Yet, while he earned many impressive achievements, his sense of humor remains juvenile, and he has little genuine empathy for others. His style of humor, exemplified in the form of practical jokes, is also a bit of a giveaway. The prospect of a box of exploding cigars is really a clue pointing right at him, as who else would come up with the idea of such a means of murder? The exploding cigar concept is essentially a calling card he left incriminating himself.

Once Stanford has been appointed the head of the company, he changes his dressing style from 1970s casual to a formal suit and demands respect from his employees. He acts far more seriously, which leads to many questions. Was he playing up the role of the joker earlier? Was he always capable of adopting a much more somber attitude? If so, did he act as he did to make people underestimate him as a cold-blooded killer and schemer? If he was exaggerating his immaturity, didn't he realize that it would make it harder for other people to treat him seriously as a leader? Or is the straight-laced company man the real façade, and if so, how long can he keep it up? Logan may not have been particularly warm towards Stanford, but he was never cruel or openly disrespectful towards him. Stanford simply tried to crush him because Logan blocked his path on the corporate ladder. And Bishop genuinely cared for Stanford, but he had no qualms about exploiting sensitive images of her and besmirching her good name. After getting her fired, he tried to soften the blow by banishing her to another state to be closer to her mother, promising to visit her often, even though it's pretty clear he doesn't intend to give her a second thought. As she has now played her part as a pawn in his game, Stanford is now content to shove her aside. Stanford is a fundamentally callous person, with no concern for others and feeling no guilt for his betrayals and the damage he causes. While a diagnosis of sociopathy is frequently hazardous, especially for a fictional character, it is fair to say that Stanford is a man who cares only about himself, and he is never upset by the fact that he is the only one who finds his jokes funny.

In his interactions with Columbo, Stanford sees the detective as a figure to be manipulated and pushed into the desired direction. When they first meet, Roger doesn't realize Columbo is with the police and treats him disrespectfully, illustrating the contempt he feels for people who can't help him in some way. When he learns Columbo's profession, his attitude changes for the better, though he still criticizes Columbo's car, comments which the lieutenant takes in stride.

Stanford starts laying his trail of red herrings very early in his acquaintanceship with Columbo, preemptively telling him that his uncle's money goes to his aunt, not him, and subtly hinting that his uncle may have been up to secret activities that were neither his business nor Columbo's. When Columbo accidentally sprays himself with silly string, Stanford is amused. Columbo realizes early on that if there was a bomb in the car, the only place to hide it was in the cigar box. Stanford tries to force the false point that the box must have been switched in the office, and he had no opportunity to change the boxes, though this is a very flimsy alibi that a skilled investigator could easily discredit, as Columbo does effortlessly.

Throughout Columbo's investigation, Stanford tries to misdirect him, pretending he can't remember clues that could lead to Quincy's hidden files and laying his supposed devotion to his aunt on thickly. Lacking the control to hide his loathing for his uncle, Stanford pushes his uncle's photograph face down in the office, a point that Columbo catches immediately.

As is often the case, Columbo sees through all of the manipulations, and the lieutenant is far more skillful at covering up his own tricks and traps. Notably, the first time Columbo rides in the funicular, he's motion sick, but in the episode's climax, he's completely unfazed by the mechanism. Based on other episodes, Columbo doesn't fake his queasiness. It seems as if he's so focused on trapping Stanford that he's unaware of the jostling. Or perhaps someone adjusted the controls, and the mechanism ran a bit smoother that day. In any case, Columbo succeeds spectacularly at making Stanford crack and incriminate himself, and though Stanford doesn't actually confess, between peals of laughter, he removes a medal for outstanding scientific work from his own neck and puts it around Columbo's. This could be construed as an amiable tribute, a good sportsman's recognition of the superior mind. It could also be seen as a less meaningful action caused by a mental break.

Ambiguity remains as to whether Stanford was an amoral monster, an unpleasant man with a twisted sense of humor, or a person suffering from serious mental health conditions that ultimately overwhelmed him. Viewers will never know what exactly was going on in Stanford's mind, but it is unquestionable that Stanford was a man focused solely on himself and his own goals, a man for whom other people's lives and reputations meant nothing and who took delight in the embarrassment of others. For him, causing destruction and humiliation were sources of humor, and he intended to laugh all the way to the presidency of his family business. Thanks to Columbo's investigation, the final joke was on Stanford.

Chapter Nine: Blueprint for Murder

Elliot Markham (Patrick O'Neal)

Elliot Markham is a man with a vision, an architect, and a city planner with a dream so vast that it can only be fulfilled through the use of another man's fortune. When the fabulously wealthy Bo Williamson (Forrest Tucker), who had initially signed on for a much more modest construction project, decides to keep his wallet securely in his pocket in the wake of spiraling costs, Markham becomes desperate. He's not about to let a little point like needing to drain another man's bank account stand in the way of fulfilling his architectural dream.

Before Williamson can cut off all funding, Markham confronts him and leads him to an isolated place at gunpoint. This is the first time that a murder is not explicitly shown onscreen, but there's no twist here–just because viewers don't see the crime committed doesn't mean that there's any doubt that Markham pulled the trigger and fatally wounded Williamson. The big question is what happened to the body. With Williamson's corpse undiscovered, it's officially a missing persons case rather than a homicide.

When Columbo is called in twelve minutes into the episode, it's due to the concerns of Goldie Williamson (Janis Paige), Bo Williamson's first wife, who he divorced in order to marry the much younger Jennifer Williamson (Pamela Austin). Goldie Williamson has taken the abandonment in stride, as she still cares for her ex-husband's well-being and treats her replacement rather like a headstrong niece, bearing no discernible rancor, just some mild pique. Goldie Williamson is convinced her husband has been murdered, and after a little questioning, Columbo agrees, even without a body. Jennifer Williamson has no knowledge of the murder, but she's a firm believer in the construction project. With her husband supposedly overseas, the second Mrs. Williamson has the right to keep funding the project in his absence.

Columbo quickly figures out that this is Markham's plan and starts trying to figure out the corpse's location. Notably, Markham himself plants the idea in Columbo's head that a body could be buried at the construction site. Columbo keeps peppering Markham with questions, causing consternation. Ironically, Columbo has to save Markham from a frame-up job when a bloodied cowboy hat of the style Bo Williamson wore is discovered. A little investigation proves that the gory hat was planted by Goldie Williamson, who is convinced of Markham's guilt and wants to see him punished.

But it'll take hard facts and a cold corpse to get an arrest, so Columbo goes through a lot of trouble to get permission to have one of the construction foundations drilled and searched for the body. After a long day of excavation in the foundation that was being prepared the day of Bo Williamson's disappearance, no trace of a corpse is found, and a triumphant Markham trumpets the lack of a discovery to the press.

After sunset that evening, the extent of Markham's plan is revealed. He takes Williamson's corpse from the hiding place near the scene of the crime and drives the body across town, planning to plant it in the foundation, where it'll be covered up, and Columbo will never get permission to excavate the area again. But before Markham can toss the body into the foundation, Columbo and other police officers appear, revealing that they anticipated this development all along. Columbo notes that Markham was trying to force the issue without being too blatant about it, revealing that he knew that "you kept trying to finesse me into digging that pile." As Columbo knew Markham wouldn't transport the body until he was sure it was safe, Columbo "had to play along" in order to get Markham to make his move.

In most cases, when a person who has recently committed a murder meets Columbo, the killer is on the defensive. In "Blueprint for Murder," Markham is also on the offensive, trying to draw Columbo into a position that will leave him humiliated and discredited and leave him forever safe, as no one will dare to search that location twice. In order for his plan to work, Markham has to take the role of a manipulator, trying to force Columbo into a course of action. It's a tricky procedure, and Markham tries to be subtle about it, but he's not as skillful as he thinks he's being. He effectively plants the idea of the corpse being concealed in the foundation into Columbo's mind without being too blatant about it, but his mistake is in failing to provide alternatives. An innocent man brainstorming about places to hide a body might spend equal amounts of time talking about out-of-the-way places where a corpse could be buried, immersed in a body of water, or otherwise destroyed. Markham was much like the magician saying, "mentally select any card you see from the deck," while flipping the deck in front of a person's eyes. In this trick, the magician arranges the deck so as to pause the flipping for a fraction of a second on the card he wants the subject to select, and because that one card is the only one the subject gets a good look at, ninety-nine times out of a hundred, the subject will pick the card he saw for the longest amount of time.

The relationship between Columbo and Markham is not particularly warm. Markham is frequently standoffish and abrupt to Columbo, though for his part, Columbo does his part to unnerve Markham from the beginning, delaying Markham's dinner with a question and offering some raisins from the pocket of his coat to tide him over, a suggestion Markham finds unpleasant. The offer of half a candy bar (presumably Columbo bit off the other half) is similarly declined. The bitten chocolate and the pocket raisins are an effective way of unsettling Markham, forcing him to disguise the disgust he feels.

Columbo's suspicions are raised by the usual little details, including the fact that the model of the building project was smashed up in Markham's office, and he correctly deduces that the victim attacked it. Not only that, but Markham made a mistake when driving Williamson's car by setting the radio to the classical music that he likes, as opposed to the country music Williamson preferred. As Markham's record collection makes it clear, he's a classical music fan, and this simple point being overlooked points Columbo in the correct direction.

Markham is fairly unpleasant and derisive over the course of his acquaintance with Columbo, snapping, "I assume I can look forward to another visit in the near future?" as the detective is about to leave and telling Columbo at the construction site that "you're very much like an arachnid," calling him a tick that hangs on and only lets go with a lot of effort. At times, Markham seems to be unnecessarily hostile, but this is a psychological strategy. Markham *wants* Columbo to dislike him. He *wants* Columbo to suspect him, so he'll dig where he wants him to, thereby providing him with the safest possible hiding place for the corpse. That's why he doesn't bother to charm him or befriend him—according to his plan; Markham needs to antagonize Columbo so that the detective will go to considerable lengths to catch him. It's logical, but it's also counterproductive because it encourages Columbo to keep going after him, and once Columbo has seen through Markham's ruse, Markham's continued rudeness does nothing to help him.

Elliot Markham became a murderer as a result of his need to see his dream construction project come to fruition. It's not excessive to conclude that his plans are actually a massive tribute to his own ego, as the architectural plans are about more than a desire to provide a useful new branch of the city, but are truly a means of assuring his own immortality. Some men might consider that they have created a permanent contribution to a city in the form of a single building, but that is not enough for Markham. Markham needs to create an entire business district, a massive structure that will become a supporting pillar of southern California's economy and one that might stand for many decades, even centuries.

The murder of Bo Williamson was, therefore, a human sacrifice to bring Markham's dreams of secular longevity into reality. It was a cold-blooded gambit to do more than simply profit, but to create something that would outlive him. Ironically, it was his desire to be ingenious that wound up dooming his dreams. Had he buried Bo Williamson in the woods or thrown his body into the ocean, the corpse might have been found eventually, but he might have had a chance to complete his dream project, or at least build it to the point where it would have had to have been finished in order to prevent the construction from becoming a total loss. Markham tried to be too clever for his own good, but unfortunately for his hopes for lasting glory, Columbo was cleverer than he was, and the detective countered Markham's vanity with the humility to endure several hours of public ridicule in order to see justice done.

II

SEASON TWO

Chapter Ten: Étude in Black

Alex Benedict (John Cassavetes)

Alex Benedict can lead an orchestra, but he can't wave his baton like a magic wand and fool Columbo. Alex Benedict is the conductor of a prominent California symphony, married to a loving, beautiful, and extremely wealthy wife, Janice Benedict (Blythe Danner). With a brilliant career and plenty of money, one might think that he has everything he could possibly want out of life, but all of this isn't enough for him, and he has been having an affair with Jennifer Welles (Anjanette Comer), a pianist in the symphony. While the conductor is happy to sleep with her, he has no plans to leave his wife for her. Welles decides to apply a little pressure to get him to get a divorce, but instead of becoming his second wife, she becomes his murder victim.

Right before a big concert, Alex Benedict slips out of his dressing room, dons a trench coat and sunglasses over his conducting tuxedo, and makes his way to Welles' home. When she announces that she's going to tell his wife everything so they can be together, he strikes her over the head, knocking her unconscious. He carries her into her kitchen, and arranges her on the floor. The impression he's trying to create is that she opened the oven and turned on the gas in order to commit suicide, and as she passed out from the gas, she fell off her seat, causing her recent head injury. To complete the staged scene, he plants a prewritten suicide note in the typewriter and returns to the Hollywood Bowl to conduct the concert.

Unfortunately for him, the pink flower falls out of his boutonniere before he leaves the murder scene.

Columbo first appears nearly twenty-six minutes into the episode at the veterinarian's office. This episode marks the first appearance of the lieutenant's beloved basset hound, known only as "Dog." The veterinarian is a classical music lover and watches the concert on television. Soon, Columbo is called to the scene of the crime, even though, at the time, it looks like a suicide. Columbo's dejected, declaring, "I can't stand suicide. Murder is sad, but suicide is sadder… Every time I see a dead body, I think it's been murdered…I like to see everyone die of old age." Meanwhile, Alex Benedict is informed of the pianist's death and, after dodging some news reporters and their cameras, makes his way to the crime scene. When he arrives, he notices his lost flower on the floor and quickly replaces it in his lapel. This is a mistake, as Columbo sees him do it, though the detective doesn't confront him about this. The conductor would have been wiser to stuff the flower in his pocket. Going further, had he changed into street clothes before committing his murder, not only would he have been less conspicuous, but it would have prevented the whole problem with the dropped flower.

Over the course of the episode, Columbo visits Alex Benedict frequently, often annoying him despite always being polite and friendly. Columbo explores his mansion, commenting on the cost of the house and furniture, and visits the garage where the conductor keeps his very expensive car. Columbo explains that the gas from the kitchen killed Welles' pet cockatoo and notes that if it was really a suicide, she would have moved it out of harm's way. Alex Benedict tries and fails to explain away this and other observations Columbo makes.

Columbo meets the conductor again at the Hollywood Bowl (where he happily plays "Chopsticks" on the piano) and explains that close examination proves the "suicide" note was typed elsewhere due to the bends in the paper and also observes that the mileage on the car doesn't fit the records at the garage, and though Columbo doesn't come out and say this, the discrepancy was caused by the use of the car to drive to and from the murder scene. Alex Benedict doubles down on the suicide theory, even though Columbo is confident it's murder. This marks a turning point in their relationship, as Alex is increasingly hostile towards the detective from this point onwards.

When Columbo speaks to Janice Benedict, he alerts her to the possibility of her husband's infidelity, thereby further infuriating her husband. Columbo thinks he's got Alex dead to rights when Audrey (Dawn Frame), a young neighbor of the victim, says she can identify a frequently-visiting boyfriend, but it turns out to be the innocent Paul Rifkin (James Olsen). Now Columbo has to build a case against Alex while clearing Rifkin. A conversation with the conductor's mother-in-law, Lizzy Fielding (Myrna Loy), who runs the orchestra, informs him that she will gladly fire her son-in-law if he steps out of line.

At the climax, Columbo invites the Benedicts to a meeting. Alex doesn't want to go, but Janice insists, and Columbo shows a recording of the concert and the news reporting afterwards, showing that Alex was missing his pink lapel flower at the concert, but had it again after visiting the crime scene. It's not conclusive evidence, and Alex is contemptuous, but his wife's devastated reaction changes everything. It's clear that though she'd been giving him the benefit of the doubt earlier, she now believes he killed his lover, and she tearfully declares that she could have forgiven him for all of his transgressions except murder. Realizing that he has lost his wife, Alex surrenders, shaking Columbo's hand and exiting with a respectful "Goodbye, genius."

From the moment they meet, Alex Benedict's general attitude towards Columbo is one of superiority. He knows he's far wealthier than Columbo (even if he married money rather than earned or inherited it), but there's also the "I'm better than you" attitude that comes with believing himself to be more cultured and important. The snobbish attitude is evident from their first meeting, but it's best exemplified in his reaction to Columbo plunking out "Chopsticks" on the piano—he sees Columbo's choice of music as so far below his own tastes of the finest classical pieces, that the chasm in their tastes is enormous. By sniping, "I haven't heard "Chopsticks" since I was a little boy," he mocks Columbo as being childish as well. As usual, Columbo displays no hurt feelings nor attempts a counterattack. He very gently reveals his suspicions by dropping lines like "suppose it was you" when recreating the murder. By the last third of the episode, Alex draws attention to himself with unjustified outbursts of anger and complaints about "harassment." His responses to Columbo are constant overreactions of hostility, reflecting anxiety over the investigation.

Notably, Alex's attempts to dismiss Columbo's theories are not very convincing. He has no logical explanation to wave away details like the death of the pet bird or the extra curls in the "suicide note." All he offers are flat denials and insistence on suicide, but no alternative theories or counterarguments. He seems to be trying to dissuade the lieutenant through sheer force of will, and he fails, as insistence is no substitute for evidence.

At the end, when the conductor admits he has been caught, he admits the experience is "humiliating." The blow to his ego is intensified by his belief that his intellect is so far above Columbo's, but also by his underestimation of his own wife. He may have thought that he would be able to convince her to say anything to protect him out of the same misguided belief of his own ability to persuade Columbo that the death was suicide. Additionally, his wife's reaction illustrates that perhaps the whole murder was unnecessary, as she could have forgiven him the adultery and persuaded her mother to allow him to keep his position. By misjudging both his opponent and the person closest to him, Alex comes to realize that he is not as perceptive as he thought he was.

Alex Benedict was a man with a problem of his own making. Had he been a faithful husband, the entire situation that led to the murder would never have happened. As the closing scene indicates, he really did have some genuine affection for his wife, though it is open to interpretation just how much he cared about her and how much his entrance into the marriage was based upon money. Given the callousness of the murder, it is reasonable to presume that he never had deep feelings for Welles and that his affair with her was based entirely on physical pleasure. His actions, therefore, prove him to be a selfish man, and when combined with his previously discussed character flaw of self-superior arrogance, it can safely be asserted that Alex Benedict was a classic example of a narcissist, a man who followed his desires without concern for the consequences, and who for whom other human lives meant nothing compared to his own prestige and safety.

As a conductor, Alex Benedict told many talented people exactly what to do and expected them to obey. Certain people's heads are turned by the slightest exposure to power, and perhaps Alex's mind was warped by his job. His conducting position required him to present other people's musical creations in the most compelling way possible, but to his chagrin, his skills as a creative artist—in murder—proved deeply lacking.

Chapter Eleven: The Greenhouse Jungle

Jarvis Goodland (Ray Milland)

Jarvis Goodland was a man filled with contempt. He believed himself to be surrounded by fools and held his closest relatives in scorn. His low opinion of the world extended to the police, and he believed that he could commit a murder without consequence. He was wrong.

Jarvis Goodland's nephew Tony Goodland (Bradford Dillman) was not in a healthy marriage. His wife was unfaithful, as was he, but Tony still loved her and decided that the best way to get her back was for her to worry about his safety, so he decided to arrange for a fake kidnapping. This premise is quite similar to "Ransom for a Dead Man," with the main difference being that the supposed kidnapping victim is involved in the plot, but the unfortunate nephew doesn't realize that his uncle planned to extract a small fortune from the family trust for the ransom, fatally shoot his young relative, and keep the money. The two set up a fake kidnapping scene, and Tony's car is left at the bottom of a slope while the supposed kidnapping victim hides.

Columbo enters nearly ten minutes into the episode. As part of a running joke in the series, an officer at the scene doesn't believe that Columbo is an actual police officer, and it takes another policeman to confirm the lieutenant's identity. When Columbo goes to speak with Tony's wife Cathy (Sandra Smith), Uncle Jarvis is there as well. After Columbo reports on the damaged car, he watches the pair closely for their reactions. While Cathy is reluctant to say anything, Jarvis pressures her to reveal the truth about the ransom demand.

Later, when Jarvis is tasked with delivering the ransom money, he receives a call from Tony, playing the role of the kidnapper. When Jarvis delivers the cash, it's a masked Tony who comes to collect it. Jarvis helps Tony escape and pushes away the police with pure orneriness, and later, when the two have gotten away and have some privacy, the uncaring uncle shoots his nephew. Instead of a happy reconciliation with his spouse, the foolishly trusting Tony Goodland winds up dead.

Soon, the body is discovered, and Columbo begins his investigation, focusing on the two people closest to the victim. Columbo shows up at Jarvis's fancy greenhouse, commenting on his lovely flowers, and starts questioning the cranky uncle. At a later visit, Columbo brings an African violet of Mrs. Columbo's that's been doing poorly, but everything he does seems to annoy Jarvis. Jarvis does mention an earlier incident where he shot at an intruder in this greenhouse, though he missed the burglar, and the bullets only struck an enormous planter filled with soil. Eventually, Jarvis goes to Columbo's superiors to complain about the lieutenant's questioning.

Meanwhile, Columbo, who has deduced Cathy's relationship with a fellow named Ken Nichols (William Smith) through their overly familiar behavior with each other, starts questioning her, noticing her lack of sorrow. Cathy's very defensive about her love life, and Columbo punctures her by mentioning the "malicious gossip" that her lover had been offered a $50,000 bribe to leave her, but stuck around after her husband was killed.

Jarvis, who despises his niece-in-law as much as he does his nephew, plants the murder weapon in her home, expecting her to be arrested for the murder.

At the episode's climax, Columbo makes a late-night appearance at Jarvis's greenhouse, revealing that he's used a metal detector to search the greenhouse and find the bullets from the earlier shooting incident. After a ballistics test, it's proven that these bullets came from the murder weapon, which proved that Jarvis owned the fatal gun. Caught, Jarvis coldly and silently allows himself to be led away with no confession, no word of remorse, and no appeal to Columbo's mercy.

Up to this point, Columbo has always had fairly cordial relations with the killers, at least at the beginning of their acquaintance. This is the first time when there is a killer who is rarely anything but curt and dismissive towards him. Jarvis never hesitates to show his disapproval of others, including towards Columbo's handling of the investigation. In their initial meeting, Jarvis is quite brusque, though Columbo acts as if he understands and displays no offense to the older man's rudeness. He's bluntly dismissive towards the police after he finishes the ransom charade, and his focus on his "fatiguing and frightening evening," stressing his own mental state rather than his nephew's physical safety, make him seem almost exaggeratedly self-absorbed and callous.

Many murderers do a bit of acting when they commit their crimes, pretending to be far more saddened or worried than they really are. Jarvis makes no such attempt, and given his character, that may be a wise decision. His contempt, as cold and unfeeling as it may be, is at least genuine. He probably knew his limits and was correct not to attempt crocodile tears. At the same time, when someone doesn't display detectable emotion when his only blood relative is allegedly facing mortal danger, it's suspicious in itself. Jarvis might have done better to play up anger towards the imaginary people who kidnapped and killed his nephew– channeling rage would have made him more relatable. Instead, he openly declares how much he despises his nephew, and while this may be true, it's also openly cold-hearted and illustrates the cruelty that is central to his character.

Later, his public face is more humane, as he's softer to Columbo, and even manages something that might be construed as a few seconds of very mild sadness to a sympathetic observer. But these moments are brief and are overshadowed by his coldness and verbal nastiness.

The relationship between Columbo and Jarvis is not especially deep, as they have somewhat less interaction than most killers have with the detective. This is due to Jarvis' refusal to attempt to build even the slightest semblance of a relationship with Columbo. Columbo tries to build a bond with him with his wife's ailing violet, but Jarvis is having none of it, keeping his responses to Columbo short and blunt. Jarvis sees Columbo as a waste of his time and never does anything to charm the lieutenant or make himself appear as anything other than a cantankerous and supercilious man.

Noticeably, Columbo does not prove Jarvis' guilt through a *psychological* gambit, as he does when he understands the mental workings of the person he's investigating. Jarvis was brought down purely by forensic evidence, with no mental manipulation or trickery involved. Unlike other killers, who acknowledged Columbo's triumph with some show of respect, Jarvis gives nothing but a frigid, silencing glare when an attempt to read him his Miranda rights is made.

When Columbo isn't around, Jarvis refers to him as "stupid lieutenant." The fact that he overlooked a detail that could link himself to the murder weapon must have weighed heavily upon him, and there is nothing more galling to a narcissist than being forced to acknowledge someone else's superiority. Jarvis had no qualms over killing his nephew and framing his niece-in-law. It was all for the sake of money, and no human being generated any warmth or affection in that disdainful iceberg of a man.

Chapter Twelve: The Most Crucial Game

Paul Hanlon (Robert Culp)

Professional sports aren't just a game; they're big business. Sometimes, they can even be deadly. Paul Hanlon is the general manager of the Los Angeles Rockets football team, and he has a contentious relationship with Eric Wagner (Dean Stockwell), the brash and vulgar owner of the team, who treats Hanlon with disdain. Hanlon decides that murder is the best way to handle his nemesis. In the middle of a game, Hanlon makes sure he's left alone in his office, and after dressing up as an ice cream man, he makes his way down to a Ding-a-Ling brand ice cream truck and drives towards Wagner's lavish mansion. Along the way, he stops by a pay phone and makes a call to Wagner, using a portable radio to create the illusion that he's still at the noisy stadium. When he arrives, he takes a large chunk of ice from the truck, fatally bludgeons Wagner, leaves the ice in the pool to melt, and sprays the hose along the ground to cover up his footprints. Hanlon quickly returns to the stadium to cement his alibi.

When Columbo arrives on the scene (over nineteen minutes into the episode), he's immediately suspicious, as he correctly infers that the extra water sprayed around the pool indicates someone is trying to obscure his presence. Though Hanlon had hoped that the death would be written off as a simple accident, the result of a head wound suffered from a fall or slip caused by alcoholic overindulgence, Columbo looks over the crime scene carefully, though not carefully enough to save his own shoes from getting ruined by pool water.

When Columbo starts questioning Hanlon, the killer initially responds to the news with an "oh, no, no," which is not so distraught as to be over-the-top, as so many murderers overplay their grief and shock, but perhaps there's a wrong note that the astute detective catches. It's not long before Hanlon becomes annoyed by Columbo following him around and asking questions. Hanlon evades Columbo's questions about the big party the deceased held right before his death and tells Columbo that he did his duty, implying that there's nothing more to be done and that Columbo should leave. Hanlon makes a tactical error by insisting the death was an accident without any examination of the evidence, and this raises Columbo's suspicions. While Hanlon doubles down on the accident theory, he does suggest that if foul play was involved, one of the "crazy hippie girls" Wagner liked to party with is to blame.

Over the course of the episode, Columbo observes that Hanlon has a tense relationship with the Wagner family attorney, Walter Cunnell (Dean Jagger), but is quite friendly with Shirley Wagner, the deceased's widow. A bit of canvassing reveals that the Ding-a-Ling ice cream truck was seen close to the mansion, but the company doesn't sell in that neighborhood. Ever alert to little details, Columbo hears some unusual noises that indicate that the phone lines are getting tapped, and after a stakeout that catches a shady private eye trying to extract the listening devices, Columbo gains control of several tapes full of recorded conversations. Though the lieutenant suspected Hanlon, it was actually the lawyer, Cunnell, behind the surveillance operation, claiming he wanted evidence of Wagner's womanizing and Hanlon's complicity. After a heated exchange, Cunnell has egg on his face, and Hanlon manages to smell of roses, at least to Shirley Wagner.

Hanlon's phone call to Wagner is on the tapes, which gives him an alibi. Hanlon had originally acted stunned to learn that his conversations were being recorded, but a little more digging leads Columbo to discover that

Hanlon was fully aware of the wiretapping and, therefore, knew he could use this information to make it look like he didn't know he was establishing an alibi by making the call. Columbo goes to work studying the tape, hoping to find some audial clue that will prove that something was wrong with the phone call.

In the final scene, Columbo confronts Hanlon at his office at the stadium, explaining that he knows how Hanlon faked the alibi call and that he realized the fatal clue was what was *not* on the tape. Hanlon has a clock with a very loud chime in his office, so when he made the call at two-thirty, the chimes should have been recorded. That proves that the call wasn't made in the office. Aghast, Hanlon is absolutely flabbergasted as he speechlessly wipes his face, gulps down a drink, and stares at the tape. Though he doesn't make an official confession or say anything incriminating, he knows he's stuck.

Columbo and Hanlon's relationship is fairly shallow. There is no bond of friendship, no attempt on Hanlon's part to charm the detective, nor are there any attempts to intimidate Columbo or force him off the case. Hanlon is reasonably civil most of the time to Columbo, such as when the detective says that he hopes Hanlon won't take offense to his investigating his alibi. Hanlon graciously replies that he takes no offense and that it is Columbo's job to double-check all statements. Hanlon does snap and explode here and there throughout his conversations with Columbo, illustrating that he doesn't much care to put in the effort to be on his best behavior with Columbo.

If anything, Hanlon treats Columbo with the bare minimum of respect, showing him enough courtesy to not antagonize the authorities, but no real warmth or cordiality. Hanlon does seem to look down on the detective, as if the policeman is on a lower social class than a sports manager. To Hanlon, Columbo is an annoyance, someone who he needn't bother with, even to be nice enough to make the lieutenant think, "this fellow is too good a guy to be a killer." This shows the level of confidence Hanlon has in his murder plot. He's sure the alibi is so strong that he doesn't have to worry—it's unbreakable. He can snap or sneer, and it will make no difference—Columbo can't arrest him for being rude.

In Culp's previous performance in "Death Lends a Hand," he played a man who killed unintentionally and out of anger and desperation. In "The Most Crucial Game," anger is once again a serious character flaw, but it is not what drives Hanlon to actually commit a murder. On the contrary, the crime is carefully premeditated, and even though Hanlon loses his temper on occasion, it's not losing his cool that eventually puts him in handcuffs, but rather overlooking a little detail. Indeed, this aggressive Type-A personality has probably been a benefit to him over the course of his career in sports. Hanlon probably taught himself to make a plan, carry it out with confidence, and win. But he focused on the big picture, and the minutia wound up bringing him down.

The title of the episode reflects Hanlon's mentality. For him, murder was a game, and he played to win. From this perspective, he figured that he had built himself an absolutely impregnable defense in the form of an alibi. While he had some inspired aspects to his plan, like a murder weapon that would dissolve without a trace and his plan to discredit a rival by using Cunnell's wiretapping plan against him, he couldn't think of everything. In some ways, this reflects his executive mindset– in the corporate world, such as when running a sports team, the man in charge often makes big, sweeping decisions and promotes a vision, while the underlings patch the holes and clarify the minutia. Hanlon was much more comfortable being on the attack, so he neglected to notice the Achilles' heel in his alibi. Hanlon's bullying and gruff manner were likely of help to him in his chosen career, as he could intimidate adversaries and keep underlings in line. Unfortunately for him, in Columbo, he found an observant man who couldn't be browbeaten, and so the most crucial game of Hanlon's life turned out to be his last, and it ended in a loss.

Chapter Thirteen: Dagger of the Mind

Nicholas Frame and Lillian Stanhope (Richard Basehart and Honor Blackman)

Some performers take method acting a bit too far. British thespians Nicholas Frame and his wife Lillian Stanhope get rather lost in their roles as Lord and Lady Macbeth. Stanhope has been flirting with their producer, Sir Roger Haversham (John Williams), to keep the funding coming for their Shakespearean revival, and when Sir Roger realizes that Stanhope has been manipulating him for more money, he gets furious and gets into a physical altercation with Frame in the couple's dressing room, leading to the destruction of Stanhope's pearl necklace. In an attempt to break up the fight, Stanhope throws a jar of cold cream, and the heavy container hits Sir Roger on the temple and accidentally kills him.

Not wanting to deal with the legal consequences of this arguably justified action, the pair bring Sir Roger back home and leave his body at the base of a stairwell, making it look like an accidental fall. They might have gotten away with it if Columbo hadn't taken a trip across the pond to talk about new investigative methods with Scotland Yard. Appearing seventeen minutes into the episode, Columbo partners with Detective Chief Superintendent William Durk (Bernard Fox) and quickly notices something's not right at the crime scene. Why would Sir Roger go downstairs when he could ring for the servants? The butler, Tanner (Wilfrid Hyde-White), notes that the deceased was a considerate man who didn't like to bother the staff at night. Columbo also notes that a valuable book was left upside-down on the table, which could damage the spine. He also wonders where the dead man's reading glasses are, and when he finds them in the deceased's pocket, he observes that they weren't broken going down the stairs.

Not content to kick back and enjoy a vacation, Columbo keeps digging and, at the visitation, notices that Stanhope's going overboard with her display of grief. Later, at Sir Roger's mansion, Frame and Stanhope hint that a valuable edition of *Macbeth* is missing, trying to suggest that there may have been a robbery, though Columbo wonders why just one book would be taken, and observes some rain marks on the dead man's car, even though the rain didn't reach the countryside. Columbo questions the duo and notices some of the pearls on the floor of their dressing room.

Over the course of the episode, Frame and Stanhope try to divert suspicion, casting red herrings and laughingly explaining away discrepancies. They made one mistake when they left the wrong umbrella at the crime scene, and they are forced to track down the right umbrella and bring it to the wax museum where a figure of Sir Roger is being prepared with his own belongings, switching out the umbrellas right before Columbo can prove the mistake.

But just as Frame and Stanhope are basking in their rave reviews and believe they've gotten away with it, Tanner shows up at their door with croissants and subtly blackmails them for a job in exchange for silence about his knowledge of their actions. Not wishing to be in his power, the pair cross the line and become actual murderers, hanging Tanner and making it look like a suicide, hiding stolen books from Sir Roger's library to frame him.

Even though Columbo has no solid evidence to bolster his suspicions, he still feels compelled to try one last trick before heading home. At the wax museum, he expounds upon his theory of the crime, correctly deducing that Sir Roger was killed at the theatre and that Stanhope's necklace got damaged in the struggle. Columbo suggests that a pearl may have found its way into the dead man's umbrella, and when a search confirms this, Frame and Stanhope crack. Mirroring their characters, Frame has a psychotic break and rambles lines while Stanhope frantically confesses. After the pair's led away, Columbo reveals that he developed a talent for tossing little objects while getting into mischief in grade school, and though he couldn't get close to the umbrella without risking an allegation of planting the pearl, he reveals that he was fully capable of tossing the pearl into the umbrella with uncanny accuracy from a few yards away.

It's unlikely that Frame and Stanhope ever form a genuine connection with Columbo, as they are always acting. The first time Columbo meets them is at Sir Roger's visitation when Stanhope is rather overdoing her sobs of grief. Columbo kindly comes up to her and gives her a handkerchief. It's up for debate if her being the loudest crier is the initial reason why Columbo comes to suspect her, but later, when they suggest that Henry Irving's own copy of *Macbeth* is missing, their heavy stress on a potential robbery may also affect Columbo's instincts, as it seems like they're trying to push a solution to the mystery once the accidental death theory is called into question. An anonymous, nonexistent burglar is a perfect patsy.

Part of the reason Columbo suspects them is because they're behaving so theatrically. Their posture, cadence, and mannerisms tend to be more suited for the stage than they are for natural conversations. When Columbo confronts them about the overheard fight (which was actually the murder), they laughingly claim it was an argument of their own and casually explain how they were arguing over a trifle, as long-married couples often do. Some observers might find their light attitude convincing, but Columbo notes that they made a tactical error. He explains that when he and his wife try to discuss what happened the previous day, they don't agree on any point, whereas Frame and Stanhope not only concur on every detail of their fight, but they use near-identical wording to describe it. It's a classic giveaway that's easily caught by experienced investigators, and it's a particular failing of actors. They weren't convincing because they rehearsed their response together.

There's an element of condescension and national superiority in Frame's dismissal of Columbo's subtle suggestion that there may have been a love triangle between the couple and Sir Roger. He sneeringly dismisses such an idea as an "American" notion, though why such a theory is more typical of someone from the United States is never explained. Frame later says that he "didn't mean to be nasty." As usual, Columbo shows no offense.

When Columbo finally puts his cards on the table and accuses the pair at the wax museum, Stanhope initially tries to laugh it off, saying, "Just when I was beginning to like you." The reveal of the pearl in the umbrella has an electric effect on both of them. Not just because they were caught, but because of who caught them– a common little policeman, and worse still, an American! It's enough to drive someone mad…

Frame and Stanhope were both egoists and snobs. At one point, Stanhope wishes Frame had taken a role in an Agatha Christie play so he'd know how these investigations worked, and Frame dismisses such a part as beneath him, a quip that earns him no warmth from Christie fans, and also ignores how many of the U.K.'s greatest actors have played Christie roles. The remark shows Frame's wholehearted embrace of the class system of authors, as some writers and their roles are seen as insufficiently "serious" or "highbrow." It's telling that Frame wanted to set himself up as one of the greats, and in doing so, he only wished to be associated with the highest class of actors. Mystery plays are seen as second-rate fare at best in his preferred circles, and there's a distinct irony in the fact that Frame considers himself too dignified to act in a crime drama, yet he's playing the leading role in a real-life murder case, and he's failing to catch all of the mistakes and plot holes he and his wife have created in a narrative. Plotting a murder is harder than Frame thought.

Likewise, Stanhope was willing to flirt with a man she had no feelings for simply to keep his money flowing into her passion project. She wasn't quite good enough an actress to keep her mark entranced, and he eventually saw through her. The play was quite literally the thing—the pair were completely driven by their desire to play roles that they believed would make them legends. Notably, they weren't out for wealth– they'd hire agents to try to get them cast in Hollywood blockbusters for that– they were out for prestige and respect, though they wanted London theatre fame rather than worldwide movie stardom.

Their mental breakdowns at the end are clearly a reference to *Macbeth*, but if the viewer is to consider why Frame and Stanhope crumbled in a way unlike any other Columbo killers and treat their psychological states as a logical progression of what came earlier and not as a mere contrivance of the screenwriter, one must delve deeper into the reasons for their collapses. Part of it stems from the realization that they may have lost everything. Even if they were able to triumph in court, the scandal connected to a double murder trial would be a permanent blight on their careers. No one would be able to watch them play in *Macbeth* without chuckling at the meta nature of every line. They went from being leading Shakespearean actors to punchlines in a moment, and they knew that they could only blame themselves. It's unclear whether Frame had a permanent mental breakdown or only had a temporary collapse, but their theatre careers and reputations were everything to them, and when their dreams shattered, so did their psyches. They "strutted and fretted their hour upon the stage, and then were heard no more."

Chapter Fourteen: Requiem for a Falling Star

Nora Chandler (Anne Baxter)

Hollywood is a ruthless town, especially for those in the entertainment industry. No matter how big a star you are, long and successful careers marked by fame and fortune are rare. Nora Chandler is a legendary film actress, but she's no longer at the top of the A-list. Instead of contending for Oscars, she's currently starring in less prestigious television productions, but at least she's working. She's able to keep going thanks to the support of her loyal assistant Jean Davis (Pippa Scott), but after years of serving Chandler, Davis is now looking out for her own happiness and is pursuing a relationship with Jerry Parks (Mel Ferrer), an unscrupulous gossip columnist.

Chandler doesn't like this one bit, especially because Parks knows an unpleasant secret of hers. A while back, she cheated the movie studio out of millions of dollars, and now Parks wants hush money to stay silent. Chandler stands up to him, but after Parks leaves, Davis announces her plans to marry him and quit her job. Though Chandler can't convince her assistant to jettison her fiancé, she does convince her to take care of some tasks for her instead of spending the evening with Parks. Chandler secretly follows Davis to the bookstore where Parks is promoting his latest tell-all and deflates her car tire. After rushing to Parks' house, Chandler pours gasoline over the driveway, and when Parks' distinctive car pulls up over the puddle of fuel, Chandler sets it alight.

Later, Chandler is calmly having a meal with friends and colleagues, but it's interrupted by the news that her assistant drove Parks' car to his house. Parks is fine, but Davis is dead. Nora collapses at the news, creating the impression in the viewer's mind that she thought she'd killed Parks.

Thirteen minutes into the episode, Columbo enters. Though he often says that he's a fan of the celebrities he meets on the job, in this case, it's unquestionably true, as he's clearly excited to be in Chandler's presence. Columbo and Chandler talk, and a bit of Chandler's backstory is revealed, as over a decade earlier, her husband Al Cumberland, a ring-wearing Shriner, presumably died in a boating accident, though his body was never found. It's a very amicable conversation and Columbo remarks upon the fountain in her backyard that doesn't run water. When Chandler views the scene of the crime, she's visibly upset.

The gossip columnist Parks, not saddened at all by Davis's death, later tries to blackmail Chandler, accusing her of the crime. Chandler counterattacks, noting that he's strapped for cash and took a large sum from Davis. She suggests he killed her so he wouldn't have to pay her back, or worse, actually marry her. It's a hostile standoff, broken only by Columbo's interruption.

As Columbo continues his investigation, he learns that Chandler isn't actually particularly wealthy anymore, as most of her fortune went into producing box-office bombs. She could make a tidy profit selling her bungalow situated on a half-acre of prime real estate in the middle of the studio lot, but she refuses to consider that possibility. In response to Columbo's questioning, Chandler launches a charm offensive, flattering him, getting him a new tie, and taking him to meet Edith Head (the actual clothes designer, cameoing as herself).

At a meeting, a studio head reveals in front of Columbo and Parks that he knows all about the two-million-dollar discrepancy, and he says that he and Chandler have found a way to resolve the situation. As Chandler came to him well before the murder, she, therefore, had no reason to either submit to Parks' blackmail or kill him. After Chandler leaves, the studio head threatens Columbo, telling him to stop investigating her. Columbo isn't fazed.

At the climax, Columbo confronts Chandler with the possibility that Davis was indeed the intended victim, and an anxious Chandler drives a car in Parks' direction to make it look like he was the target of a failed hit-and-run attack, though she doesn't seriously try to kill him. Soon afterwards, Columbo meets Chandler at the studio and reveals that Parks intended to use a piece of evidence against her—a Shriner's ring. Columbo claims not to know the meaning of it, but right after their conversation, Chandler rushes back to her bungalow.

Columbo confronts her there, revealing that he realized, after watching a scene from one of her films where she wore a man's clothing, that she could have dressed as her husband and pretended to be him when he took his supposedly fatal boat ride. He further deduces that her husband is buried in her yard, and the reason why the fountain doesn't work is because Chandler can't have workmen digging up the lawn to lay new pipes because of the body. He borrowed someone else's Shriner's ring to see her reaction.

Chandler breaks down and confesses, confirming all of Columbo's suspicions. When she and her husband had a violent fight, she struck him with a bottle and buried him in the yard, faking his boating accident later. Davis helped her, telling no one for twelve years, but Chandler was convinced she'd eventually let the deadly secret slip to Parks if she married him, so she decided murder was her only option to make sure her husband stayed buried. With quiet acceptance, Chandler leaves with Columbo, knowing she'll face punishment for both deaths.

Columbo and Chandler have the most amicable detective/killer relationship since Carl Brimmer in "Death Lends a Hand." It would not be accurate to view their interactions as a meeting of equals. Many movie stars, even ones who haven't made many hit films in a while, have a certain level of glamorous status brought about by continual media attention and a system that pampers them, convincing all but the most humble of them that they're on a higher plane than "ordinary" people. As such, Chandler is used to a level of deference from the average person, though notably, the studio boss makes it clear who's in charge, and Parks gives her no respect. Columbo certainly behaves differently around her than he does towards most suspects. He actually makes an eighth-hearted attempt to straighten up his appearance when he meets her, patting his hair and tugging at his coat. He's clearly a genuine fan of her work, as the comment, "You never expected to meet a legend," hits home.

Their rapport is instantly amicable, as Chandler graciously agrees to talk to Mrs. Columbo on the phone, though the detective's wife is out at the time, but his brother-in-law is there and gets a thrill, and Chandler actually laughs during the conversation. Notably, there is never any point when Columbo and Chandler's relationship crumbles. In most cases, there's a steep decline in affability on the killer's part in all subsequent meetings, but she's very gracious, albeit a bit impatient to get back to work when Columbo questions her on the film set. Even late in the episode, when Columbo's questions get ever-closer to the truth, she's always friendly, even if she can't cover up her stress, which is made evident through perspiration and fleeting facial expressions. She could have turned nasty, ordering him to leave or refusing to cooperate, but nothing like that ever happens. When the studio boss tries to pressure Columbo, it's unclear if Chandler has any idea of what he's doing. (It's possible that the studio boss suspects her, but he doesn't want her arrested as he'll potentially lose out on the investment he's made in her.) Chandler certainly has the potential to be tough and aggressive, as expressed through her handling of Parks, but she's invariably cooperative towards Columbo, save when she begs off for work or exhaustion.

Rather than using threats in a futile attempt to scare off Columbo, she tries to win him over, for as previously mentioned, she showed him a bit of Hollywood glamour by meeting with Edith Head, giving him a more stylish tie, and plying him with flattery. This is a tactic that will be used much later in the series in "It's All in the Game" by Faye Dunaway's character, but in that case, the woman in question likely developed genuine feelings for Columbo. Chandler almost certainly has not started seeing Columbo in a romantic manner, but she does believe that a little flirtation and attention might throw the detective off her trail. Honey attracts more flies than vinegar.

But her attempts don't work, and when Columbo finally confronts her with his conclusions, she delivers her first dismissive comment towards him, declaring, "I find you amusing up to a point, Lieutenant, but you've gone past that." He qualifies his accusation with the statement that he doesn't want it to be true, and from the expression on his face, that's almost certainly the truth. Chandler's attempts to dismiss his deductions as "rambling speculations" fade in the wake of the possibility that he'll dig up her husband's body in her backyard, and she quickly folds. There's a moment of genuine sympathy between them as Columbo helps her with her coat, and no handcuffs are needed as she quietly walks away with him.

Does Chandler deserve this sympathy? She could make a case for self-defense regarding the death of her husband, as she wouldn't have hidden his corpse in her backyard if she'd planned his murder ahead of time, and the nature of the wound might indicate it happened in a fight. But the death of Davis was a different matter. She wasn't really an innocent person, as she was an accessory after the fact for the demise of Chandler's husband, but she was loyal, and Chandler may have been wrong in thinking Davis would eventually betray her secret to her scandal-mongering husband.

Like several other Columbo killers, Chandler's first killing was either accidental or arguably justifiable, but in her attempt to cover up her dark secret, she committed a cold-blooded and particularly heinous murder of someone who'd served her loyally for many years. It's a curious paradox of the *Columbo* series that some of the most likable and sympathetic killers who get along best with the lieutenant are the ones who treat their victims the worst. Some utter slimeballs may dispatch their victims quickly and painlessly with a single shot to the head, but Chandler killed her assistant by setting fire to a car, which almost certainly caused the poor woman to suffer several minutes of agony as she burned to death. Surely, there could have been a less painful way to have committed the crime while still attempting to create the illusion that the wrong person was killed.

It's a surprisingly brutal act, even if it's largely shown off-screen, and it's arguably the grisliest death in all of *Columbo*. Perhaps Chandler chose this method, albeit unconsciously, because it appealed to her dramatic instincts.

The death is made all the more horrific by how unnecessary it truly was. Yes, Chandler was always in danger of having her husband's body discovered, but was this really a disaster? Her career was already on the decline, but she still had a lot of goodwill from her fan base, as evidenced by Columbo himself. Had she revealed the truth, declared that it was a case of self-defense, and used her acting skills to mount a publicity campaign, it's possible that she could have been acquitted at a trial. The studio's determination to protect its investment in her might have led to it funding her defense team. All of the publicity and the possibility of an outcoming of public support towards a woman painted as more sinned against than sinning could actually have invigorated her career.

Chandler's actions were driven by her fear of scandal. Fame can be an addictive drug, and movie stardom, where a press machine can turn a lucky actor into something approaching a demigod, can lead the target of this acclaim to believe all the hype. The idea of having her hands stained by the blood of her husband or a tale painting her as an abused wife might have soiled the dazzling public image she was so desperate to maintain. But promoting an image of perfection to the wider world cannot last forever if one's real life is deeply corrupted. Had Chandler thought that the studio might try to regain its money by making a television movie based on her life, the episode's final moments might have gone rather differently. Ironically, being arrested for murder probably helped to make Chandler a household name again, but infamy is a very different beast from movie star fame.

Chapter Fifteen: A Stitch in Crime

Barry Mayfield (Leonard Nimoy)

Dr. Barry Mayfield has no respect for the Hippocratic Oath. He's an ambitious doctor who commits two murders to rise in the ranks of the surgical profession, and it's only thanks to Columbo's actions that he doesn't kill a third person. Due to his work on a potentially revolutionary heart medication in the pipeline, Mayfield is a heartbeat away from unimaginable prestige. Unfortunately, it's the heartbeat of Dr. Edmund Heideman (Will Geer) that stands in his way.

Heideman wants to take a lot more time to study the medication, and fearing that any delays will lead to a missed opportunity, Mayfield decides that the perfect time to get Heideman out of his way is Heideman's upcoming heart surgery. Mayfield doesn't kill Heideman immediately on the operating table—that would look too suspicious. Instead, he plots a cold-blooded crime that will produce the results he wants in a few days. Mayfield acquits himself brilliantly during Heideman's surgery, but Nurse Sharon Martin (Anne Francis) suspects that Mayfield doesn't believe in "Do no harm." Immediately after the surgery, she scrutinizes a leftover piece of the suture used in Heideman's operation and notes that it doesn't feel right. Rather unwisely, she confronts Mayfield with her suspicion, and immediately afterward, he beats her to death with a tire iron in the parking garage and takes the suture thread. Mayfield attempts to set up a motive for the crime by planting vials of drugs from the hospital in the dead woman's apartment and then ransacking the place, trying to frame Martin as being involved in dealing narcotics.

Columbo arrives fifteen and a half minutes into the episode, and he's very tired. Apparently, Mrs. Columbo is sick, and he hasn't gotten any rest. The lieutenant's not at his best, but even through his brain fog, he notes how focused a man Mayfield is, observing that even when he's seemingly shocked by the murder, he's still concentrating enough to reset his desk clock. At the late woman's apartment, Columbo is there when the drugs are discovered and notes how odd it is that no fingerprints are on the little glass vials.

The detective decides to share his thoughts with Mayfield at a party the doctor's holding, and characteristically, Columbo can't resist helping himself to the buffet. Columbo goes over some discrepancies in the case with Mayfield, and later, Mayfield has a chat with Martin's roommate Marcia Dalton (Nina Talbot) to lay some metaphorical breadcrumbs in the direction of Martin's ex-boyfriend, Harry Alexander (Jared Martin), a recovering drug addict whose relationship with Martin ended when his reliance upon her became unhealthy.

Meanwhile, Columbo's becoming more overt with his suspicions, and when he declares that the drugs were planted in the victim's apartment, Mayfield asks if the lieutenant believes he is responsible. Tellingly, he doesn't deny the action; he just claims that he doesn't have a motive.

In Mayfield's determination to find a patsy for the crime, he tracks down Alexander and ambushes him in his apartment, giving him a massive overdose of drugs. A short while later, Alexander awakens but dies in a fall. The evidence Mayfield plants is meant to incriminate Alexander for Martin's death, but Columbo doesn't buy it, especially when he realizes the drugs were injected into Martin's left arm, and Martin was left-handed. Mayfield dismisses Columbo's murder theory, but he's more upset when Columbo starts talking to Heideman and starts suggesting the heart patient seek outside medical advice.

After a little more digging, Columbo learns about dissolving sutures and deduces the plan to kill Heideman. Mayfield's dismissive, but Columbo's confident and informs Mayfield that if Heideman dies, he'll have an autopsy performed that will prove that dissolving sutures were responsible for the death. Trapped, Mayfield convinces Heideman that a second operation is necessary, and when Mayfield prepares to swap out the dissolving sutures for proper ones, Columbo's watching him like a hawk (notably, Columbo's always been squeamish about blood before, but in this instance, he's not even a little pale).

As soon as the operation's over, Columbo launches a search to find the dissolving sutures. Mayfield has a brief tantrum and puts his hands on Columbo, but quickly regains his composure. The search produces nothing, and Columbo reluctantly concedes defeat. A triumphant Mayfield luxuriates in his victory—for about five seconds. Columbo rushes back into Mayfield's office, commenting on how out of character Mayfield's outburst of anger was. Columbo realizes the one thing he didn't search was *himself*, and finds the dissolving sutures coiled up in a pocket of the surgical scrubs he wore. All Mayfield can do is respond with an agonized look.

While many of the Columbo/killer relationships quickly become contentious, Mayfield is one of the few murderers who really makes Columbo mad, so much so that the detective actually yells at him. Their connection didn't start out with that level of hostility. Their initial interactions are fairly cordial, with Columbo disarming Mayfield by playing up how he got lost in the big hospital and sometimes passes out in hospitals as well. Their conversation at Mayfield's party is similarly friendly, even as Columbo starts to chip away at the narrative Mayfield's trying to construct.

The tension starts to grate at their relationship when Columbo first guesses Mayfield's plan to allow Heideman to die soon after surgery. Mayfield makes a bit of an error by allowing his imperturbable demeanor to crack, threatening to go to Columbo's superiors. A skilled surgeon can be excused for having an ego, but the vehemence towards preventing Columbo from assuring Heideman's health and safety is a giveaway. Under normal circumstances, Mayfield might not like having someone question his diagnoses, but he'd be so confident in his own correctness that he'd be certain that any other halfway decent medical expert would confirm anything he suggested. The indignation and aggressiveness make it look like he has something to hide, and this little lapse is a dead giveaway that Columbo's found a sore spot. When Columbo asks Mayfield if he has a match right after the doctor threatens to complain to his bosses, it's asked in all innocence, but in reality, it's a careful taunt that shows just how little Columbo cares about Mayfield's attempt at intimidation.

Mayfield responds in kind later on when he tries to belittle Columbo's accusations, laughing and saying that the detective can't honestly believe the "ridiculous" claims he's alleging. He sneers, "Lieutenant Columbo, you're remarkable. You have intelligence. You have perception. You have great tenacity. You've got everything except proof." This leads to one of Columbo's very rare shows of temper, an absolute explosion of fury, as he confronts a man who's taken two lives and is on the cusp of murdering a third. Most of the time Columbo is playing catch-up, but this is one of his occasional opportunities to save a life. The lieutenant makes it clear that he has no fear of Mayfield, and that Heideman's death will convict, not protect him. Columbo's successfully put the doctor into check, leaving Mayfield with no choice but to save the life of the man he's trying to kill and forcing him to abandon his bloodthirsty plan to rush the medicine to market. It's a show of both power and righteousness on Columbo's part, driving the characters of the two men into sharper contrast.

Part of what makes Mayfield such a cold and unnerving villain is that his victims are all so sympathetic. Nurse Martin is a kind woman who seeks to save a man she deeply respects. She's clever enough to figure out that something's wrong, though she's not sufficiently sharp to realize that she'd better not give Mayfield any indication she suspects him. Alexander served his country and is successfully overcoming addiction. And Dr. Heideman is a very amiable fellow, a man who's devoted his life to helping others and doesn't deserve to die just because he wants to proceed with care and caution when testing a new medication.

The whole murder plot stems from Mayfield's desire for more wealth, fame, and prestige. He's so anxious to achieve success by rushing this new drug to market that he's acting like he's already booked tickets to Stockholm that autumn to pick up his Nobel Prize for Medicine, and he can't get a refund. This is a critical difference in attitude. Heideman and Martin are in the medical business because they have compassion for people with health problems. Mayfield cares only for his own reputation, and saving lives is incidental to him. Having his peers pat him on the back for performing a skillful operation is more important than having the patient survive.

Mayfield's lack of regard for human life is obvious when looking at his murders. He was so confident in the medication and so desperate not to be beaten to the release by some other pharmaceutical company that he didn't stop to worry about heart patients who might suffer from a faulty drug. While the reasons for killing Heideman and Martin are at least understandable from Mayfield's warped and ambitious perspective, the murder of Alexander is absolutely unnecessary. It's committed solely to wrap up Martin's murder in a neat little bow, but there's no reason for it. All Mayfield had to do was leave the matter alone, and without any evidence against him or anybody else, it could be explained away as a random mugging gone wrong. It was just one more death added to Mayfield's tally, an unnecessary crime explained only by an obsession with tying up loose ends– or possibly an indication that Mayfield enjoyed playing God and took pleasure in holding life and death in his hands. Fortunately for Heideman and his less lucky victims, Mayfield was brought down by an observant man whose great professional pleasure was bringing the guilty to justice.

Chapter Sixteen: The Most Dangerous Match

Emmett Clayton (Laurence Harvey)

Chess is only a game…until one of the players would rather kill than lose. Emmett Clayton is a champion player who gained the ranking of the best player in the world when his strongest challenger, Tomlin Dudek (Jack Kruschen) from the Soviet Union, was too ill to compete. A while later, Dudek's health has improved enough for him to go to Los Angeles for the match-up the chess world has been longing to see.

But the pair can't wait for the official match. Dudek, who loves fine dining despite his diabetes, sneaks off to a restaurant for escargot and other treats. Clayton follows him, and the pair start playing each other, using a red-and-white tablecloth and assorted table items instead of a proper chess set. Eventually, Dudek triumphs in spectacular fashion, and Clayton is devastated, having nightmares at the prospect of being humiliated on the world stage. Rather than attempting to up his game or accept defeat like a gentleman, Clayton decides to turn to murder. After tricking Dudek into writing a letter in Russian (supposedly to a Russian paramour of Clayton's that he's running out on), Clayton words the missive so that it could be interpreted as a suicide note from Dudek and then shoves poor Dudek into a gigantic trash compactor at the hotel.

Columbo first appears sixteen minutes and forty-five minutes into the episode, playing checkers with the veterinarian. Clayton is superior and curt to Columbo, and one suspects that if he could pretend that he couldn't hear the detective due to his hearing aid malfunctioning, he'd try to get away with that gambit. Clayton gives himself away a bit by assuming Dudek is dead, but in fact, he survived the trash compactor when it shut down due to the mechanism jamming. He's in the hospital, unconscious but with a fair shot at survival.

As Columbo investigates, he quickly identifies numerous points that prove that Dudek wasn't suicidal and suggests that this was really an attempted murder. Clayton is dismissive of Columbo's correct conclusions and is consistently brusque towards the lieutenant. Eventually, Columbo uncovers Dudek's notes. The grandmaster's incredible memory allowed him to remember the match's moves, and the notes indicate that he handily won their match. Clayton lies and claims he won their game, but Columbo keeps bombarding him with evidence, getting Clayton increasingly flustered.

With Dudek having a fair shot at survival, Clayton tampers with Dudek's medications and makes sure that his rival dies from poisoning. Inspired by Dog's behavior, Columbo realizes how to trap Clayton. He takes Clayton to the noisy, gigantic trash compactor and reenacts the crime. At a signal from Columbo, the functioning compactor is shut down, and Columbo continues to speak in a raised voice. When Dudek doesn't realize that the compactor is no longer making noise, Columbo is triumphant. The compactor stopped as soon as Dudek was pushed into it. Only a deaf person wouldn't have realized that it had stopped functioning, and since Columbo has disproven the suicide theory, Clayton is the only person who fits the criteria for being the killer.

The interactions between Clayton and Columbo are very much a human chess game, with Columbo continuously on offense. Clayton is certainly no fool, and he's a skillful planner, but like most Columbo killers, he overlooks critical details, and when he's outside the easily controllable eight-by-eight grid of the chessboard, he's unable to detect some of the serious holes in his plans. Colombo's demeanor towards Clayton is consistently polite, occasionally even deferential, but he is suspicious of Clayton from the beginning, and with each passing conversation the lieutenant has with him, his opinions of Clayton become increasingly clear. Columbo performs his standard scrutiny of his suspect as he explains how little discrepancies in the room prove Dudek didn't pack his own suitcase. Clayton, who made the mistake of packing the wrong toothbrush for Dudek, has the presence of mind to provide the suggestion that a bellhop might have done the packing. It's a clever possibility, but one that would explain away nothing in the long run since no hotel employee would admit to doing that. Columbo's observation about issues connected to the stationary used to write the unsigned "suicide" note, when the good hotel stationary wasn't used, and the cheap paper pad wasn't found in the room, is dismissed by Clayton as "picayune little things." It's an example of the dismissive and superior attitude Clayton loves to adopt.

Clayton never tries to befriend or charm Columbo, he only tries to diminish him by belittling the Lieutenant's observations, or by displaying his own aptitude. When Columbo sets a trap to prove that Clayton could have memorized a list of Dudek's medications after just a quick glance, Clayton can't help but show off his prodigious memory skills and demonstrate how they make him a chess champion. No opportunity to make himself shine is missed. Towards the climax, when Columbo confronts Clayton while he plays multiple games of chess at once, the detective manages to shake the grandmaster up so badly that he makes a basic mistake and loses a game. The rookie mistake and the unexpected loss hurt Clayton like a slap in the face, and Columbo seizes upon this moment to pressure Clayton while he's still wounded. It's a clever strategic move on Columbo's part, knowing that it's best to attack when his suspect's morale is at its low point.

Clayton's greatest shortcoming is his pride. It's rare that *Columbo* goes outside of the confines of real life, but there are a couple of brief dream sequences that show the deepest fears of Clayton's psyche as he staggers around a gigantic and surrealistic chessboard, and faces the ego-crushing prospect of being revealed to the world as Dudek's inferior. Being arguably the second-best chess player in the world is no small feat, but being defeated is a devastating blow to Clayton's entire identity. His decision to kill rather than try his hardest to win honestly or accept an honorable loss illustrates that it's the title of "best in the world" that means everything to him and whether or not he's actually worthy of such an accolade is unimportant. Certainly, Clayton had options, even if they only meant postponing the inevitable. He could have staged some sort of accident for himself, such as a slip down a flight of stairs, and then claimed the pain or the medications he received made it impossible for him to focus on a game, and given the international issues connected to the match, it could be months, even years before a rematch could be scheduled. But Clayton was so obsessed with projecting superiority that he couldn't bear to make himself look weak in any way. By staging a suicide and arranging for a suicide note that made Dudek look like he was crushed by his own impending defeat, Clayton was destroying Dudek's reputation as well as his life. Clayton's actions seem all the more heinous because Dudek is one of the series' most likable victims. He did nothing wrong; he only wounded Clayton's pride by being a superior chess player.

Clayton's refusal to admit any failure ultimately helped Columbo build a case against him. Between the notes Dudek left behind and the testimony of the waiter, it was clear that Dudek had won their informal game. Clayton's insistence that he had won only made him look guiltier in Columbo's eyes, and not only that, being reminded of his own defeat only served to shake him to his core. Had Clayton been a better strategist, he could have explained away the loss in a way that made him look like an even more cunning opponent. All he had to do was say, "Quite right, Columbo. Dudek won our match, and though you may think me a poor loser for saying this, I made sure that I lost. You see, I wanted to gain a psychological advantage over Dudek by making him think I was really a weaker opponent than I truly am. That way, when we played our official match, I could have an advantage of surprise strength over him. Not only that, but I wanted to get a clearer picture of his offensive strategy, and I was careful not to play so poorly that he knew I was holding back. There's no shame in throwing an unofficial match in order to gain a stronger tactical position when you play for the championship, Lieutenant." But Clayton didn't use this option, possibly because his grandmaster's brain wasn't nimble enough to see the advantage of this strategy, but arguably more likely because his ego wouldn't let him admit weakness. Earlier, he was capable of coming up with an explanation of why he didn't tell Columbo about his dinner with Dudek, claiming that he didn't want to besmirch the dead man's reputation by announcing to the world that he beat him. It's a hollow bit of false modesty that only serves to make him look insincere, and it illustrates to Columbo the kind of lies his quarry tells—his untruths are designed to burnish his self-image, creating a noble, brilliant persona that's quite far from reality.

It's worth questioning just how mentally stable Clayton really was. Certainly, his dreams were indications of nervous tension. Throughout Columbo's interrogations, the pressure and irritation are evident in Clayton's face, posture, and cadence. G.K. Chesterton once quipped, "Poets do not go mad, but chess players do. Mathematicians go mad, and cashiers; but creative artists very seldom. I am not, as will be seen, in any sense attacking logic: I only say that this danger does lie in logic, not in imagination." That line might well be Clayton's epitaph. Though the chess player did not have a full-fledged mental break comparable to Nicholas Frame in "Dagger of the Mind," he frequently looked and acted like he was not too far from a breakdown. His self-image and reputation were sacrosanct to him. He had to flaunt his intellectual and strategic superiority to others, not only through chess, but through the act of murder as well. It wasn't just vanity; his unquestioned brilliance was a monomania to him. In the closing moments, unlike many *Columbo* villains, Clayton neither confesses nor complements the detective. He's been checkmated, but he refuses to tip his king on its side in recognition of defeat.

Chapter Seventeen: Double Shock

Dexter and Norman Paris (Martin Landau)

At the end of its second season, *Columbo* finally presents something it's never attempted before: an actual whodunit. The suspect list isn't very large, only two people, but for the first time in the series' history, there's an actual question regarding who is responsible for a crime, even though the murder is still shown on-screen.

This is due to the fact that the suspects in this case are Dexter and Norman Paris, a pair of identical twins, both played by Martin Landau. Despite their matching DNA, the Paris brothers allegedly don't get along. At this point in their adult lives, with one a television chef and the other a banker, and the pair living separate lives, the one link between them is their uncle Clifford Paris (Paul Stewart), a wealthy fitness enthusiast.

Uncle Clifford is about to marry a much younger woman, which would mean that she and any children they might have would inherit his fortune. So, right before the wedding, one of the brothers slips into the bathroom while Uncle Clifford is bathing, plugs in an electric mixer, and drops it in the bath water. Poor Uncle Clifford is electrocuted, and his body is dressed and thrown on top of an exercise machine in the presumed hopes of making the death look like a heart attack while exercising.

Columbo starts his investigation thirteen and a half minutes into the episode, and the reveal that the brothers Paris are twins comes as a shock to him and any viewers who haven't read the episode description before viewing it. However, the viewer doesn't know which of the brothers dropped the mixer. It looks like both of the feuding twins are set to inherit, until their lawyer Michael Hatheway (Tim O'Connor) reveals a will in favor of the fiancée, Lisa Christie (Julie Newmar). Hatheway offers to conceal the will for a fee, but soon afterwards, Christie is tossed from a balcony, though the viewer doesn't see who killed her.

As Dexter and Norman start divvying up their inheritance, Columbo reenacts the murder and proves that one person couldn't have pulled the dead man out of the tub. This was a two-man job. The brothers got along much better than they let people know, and they worked together to murder their uncle and his fiancée, though it's not made clear which brother committed the actual crimes, or if they each took one life. In any case, they were a homicidal tag team, and Norman accepts his fate and confesses, even though a horrified Dexter screams at him to "shut up!"

Illustrating the differences in the twins' characters, Columbo's exchanges with Dexter and Norman are distinct. Dexter has the more active role, interacting with Columbo more deeply, such as when he tries to provide explanations for his uncle supposedly going for more exercise even after he had already worked out and bathed a short while earlier. Dexter's suggestion that the uncle was simply "insatiable" for exercise is very weak and only serves to make himself look more suspicious. Dexter does act mildly friendly towards the lieutenant, though his manner often becomes much sharper once Columbo gets too close to the truth. In their most notable scene together, Dexter invites Columbo on stage when the detective visits him at a live set, and when Columbo becomes embarrassingly camera shy, Dexter laughingly says that the lieutenant amuses him, though it's debatable whether he's covering to save the recording or if he's enjoying seeing Columbo off his game. This doesn't last long, though, and when Columbo starts asking him about electric mixers, Dexter snaps at him, telling him he has "the subtlety of a train wreck." In the end, Dexter adopts the common stratagem of trying to denigrate Columbo once he's revealed the truth, scoffing, "Columbo, you're marvelous. You're absolutely bizarre."

In contrast to his twin, Norman doesn't try to charm Columbo. He's brusque and curt in their conversations, and Columbo quickly notes how logical he is. Norman doesn't try to present himself as too moral for murder; he simply says that he'd be more likely to embezzle money if he needed it. When Norman's major gambling debts are revealed, it shows he's not as controlled as he initially seems. Norman's conversations with Columbo are short and to the point, and no real bond grows between them.

Normally, Columbo's deepest connection to another character over the course of an episode is with the killer, but not in "Double Shock." Interestingly, the most complex and amusing relationship he forms over the course of the episode is with the housekeeper, Mrs. Peck (Jeanette Nolan). Columbo's not known for being neat and tidy, and Mrs. Peck is obsessed with keeping her employer's house pristine. Shortly after the murder, Mrs. Peck is quite distraught, as it's implied that she had feelings for Clifford Paris, and she resented his relationship with a woman young enough to be his granddaughter. Columbo provokes her fury by sprinkling cigar ash and grinding it into the carpet and then knocking over a glass vase so it smashes on the ground. When Columbo notes the irregularities that indicate foul play, such as a missing towel found damp in a hamper, Mrs. Peck takes this simple observation as a slur against her housekeeping skills and responds with rage. The situation worsens after Columbo uses a valuable piece of silver as an ashtray, causing her to scream at him and call him a "bum!" This leads to one of Columbo's finest lines of dialogue, where he shamefacedly tells her:

"Mrs. Peck, I made a very poor introduction of myself to you. I know that. I'm a stranger in your house that you love, and I'm here to do something that's not very pleasant, so I don't expect you to like me, but I have feelings too, Mrs. Peck. Now, I'm sorry about being untidy. That's something that I can't control. That's a fault of mine that I-I, I don't know, I just can't correct that, and I've tried many years. I'm just very untidy. That's my nature, but I've never been un... I-I-I've never been rude to you, Mrs. Peck, and-and i-if you keep on treating me like an enemy just because I'm here trying to find who killed a man that you worked for thirty-three years, well, then...well, then I think you're a very unfair person."

It's a great character moment for the lieutenant, as he reveals both his own awareness of his own shortcomings and how he knows how to disarm and emotionally connect to another person. It leads to the housekeeper softening and offering Columbo some of her late employer's favorite health cookies and a glass of milk. Unfortunately, this new friendship is short-lived. As much as Mrs. Peck cares about her work, she also enjoys a quiet sit-down in front of the television, and her favorite entertainment was damaged by the power surge caused by the electrocution. When Columbo's attempt to fix the television failed, her wrath was fierce, and their temporary truce crumbled like a health cookie. Not until the closing moments, after the twins, who Mrs. Peck cared for like they were her own nephews, were arrested, is there a reconciliation, as Mrs. Peck leans on Columbo for comfort. It's a little moment that shows Columbo's compassion for innocent people caught up in murder and a bittersweet end to their character arc. Normally, the ending of an episode is a moment of pure triumph for Columbo, but this moment illustrates how catching a killer doesn't necessarily mean a happy ending for the innocent.

While Dexter and Norman Paris were twins, they were not identical in temperament. It's not clear, however, how much of the brothers' personalities are genuine and how much affectation they use to differentiate themselves. Given the differences in their career choices, Dexter's job as the host of a television cooking show indicates that he enjoys attention and has an artistic and dramatic flair, whereas Norman's banking career indicates a more conventional, mathematical mind and a preference for an unglamorous but potentially profitable job. Their dressing styles similarly reflect Dexter's flashier character and Norman's more staid personality. Their different wardrobes were also probably a conscious choice on the part of the production team to make the twins easier for the viewers to differentiate.

Did the twins genuinely have a strained relationship, or was this simply an act? Siblings often have complex and sometimes tense interactions, so it's not too much of a stretch to conclude they didn't always get along. Nevertheless, since they were willing to trust each other as partners in crime, that indicates that there was always a strong bond between them, and the supposed feud between them was played up for the sake of diverting suspicion from the possibility that they might be working together.

With some reflection, the initial murder weapon, the electric hand mixer, becomes something of a metaphor, with twin beaters working together to perform a task. The plan was clearly the work of two men with different mindsets. The murder method had the flamboyance of a television performer, but the plan also had the precision, care, and calculated risk that comes from being a professional banker. But it was Norman, the experienced gambler, who folded, choosing to surrender rather than fight for his freedom in court. This decision took his brother Dexter down with him, and it illustrated how a murderous partnership is only as strong as its weakest link.

III

SEASON THREE

Chapter Eighteen: Lovely But Lethal

Viveca Scott (Vera Miles)

Cosmetics can disguise a multitude of blemishes, but they can't cover up a murder. Viveca Scott is the head of a makeup company, though her business is on the ropes. When Karl Lessing (Martin Sheen), an ex-boyfriend of hers who bears a grudge, gains hold of a wrinkle cream formula that could potentially save Scott's business, she at first tries to buy it back, even scribbling the price she's willing to pay on a magazine with an eyebrow pencil. But Lessing doesn't want to do business with her; he wants her humiliated, and in a fit of rage, she picks up a microscope and beats him over the head. She seems genuinely shocked to realize she killed him, making her actions arguably manslaughter rather than murder, but she still has the presence of mind to take the only known sample of the wrinkle cream with her, though she leaves behind the magazine with the numbers she wrote upon it.

Nineteen minutes into the episode, Columbo arrives at the crime scene and starts investigating. A dartboard with Scott's picture on it leads him to her, and he quickly starts talking about Scott's wife, who is a big fan of Scott's cosmetics. He eventually notices that Scott places a fake beauty mark on her face with a black eyebrow pencil and makes the connection to the notes on the magazine.

Columbo keeps interviewing her at the health spa Scott runs, and her initially friendly demeanor quickly grows hostile. Away from Columbo,

Scott spars with her business rival David Lang (Vincent Price). Lang tries to bribe Lessing to gain control of the wrinkle cream, but Lang's secretary, Shirley Blane (Sian Barbara Allen), suspects Scott of the crime and tries to blackmail her, albeit subtly. Scott pretends to be happy to work with Blane, but secretly spikes a cigarette with hallucinogenic drugs, so when the heavy smoker Blane consumes the tainted cigarette while driving, she gets into a car crash and is killed.

Meanwhile, Columbo keeps questioning the increasingly prickly Scott, and notices that he's gotten a nasty rash, and she's constantly scratching her hand as well. Columbo realizes that Lessing was studying poison ivy on his microscope after realizing the slide on the microscope was missing. They both came into contact with the poison ivy extract at the crime scene, proving her presence there. Caught, Scott coldly congratulates Columbo and calls an officer herself to take her away.

This is not one of the warmer detective/killer relationships, but this isn't Columbo's fault. The tension is all on Scott's side, and the tone of their interactions is completely controlled by how Scott happens to feel at a certain time. When they first meet, Scott is far from impressed by the shabby detective, illustrating the importance she places upon appearances. After a bit of conversation, she's far friendlier to Columbo, especially when he tells her how fond his wife is of her cosmetics. Whether this is true or not is, as always, open to interpretation.

As the episode progresses, her demeanor changes, possibly due in part to the growing stress she's enduring. Columbo's continued questioning is met with a snappish "I'm sorry, but you've taken up enough of my day." Later, when she's angered after seeing the dartboard Lessing created with her face upon it, she lashes out at Columbo, telling him, "You belong in a museum." When the lieutenant queries her about her dating life, she attacks him for his supposed "ancient masculine double standard," completely unaware that Columbo asks men the same sorts of questions in other investigations. For his part, Columbo apologizes, but from the look in his eye, it's not because he's contrite, but because he's aware that her anger is a feint to unnerve him. It's an insincere attempt to placate his quarry and leave the door open for further questioning. It works, because she's far more cordial at their next meeting, a change in attitude that Columbo thanks her for at their final confrontation, right before he has her arrested. When he searches her office, she's snappish again, telling him to complete his search and leave.

At one point in their interactions, Scott makes a largely ineffective attempt to convince Columbo of her innocence, saying, "I couldn't kill a fly." There's nothing particularly persuasive about her statement, and it doesn't sway Columbo in the least. It's meant as an Easter egg, referencing the fact that Miles was in the movie *Psycho*, and the killer used a similar line in that film.

Throughout their interactions, there are moments of condescension on Scott's part. Early on, when Columbo asks about a black eyebrow pencil, she's a bit dismissive over his lack of knowledge that black eyebrow pencils are used by brunettes, and she's a redhead. This is a tactical error, as her neglect to mention she uses a black eyebrow pencil to draw a beauty mark on her own face makes her possession of the instrument all the more suspicious. Later, when Columbo explores her wellness spa and inquires about his wife potentially visiting, she informs him that the cost is two hundred dollars a day, a sum that she knows full well is likely outside his reach on a policeman's salary, and she states the cost in a manner that makes it clear she knows this fact. There's a constant undertone emphasizing that she believes she's better than him due to her wealth and appearance, and the fact that he proves himself capable of outwitting her is clearly a painful experience.

Scott's career emphasizes her critical character flaw. Her business empire is based on cosmetics and running a "wellness" resort, and her greatest personality defect is vanity. It's not just personal appearances that matter to her, but also her general public image. She doesn't just want to look physically beautiful; she is also compelled to be financially successful. The prospect of her business going bankrupt is as abhorrent to her as physical disfiguration. In addition to people envying or desiring her for her physical attractiveness, she also wants people to respect her for her corporate leadership acumen, even though her skills aren't as strong as she wants the world to believe. The fact that the rumpled policeman Columbo is the one to bring her—and quite possibly her entire empire– down is a blow to her, and from the cold look on her face at the end, she respects his ability, but she loathes him for his triumph.

Scott's pride and ambition were pivotal to her success, but it was also a component of her downfall, as she would not have gone down her murderous path if she wasn't so concerned with keeping up appearances in every way. Her final act was one of asserting control, as she directed her own arrest. Ultimately, Viveca Scott is the embodiment of beauty only being skin deep, and viciousness and vanity go down to the bone marrow.

Chapter Nineteen: Any Old Port in a Storm

Adrian Carsini (Donald Pleasence)

In polls of *Columbo* fans, "Any Old Port in a Storm" often ranks as one of, if not *the* most popular episodes. Part of this is due to the unusually likable killer, Adrian Carsini, and the remarkably amicable relationship he builds with the lieutenant.

Adrian Carsini loves wine. It's his passion and his career, though since he focuses on quality over quantity, the Carsini winery isn't very profitable. Alas for Adrian, his half-brother Enrico "Ric" (Gary Conway) inherited the vineyard from their father, and since Ric needs cash to fund his latest marriage, he's decided to sell the land to the Marino Brothers, who produce large quantities of cheap, poor quality wine. Adrian's enraged, and after a brief but intense argument, Adrian strikes Ric on the head with a blunt instrument. Ric isn't killed outright, and Adrian hatches an impromptu plan. He brings his half-brother's tied-up body to his wine cellar, leaves it there, turns off the circulating air, and flies across the country for a business trip with his secretary Karen Fielding (Julie Harris) while Ric suffocates. Several days later, Adrian returns and brings Ric's body out from the wine cellar and arranges the corpse to look like the victim of a scuba diving accident.

Twenty and a half minutes into the episode, Ric's fiancée visits Columbo and asks him to find her missing lover. Columbo starts his investigation, and soon learns the brothers had a very strained relationship and that Adrian Carsini is a notorious snob in all ways. Columbo and Adrian don't meet until nearly halfway through the episode's run time, but once they do, it's one of the friendliest interactions yet. Adrian's a bit put off at first by Columbo's appearance, but he insists that Italians should know how to appreciate good wine, and soon, the two are tasting some of the Carsini winery's best together. Adrian even shows Columbo the wine cellar where his unconscious brother spent his last days.

When Columbo reveals that Ric's death is being treated as a homicide instead of an accident, Adrian's visibly unnerved, but not angry or antagonistic to Columbo. Fielding is a bit upset by Columbo's questioning interrupting her late-night movie, but even though neither has been particularly inconvenienced by Columbo's questions, Columbo insists on taking the two of them out to a top-notch restaurant to apologize for bothering them.

Upon their arrival, Adrian browbeats the staff into giving them a better table, and the trio enjoy a wonderful meal, to be capped off by a bottle of rare Ferrier port. Adrian's thrilled…until he actually tastes the port and declares that it's been ruined by being left in excessive heat. While Fielding and Columbo think the port tastes wonderful, Adrian explodes, excoriating the staff for mistreating the wine and dismissing it as *"liquid filth!"*

As they leave, Columbo notes that while Adrian and Fielding were away, California had a terrible, unexpected heat wave. Adrian is shocked to realize that by turning off the air conditioning in his wine cellar, he inadvertently overheated his rare wine collection. He's even more disturbed to learn that Fielding has lied and told Columbo that she saw Ric leave the winery alive that fateful day, thereby giving Adrian an alibi. Later, when the pair are alone, Fielding asks Adrian to marry her in order to keep her silence.

Adrian doesn't like being extorted, and he's devastated by the realization that he accidentally ruined his own precious wines. After gathering the entire collection up into baskets, he carries them down to the ocean and tosses some of them away in disgust, smashing them on the rocks. Once he finishes destroying one batch, he returns to collect more, only to find Columbo there. Columbo reveals that the port served at that night's dinner was actually from the wine cellar—he took the bottle when he was briefly left alone in there. Adrian is blindsided, noting that he's one of a very small number of wine connoisseurs who could have detected the heat oxidation in the wine. Preferring prison to marrying Fielding, he agrees to confess to the murder. As Columbo drives him to the station, Adrian worries about his beloved vineyard, and a sympathetic lieutenant comforts him. As the episode closes, Columbo produces a bottle of a first-rate dessert wine, and the two share a drink. Columbo declares that the dessert wine is "Very suitable for the final course." Adrian tells him, "You've learned very well, Lieutenant," and Columbo replies, "Thank you, sir. That's the nicest thing anybody's ever said to me."

Exemplified by this closing scene, the relationship between Columbo and Adrian is unquestionably one of the friendliest and most respectful connections between the detective and a killer in the series. But why is this? Why are the pair so amicable here, especially when, in many other cases, the murderer's attitude towards Columbo drips with self-superior scorn, and the slightest progress in the investigation is met with threats to complain to Columbo's superiors? At first glance, one would think that Adrian, described by all who know him as an incorrigible snob, would have nothing but contempt for the scruffy little policeman with no knowledge of wine. And yet, after their first introduction, aside from Adrian's strong admonition that Columbo should not smoke his cigar while drinking wine, Adrian never treats Columbo with disdain.

On the contrary, Adrian, though he's initially a bit put off by Columbo's disheveled persona, soon comes to appreciate him, and when he gives Columbo wines to sample, one never gets the sense that he's trying to manipulate or distract Columbo. Adrian seems to have a genuine interest in seeing Columbo's palate develop. Perhaps he sees it as a public service to educate Columbo. When Columbo deduces the type of wine he's sampling through deduction rather than taste and smell, Adrian seems genuinely delighted.

So why does Adrian, known to all as an incorrigible snob, become sincerely charmed by Columbo? When other killers quickly morph from ersatz warmth and friendliness to aggressive hostility and desperate threats, Adrian even fails to raise his voice to Columbo in anger. Poor treatment of wine sends him into a rage against waitstaff, but though Columbo's subtle pressure indicating that the walls may be closing in on him may make Adrian a bit nervous, the oenologist never attacks or belittles Columbo. This cannot be attributed solely to the "breeding" that Adrian prides himself upon, as impeccable manners would prevent him from throwing a fit at the expense of a hapless waiter and maître d'. Throughout the episode, from their wine tastings to their final conversation, it seems as though Adrian has a genuine liking for Columbo, and Columbo seems to reciprocate, though the detective's positive reactions towards the winemaker as a drinking companion do nothing to deter him from bringing the man to justice.

As is often the case, Columbo determines his quarry's Achilles' heel and applies pressure to it in order to help crack the suspect's resolve. Columbo's rough handling of certain wine bottles makes Adrian very anxious, though Adrian's temporarily flustered demeanor doesn't lead to an outburst. Columbo's perceptive question about Adrian allowing someone else to decant the wine at his earlier meeting leads to stuttering and a nervous comment about it being a nice gesture. Columbo isn't fooled—he correctly suspects that the delegation is connected to Ric's demise, and by the time Columbo silently implies his shrewd conclusion of how the crime was committed, Adrian has recovered sufficiently to respond to Columbo with an almost admiring "Lieutenant, you really are one of a kind."

Adrian is a snob, and snobbery is based in part on feelings of self-superiority, as well as distaste for qualities different from those one personally embodies. If Adrian treats Columbo with more respect than anybody else in his orbit, it must be because he sees something commendable in the detective. Perhaps Adrian detects Columbo's intelligence when other killers dismiss him as a bumbling fool. Maybe it's Columbo's determination and quest for excellence in his chosen profession that leads Adrian to develop a respect for the man. Friendships aren't always based on similar interests and personalities. It's possible that Adrian noticed that Columbo possessed characteristics that he himself lacked, such as an ability to form connections with people. Normally, when a killer tries to terminate the investigation, that person delivers a cutting remark to Columbo about not expecting to see him again. Columbo reverses this after his dinner with Adrian, telling him he doesn't think they'll meet after this, right after delivering his comment about the heat wave that may have spoiled the wine in the cellar. This is a double blow to Adrian. Not only has his prized collection been "ruined," but Columbo's withdrawal from his life means that he has also lost the closest approximation of a friend that he has in his life. He didn't get along with his half-brother and Karen Fielding was just an employee to him. Yet, for some indefinable reason, he bonded with Columbo, and in the space of a minute, Adrian's life became much emptier.

After referencing Adrian's secretary Karen Fielding, it should be explained that even though she lied to provide her boss with an alibi, she does not quite qualify as an accessory after the fact, as she was not an active partner in the crime, and she does not have definite knowledge that her employer was responsible for his half-brother's death. Her statement was made out of love for her employer (or, if a viewer chooses to be less charitable, a desire for financial security and companionship after too many years of solitary late-night movies). An intelligent woman like Fielding would also know that if her boss was arrested, she'd be out of a job as well. Fielding's lie was certainly ethically dubious, yet her level of complicity does not quite rise to the point where she can be qualified as a killer.

But Adrian is most certainly a murderer, and while by his own admission, he felt no guilt for his crime, he was devastated by the fact that the method he used to kill Ric wound up "ruining" his wine collection. Adrian really didn't have to destroy the wine that had been exposed to heat. Had he not been so distraught, he could have realized that this may have been a trap, and he could have simply waited to dispose of the wine. He could have sold it to buyers with less discriminating palates, who couldn't possibly have detected the effects of the warmth on the wine. Instead, he was so upset and filled with self-loathing that he felt the need to smash the bottles by the ocean in a dramatic manner. As a matter of fact, Adrian doesn't know for sure that all of the wine was damaged from the heat, and for all he knows, it's possible that some of his wine had already been exposed to high temperatures before he bought it.

The collection of wines he built wasn't just for drinking. He may have planned to consume a few here and there, but when he bought a bottle of wine for five thousand dollars and carried the well-wrapped-up bottle with him on the flight home with as much care as most people would transport a baby, he made it clear that he didn't buy it because he was excited about consuming it. His main reason for shelling out a substantial sum was because he didn't want anybody else to have it. It was a status symbol, a power play in the small, insular, but easily impressed world of wine connoisseurs. Owning it made it clear that he had both the wealth and the determination to expand his collection. This was an unusual form of gluttony, where he wanted to possess wine and deny it to others without consuming it himself.

Wine was a critical part of Adrian's self-image. He prided himself on his extensive knowledge and his ability to detect imperfections through his highly refined palate. He saw himself as more than just a collector, but as a curator, the temporary custodian of something more than mere fermented grape juice. For him, a bottle of fine wine was a work of art. His belief in his aesthetic superiority led him to ignore the fact that the winery was a business. Had he sold his specially made wine to rich enthusiasts for several hundred dollars a bottle instead of serving it at important occasions (he used the term "friends," but in reality, they were simply fellow wine enthusiasts for whom he felt no affection), he could have made sufficient profit to convince Ric not to sell the winery. Instead, he acted as if he were above such petty concerns as financial viability, and all proved to be vanity.

Adrian Carsini sought perfection in winemaking. If he had only applied this level of scrutiny to his moral character and his connections with other people, he might have been a happier man and a free man as well. But as Adrian mourns, "freedom is purely relative," and living in a loveless marriage and wrestling with the knowledge that he was responsible for despoiling hundreds of bottles of rare wine was a "great weight" upon him. He is far more upset over "ruining" the wine than he is over killing his brother. As Carsini gulps down his dessert wine and grasps the bottle, knowing it may well be the last high-quality wine he ever drinks, there is an uncharacteristic level of pathos in the final moments. Certainly, the prospect of consuming prison wine for the rest of his days was cruel and unusual punishment to him. Adrian Carsini may have been a snob and a killer, but beneath all of his refinement and character flaws, he still had a heart.

Chapter Twenty: Candidate for Crime

Nelson Hayward (Jackie Cooper)

"Candidate for Crime" is Columbo's most high-profile case to date (in the context of the show's fictional universe), featuring not just a wealthy and socially prominent killer, but a potentially powerful political figure. It's also one of the very few cases to be referenced in multiple future episodes. But while the murderer's career made the case arguably the most famous of Columbo's career in terms of the detective's fictional world, does the interaction between Columbo and Senator Nelson Hayward rank as one of the deepest and most memorable connections between detective and killer? In the wake of the lieutenant's unusually cordial relationship with Adrian Carsini in "Any Old Port in a Storm," the connection between Columbo and Hayward pales in comparison, but it's still a classic example of how Columbo is able to crack a confident killer's façade.

For the first time, Columbo appears onscreen long before the murders. Less than a minute into the episode, he's caught up in a crowd of reporters questioning the senator. A critical election is coming soon, and one might think that Hayward would be on his best behavior. But Hayward is the sort of man who allows his passions to conquer prudence, and the married senator is currently in the middle of an affair with Linda Johnson (Tisha Sterling), a secretary working with the campaign. When his campaign manager, Harry Stone (Ken Swofford), politely but firmly tells the senator to cool down the relationship until all of the ballots are safely cast, Hayward pretends to acquiesce, but the politician doesn't like being told what to do. Stone knows where all of Hayward's bodies are buried, and the senator decides that murder is the best way to escape his campaign manager's control.

On the pretense of ending the affair, Hayward and Stone make their way to Hayward's second home, swapping clothes and cars in order to shake the security detail that's supposed to protect him. After a few evasive maneuvers, they finally arrive, and inside the garage, Hayward shoots and kills Stone, slips a cheap watch on his victim's wrist, commits the old, old gambit of setting the hands to a different time for the sake of an alibi, and smashes it. Hayward then returns to his home to establish an alibi at a party.

After the murder is uncovered, Columbo visits the Hayward household, leading to the breakup of the party. This begins the standard series of frequent conversations, with Columbo frequently visiting Hayward's campaign offices and home, steadily puncturing the idea that Stone may have been killed because he was mistaken for Hayward, illustrating that the broken alibi watch was all a sham, and when Hayward receives a new sport coat identical to the one ruined when Stone was shot wearing it, Columbo realizes that Hayward ordered it long before he could have known he'd need to get a replacement.

Hayward knows that Columbo suspects him, so he crafts a ploy to distract suspicion. He locks himself in his office, saying he's going to make some calls, and fires a shot from the murder weapon into his wall. A while later, he returns to his office and lights a firecracker, and when others rush in to check on him, he makes a dramatic show of claiming someone tried to shoot him and demands that Columbo match the bullet in the wall to the bullet that killed Stone.

Columbo, completely unfazed, tells him he already has. Columbo was waiting in a nearby room that day, and he could tell from the phone switchboard that Hayward made no calls. After Hayward left, Columbo had the room searched, found the bullet, and tested it. The man who fired the gun is still in the room, and Columbo accuses Hayward. With his duplicity revealed, Hayward doesn't confess, but his brow does break out in nervous perspiration.

One of the qualifiers that shapes any analysis of Hayward is the fact that, as a politician in the public eye, he's constantly forced to maintain a false persona for the sake of his constituency. The adulterous senator is compelled to present himself to the world as a loving spouse, and the nervousness he exhibits is palpable w Columbo gets ever-closer to the truth could doom his electoral prospects if it were caught on camera and broadcast on the news. When Hayward tells Columbo, "You're a very nice man, I like you very much… [but I'd] hate to depend on you if I'm in a hurry," one can assume he's genuine in his belief that Columbo's slowness is an aggravation to him, but whether or not he truly likes Columbo is questionable. As his interactions with party guests show, the senator is a glad-hander, skilled at making the person he's talking to feel like the most important person in the room for a few minutes before moving on and treating the next person the same way.

Certainly, those close to him know when he's lying. From the comments Hayward's wife Vicky makes after she sees him respond to the news of Stone's murder, she knows that he's putting on an act of false grief, though she doesn't seem to suspect that her husband might be involved in the crime until Columbo sows the seeds of suspicion in her mind. The Haywards are clearly not in a loving relationship—they interact well in public, and she provides him with the respectability he needs to promote his career. It seems like the coolness of their relationship has had a negative effect on Vicky Hayward's well-being, as she self-medicates with plenty of alcoholic beverages. Given the cavalier way that the senator treats his wife and how little concern he has for her health and happiness, it emphasizes just what a self-absorbed and ambitious man Hayward is. His wife may just be a prop to him that he uses for boosting his public image. Could he genuinely care for her, but not enough to be faithful to her? It's hard to tell, but there's a sense that Hayward's true love is his political power.

Does Hayward really like Columbo, as he claims? It's notable that many other murderers who are prominent members of the community, after only a mild amount of rattling, threaten to use their friendships with powerful people to influence Columbo's superiors, potentially damaging his career. Yet Hayward, arguably the man with the most social clout to appear on the series to this point, never threatens to use his authority to break Columbo down to traffic patrol or to call the IRS to audit the lieutenant's finances until they bleed. A man who *could* use his position to destroy a man who threatens him doesn't. Why is that? Instead of a direct attack, Hayward chooses to play a deceptive gambit to make himself look like a victim. Maybe, in the tit-for-tat world of politics, he didn't want to call in a favor or put himself in someone else's debt to take down a threat. Perhaps Hayward, always concerned with his optics, didn't want to do or say anything that might make him look aggressive or bullying or anything that would stop him from projecting the sort of likable respectability that would make people like to vote for him. In Hayward's estimation, sincerity is unimportant; appearances are everything.

While Hayward isn't a genuine person, it's important to remember that while Columbo is almost always a version of himself, a certain level of guile is all part of Columbo's stock in trade as well. Columbo is quite coy about who he plans to vote for, telling the senator he's "still a little bit on the fence." It's a subtle way of implying that Hayward has to earn his approval, so the politician should be nice to him. Columbo has to act deferential even when he's trying to crack Hayward's veneer. When Columbo makes a point of questioning the misdirection Hayward tried so hard to arrange, Hayward shatters, screaming how absurd Columbo's suspicions are, leading the detective to wonder why Hayward isn't more relieved. The first sign of danger shook Hayward to the point that he practically gave himself away.

The results of the election are never revealed, which leaves the viewer wondering if the citizenry sensed that Hayward wasn't fit for public office, or if the duly elected senator will need to be replaced. Hayward's reactions to Columbo's questioning show that he wasn't built to withstand pressure, and his refusal to take simple precautions to protect his candidacy by pausing his affair shows that he was a man of limited self-control. Hayward wasn't a true leader or public servant, only a man who sought power and pleasure. It's said that people get the elected officials they deserve, and they deserve to get them good and hard. Columbo made sure that the citizens of California weren't led by a murderer.

Chapter Twenty-One: Double Exposure

Bart Keppel (Robert Culp)

In Robert Culp's third and final portrayal of a killer (though he would appear as the father of a murderer in "Columbo Goes to College"), he plays Bart Keppel, an expert in psychology and manipulation and also a blackmailer. Dubbing himself "a motivational research specialist," subliminal messaging is Keppel's stock in trade, exemplified through undetectable stills spliced into films, like images of popcorn making people desire snacks. This is based on a real and controversial tactic that was used in the years shortly before the episode aired, encouraging moviegoers to buy treats in the middle of a movie. Once these tactics were made public, widespread outrage led to the banning of the practice, a point referenced by Columbo midway through the episode.

Vic Norris (Robert Middleton) is a client of Keppel's who is also being extorted, as Keppel has taken pictures of the married Norris having an affair. Once Norris announces his intention to stop paying and start reporting Keppel to the authorities, Keppel launches his murder plan. He places some images of cool beverages into the sample business film he's showing with Norris in the audience, fills Norris with salty caviar, and heats up the movie theater, all to encourage Norris to desire liquid refreshment. Keppel claims to narrate the production off-stage, but a recording provides him with an alibi. Norris, as expected, steps out for a drink of water, and Keppel shoots and kills him, replacing the gun back in a display case in his office and returning to the theater.

After the body is discovered, Keppel records the commotion over the narration on the tape he used for an alibi. Columbo arrives to investigate fourteen and a half minutes into the episode, saying he was "working late on the Hayward case," a rare bit of direct continuity from the previous episode. This also illustrates how, in the *Columbo* universe, the lieutenant's work doesn't end with the big "gotcha!" moment at the end of the episode—with no signed confession and a high-profile perpetrator, there's still plenty of investigation and tying up loose ends to go after the arrest.

Columbo, never one to pass up free food, helps himself to the caviar, enjoying it at first, but realizing that the saltiness soon made him extremely thirsty. Keppel, like many other killers, is initially uncertain as to whether Columbo is even with the police and insists that the detective call him *Doctor* Keppel, a title that Columbo can't seem to remember, which may be absent-mindedness, but more likely is a deliberate ploy to rattle Keppel.

As they talk, Keppel tries to point the finger of suspicion towards Norris's wife (Louise Latham), though Columbo doesn't consider her a serious suspect as her alibi's so weak. Keppel sent her on a wild goose chase with a phone call, assuring she'd be alone at the time of the crime. Columbo begins his standard tactics of catching little inconsistencies in his target's story, wondering why Keppel switched on the tape recorder after the murder, and Keppel reasonably explains he turned it on with the intention of preserving his audience's reactions. The next day, Columbo meets Keppel at a supermarket and learns how cameras study consumers for their body language. By this point, Columbo's discovered proof that Norris wanted to sever his business relationship with Keppel, though the motivation research specialist insisted that Norris would hire him again as soon as he needed him.

Columbo keeps visiting and asking questions, and Keppel reveals Norris' affair. The professional manipulator still hasn't given up on framing Mrs. Norris, and he gets another chance to build a case against her when Roger White (Chuck McCann), a projectionist, reveals that he has seen the edited version of the movie Keppel used to draw a thirsty Norris out to the hall, and amicably blackmails Keppel for a large sum.

Had White seen a single episode of *Columbo*, he would have known that any attempt to extort money without Columbo's prior approval and assistance is tantamount to suicide, and Keppel steals a gun from the Norris home and shoots White at his other job at a movie theater. Columbo brings Keppel along to investigate, and though Keppel tries to make Mrs. Norris look guilty, Columbo makes it increasingly clear without coming right out and saying that he suspects Keppel. Keppel reminds the lieutenant that he has no proof, and Columbo, who has tested the gun in the display case in Keppel's office and determined it's the wrong caliber, has to agree. Columbo is discreet in his implications until he confronts Keppel on a golf course and flat-out accuses him.

Soon afterwards, Keppel is viewing one of his own films in his office theater and swiftly becomes increasingly nervous. Columbo has introduced subliminal edits of himself searching Keppel's office, and though Keppel doesn't realize what's happening, he rushes to his office and retrieves the calibration converter he used with the gun in the display case, having hidden it in a lamp. Columbo catches him and remarks that he never thought of a device to change the bullet size used on a gun.

Flustered and gently giggling, Keppel remarks "You would never have solved it without my technique." Columbo responds by telling him, "If there was a reward, I'd support your claim to it."

This comment is the culmination of an extended war of attrition between the pair. Like other prominent *Columbo* killers, Keppel's personality is colored by his unabashed and confident self-superiority. There is no doubt in Keppel's mind that he is a brilliant man, capable of committing the perfect, unprovable time. Up until the episode's final minutes, Keppel practically pities the lieutenant for wasting his time in a futile attempt to bring him to justice. Columbo's aware of his quarry's belief in his own intellectual predominance, and the detective's not immune to being rankled by a criminal's patronizing attitude. Columbo's refusal to address Keppel as "Doctor" is his own way of putting his opponent in his place—the excuse that it's simple absent-mindedness that leads to the slip-up does not fool

Keppel.

At the same time, Columbo makes it clear to Keppel that he doesn't underestimate his adversary's intellectual abilities. After reading his book, Columbo informs Keppel he's a "genius." Keppel appreciates the compliment, and once he realizes that Columbo suspects him, Keppel takes a certain measure of pleasure in their interplay, enjoying it when he thwarts Columbo's little traps. For example, when Columbo asks Keppel to join him while investigating the murder of White, Columbo hopes that Keppel—who is driving– will betray himself by heading to the scene of the crime without being told where it happened. Keppel takes great pleasure in avoiding the trap, and Columbo good-naturedly concedes that Keppel has won the trick.

But in the final scene, Columbo seems to take a quiet but obvious triumph in his victory, clearly taking pleasure not just in cracking Keppel's façade, but in rubbing it in regarding how Keppel sowed the seeds of his own destruction. It's a case where Columbo takes pride in crushing another man's pride.

Keppel believed himself to be a master manipulator and figured that his skill at implanting mental messages through film could translate into being able to use deflective techniques to get away with murder and frame an innocent woman. Keppel failed to realize that his techniques worked in part because they were used on unconscious subjects who didn't realize that they were being guided to respond to certain stimuli. If someone anticipated deception or misdirection, as the ever-suspicious and perceptive Columbo did, the wary would-be victim would be able to peek behind the curtain, both literally and figuratively. Columbo read Keppel's books to learn his tricks, meaning that Columbo knew what to expect and to combine his existing critical skills to figure out how to identify and deflect Keppel's maneuvers.

Keppel wasn't superior to other people because he knew how to utilize subliminal messages and stimuli to achieve his ends. As Columbo's final trap proved, he was just as susceptible to suggestion as anybody else. Knowledge of how unconscious persuasion worked didn't immunize him against it being used against himself. Being no fool, Keppel realized when Columbo was laying traps against him and deflected them, but by the end, the mental strain of trying to evade capture left him vulnerable to Columbo's ploy. It was not guilt that led Keppel to fall prey to Columbo's trap, but fear of getting caught, however unconscious his feelings might have been. The "Double Exposure" in the title was more than just Keppel's exposure as a killer. It was also the exposure that for all his expertise in motivational research, Keppel was just as susceptible to stimuli as the people he prided himself on manipulating.

Chapter Twenty-Two: Publish or Perish

Riley Greenleaf (Jack Cassidy) and Eddie Kane (John Chandler)

Two of the great repeat *Columbo* villain actors appear in back-to-back episodes, as Jack Cassidy takes on the role of Riley Greenleaf, a publisher who just can't stand the prospect of one of his bestselling authors defecting to a different house. Alan Mallory (Mickey Spillane) has enjoyed healthy sales numbers writing erotic novels for Greenleaf, but with the encouragement of his agent Eileen McRae (Mariette Hartley), Mallory plans to write a more "literary" war novel, and as soon as his contract with Greenleaf runs out, he'll take it to a new publisher. Seeing an opportunity to make a fortune and feeling betrayed by an author he feels owes him everything, Greenleaf decides to commit a pair of murders.

In the opening scene, Greenleaf consults with Eddie Kane (John Chandler), an obviously unstable war veteran who has a fondness for explosives and who wants Greenleaf to publish his book on all sorts of things that go "boom." Greenleaf offers Kane a deal—kill Mallory with Greenleaf's gun (taking care to preserve Greenleaf's own fingerprints), and he'll publish Kane's book and make him rich and famous. Kane joyfully accepts the offer, but it's obvious to all but the most criminally dense viewers that Greenleaf has no intention of printing one word of Kane's work.

Greenleaf crashes a party attended by Mallory and McRae, acting more intoxicated than he really is. He makes a scene, threatens Mallory, and staggers away. Mallory heads to his office to continue dictating his manuscript into a tape recorder, leaving the door open for air circulation on a stuffy night. Kane arrives and fatally shoots Mallory, leaving the key Greenleaf gave him (that he didn't have to use) on the floor. At the moment of the murder, Greenleaf deliberately crashes into another car, playing up his drunkenness, leaving his contact information with the couple whose vehicle he struck and being generally boorish and insulting. It's all part of his plan to be memorable when creating an alibi.

Columbo staggers into the crime scene sixteen minutes into the episode, wiped out from insufficient sleep after his wife roped him into watching late-night movies two nights in a row. Soon afterwards, Columbo interviews Greenleaf in an interrogation room, with Greenleaf's lawyer David Chase (Alan Fudge), in tow. Greenleaf dramatically expresses his grief over Mallory's death and declares that he was too drunk to remember what he was doing the previous night. This is a clever bit of psychological manipulation, for if Greenleaf presented his alibi right away, it might raise suspicions, but by making the police work for the alibi, they would theoretically be more willing to accept it.

Outside of Columbo's earshot, Greenleaf mourns to his lawyer that he might have killed Mallory without realizing it. At Greenleaf's house, Columbo notices some scratches around the lock of the glove compartment where the gun was kept, which was carefully left there by Greenleaf. Columbo's conversation with his chief suspect is interrupted by Chase, who has received a phone call informing him of Greenleaf's alibi. Triumphantly, Chase harangues Columbo for jumping to conclusions about Greenleaf's guilt (how dare Columbo suspect Greenleaf just because a gun with Greenleaf's fingerprints on it was found at the scene!), while Greenleaf expresses gratitude that the passengers in the car he damaged remembered him. Columbo catches the error, as Chase didn't mention that two people were in the car. Chase saves his client, suggesting that Greenleaf remembers the pair subconsciously.

Later, Columbo visits Greenleaf, stating that the alibi checks out, and then questions Greenleaf about the million-dollar insurance policy the publishing house holds on Mallory. Greenleaf claims to have forgotten about it, a statement thrown into question by the fact that the policy was recently renewed, though Greenleaf says the billing department handled it. As he leaves, Columbo informs Greenleaf that Mallory changed the locks a few weeks prior, and the key left on the floor couldn't have opened the door.

Late at night, Greenleaf visits Kane, declaring his excitement over publishing Kane's book. The murderous publisher slips a knockout drug into the champagne he serves Kane, leaving the explosives expert unconscious. After typing out a synopsis for Mallory's novel on Kane's typewriter and hiding it away safely at the scene, Greenleaf leaves, but not before rigging a hand grenade to explode right after his departure.

Columbo interviews Mallory's agent and would-be new publisher at a restaurant and learns that the original plan for Mallory's novel was for the central character to die. After a film studio pursued the rights to adapt the book starring Rock Hudson, the agent suggested a happier ending where the flawed protagonist seeks redemption at the end by joining a monastery, as a star like Rock Hudson wouldn't be killed at the film's conclusion.

Columbo is called to the scene of Kane's death, and he discovers the supposed outline for the novel. When he shows it to Greenleaf, the publisher lies and claims Kane sent it to him several months earlier, but as Kane was a good plotter but a poor prose stylist, he rather unethically asked Mallory to write it for him. This is all meant to give Greenleaf the rights to Mallory's novel.

At the episode's end, Columbo summons Greenleaf to Mallory's office and confronts him with his summation of the case. Mallory left the door open in the heat, and Kane, hired to kill him, left the key behind anyway. When Greenleaf says he couldn't possibly have known what Mallory was working on, Columbo produces a messenger boy who picked up Mallory's tapes regularly to have them transcribed. Greenleaf bribed the messenger to give him copies of the transcriptions. Columbo points out that the synopsis found amongst Kane's things had to be a fake, as its ending shows the protagonist going to a monastery, a finale that was only created by McRae a short while earlier. Columbo smiles with triumph, though Greenleaf doesn't confess.

Greenleaf's connection to Columbo is, to a significant extent, more deeply marked by artificiality than most detective/killer relationships in the series. Certainly, all murderers adopt a false persona to some extent, attempting to seem more benign than they are. Arguably, the most genuine killer in the series to date was Jarvis Goodland ("The Greenhouse Jungle"), who never hid his cantankerous attitude or his disdain for Columbo, with Adrian Carsini ("Any Old Port in a Storm") being another candidate, due to his sincere connection to the lieutenant. Most of the other killers adopt a more benign or amiable persona, though few of them can maintain that level of pretense for more than a couple of meetings. Others, like Dr. Ray Flemming ("Prescription: Murder"), feel comfortable dropping the mask and revealing their true, smug natures once they are aware Columbo knows they did it, but they are still wrongly positive that he'll never be able to prove their culpability.

From their earliest moments, Greenleaf fakes most of his emotions in front of Columbo, relishing his portrayal of a man suffering from alcohol-induced amnesia, with this impairment leaving him unable to defend himself. He feigns grief over his first victim's death, as well as concern that he might be a killer without knowing it. Once his carefully arranged alibi is revealed, Greenleaf adopts an attitude of false geniality towards Columbo, one that is shattered every time his natural, antagonistic short temper is tried.

Greenleaf's inherent irritability is revealed when his assistant tells him, "there's a strange man wandering around the editorial section," and when Greenleaf tells her to call the police, she replies "he says he *is* the police." Greenleaf is speaking through an intercom, so he's not being watched at that moment. From the instant he realized that Columbo was there, he should have known that he needed to take a moment to compose himself before meeting the detective. But instead of preparing the proper attitude, Greenleaf comes out snappish and hostile towards Columbo. He quickly becomes more amicable when he learns that Columbo has confirmed his alibi, but the damage has been done, even if he doesn't realize it. Columbo has seen the unpleasant side of Greenleaf's nature, and a hastily donned mask is still easily identifiable as a mask. After a seemingly friendly Greenleaf sends Columbo on his way, calling him "the man," he barely has time to shut the door before his face cracks with amused contempt towards the man he thinks is so easy to fool.

In their final meeting, Greenleaf can barely master the strength to be civil to Columbo, with his impatience obvious to see. He has no interest in hearing Columbo talk about his thoughts on turning his investigation in "Candidate for Crime" into a book, saying he "doesn't care" about that case or the senator. (Surely, this is a flawed business decision, as a book based on one of the most publicized crimes in recent memory, told from the perspective of the detective who brought down a powerful politician, would have a strong shot at the bestseller lists.) Greenleaf's poor temper is evident, and he's reckless enough to come to the meeting without his lawyer.

These actions and reactions all illustrate the true man that Greenleaf was. He was petty and vindictive and allowed his desire for vengeance and profit to overwhelm his instincts for self-preservation. Easily annoyed but equally adept at faking geniality, his pettiness and hostility were the factors that fueled his self-destruction and led to a murder plan that appealed to his personal flair for the dramatic.

Greenleaf's plan for escaping punishment illustrates how his mindset differs from most other killers on *Columbo*. Most murderers seek to avoid suspicion altogether, trying to create a situation where they would never be suspected of being involved at all, whether it's by making the crime look like an accident or pointing the finger in a different direction. But Greenleaf went out of his way to make himself the most likely suspect from the start, and this was an added reason for Columbo's initial suspicions. Greenleaf was obviously relishing the spotlight, and Columbo always has a sixth sense for detecting insincerity.

Ironically, Greenleaf's alibi is one of the most common and easiest to crack. While other killers had the imagination and creativity to generate original, seemingly unbreakable alibis, Greenleaf used a tactic that's been done many times before—hire someone else to commit the crime for him. Once the prospect of someone else acting for him is accepted, his entire alibi becomes worthless.

Why did Greenleaf become a killer? It's not like he was in any physical or economic danger from Mallory's defection. All he needed to do was let the man go, and that would have been the end of it. It would be easy to find another wannabe bestselling writer willing to commit to turning out sexually charged novels that would appeal to the mass market. But there are two factors involved. One is possessive pride. Greenleaf is genuinely insulted by what he sees as Mallory's base ingratitude. In the publisher's estimation, Mallory's success is completely due to him, so he owns Mallory. In Greenleaf's narcissistic worldview, Mallory is guilty of treason, and treason is punishable by death. The second factor is financial. The "routine" million-dollar insurance policy on Mallory will bring some nice revenue to the company coffers, and thanks to the additional deception, he now has all the rights to Mallory's epic war novel, including a cut of the already set-up film deal. Being able to tweak the nose of a rival publisher is an added bonus for Mallory. Jack Cassidy's killers always take other people's lives with twinkles in their eyes, and there's a sense throughout the episode that Greenleaf is enjoying the opportunity to kill while expecting no negative consequences. Remorse and guilt are absent in Greenleaf's psyche. He feels a man has wronged him, and he shall not only have his revenge, but a sweet stack of cash as well.

Riley Greenleaf's descent into homicide was fueled by his narcissism. He couldn't bear the public embarrassment of losing a star author, and once he had decided on murder, he had to be the star of the show he had written and directed, even if it would have been more prudent to play a laid-back role. Greenleaf took two lives in order to assuage his wounded ego, but it culminated in far greater injury to his pride when Columbo unraveled his plans.

Chapter Twenty-Three: Mind Over Mayhem

Marshall Cahill (José Ferrer)

Murdering the man who could expose one's son's intellectual dishonesty to the world doesn't make one Father of the Year material, but it does make Dr. Marshall Cahill a *Columbo* adversary. Cahill is a scientist who works with complex computer technology for government and military matters. However, it's not his work, but that of his son Neil (Robert Walker) that leads to a deadly crime. Prof. Howard Nicholson (Lew Ayres) visits the elder Cahill and informs him that Neil does not deserve a major scientific award he's due to receive shortly. Nicholson accuses Neil of plagiarizing the molecular matter theory of the late Carl Finch, taking Finch's unpublished work and claiming it as his own. Nicholson insists that "Neil's a competent computer analyst, and that's all he is" and demands that Neil repudiate the award and admit to his appropriation of Finch's ideas. Otherwise, he'll expose Neil to the world as a fraud himself.

Concerned that the scandal will not only destroy his son's reputation but his own as well, Dr. Cahill decides to turn his brain to crime. After arranging for a boy genius named Steve Spelberg (Lee Montgomery—the character's name references the famous director who was behind the camera for "Murder by the Book" and is deliberately spelled differently) to have a night of fun, Dr. Cahill commandeers MM7, the giant programmable robot Spelberg designed, and uses MM7 to man the controls in his private office, out of sight of the rest of the staff. Later that night, as other members of the institute run war simulations, MM7's work allows Dr. Cahill to slip out unnoticed.

Arriving at Nicholson's house, Dr. Cahill lures his colleague out and immediately runs him over with his car, causing Nicholson's pipe to go flying. Carrying Nicholson's body back inside, Dr. Cahill deposits him on the living room floor, sets up a couple of drinks and lights a match, then arranges the scene to look like a scuffle. He then takes a few items to make the crime look like a burglary, including the victim's wallet and a can of heroin that Nicholson used strictly for chemistry experiments, all to make it look like the crime was the work of a desperate drug user. Dr. Cahill returns to work, establishes his alibi, and returns home, but not before staging a car accident to account for the damage to his automobile.

The next day, seventeen and a half minutes into the episode, Columbo receives some unfortunate news from the obedience school Dog is attending. Apparently, Dog isn't learning his lessons properly, and he's having a negative effect on the other students, so he's being expelled. When Columbo and Dr. Cahill meet soon afterwards at the scene of the crime, Columbo doesn't accept the homicidal addict theory. The heroin jar in Nicholson's laboratory was marked with the chemical formula, and an addict is unlikely to have known what that collection of letters and numbers meant. Columbo also discovers the broken pipe in the driveway, and when combined with a black smear of shoe polish on the door, the lieutenant correctly deduces that the chemist was killed outside and carried in by the killer. After examining the burned-down match, Columbo sets his sights on Dr. Cahill for the crime, telling him, "All I know, the person who did this, he had a brain."

Columbo starts digging, and his suspicions grow when young Spelberg tells him how Dr. Cahill treated him to a night at the movies for the first time ever, an uncharacteristic act of benevolence Columbo immediately finds dubious. At first, the relationship between Columbo and Dr. Cahill is cordial, with Dr. Cahill even giving Columbo an expensive cigar, which Columbo says he'll save for a special occasion. Without being asked, Dr. Cahill makes a point of telling Columbo where he was at the time of the crime, and Columbo replies, "[I] can't believe I forgot to ask that question." Things sour when Columbo, with Spelberg's help, uses MM7 to demonstrate just how Dr. Cahill set up his alibi. Dr. Cahill is coldly furious, both at the use of the robot and at how thoroughly Columbo has seen through his plan. Not only that, but when Dr. Cahill stopped MM7, he proved that he knew how to work the robot. Columbo makes a sincere-sounding apology, and Dr. Cahill, from this point forward, replies to Columbo with curt insults.

Soon afterwards, Columbo makes a much more dramatic public apology, saying that he knows for a fact Dr. Cahill is innocent. He provides a witness who claims that Neil was having an affair with Nicholson's much younger wife, Margaret (Jessica Walter). Columbo has Neil arrested, while the younger Cahill loudly denies the affair. Dr. Cahill knows something's fishy about the allegation, but after a brief moment of soul-searching, he decides to concede and confess to the murder in order to save Neil, as he won't risk calling Columbo's bluff. Columbo informs Dr. Cahill that he suspected him "ten minutes after I met you," as the match was burned down in a way that indicated a cigar smoker. As the episode ends, Columbo assures Dr. Cahill that Neil will be released right away and hands Dr. Cahill a cigar, which he smokes.

Notably, Columbo gave Dr. Cahill his own cigar back. It shows that Columbo couldn't accept a gift from a man he knew to be a killer, but given Columbo's recognition of Dr. Cahill's reasons for his confession, he felt like the man deserved one last little comfort, much like the dessert wine he gave Adrian Carsini in "Any Old Port in a Storm." Perhaps this was a way of returning a potential bribe. Only a handful of *Columbo* killers receive any sort of warm consideration from the lieutenant at the end of the episode—the most arrogant and unpleasant killers receive only the humiliation of getting caught and the sight of triumph flushing over Columbo's face. And yet Dr. Cahill, a man who showed Columbo precious little warmth or friendliness, closes out his appearance with a surprisingly compassionate moment alongside the detective.

There is no friendly relationship developing between the pair. After the initial graciousness in the original meeting, Dr. Cahill quickly fell into the habit of attacking Columbo when he got too close to the truth. When Columbo reveals he knows how the robot was used to set up the alibi, angering Dr. Cahill, Columbo tries to accept the blame to protect Steve from repercussions, but Dr. Cahill snaps, "You haven't got the brains for it." When Columbo apologizes for suspecting Dr. Cahill, the acceptance is sharp and hostile. Later, Dr. Cahill tells Columbo, "You have a very transparent mind, which in no way implies clear thinking." These are insults meant to assert Dr. Cahill's intellectual superiority over the lieutenant, but this sort of language leaves no scars on Columbo. Dr. Cahill is used to people folding before him when he vents his wrath. Columbo failing to crumble is a new experience for the doctor.

Throughout the episode, Dr. Cahill comes across as a cold, rather austere man who demands perfection from everybody around him. It's unlikely that his son had an easy time of it growing up, and Dr. Cahill is perceptive enough to know that Neil likely stole a dead man's work in order to earn his father's approval. The closing moments are the only time the viewer sees any signs of softness or tenderness in Dr. Cahill, and it's clear that Columbo is correct in deducing that Dr. Cahill truly loves his son and the entire murder was committed to protecting him (although he certainly had the additional motive of shielding himself from the repercussions of scandal as well). One wonders if Dr. Cahill realizes that if his style of parenting had been different, there would never have been any need for the murder in the first place.

The denouement is one of the rare times when Columbo veers into ethically shaky territory by arresting a man he knows to be innocent, though it's made clear that Neil is in no danger of being formally charged or having any stain on his record. Indeed, it's not even definite that this is a legal arrest or just a bit of theater. Surely, Dr. Cahill could realize that this is simply a high-stakes game of chicken, but Dr. Cahill acts as if his son is at a very real risk of conviction. Does Dr. Cahill misjudge Columbo, or does he confess out of sudden feelings of guilt that distort his judgment? However the viewer evaluates Dr. Cahill, he's cold and calculating man whose heart still has a soft spot for his son.

At one spot in the episode, a psychologist says of Columbo, "He's a lot wiser about people than he cares to show, or perhaps that we recognize." Usually, Columbo cracks the case by finding crucial evidence or forcing the killers to reveal themselves. In this instance, Columbo broke a killer's resolve by appealing to his humanity and paternal protectiveness. Few people would have thought Dr. Cahill had any weaknesses at all, least of all for his son. Yet Columbo realized that Dr. Cahill was thoroughly capable of love, and that emotion had led him to murder, and it would also lead him to a confession.

Chapter Twenty-Four: Swan Song

Tommy Brown (Johnny Cash)

It was only a song when Johnny Cash said he shot a man in Reno just to watch him die, but when Tommy Brown killed his wife and underage lover in a plane crash, it was to escape blackmail and to live a more luxurious lifestyle.

Tommy Brown is a gospel singer whose deeds don't match his words. He's incredibly successful thanks to the promotional efforts of his wife Edna (Ida Lupino), who has partnered Brown with The Lost Souls Crusaders choir and created a high-revenue musical group. The deeply devout Edna allows her husband only a skimpy living allowance and funnels the entirety of the remaining profits into funding religious outreach programs. Brown resents the fact that he doesn't even have an automobile of his own, and when he demands that Edna give him more money, she refuses, informing him that she built him up from nothing and that she's fully aware of his sexual relationship with one of the members of the choir, Maryann Cobb (Bonnie Van Dyke). It began when she was only sixteen, and since Edna has the evidence to prove the affair, that means that if she wishes, she can get him convicted and jailed for statutory rape.

Although this confrontation seems to provoke Brown to murder, he's clearly been planning this for some time. Brown flies himself, Edna, and Maryann in a private plane. The women are given a thermos full of drugged coffee, and once the pair are unconscious, he jumps out of the plane with a parachute, leaving the women to die in a crash. Brown survives his jump with an injured leg, planning to claim that he was thrown clear of the wreckage and miraculously landed safely and ready to enjoy life as a wealthy widower.

Columbo's arrival at the crash site twenty-three minutes into the episode upsets Brown's plans. The lieutenant impresses the professional plane crash inspector with his skills, but doesn't see anything particularly suspicious until Edna's brother arrives, accusing Brown of engineering her death.

Columbo's not immediately suspicious, though, when he arrives at Brown's new house, an enormous place where the rent is $2,000 a month (Exactly fifty years after this episode aired in 1974, after inflation, that would be the equivalent of $12,720.00 in 2024 dollars[1]), and sees a harem of bikini-clad young women there, Columbo's instincts lead him to treat Brown as a suspect. Yet despite Columbo's growing belief that Brown is a murderer, the two have one of the most amiable relationships in the series. Brown takes all of Columbo's questions in stride and never gets seriously upset, other than a quick look of dismay when Columbo makes a comment that gets too close to the truth.

Columbo performs his standard investigation, noting all sorts of inconsistencies and observing how Brown is acting like a man who's enjoying being newly single. Throughout, Brown is genuinely cordial to Columbo, offering him refreshment and treating him with respect. Columbo, for his part, becomes a fan of Brown's music, and there's never any animosity between the two.

The culmination of the episode begins when Columbo explains that barbiturates were found in the bodies of the two women, and Columbo suggests that some unknown party was trying to kill Brown as well by spiking the thermos. Columbo suggests that a search for the coffee thermos will help them find the killer, and he's willing to scrutinize the entire crash scene to locate it.

Brown acts unconcerned and denies Columbo's offer of police protection, and when he sees Columbo watching him at the airport, he laughs, pleased that Columbo's looking out for his safety. Later that night, however,

Brown doubles back from his destination and returns to where he hid his parachute a short distance from the crash site. When he emerges with the incriminating evidence, Columbo's there to catch him. The talk of retrieving the thermos was meant to scare him into removing the parachute. Caught, Brown joins Columbo in his car and asks, "Aren't you afraid being alone up here with a killer?" Columbo isn't, noting that he doesn't think Brown will attack him, and observes that he's already suffering from conscience, saying, "Sooner or later you would've confessed, even if I hadn't caught you." Brown agrees and expresses relief that he no longer has to worry about hiding his murderous secret. With a look of compassion, Columbo plays Brown's music and says, "Any man who can sing like that can't be all bad."

It is with this observation that Columbo touches upon a point that makes Brown practically unique amongst all of the Columbo killers. *He actually feels guilt for his actions.* Few other murderers feel real shame for their actions. Most of their consciences are so deadened as to border on sociopathy. They had their motives; the victim stood in the way of their goals, and they just didn't care that another human being was dead. Carl Brimmer, in "Death Lends a Hand," regretted his role in a woman's death, but it was an accident caused by an angry outburst, as opposed to a carefully premeditated crime. A couple of other sympathetic killers in future episodes will explain their absence of guilt by explaining that their actions were justified due to the way their victims treated the women they loved.

And it should be noted that Brown's actions are certainly odious. He's the only murderer who is also a sexual offender, and one of the victims was the girl he had an affair with while she was still underage. In terms of his murder plot, it's unquestionably the most reckless of any *Columbo* killer's, as even with a parachute, he stood a very real risk of death, or, at the very least, serious injury. The psychological theory that he may have subconsciously been trying to punish himself for his crimes cannot be discounted.

Though these critiques are designed to focus on the killers, in this case, certain focus should be directed towards the victim as well, as a means of understanding Brown's motives more thoroughly. In many reviews, critics refer to Edna as shrewish or worse, but is this fair to her? There's no proof of her knowing about Brown's sexual actions until after their marriage. She may not have been fully aware of the character of the man she married. It's possible that being cheated on and the knowledge that her husband committed statutory rape on numerous occasions embittered her. But she did nothing in order to protect the cause, which was her obsession. She's raised a great deal of money for religious purposes, and by all accounts, she's not living in luxury off the largesse of the faithful. Aside from the funds used for keeping the Crusade going and for transportation, she lives modestly and expects her cheating husband to do the same. Certainly, they're not deeply in love with each other, and clearly, she despises him. To her, their relationship is strictly business. His talent brings in money, which she then puts towards a higher purpose. The viewer sees their relationship largely through Brown's perspective, but it's certainly possible that an unsympathetic view of Edna might have been reversed if only there had been a brief scene that might have explained a bit better how she felt, her reasons for staying in the marriage, and her religious faith. Flashing forward a few decades in television history, most of the detectives on *Law & Order: Special Victims Unit* use harsh language towards statutory rapists that mirrors what Edna tells her spouse. From the way she places a protective arm around Maryann, there's reason to think she feels genuine maternal and protective feelings towards her, more than just attempting to maintain a pleasant relationship with the proof she needs to keep her spouse in check. However viewers might feel towards Edna, there is absolutely no justification for his murder of the girl he took advantage of when she was in her mid-teens.

Given everything that Brown did, why do he and Columbo get along so well? As the lieutenant himself indicates, Brown had his sins, but he wasn't purely evil. People aren't always one way or another, and most of the murderers in this series may be vile and cruel on the inside, but charming on the outside. Brown may have been a double murderer and a statutory rapist, yet it is in no way meant to diminish his terrible crimes to say that there was goodness and contriteness in him as well.

At their initial meeting, Brown's a bit hostile to the prospect of a detective investigating him, but Columbo defuses him immediately by explaining that such an inquiry is purely routine and he's just doing his job. From that moment on, Brown is consistently cordial and warm to Columbo. He never tries to flaunt his celebrity or wealth, or pat himself on the back for being cleverer than the lieutenant. There are no power plays, only amicability. The only bumpy parts in their relationship are when Brown becomes visibly worried, such as when Columbo reveals he knows about Brown stopping work on a religious building construction project, or realized that he rearranged the choir's singing arrangement to downplay Maryann's part long before he ought to have known she'd die. When Brown tells the detective, "I know how bad you hate to ask all of those stupid questions," it's not entirely sincere. Brown knows that Columbo is a dog that's on the scent, and the singer feels the need to discount the investigation as a "stupid" waste of time, perhaps hoping that his mocking the situation will put Columbo off the case. Of course, this doesn't work. While Columbo is determined to prove the truth, there's none of the triumphant attitude that comes from checkmating the most arrogant killers. The friendly final conversation in Columbo's car directly mirrors the similar one with Adrian Carsini in "Any Old Port in a Storm."

Columbo is not a crime series that dwells much on the possibility of redemption. In most cases, it's implied that the killer will either fight the accusations in court or spend a lengthy prison term fretting over mistakes and cursing Columbo's name. Even Carl Brimmer of "Death Lends a Hand" stressed that it was an accident, and Adrian Carsini in "Any Old Port in a Storm" made it clear that he was relieved to be caught, but he didn't feel the least bit guilty over his brother's death. This is the first case where it seems like the killer is deeply haunted by a troubled conscience (the killers in "Dagger of the Mind" arguably snap from the shattering of their public reputations—not from guilt). The guilty feelings aren't strongly stressed in the episode, though Brown's initial hedonism in the wake of becoming a widower tempers off quickly. Columbo's statement at the end makes it clear that he's seen Brown's crumbling façade.

Tommy Brown committed awful crimes, but almost uniquely amongst the series' villains, he felt the weight of culpability. Columbo had a partner in this investigation: Brown's own conscience. Brown possibly accepted Columbo in a friendly manner because he subconsciously saw the lieutenant as an avenging force that would bring the singer to well-warranted justice.

[1] * https://www.usinflationcalculator.com.

Chapter Twenty-Five: A Friend in Deed

Mark Halperin (Richard Kiley) and Hugh Caldwell (Michael McGuire)

Longtime viewers often wonder why Columbo was never promoted higher than a lieutenant. Certainly, with his investigative skills, he should have been recognized as one of the LAPD's brightest lights. But great detectives are often passed over for higher-level administrative jobs, as skillful sleuths are needed in the field, and many able people fail to do well on the official tests for promotion. It's said that a surefire way to stall your career is to make your superiors look bad. Columbo's arrest of the Deputy Police Commissioner for murder may not have been the savviest career move, but it was all in the cause of justice.

Hugh Caldwell is in the minority of *Columbo* killers: a homicidal man without a plan of his own. He committed the unpremeditated murder of his wife (not shown onscreen), and he has no idea of what he should do next, so he calls his good pal Mark Halperin. Caldwell got into a fight with his wife and strangled her without realizing what he was doing until it was too late. Halperin sends Caldwell out to get himself an alibi, and Halperin makes the scene look like a robbery. Caldwell goes to a bar, and a little later, the two have a public phone call with Halperin pretending to be the late wife, thereby creating the impression she's still alive. But before anybody nominates Halperin for an award for "Most Murderously Altruistic Friend Ever," it should be noted that Halperin has an ulterior motive. His wealthy wife Margaret (Rosemary Murphy) gives too much money to charity and not enough to him, so he plans to kill her and have Caldwell help him establish his own alibi. In the meantime, Halperin returns to his nearby home and, in the presence of his wife, pretends to see a shadowy figure running from the Caldwell home and summons the police.

Columbo appears on the scene sixteen and a half minutes into the episode. He interviews Caldwell and notes little details that call the robbery narrative into question, such as the fact that a nightgown was left on the bed (a detail arranged by Halperin), but there was another nightgown underneath the late woman's pillow. Columbo realizes that this isn't a simple robbery, and that certain aspects of the scene have been staged, leading him to immediately suspect the husband with an alibi. Yet since the husband knew all about his wife's habit of tucking a nightgown under her pillow to use again, he wouldn't have taken out another one, leading him to realize that another person, less aware of the late woman's habits, must have been involved.

Halperin oversees the early stages of Columbo's investigation and pressures him to focus on the theory that the murder was committed by a burglar. Soon afterwards, he's ready to commit his own murder, drowning his wife in her bathtub. He arranges to be up in a surveillance helicopter that night, and Caldwell, under Halperin's instructions, carries the late Mrs. Halperin out of the house and drops her into the swimming pool before running off, all in full view of the helicopter's passengers.

When Columbo questions Halperin, the Deputy Police Commissioner is faking hysterics of grief, claiming that since he "misspoke" at a press conference and implied to reporters that his wife witnessed Mrs. Caldwell's killer running away, the killer came back and murdered her, fearing she could identify him. Columbo later tells Halperin he thinks the murder of Mrs. Caldwell was staged to look like a robbery, and Halperin, no longer grieving as hard as he was a short time earlier, patronizingly but firmly tells Columbo the killer had to have been a burglar.

Columbo continues his investigation, finding little inconsistencies, including soap in Mrs. Halperin's lungs, making him realize she drowned in the bathtub. There have been a string of genuine robberies in the neighborhood of the murders, and after some digging, the lieutenant tracks down the true thief, Artie Jessup (Val Avery), a career criminal, but not a murderer. Despite some initial hostility, Columbo's able to forge a connection with him and convinces Jessup to blackmail Caldwell in an attempt to uncover the truth. Jessup meets with Caldwell, noting that as he didn't kill Mrs. Caldwell, it seems likely that the husband is the most likely suspect. Threatened and nervous, Caldwell turns to Halperin, who plans a frame-up.

That evening, while Columbo's looking through his files on known burglars, Halperin casually picks up Jessup's file and makes a quick note of his target's address. The next day, while Caldwell hands Jessup a bit of hush money, Halperin sneaks into Jessup's apartment and plants some of the items he took from the Caldwell household to bolster the robbery theory. Soon afterwards, Halperin leads a raid, as Jessup is arrested and the police search the apartment. Once the stolen goods are discovered, it looks like a solid case, until Jessup is brought to the scene and denies that this is even his apartment. Columbo, who has been present at the raid, warning Halperin against it the whole time and even accusing Halperin of murder, agrees. Columbo rented the apartment as a trap, leaving a fake dossier on Jessup for Halperin to read and filling the apartment with his own possessions. As Halperin was the only one who saw the ersatz apartment address, he was the only one who could have planted the items there. Realizing that he's incriminated himself, Halperin exercises his right to remain silent, though Columbo is confident in his ability to crack Caldwell. Interestingly, Columbo hasn't completely figured out the crime, as when he accuses Halperin of his wife's murder, he's not sure whether or not Halperin killed Mrs. Caldwell or if Caldwell killed her.

It's notable that Columbo, being known to the killers already, doesn't have to play up his absent-minded persona. In his first scene, he's dropped his cigar in a car and his having trouble finding it, indicating that his awkwardly bumbling moments aren't entirely a sham. At first glance, one might think that Halperin would make sure that a second- or third-rate investigator was placed on the case, but upon reflection, as the wives of police officers were targeted, it would seem suspicious if the cream of the crop wasn't in charge of the investigation. Still, just because Columbo has a great reputation, that doesn't mean that a man like Halperin, who enjoys his luxuries and cares about appearances, wouldn't underestimate Columbo, or, at the very least, overestimate his own competence and cleverness.

Columbo's interactions with Caldwell are brief and cordial, as they mostly consist of a brief interview shortly after the murder of Mrs. Caldwell. Columbo's observations lead him to find the burglar theory unconvincing, which leads him straight to the husband. Caldwell acquits himself well in Columbo's presence, but when he's talking to Halperin, he acts like a man whose nerves have frayed beyond repair, and as his crime was at most second-degree murder, it's clear that he's not a cold-blooded killer. Caldwell's actions were those of a man in a violent frenzy spurred by an argument with his adulterous wife. It was unpremeditated, and once he realized what he had done, he lacked the ability to figure a way out of it and had to turn to a friend for help. Caldwell was the weaker member of the pair, but while some investigators might have pursued a strategy of giving the third degree to who they thought was the more likely suspect to crack, Columbo realized that as long as Caldwell had the presence of mind to ask for an attorney and be quiet, that approach would fail. The safest way to break Caldwell would be to build a solid case against his partner, leaving Caldwell with no escape.

Halperin, in contrast, is portrayed from the beginning as a man who luxuriates in enjoying vices, including gambling and attractive women who are not his wife. He's a man who appreciates wealth and all of its trappings, and when he learns what Caldwell has done, his first reaction is not one of shock at the crime, but instead, he quickly calculates how he can take advantage of this death.

In addition to money and pleasures, Halperin also is a man who enjoys power. He clearly relishes his authority over Columbo, and Columbo is always aware of his subordinate status in this case. Columbo's explanation of his logical conclusions is solid and intelligent police work, but when

Halperin dismisses his ideas for no reasons other than his own desire to push his preferred narrative, Columbo shows no anger or belligerence. After a few attempts to defend his theories, he either says nothing or agrees to follow Halperin's directives. It's a remarkable show of humility, or at least going along to get along, especially when Halperin becomes aggressive and bullying, such as when he bluntly tells Columbo he's wasting his time, "and it's gonna stop, now." Columbo's track record is glossed over with the declaration that "Nobody can be right all the time." A less controlled man would have thrown that remark back in Halperin's face, but Columbo is skilled at playing the long game. The lieutenant knew that he couldn't bring down his boss head-on, not without a bulletproof case.

In their final scene, Columbo quietly and calmly lays out his case against Halperin, explaining his reasons why he suspected Caldwell and why Halperin's alibi doesn't hold. It culminates with a flat accusation against Halperin, leading to Halperin declaring, "You just lost your badge, my friend." It's a pure power play, but Columbo isn't fazed. He knows his job isn't in any danger, and he's sure enough of the strength of his case that he doesn't fear that Halperin's connections will lead to repercussions. Columbo doesn't luxuriate in his triumph, and his statement of the solidness of his accusation is that of a man simply stating a fact rather than gloating over a fallen foe. There's no attempt on Columbo's part to declare a victory or humiliate the man who lorded his position over him. Perhaps this is a professional courtesy to a man who is, after all, a fellow member of law enforcement. Maybe Columbo is aware of the shame this will bring to a department he cares about, and perhaps Columbo knows that bringing down a superior officer may hurt his career in some way. It's a restrained performance on Falk's part, with very little emotion shown. Sometimes, Columbo twinkles with glee as he sends a killer to jail, but in this case, he's quite somber.

Caldwell became a killer because he snapped and acted violently. Though he committed a horrific crime, there's a sense he could have been an honest detective once. Halperin, in contrast, gives the impression that he was always a venal and corrupt man who married for money and sought out the position of Deputy Police Commissioner not because he had deep and genuine respect for justice but because he enjoyed power and influence. There's no indication he was using the job as a stepping stone for higher office, though that possibility cannot be ruled out completely. If his approach to his job was as mercenary as his approach to his marriage, it's actually rather likely, especially as public service positions, even those of considerable authority, have salaries that pale in comparison to the private sector.

As this episode proved, Halperin collected favors. When Caldwell strangled his wife, Halperin immediately saw a chance to turn the situation to his own advantage. It's not too much of a stretch to theorize that as he climbed the power ladder and as he held his current position, Halperin provided less murderous assistance to people in positions of influence in exchange for favors to be cashed in as needed, and it's possible that's how a man with so little respect for human life and the law made his way to that position.

Like many killers before and after him, Halperin was utterly confident in the narrative that he created for covering up murder. When Columbo discovered inconsistencies, he became aggressive in his defense of his preferred narrative, to the point where his refusal to consider alternative possibilities became suspicious. After all, every experienced law enforcement professional ought to know that any halfway competent defense attorney can create reasonable doubt through an alternative theory of the crime. Police officers can be pilloried on the witness stand for not investigating and discounting all of the possibilities and leads. The insistence on demanding that Columbo follow the planted trail of breadcrumbs was a giveaway, and it shows how, like many others of his kind, the prospect of having his lies challenged was not just a blow to Halperin's safety but to his ego as well.

The Caldwell/Halperin alliance was born out of necessity, and given the fact that Halperin was clearly the dominant partner, the imaginative viewer can reflect on the steps that Halperin might take if he suspected there was any chance of Caldwell confessing. The relationship between the two men was clearly a friendship of convenience, at least on Halperin's part. The ending is also a testament to Columbo's integrity, as a less ethical man might have parlayed his theories and evidence into career advancement. Instead, Columbo put the truth above personal profit and even the reputation of the department.

IV

SEASON FOUR

Chapter Twenty-Six: An Exercise in Fatality

Milo Janus (Robert Conrad)

Milo Janus may have been in terrific physical condition, but he was quite weak in a moral sense. A fitness instructor, Janus is the public face of a chain of athletic centers. Gene Stafford (Philip Bruns) bought the franchise from him, but Janus kept control of the supply companies that provide the exercise equipment, keeping that business going. With a huge mark-up, Janus is raking in money. Furious at having his pocket picked, Stafford threatens a class action suit and an SEC investigation. To prevent this, Janus attempts to choke Stafford, but Stafford breaks away, only to be cornered and throttled by a bar against his throat. Janus changes Stafford's clothes, dressing him in sweats and sneakers, lays him down on an exercise bench, and places a barbell over his throat, making it look like an exercise accident. He even sets up an alibi with a tape recording of Stafford and plays it over one house phone while talking on the other, making it sound like Stafford's exercising while Janus is at a party with friends.

Eighteen minutes into the episode, Columbo appears to question this pat little scenario. Columbo gets down upon a freshly waxed floor and sees brown scuff marks on it. None of the police have shoes with that color sole. Furthermore, Stafford supposedly locked away his personal items even though he was the only one there. About a third of the way through "An Exercise in Fatality," the lieutenant meets Janus for the first time, telling him how Janus's exercise television program saved his marriage, as Mrs. Columbo was depressed for a while, but the exercise helped her.

As the investigation continues, Janus acts as if his superior physical condition is enough to break Columbo, insisting on answering questions while jogging on a beach, leaving Columbo breathless and sweaty. The exercise maven claims he saw Stafford dressed for a workout. Janus is insistent upon the accident theory, despite Columbo's observations that Stafford would have followed exercise safety protocols and that the barbell was too heavy for most men to lift.

Mrs. Ruth Stafford (Collin Wilcox Paxton), the dead man's widow, continues to make the same allegations her husband did and eventually ends up in the hospital due to an overdose of alcohol and prescription medication. Columbo, furious at what's happened to her, openly blames Janus for driving her to this, and Janus calmly calls the detective "a devious man." With a quiet and undeniable threat, Janus tells Columbo, "If you are smart, I won't be seeing you again."

But Columbo is intelligent, and he finds the tape recording that destroys Janus's alibi. In addition, he shows Janus the dead man's shoes and illustrates how the knots prove that they were tied by someone other than Stafford. Some other person put the shoes on the dead man's feet and tied them for him. This discredits Janus's testimony, leaving him silent but stunned as a slightly more triumphant than usual Columbo declares, "It's your perfect alibi that's gonna hang you."

Columbo and Janus do not have a chummy relationship. Continually, Janus treats the lieutenant dismissively, seeing him as an annoyance. Even when Janus is polite, his contempt for the detective is evident on his face. Janus's treatment of Columbo is invariably that of a bully trying to intimidate someone he sees as weaker than he is while avoiding overtness. The larger, more muscular man often stands over Columbo or strikes a pose that emphasizes his superior stature and strength. In the jogging on the beach scene, Janus is clearly trying to wear down Columbo, leaving him exhausted and unable to concentrate.

But these attempts to assert dominance *physically* are met by Columbo's eventual assertions of *mental* and *moral* superiority. Columbo illustrates how much cleverer he is in the climactic scene, as he builds his solid case in front of Janus, but it's the hospital scene where Columbo rails at Janus for how his actions led Mrs. Stafford to either a suicide attempt or an accidental drug overdose, and it's this righteous anger that shows that the case has become personal for Columbo. To the lieutenant, Janus is an ethical monster who leaves a trail of destruction in his wake, and Columbo loathes him for taking a man's life and leaving a decent woman emotionally devastated. Columbo always wanted Janus arrested, but now he's truly on fire to see justice done.

By the end, Columbo is certain of the solidness of his case. Columbo asserts his authority in the climax, countering Janus's question of what gives him the right to putter around his office with the blunt declaration that his warrant gives him the right. Even as Columbo explains the holes in his murder plot, Janus dismisses each point with put-downs, such as comparing the lieutenant's clues to "more cigar ashes." This is one case where Columbo is open about how he despises his quarry. At the end, when Columbo confronts Janus with the critical mistake in his testimony, he declares, "It could only be you. By your own admission, it had to be you." There's intense triumph in Columbo's face as he's bringing down a man he sees as a danger to society.

In terms of the actual murder he committed, Janus is a more brutal villain than most of the others in the series. While most (though certainly not all) of the crimes take place in the space of a few seconds, consisting of pulling a trigger or swinging a blunt instrument. The strangulation scene in "Prescription Murder" is largely shown in bits and cutaways, and the actual squeezing of hands on a woman's neck is largely kept off-screen. When Janus commits his murder, viewers see a brutal attempted choking, followed by a chase scene as Stafford flees for his life, followed by a full scene of Janus pressing a bar against a struggling man's throat until he dies. The violence characterizes Janus as one of the darkest killers yet.

The crime is debatably planned, as Janus anticipated the need for an alibi later, but his actual murder was not well choreographed, showing poor planning. In the legal sense of the word, it is definitely premeditated. The initial attempt to choke Stafford was an impulsive move to silence a threat, but after chasing Stafford, enough time elapsed to provide Janus with sufficient time to reflect upon his actions, making the crime first-degree murder. Noticeably, Janus failed in his first attempt to kill Stafford. Stafford, despite being far weaker than Janus, managed to escape, and it's possible that this was due in part to Janus's initial hesitancy to take a life. Perhaps this may be giving Janus too much credit. Perhaps he simply underestimated his victim's strength, and Stafford had a sudden and unexpected burst of power stemming from his desire to survive.

Milo Janus started on the road to murder by building his fitness empire on unethical behavior. He was an unethical businessman who exploited people who worked with him, and his plan was not particularly well-hidden. Anybody with a basic knowledge of forensic accounting could have uncovered his scheme, as Stafford certainly did. Certain labels might be applied to Janus's callous treatment of both Staffords—cruelty, narcissism, sociopathy, and many more. It was the inhuman treatment of others that made his relationship with Columbo so antagonistic. As much effort as Janus put into bodybuilding, the most important muscles in his body-those in his heart- were miserably weak.

Chapter Twenty-Seven: Negative Reaction

Paul Galesko (Dick Van Dyke)

A picture's worth a thousand words, and when used properly, it can also be the next best thing to a confession. Paul Galesko is an acclaimed photographer who loathes his wealthy wife, Frances (Antoinette Bower). As the episode opens, Galesko is preparing a ransom letter made from letters cut from a newspaper, and Frances takes a short break from day drinking to argue with him. The two go to an abandoned farmhouse, where he overpowers her, ties her up, takes a photograph of her with a self-developing camera, takes another picture after the first one turns out badly, and then shoots her. A little clock in the background, set to the wrong time, is Galesko's plan to give himself an alibi.

Galesko takes steps to create the illusion that his wife has been kidnapped, including pretending to receive a phone call from the abductors in front of his housekeeper and scribbling a note to further convince her that he's paying a ransom. Galesko has befriended a former prisoner, Alvin Deschler (Don Gordon), under the pretext of helping him find work. Meeting Deschler at a junkyard, Galesko shoots him and then places the murder weapon in Deschler's dead hand and fires into his own leg. The self-wounded Galesko hobbles into his car and leaves to alert the authorities, the only witness being an inebriated derelict hiding out in the junkyard.

Columbo arrives twenty-two minutes into the episode, and the twin running gags of Columbo being unrecognized by his peers and the shabbiness of his vehicle are revived when one of the officers at the scene thinks Columbo's dropping his car off at the junkyard. Columbo finds it odd that Galesko didn't try harder to learn his wife's location and make sure that the homeless man is properly interviewed. Columbo and Galesko meet a few minutes later while the murderous photographer is having the bullet removed, and Columbo quietly finds the positioning of the wound suspicious. The investigation continues, and the police find cut-up newspapers from the ransom note at Deschler's motel room, carefully planted by Galesko. Columbo considers the evidence to be a bit too obvious, as even the least intelligent criminal would know to dispose of the newspaper scraps.

When the police discover Mrs. Galesko's corpse at the farmhouse, Galesko arrives and plays up his devastation. At the crime scene, Columbo notes that the alibi clock doesn't have the dust that covers the rest of the room and begins his investigation in earnest, going from a camera shop to St. Matthew's Mission, where in a classic comedy scene, the extremely helpful Sister of Mercy (Joyce Van Patten) believes Columbo's down on his luck, plies him with stew, and offers him a new coat.

Armed with new information about Deschler, Columbo begins his questioning of Galesko, querying about photography and other issues until Galesko begs off, pleading exhaustion. Later, at the funeral, Columbo distracts the not-so-grieving widower, taking photographs and telling an increasingly irritated Galesko that he believes someone else was involved in the crime. Columbo continues digging, eventually finding a book of photographs Galesko took of inmates at a prison. Deschler appears in it multiple times, proving the two knew each other. Galesko gets increasingly frustrated, threatening to complain to Columbo's superiors. An inquiry with a driving instructor provides Deschler with an alibi for the crime, leaving Galesko's narrative in disarray.

The episode ends in the evidence room at police headquarters, where Columbo says he has proof against Galesko. Upon blowing up the picture at the murder scene, Columbo reveals that the clock on the mantelpiece actually says ten o'clock, not two, thereby destroying Galesko's alibi. Amused, Galesko declares that the image was reversed when it was enlarged. When Columbo denies this, Galesko seeks to show him how easy it is to reverse an image, grabbing one of several cameras from the evidence shelves, photographing the blow-up, and declaring that the negative will show the reversed image. Triumphant, Columbo asks the other officers if the witnessed what Galesko just did. With about a dozen other cameras available, Galesko just happened to grab the camera found at the crime scene, the one used to take the victim's photograph. Only the killer would know which one to use, and Galesko is led away, shocked and self-recriminating, realizing that the reversed photograph was deliberate and that his own impulsive actions proved his guilt.

Galesko does not befriend Columbo. His general attitude towards the lieutenant can be described as curt and condescending. He consistently treats Columbo as if every word the detective speaks is a massive infringement upon his time. There's often no attempt at politeness, such as when he says, "Columbo, you're becoming very annoying, do you know that?" at a photo exhibition, or when he compares the detective to "a little shaggy-haired terrier…[who] won't let go." His tone is that of a man who believes that if he's sufficiently dismissive, the detective will slink away, chastened and afraid to ask further questions out of trepidation of receiving further insults. Like other killers failed to realize, there is nothing to gain through his open curtness. When Columbo doesn't get the hint, Galesko turns to threatening his job, saying, "I'll scream until the beams of City Hall shake." Viewers get a rare glimpse of Columbo's superiors, who think he's wasting his time. It illustrates how Columbo isn't always supported by the top brass, but he still presses on alone, determined to seek out the truth even without the support and possibly with career annihilation facing him even if he's wrong. Galesko never even tries to understand what sort of man his nemesis is.

Galesko makes multiple errors of characterization in the wake of his murder. Like many other killers, he can't keep up his pretense of grief. It's like he has only enough devastation to last through the initial discovery of the body, after which point he's clearly not the least bit saddened and ready to begin living his happy widowerhood. A wiser man would have been willing to set aside several months of grieving before returning to the world. He also forces the narrative he wants to create too hard, becoming agitated when Columbo notes substantial gaps in his timeline and pressing his points as if an aggressively patronizing tone is the best way to be convincing.

For his part, Columbo never seems offended or outwardly hostile to Galesko. After tricking Galesko into proving he knew more than he should, Columbo has a brief moment of quiet success, but not the kind of flushed triumph that he enjoys when he's defeated an opponent who's particularly gotten under his skin. There's minimal emotional connection on Columbo's part, and that's surprising, given Galesko's snideness and the fact that Columbo tends to feel particular antipathy towards men who murder their wives. This isn't a personal case for him, and Galesko is just another murderer.

The essential defining characterization of Galesko is that he is first and foremost a photographer who demands perfection in his work. Taking a second photograph of his wife is the action of a man who can't bring himself to release an inferior product to the world, even though a poor picture might be subconsciously more convincing to the authorities. The photo didn't need to be flawless, just enough to show Mrs. Galesko and the time on the clock. But Galesko just couldn't produce a low-quality image, and the way he tossed away the first photo when he really ought to have pocketed it and destroyed it later shows the disdain he holds for bad photography. When Columbo shows him his pictures of the funeral, asking him if he recognizes anybody in the crowd of mourners who might potentially be involved, Galesko forgets that he's supposed to be anxious to help bring anybody involved in kidnapping and killing his wife to justice. Instead, he criticizes the photos, saying, "Lieutenant, these are the worst pictures I have ever seen." Like with Adrian Carsini, Galesko's vocation is an overwhelming passion, and his dedication to perfection in his preferred field leaves him vulnerable to self-exposure.

Galesko developed a murder plan that was unusually full of holes. He could capture a real-life situation beautifully with his camera, but his talents lay in preserving existing imagery. When he tried to create his own murder tableau, he failed to notice all of the errors he'd made and the unexpected clues he left behind. When challenged, he became abrasive, as Columbo's observations were not just a danger to him, but also a blow to his pride. Poor planning and boorish behavior led to his downfall. Galesko may have devoted his career to capturing perfect images on film, but Columbo's trap produced a picture-perfect result.

Chapter Twenty-Eight: By Dawn's Early Light

Lyle Rumford (Patrick McGoohan)

Of all the *Columbo* killers, Colonel Lyle Rumford is one of the most respectful towards the lieutenant. He never attacks or insults him, and by the end, he may genuinely see him as a friend, or at least an opponent worthy of honor. Patrick McGoohan, one of the great recurring *Columbo* killers, makes his first of four appearances in this episode.

Colonel Rumford is the headmaster of a boy's military school, and he's preparing for war. In the opening scene, he tampers with the explosive powder in a shell, but it's not clear what his reasons for doing so are until shortly afterwards, when he meets with William Haynes (Tom Simcox), a brash and influential alumnus who wants the school to go co-ed and kick out Rumford. The colonel believes this will destroy the school and places the shell in a cannon, observing a bottle of cider hanging from a window and fermenting. Haynes insists on firing the cannon on Founder's Day, and as the Colonel watches from the safety of his office, the cannon explodes, killing Haynes.

Seventeen and a half minutes into the episode, Columbo arrives. The detectives at the scene are convinced it's all a tragic accident, but the lieutenant being the lieutenant, Columbo, sticks around and starts asking questions. After a brief bit of awkwardness where Rumford doesn't realize Columbo's the lead investigator, the Colonel gently pushes the accident theory while Columbo keeps asking questions, noting that any blockage in the barrel could cause an explosion, which leads to the possibility that a student left a cleaning rag in the cannon, leading to the tragedy.

Columbo asks permission to stay and investigate, which Rumford grants without any resistance. As Columbo digs for clues, he's surprised by the Colonel's strictness towards the students and discovers blueprints for girls' facilities in the victim's car. Columbo addresses a couple of theories, including the possibility that a student's negligence caused the explosion and that the Rumford might have been the true target, as he traditionally fired the cannon. When Columbo explains that the forensic report found gelignite in the remains of the shell, making this a murder case, the Colonel is concerned about the academy's reputation, but he admits he's an expert in explosives.

After a couple of additional friendly conversations between the two men and Columbo tracking down an AWOL student who fears he may be blamed for causing the explosion through negligence, the colonel starts a search for the cider he noticed as he rigged the cannon, but Columbo retrieves the fermenting alcohol and hides it before the school authorities find it. The detective, who has been staying in the dormitories, confronts some of the students about the jug of cider he found and asks about their fermentation process.

The following morning, the cider is hanging from its original window, and Rumford is ready to punish the culprits. Columbo asks when he last saw the cider, and the colonel admits that he saw the cider hanging from that very window earlier. Columbo reveals that the students only hung that cider up at night, and it was only in that position the morning before the explosion. As Columbo notes, due to the layout of the campus, the only place where Rumford could have seen the cider is from the cannon, and given the time of sunrise and when the boys removed the cider, there was only a very narrow window when he could have seen it. Without meaning to, Rumford has placed himself at the cannon on the morning of the explosion, contradicting his earlier statements, and the lie is indicative of guilt.

The colonel surrenders, but he is unrepentant, seeing his crime as necessary for the well-being of the school and the nation. Rumford tells Columbo he did "a very nice job," asks to address the students one last time as a favor, and then quietly leaves with the lieutenant.

What's notable about the Columbo/Rumford relationship is its quiet cordiality. Rumford is a man who's used to using his authority to punish those who don't live up to his expectations. The colonel is no fool. He knows early on that Columbo is a dogged investigator, and it's clear that the lieutenant is looking in his direction. Though the suspicion is unspoken, Rumford knows that his freedom and reputation are at risk. But while many other *Columbo* murderers would threaten Columbo's career or come up with a red herring as a distraction, Rumford allows Columbo's investigation to continue unimpeded. Why is this? Surely, a seasoned soldier would be prepared to use his defensive skills and launch a counterattack.

It's possible that he felt reluctant to slow down Columbo's investigation out of respect. There are no patronizing comments from the colonel, no complement wrapped around a sneer, no attempts to leverage his position and connections to his advantage. But why does he just let the investigation happen? Does he want to get caught? From his heartfelt speech at one point about how the nation needs tough, dedicated soldiers to keep the country safe and secure, there's no reason to believe that he's the sort of man who sees lying down and refusing to fight as an acceptable strategy. If he's not willing to fight, then it's possible that Rumford believes that there is no honor in fighting. It's perfectly acceptable to battle a man with evil in his heart, but fighting a pure-motivated man with righteous motives makes you the villain.

Throughout their interactions, Rumford declines to treat Columbo as an adversary. This is not because he underestimates him. When the two have dinner together, Rumford's responses are quietly restrained even as he learns about what the lieutenant has unearthed. At one point, Rumford tries to downplay the possibility of deliberate homicide, commenting, "I think you're working too hard…. Everything is not a murder, you know." When confronted with evidence of deliberate tampering, he immediately accepts this and does not try to advance a theory that no longer holds water, unlike other *Columbo* killers. One of Rumford's slips is that he wasn't more concerned about the possibility of being the true target of the explosion. An innocent man would have been wary, even if he might have too much pride to request protection.

In one of their later conversations, Rumford offers Columbo a high-quality cigar and even asks about his first name (Columbo replies that his wife is the only one who uses it). It's a bonding moment where the colonel acts in a friendly manner without an ulterior motive. He's not trying to dissuade or gaslight Columbo. He knows that Columbo is working to uncover the truth behind his crime, but rather than trying to fight the detective, Rumford's simply willing to allow a man he sees as a dedicated professional to pursue his work. The colonel notes that they both wear a uniform in a way, and they're both fighting their own war. Rumford sees a lot of himself in Columbo, as both are intelligent, strong-minded men who serve their country to the best of their abilities. By doing nothing to impede Columbo, Rumford is perhaps consciously, perhaps unconsciously, refusing to stand in the way of a man doing his duty. Could there be a subconscious desire to be caught, as Rumford knows he's crossed a line and deserves to be relieved of command? It's possible, but as Rumford launches into a speech about how he wants the United States to have the world's best military and how his methods turn young men into model soldiers, it's arguable that Rumford is trying to make the case that his nation needs him, and that his mission requires him to step outside the moral and legal boundaries that constrain most of the citizenry. Perhaps he's trying to convince Columbo that Haynes was a necessary sacrifice for the greater good. Rumford wants the authorities to rule the death an accident and would be willing to accept a troublesome student being charged with negligent homicide, but the colonel holds himself to the same standards to which he holds his students. If he is caught breaking the rules, he must be punished. No excuses, no free passes.

For his part, Columbo sees much to respect in Rumford, even though he doesn't have much affection for the colonel's overly strict worldview. From Columbo's disheveled appearance, it's clear that he has no great admiration for military strictures on neatness and order. He does, however, understand that the colonel is not acting out of purely selfish motives, but is acting out of a personal conception of necessity. When Rumford upbraids his students, it's not out of sadistic cruelty, but because he believes this level of tough love is necessary to make them better men. If his heart isn't entirely in the right place, it's not wholly in the wrong place, either.

Rumford's focus on making sure every infraction, no matter how minor, is punished leads to his undoing. All he had to do was ignore the cider he saw, and he could have escaped the fallout. Perhaps he didn't realize that the only place he could have seen the cider was from the immediate vicinity of the cannon, but being an intelligent man, he should have known that it was unwise to publicize anything that might have drawn attention to his position at a certain time. It was his compulsion to make sure that every rule was followed that led to his undoing. Rumford believed that any looseness or overlooking of infractions could lead to a snowball effect that could lead to the total breakdown of discipline. Little slips lead to larger problems, and Rumford embodied the stereotypical military mindset– strict adherence to the rules at all time, all orders followed to the letter. This ideology made him a dedicated soldier, but it also led to self-incrimination.

Colonel Rumford is one of the more sympathetically drawn killers, albeit strictly in terms of his personal character, not his actions. However misguided he might have been in his crime, it can, at least, be argued that he was sincere in his convictions that the academy needed to remain at his standards for the greater good of the nation. Rumford wasn't just trying to protect his own comfortable job; he believed that he was trying to keep America strong, and the death of Haynes and placing one of his students in a rather loose frame for manslaughter were simply acceptable losses. He, therefore, stands as one of the least selfish killers in the series in terms of motive, though that does not make his actions any less misguided. In his closing words to Columbo, he declares, "Don't expect me to be contrite. I did what had to be done, and I'd do it tomorrow." There's no remorse, just a complete certainty that his style of education is needed for the good of the country, one man's life, and potentially a young student's freedom. It's notable that a dedicated soldier would surrender so easily, but Rumford had no desire to do battle with the truth. While most *Columbo* killers have a tenuous grasp of morality, if any, Rumford lived by a code, and he became that seemingly oxymoronic phenomenon: a highly principled killer.

Rumford's quiet acceptance of his fate may also be a calculated military decision. With Haynes gone and no longer pushing a coed policy, there is a fair chance that the academy may remain as it is. The colonel may have had to sacrifice himself, but in doing so, Rumford may have won his personal war in the long run.

Chapter Twenty-Nine: Troubled Waters

Hayden Danzinger (Robert Vaughn)

When Mrs. Columbo wins a cruise, the lieutenant thinks that he might be able to have a well-earned vacation. His relaxing plans are marred by murder, as Hayden Danzinger believes that he can rid himself of a troublesome girlfriend without consequences. Once Columbo gets involved, it's clear that Danzinger has completely missed the boat…

This is one of the rare cases where Columbo appears before the killer, as during the opening moments, the detective is running around the boat looking for his wife, described as having black hair in a bun. Columbo even meets Danzinger, a car dealer, before he kills.

Danzinger confronts his mistress, Rosanna Wells (Poupée Bocar), in her cabin. She's extorting money from him, threatening to tell his wife about their affair. Furious, the cad smacks her and plots murder. Using the key-cutter that's apparently standard issue for car dealers, he makes himself a master key and berates his wife for leaving his golfing gloves at home. A bit later, he inhales an amyl nitrate ampule by the pool, simulating a mild heart attack. He's taken to sick bay for overnight observation, and later that evening, when the nurse is distracted, he dons a ship employee's uniform, takes a pair of surgical gloves, and sprints out to confront Wells. He shoots her through a feather pillow, draws an "L" in lipstick on the mirror to incriminate her former paramour Lloyd Harrington (Dean Stockwell) (the clue is a riff on a comparable red herring in Agatha Christie's *Death on the Nile*), hides the weapon and gloves, and returns to sick bay in time for the nurse to examine him and comment on how fast his pulse is racing.

After the body's discovered, a crewmember recruits Columbo to investigate. Columbo's rather ill from seasickness, but it soon becomes clear that detective work has more health benefits for him than Dramamine. Columbo's suspicions are first stimulated by a little feather found near Danzinger in sick bay. Though the lieutenant's first attempt to question Danzinger is thwarted by the protective doctor, as soon as Danzinger is released, Columbo talks to him again. Danzinger has brought numerous guests to join him and his wife on the cruise, and he doesn't want their fun interrupted by investigation. Columbo skillfully recruits him as an assistant, ostensibly to protect his guests' good time, and Danzinger takes on the role of a dark Watson, pretending to help the detective solve the crime he committed.

In the grand tradition of killers attempting to influence Columbo by pushing untenable hypotheses, Danzinger insists that Harrington is the perpetrator. Furthermore, Danzinger insists that Columbo stay away from his guests. Columbo starts figuring out the steps of Danzinger's plan, tracing the route from the crime scene to sick bay, discovering that a pair of surgical gloves are missing from the medical supplies, and retrieving the amyl nitrate capsule from the swimming pool filter. Pretty soon, the captain, a firm believer in Harrington's guilt, gets frustrated with Columbo, though once the lieutenant starts laying out his evidence, the ship's authorities start warming towards Columbo's theories.

Attempting to trap Danzinger, Columbo informs him that there's not enough for a case against Harrington, but finding the missing gloves could potentially make the case. Desperate to frame his patsy, Harrington swipes some more gloves, takes another gun, fires it to get the necessary power burns, and hides the gloves in a fire hose. When the gloves are discovered after a planned fire drill, Danzinger believes that the case is complete, and it is, but not in the way he expects.

Columbo pulverizes a little pencil lead and dusts the *inside* of the gloves, revealing handprints. They don't match Harrington's prints, but Columbo's sure they will match Danzinger's. After the faintest of denials, Danzinger sags and concedes defeat. Columbo explains that he first suspected him when he found the feather in sick bay—it came from the muffled shooting, and it couldn't have come from sick bay because their pillows are filled with hypoallergenic foam. Danzinger is sent to the brig, and Columbo rejoins his wife for some time ashore.

In this episode, the relationship between detective and killer isn't genuinely warm. Columbo is consistently amiable, but it's his standard pose of civility to maintain his connection to his chief suspect. Columbo's use of one of his classic gambits, drawing the killer into the investigation to see how he responds and to extract some information without the murderer realizing it, is played with a bit of a twist here. Sometimes, a killer may enjoy the thrill of looking into a crime he committed himself, but Danzinger sees it as an unpleasant obligation, as he wants to find out where Columbo is in the investigation, but he'd really be happier going back to entertaining his guests.

Danzinger doesn't attack Columbo verbally the way other murderers do, but he does lose patience at times when the investigation isn't going the way he prefers. At times, it seems like he's barely able to stay civil towards Columbo, though he consistently speaks with a level of hauteur. There's no deep friendship or warm respect here, only the unease of a man who realizes he's being hunted by a man who is not easily fooled. For his part, Columbo maintains his affable exterior towards Danzinger up until the end, though his conversation with the ship's crew towards the end of his investigation indicates that he doesn't have any particular liking for the man. For that matter, neither is there any powerful animus against Danzinger. He's just another killer to be brought to justice. From the lieutenant's facial expressions, it's indicated that he can see through Danzinger's deceptions, and upon scrutiny, it's rather striking how difficult it is for Danzinger to mimic the behavior of an innocent man.

It's notable that Danzinger neglects to scrutinize his own psychological responses. He's supposed to be a man who just had a mild heart attack, but he's not worried. Most men might insist on being flown to a first-rate hospital at the first opportunity, or would be obsessing over mortality issues, or worrying about food choices and stress levels. Instead, Danzinger is acting as if absolutely nothing is wrong, as is indeed the case. It's actually a missed opportunity, as Danzinger could have used his nonexistent condition to slow down Columbo, grabbing his chest and asking for assistance if Columbo was getting too close to a clue. Instead, Danzinger treats his supposed heart attack as nothing more serious than a bout of indigestion– briefly unpleasant, but it passed quickly and now is no more than a fading memory.

In the end, when Danzinger concedes defeat with minimal struggle, it seems a bit anticlimactic, but it also is in character for a man who has accustomed himself to a soft life. Mrs. Danzinger holds the purse strings in the relationship and exercises a firm, if not dictatorial, level of power over her husband. While she seems to be aware that her spouse has a wandering eye, a vengeful lover confronting her might be too much for her to accept. It's clearly a marriage of convenience on Danzinger's part, and the loss of his wife's money is not an acceptable prospect to him. While he runs a successful car dealership, it's supported by Mrs. Danzinger's funds, and Danzinger's heart is clearly with playing a gregarious host and living the good life, rather than putting in long hours and straining to make his business increasingly profitable.

Danzinger's murder is the sort of crime committed by a man who can't see the weakness of his ideas. It was unwise to target an innocent man in order to frame him for the crime, especially when he couldn't create a situation assuring that his target had no alibi. His determination to force this theory of the case led to him planting the evidence that led to his own downfall. Surely, even someone with minimal knowledge of fingerprints would have realized that he would leave evidence of himself on the inside of the gloves. And that is the critical flaw of Danzinger's career as a killer. He simply doesn't think through all of the possibilities and consequences of his plans. Mightn't it have been wiser to throw the gun overboard and to take the attitude that an unsolved crime was a perfectly acceptable outcome?

Really, it might have been a cleverer move to find a way to throw the body overboard as well, to remove any definite evidence of a crime. From the shortcomings in the murder plan to the flaws in Danzinger's actions, he's clearly a man who doesn't think things through for the safest possible outcome.

In the final moments, when he readily concedes the presence of his fingerprints on the gloves, he tries to advance the theory that he deliberately planted the gloves in the fire hose. When Columbo asks the very sensible question as to why he would do such a thing, he has no answer. Danzinger threw out an explanation with no rationale behind it. That shows the weakness of Danzinger's mental processes. He was either too lazy or too careless to check his plans for mistakes. He developed a flawed plot, acted without taking basic steps to verify the plan, and then hoped for the best. Danzinger's unfocused approach to murder left him vulnerable to a scrupulous investigator, and as a result, Danzinger wound up being…lost at sea.

Chapter Thirty: Playback

Harold van Wick (Oskar Werner)

When a technological wizard manipulates his home security system, he thinks he's created the perfect alibi. Unfortunately for Harold van Wick, the video recording that he thought would vindicate him proved that he wasn't ready for his close-up.

Harold van Wick, like many killers before and after him, wanted everything. He wished to marry into wealth, but he also desired to have affairs with impunity. His imperious mother-in-law, Margaret Meadis (Martha Scott) despises him, and thinks he's an incompetent head of the family business, as revenue is not meeting expectations. She's hired a private detective who has obtained proof of his adultery and demands that he step down from running Midas Electronics. Van Wick doesn't accept this ultimatum, and he shoots his mother-in-law, afterwards reprogramming the video cameras to make it look like the murder took place while he was away at an art gallery. Meanwhile, van Wick's loving wheelchair-using wife Elizabeth (Gena Rowlands) is awakened by the murder, though she doesn't understand what's going on at the time.

Columbo arrives just shy of nineteen minutes into the episode, battling a cold, but not too sick to be amazed by the automated house. Simply clapping one's hands will cause doors to open. Van Wick explains how he thinks this must be a burglary gone horribly wrong and is pleasant and helpful to Columbo, who is confused by all of this technology. As Columbo views the surveillance video of the crime, Columbo observes that the killer must have had the incredibly dumb luck to stay just out of the range of the camera. As Columbo views the crime scene, he notices the absence of clues that would prove a burglar came from outside, points that van Wick explains away with varying degrees of convincingness.

When Columbo returns to the house, he performs an experiment by firing a gun into a sandbox, illustrating that the sound of the shot opened the door to Elizabeth's bedroom, causing light to stream into a corner, illuminating an unsettling toy clown. This test causes van Wick to fly into a rage, followed by sneers and gibes directed towards Columbo.

At the climax, Columbo checks the surveillance footage one more time and accuses van Wick of the murder. He knows that van Wick manipulated the video feeds and points out the proof—van Wick's invitation to the art gallery party is visible on a desk immediately after the shooting. Van Wick presented the invitation when he arrived at the party, so he must have stepped over the body to retrieve it. He must have committed the murder.

Van Wick is enraged and orders his wife to testify to his innocence. She refuses, and van Wick is led away, while a broken-hearted Elizabeth cries while Columbo stands uncomfortably, unsettled by the sight of her tears.

Like several other killers, van Wick can only manage about ten minutes of amiability and civility towards Columbo. Beyond that point, his temper frayed quickly. The slightest challenge to his official narrative causes him to roar with anger. Initially, van Wick attempts to establish himself as the intellectual superior in his relationship with Columbo, showing off his knowledge of technology and not-to-subtly advertising his own brilliance at creating the security system and little conveniences around the house.

Columbo advances his usual gambit of pointing out little inconsistencies and setting van Wick up to explain them. Why wasn't anything stolen? Van Wick suggests the burglar panicked. Why aren't there footprints where the supposed burglar went out the window? Van Wick postulates the killer eased himself out of the window. Why didn't the burglar track mulch and soil into the house? Van Wick hypothesizes the burglar removed his shoes. These are all plausible explanations, and van Wick takes pleasure in teaching the detective his own job. Columbo, lulling van Wick into a false sense of superiority, taps his head, says he was "stupid" and professes to be "embarrassed." It's all part of Columbo's classic game, and once Columbo starts pointing out flaws in van Wick's supposedly perfect murder, the killer's temper flares.

When Columbo illustrates how the gunshot opened Elizabeth's bedroom door, van Wick tries to prevent the demonstration by feigning concern over how all of this will affect his wife. Given his treatment of Elizabeth, it's clear that van Wick doesn't really care about the stress and strain his wife may suffer. Van Wick keeps trying to belittle Columbo's efforts, calling the gunshot test a "foolish experiment" and unconvincingly explains away the opening door as part of a "sensitive system" and the test is a "parlor trick" of no evidentiary value. He sneers, belittles, and dismissively suggests that Columbo take up residence in the guest room because he visits so much. At the end, he calls Columbo's final summation "insane." As he snaps and throws a fit at every opportunity, van Wick may think that he's using intimidation to get his way, but in reality, he often makes himself look petulant and ridiculous, though he is incapable of seeing just how deeply he debases himself through his tantrums and attacks on others. Van Wick clearly believes that shabby treatment will cause a homicide detective to slink away in shame, which shows just how little understanding of psychology he has, especially for a dedicated man like Columbo, who never lets his personal ego get in the way of an investigation.

Van Wick was a man who loved power and nursed his pride. The prospect of losing his position of authority in the company was abhorrent to him, even more so when it was possible that his wife would take over, and being subservient to his own spouse was, by his own admission, an unthinkable blow to his ego. There may well have been a level of misogyny in play, as van Wick found it particularly chafing to have a woman in a position of power over him, whether it was his mother-in-law attempting to crush him, or his adoring wife suggesting that she take an active role in her own family's company.

Insecurity was very likely a driving force in van Wick's character. He filled his home with evidence of his own cleverness, and he loved to point out his technological wizardry at every opportunity. He needed to assert his intellectual dominance at every opportunity, even when the other person was clearly in the right, and all he had were *ad hominem* attacks and shouting in order to cow his opponent. At the end, his informing the officer that handcuffs "won't be necessary" was an attempt to maintain both his dignity and a small degree of control over the situation. Van Wick's coldness towards his wife after she refuses to perjure herself to save him after he killed her mother proves his lack of affection towards Elizabeth, whereas her tears show just how devastated she is by the revelation of her husband's murderousness. Van Wick had a wife who adored him, and he could not appreciate her.

Narcissism, overcompensation, and a short temper were the defining characteristics of a man who thought of himself as always being the cleverest man in the room. Unfortunately for van Wick, Columbo walked into the room and proceeded to burst van Wick's inflated self-image.

Chapter Thirty-One: A Deadly State of Mind

Mark Collier (George Hamilton)

Mark Collier is a psychiatrist with very poor ethics. He pressures colleagues to provide him with the lab results he desires, regardless of the truth of the tests. He's sleeping with a patient. And when his shady dealings are exposed, he starts killing people.

The episode opens with Collier's patient, Nadia Donner (Lesley Ann Warren), on the couch, talking about her childhood while under a form of drug-enhanced hypnosis. They're having an affair, but when Collier arrives at her house later, her husband, Carl Donner (Stephen Elliott), is there, ready to humiliate them both. When Collier tries to take Nadia away, Carl strikes his wife, and Collier grabs a fireplace poker and fatally wounds Carl. This is arguably justified– he was protecting a woman from a physical attack from her husband, but as Collier notes, he can't prove it. Therefore, he comes up with a story saying that two robbers broke into the house and killed Carl and convinces Nadia to claim she witnessed the crime. As Collier rushes away from the scene of the crime, he nearly runs over a blind man walking by the house.

Columbo enters the picture about fifteen and a half minutes into the episode. He examines the crime scene, talks to Nadia, and discovers a little fragment on the floor, which he eventually discovers is a piece of a flint from a lighter. Columbo notices a bunch of holes in Nadia's "robbery" story, and when Collier arrives to look after his patient, the lieutenant observes that the doctor uses a match when smoking. Later, Columbo finds Nadia staying at an apartment and questions her in Collier's presence. Nadia is unsettled by Columbo pointing out the gaps in her story, such as why men with guns would use a poker to kill. Columbo's also interested in the lighter Collier uses, an object that the not-so-good doctor seems to prize. By the time Columbo leaves, Nadia's barely keeping it all together, and the far more composed doctor starts seeing her as a threat to his safety.

Soon afterwards, Columbo visits Collier at his workplace, and Collier makes it clear that he believes he has taken the lieutenant's measure, telling him, "You're a marvelously deceptive man. You know, the way you get to the point without really ever getting to the point." When Columbo keeps questioning him, Collier replies with a slightly chiding, "I really think you believe there's something cockeyed about Carl Donner's death." Columbo insists that Nadia's either withholding evidence or flat-out lying, going through all the problems with her story, points that Collier tries and fails to explain.

Concluding that Nadia is bound to crack sooner rather than later, Collier has one more session with her, heavily dosing her with drugs and planting a hypnotic message in her mind. That night, Collier holds a party at his house, and when Columbo comes by to ask more questions, the lieutenant becomes the most popular guest at the gathering. Columbo deduces that the flint from the lighter proves that a smoker was in the house, but the Donners are nonsmokers, and the alleged burglars wore stocking masks, meaning that some other person, a smoker, was there, as the freshly cleaned house proves the flint was recently dropped. While the other guests are inquiring about the investigation, Collier calls Nadia. Using a code word, the hypnotic suggestion is triggered, and Nadia, mesmerized into believing she's about to take an invigorating swim, takes off her clothes and dives off her balcony, believing she'll land in the pool. Unfortunately, she hits the ground and is killed.

Columbo confronts Collier at the marina and makes it clear that he believes that Collier is responsible for the deaths of both Donners. Collier is unruffled by the accusation, but when he is invited to the scene of the first crime soon afterwards, he's much more hostile. Columbo declares that though he can't prove Collier is responsible for Nadia's death, he has a witness placing Collier at the murder scene at the time of the killing of Carl Donner, and a man with tinted glasses cautiously walks into the room and carefully makes his way into a chair. Collier sneers at the attempt to incriminate him and laughingly declares that the supposed witness couldn't possibly have seen him because the so-called witness is blind. After confidently handing the witness a magazine, Collier is dumbstruck when the man can indeed read it. As it turns out, this isn't the real witness, but the sighted brother of the true blind man who was there that fateful night. The only way Collier could have thought the so-called witness was blind was if he'd been there and seen the man himself. Just as triumphant as Collier was a minute previously, Columbo says, "I have an eyewitness... the eyewitness is you."

Columbo and Collier fail to form a friendly connection over the course of the case. Throughout their scenes, Collier is polite to the lieutenant, but he's convinced that he's sufficiently crafty to pull the wool over the policeman's eyes. There's some gracious hosting at the party, but no genuine warmth on Collier's part towards Columbo. Collier is an urbane man, confident in his own mental superiority. He never feels threatened by Columbo until the final minute of the episode. He feels no need to make threats against the lieutenant's job, but though he doesn't attack or denigrate Columbo, he seems to draw pleasure from informing the detective that he can see through him.

Columbo follows his standard pattern of being polite and deferential until the end unless the killer does something so despicable as to make the lieutenant confront him angrily. Columbo may have believed that Nadia was complicit in her husband's death, but he considers her death a particularly cruel act, and his accusation in the penultimate scene is the embodiment of his rage towards a heartless killer. Even though Nadia was an accessory to her husband's death, it was arguably self-defense or justifiable homicide, and due to the amount of control that Collier exercised over her with drugs, hypnosis, and his position as her doctor, she cannot be viewed as an equal accomplice, nor can she be definitively said to have acted out of her own free will. Indeed, given Collier's influence over her, she probably should not be viewed as a willing adulteress, but as the victim of sexual exploitation by a manipulative predator. A strong case can be made that Nadia was more puppet than partner in the crime. In contrast, Collier is amiably superior towards Columbo until the final scene, when he finally snaps and becomes gruff and sneering. It's not clear if the breaking point is caused by anxiety over the strain or if there's another explanation, but in the final scene, something's happened to make the cultured mask fall off his face.

Collier is in many ways a spiritual sibling of Harold van Wick from the previous episode "Playback." His entire persona is based upon the presumption of his own intellectual superiority. Yet there are differences between Collier and van Wick. Van Wick, for all of his ego and bluster, was surprisingly fragile. The slightest provocation could send him into a frenzy. In contrast, Collier has a stronger hold over his emotions, yet he is also obsessed with his reputation and loves to flaunt his cleverness, often to his own detriment.

It's notable that Collier's testiness fades away the moment he thinks he's seen through Columbo's trap. Why is this? Arguably, it's because he feels like he's in control again. He believes that his superior acumen has thwarted a clumsy attempt by a bumbling detective to incriminate him, and he delights in the chance to show up the lieutenant. Had Collier simply sat quietly and demanded a lawyer, there would not have been enough to arrest him. But Collier had to boast that he was just too smart for Columbo, and the result only served to prove which one of them was truly the cannier person.

Collier is indeed a sleazy individual, ignoring basic rules of ethics, demanding that tests be faked to fit his preferences, and using drugs as dangerous shortcuts in therapy, not to mention sleeping with a married patient. Right before the killing, one might think that he has genuine feelings for Nadia by the way he says he's taking her away from her husband's home, but a couple of days later, he sees the sacrifice of her life as a necessary step to assure his own safety. There's no genuine guilt for his crime. Nadia really meant nothing serious to him. His seeming protectiveness towards Nadia may actually have been protectiveness for his own reputation. He may have enjoyed their relationship, but given the choice between Nadia and his own career and safety, Collier put his own interests first every time.

Narcissism drives Collier's character. He's supremely confident in his own intellectual superiority, and paltry things like medical ethics are not allowed to stand in the way of his desires. He enjoys playing the respected mental health professional, and he takes pleasure in the role of the charming host at the party, but it's all superficial. The results of medical experiments must be altered to suit his goals; dangerous drugs are an acceptable substitute for more complex psychotherapy, and threatening his comfortable life is a capital offense in his estimation. The title of the episode, "A Deadly State of Mind," has many potential meanings, but one of the most thought-provoking is the interpretation that it is Collier's state of mind that is deadly. Collier's mental makeup saw his own reputation and desires as the most important things in the world, and his attitude towards everybody, especially Columbo, screamed, *I'm better than you!* Columbo's investigation was a blunt reply stating, "No, you're not."

V

SEASON FIVE

Chapter Thirty-Two: Forgotten Lady

Grace Wheeler Willis (Janet Leigh)

I n the *Columbo* universe, some professions produce more killers than others. Psychiatrists frequently violate their oath to do no harm, and Grace Wheeler Willis is the third actress on the series to take a life, or technically the fourth, counting the accomplice Joan Hudson from "Prescription: Murder." Wheeler Willis was once part of the celebrated dance duo "Diamond and Wheeler," opposite her longtime partner Ned Diamond (John Payne). Unfortunately, careers in show business have a habit of fading long before the performers in question are ready to leave the spotlight, and Wheeler Willis is now living in the happy memories of her once-glorious triumphs and dreaming of a comeback.

Wheeler Willis has re-partnered with Diamond and plans a brilliant return to Broadway later that year, but her husband, Dr. Henry Willis (Sam Jaffe), puts the kibosh on that hope. He declares that acting again would be "preposterous" and declares her ambitions to be the result of her living in a "fantasy world." Wheeler Willis was counting on her husband to invest half a million dollars into the new musical, but Dr. Willis refused. Not willing to let her dreams of stardom die, Wheeler Willis decides to fund her desires with her inheritance. She drugs her husband, and after her servants set up one of her old movies for her to watch, she slips out of the viewing room, uses her dancing acrobatic skills to climb up the side of the house into her husband's bedroom, shoots him, and makes it look like suicide. When she returned to the viewing room, the film projector jammed, so she had to cut and repair the damaged reel.

Twenty-three and a half minutes into the episode, Columbo arrives to investigate the supposed suicide, so tired he forgot his jacket and badge and unable to figure out how to work a borrowed pen. He's still sharp enough to figure out when something's not right at the crime scene, wondering why a man planning to shoot himself would take a sleeping pill first, and notes how a cadaveric spasm has affected the position of the deceased's fingers.

Columbo doesn't meet Wheeler Willis until forty-four minutes into the episode, the latest ever in an episode, but when he does see her, he's star-struck, much like he was in "Requiem for a Falling Star." He explains some of the issues contradicting the suicide theory, including the fact that the gun was kept in the car, and the deceased would have had to go downstairs in his robe and slippers to retrieve it, yet there was no grass or dirt soiling the bottoms of his shoes. Wheeler Willis is lucid enough to note that no one could have climbed the tree beside the house due to the branches being cut, but her mind is clearly unfocused, and she comments on her own forgetfulness. She's not even clear on what day it is. Still, she's friendly and gracious to Columbo, inviting him to watch one of her movies at her home sometime.

Later, Columbo returns to the house while she's hosting a party and tries and fails to climb the tree. Wheeler Willis is quite amused by his antics, saying "I don't think you're being completely candid to me about your frequent visits" and "You simply enjoy being around the magic of show business."

Soon afterwards, Columbo attends an evening screening party at Wheeler Willis's house, wearing a tuxedo. Diamond is also there. Columbo explains to Diamond that Wheeler Willis killed her husband and that based on the testimony of the servants, the movie she was watching the night of the crime took over ten minutes longer than normal to run. Columbo deliberately breaks the currently running reel, and Wheeler Willis proves that she knows how to fix it. Columbo reveals to Diamond that Wheeler

Willis is suffering from a terminal brain aneurysm and has at most a few months to live. She has serious gaps in her memory and, in all likelihood, has forgotten she's even committed the crime.

Diamond, who's been in love with his longtime co-star for years, falsely confesses to the murder in order to allow her to spend her final days in the comfort of her own home. Columbo notes that he'll be able to prove Diamond's innocence without much trouble, but Diamond suggests that by the time he's exonerated, Wheeler Willis will have passed away peacefully. Columbo accepts this ruse, knowing that Diamond will never be convicted, possibly never even jailed, and they leave while Wheeler Willis sits on the couch watching herself on film, oblivious to everything but her own glorious memories of stardom.

Wheeler Willis is an anomaly—a killer who doesn't realize she's a killer! Most *Columbo* episodes are a game of wits, with Columbo steadily uncovering the truth, questioning and challenging the suspect until there's enough evidence to make an arrest. But, due to her brain damage from her condition, Wheeler Willis doesn't remember what she's done, so she genuinely believes that her husband committed suicide. Columbo's traditional psychological pressures don't work because she doesn't have the guilt or anxiety or even the wariness of most killers. There is no better defense against an interrogation than a genuine belief in one's own innocence.

Rather than seeing Columbo as a threat or a nuisance, Wheeler Willis treats the lieutenant as a dedicated, possibly a little overzealous man with an understandable attraction to the glamour of Hollywood. It's genuine friendliness, tainted only by the slight self-superiority that Hollywood legends may hold towards "ordinary" people outside the business. Her forgetting the name "Columbo" might have been taken as a mild insult by some people, though Columbo was clever enough not to take it personally and to see it as a sign of the damage she's suffering. For his part, Columbo's genuinely impressed by these legendary celebrities, though insufficiently dazzled to stop his investigation. It's possible that his affection towards her work influences his decision to let her pass her few remaining days obliviousness of her crime.

But is this act of kindness warranted? She did commit a violent act against her husband, and the care with which she crafted her alibi shows just how capable and sharp she was. However, the psychological effects of committing such a crime may have caused a slight mental break, wiping her memory and perhaps accelerating her decline. She did not kill in a fit of madness, and in her mental state at the time of the murder, she still had the ability to tell right from wrong, and her memory lapses don't affect her ability to meet the legal standard for sanity. Whether or not she's sufficiently capable of contributing to her own legal defense, given her mental lapses and the possibility that the impairment will only get worse with time, would be a matter for the courts to decide.

Is Wheeler Willis responsible for her actions or not? The answer is arguably "yes," at least morally. She shot her husband for selfish motives—the revitalization of her career. One might argue that Dr. Willis was at fault for not explaining his wife's condition to her, but it's theoretically very possible that he did, multiple times, and it simply never stayed in her memory very long, especially since she was in denial about her condition. Eventually, he might have grown tired of telling her repeatedly. There is a qualification for this statement of culpability. It's possible that her brain aneurysm may have caused some additional mental defect that may have disposed her towards violent acts, affected her conscience, and drained her impulse control. Everything is conjectural, but all possibilities bear consideration. Not only that, but under the law, a person may not be able to be tried for a crime if that individual is sufficiently mentally impaired so that full participation in one's own defense is impossible. Wheeler Willis's health probably fits this condition.

The relationship between Columbo and Wheeler Willis is unique. Columbo has compassion for a seriously ill woman, and he realizes that her condition may require special consideration. Really, there's no true need for him to allow Diamond to be arrested at all—he can simply let events unfold and allow the truth to come out at some point after her death. Perhaps even Columbo balks a little at tarnishing the legend of a performer he loves. Grace Wheeler Willis has the rare distinction of being a *Columbo* killer who got away with her crime.

But not for very long.

Chapter Thirty-Three: A Case of Immunity

Hassan Salah (Hector Elizondo) and Rachman Habib (Sal Mineo)

International intrigue and diplomacy make for an unusually tricky investigative situation for Columbo. The narrative opens at the embassy of the fictional Middle Eastern country of Suaria. Hassan Salah is a leading diplomat, but in the opening scene, Salah and his young associate Rachman Habib are trashing an office, scattering papers, and spraying graffiti. Once they're ready, Salah calls in the head of security, Youseff Alafa (André Lawrence), into the room, and when Alafa's distracted, Salah bludgeons him to death. Habib later makes a phone call to create the impression that Alaha is still alive, giving Salah an alibi, and Habib recklessly drives away from the embassy.

Meanwhile, viewers get the impression that Columbo doesn't get nearly as much respect as he deserves, as one of his superiors is gruff and dismissive towards him. When the lieutenant appears eight minutes into the episode, he's been recruited to work with the Suari embassy by mistake, taking a position meant for Captain Colimo. All crimes at the embassy are investigated under the authority of the Suari government, but the Suaris need the LAPD's help, and when Columbo examines the crime scene, clues like the positioning of dust from the blown-open safe and the fact that

Alaha didn't draw his weapon makes Columbo think that this is an inside job. Coupled with the fact that a guard's rifle malfunctioned, saving Habib from being shot, Columbo believes the culprit is among the embassy staff.

Salah isn't thrilled by Columbo poking holes in the narrative he's tried to create, but he's polite and gracious to Columbo as the two work together. Soon, Columbo sees the missing Habib as a person of interest. When Salah meets Habib later, Salah knocks out his associate and places the man into a car, arranging for it to zoom down a slope and crash. The next day, after Columbo examines the crash site, he realizes that it's not a simple accident. The dead man was wearing contacts underneath the glasses Salah replaced on his face. The stolen papers contain information that could lead to the overthrow of the young, progressive king. Salah wants Columbo to think Habib was part of a revolutionary student group, but false narratives never fool the lieutenant.

Columbo attends a couple of fancy embassy parties and eventually meets and charms the king (Barry Robins). Once Salah realizes Columbo suspects him, he files a complaint with the State Department, and even though Columbo believes Salah's a killer, the powers that be don't care. They want Columbo to apologize and never go near Salah again.

Even though his career is on the line, Columbo refuses to follow these orders, and Salah, acting enraged over Columbo's accusations, declares him persona non grata. The lieutenant performs a little quick diplomacy of his own, and Salah agrees to have one last conversation with Columbo once Columbo admits Salah's untouchable. Basking in his diplomatic immunity, Salah admits that he thinks the Western-minded king will destroy Suaria, so he's plotting to overthrow him. Salah admits to the murders as well, believing Columbo can't arrest him.

After the confession, the king emerges, having overheard everything in a trap set up by Columbo. Salah now faces Suarian justice, which has a reputation for brutality. Desperate to save his life at the cost of his freedom, Salah signs away his diplomatic immunity and confesses, willing to spend his life in a comparatively humane American jail.

This episode is one of the few to provide a deeper glimpse into Columbo's character. Despite his skills as a detective (or perhaps, because along the way, he happened to arrest some prominent individual his superiors liked, such as in "A Friend in Deed"), at least one of his superiors views him with contempt. More telling about Columbo himself is just how far he's willing to go to get justice. His superiors and the State Department don't really care about the crime, and they just want the case swept under the rug. Columbo's pursuit of Salah has every opportunity to destroy his career, and he's gambling his entire future on capturing a single killer. Indeed, even if he's successful, the backlash could be devastating for him. It's only because Columbo has earned the respect and gratitude of the king, leading to much better American and Suarian relations, that Columbo can expect to continue his career without any repercussions.

Why would Columbo risk everything to bring down Salah? He doesn't have any connection to the victims. Salah hasn't done anything to threaten him or give him any real reason to dislike him on a personal level, though attempting to spark an uprising to overthrow a monarch is certainly one of the most high-stakes goals of any *Columbo* murderer. Certainly, if there was a revolution, hundreds, perhaps thousands of innocent people could be killed. Arguably, this is one of, if not *the* most impactful cases of Columbo's career, and Salah's determination to shape his nation in his preferred image, regardless of the effects on other people, sets him apart from the killers who simply want to inherit a lot of money or swap romantic partners.

It takes a while for Columbo to realize the full extent of Salah's plan, but initially, the two get along well. Salah treats Columbo with respect, appreciating how the lieutenant picked up on the little contradictions in his story. Salah complements Columbo with comments like "Excellent observation," maintaining a poker face. Despite the initial friendliness, Salah's dismissive comments regarding Columbo to the king indicate that he holds a certain level of contempt towards the lieutenant, carefully hidden behind long training as a diplomat. Salah calls the lieutenant "a simple man," indicating that he thinks him unsophisticated.

Salah does realize the danger that Columbo holds for him and uses his power and influence to block the investigation. That should have been the end of the matter, but instead, despite being under no obligation to do so, Salah chooses to meet with Columbo in order to gloat. He didn't have to confess—admitting his culpability was the height of foolishness, but Salah believed that he was safe and reveled in his own cleverness over committing a crime that could not be prosecuted. Salah smugly asserts, "You never did have much of a case," and asks Columbo simply to take pride in the fact that he has "unraveled the puzzle" and tells him to "let it be." All Salah had to do was keep his mouth shut, but he wanted the opportunity to rub his victory in his opponent's face. Salah didn't even bother to take the elementary precaution of checking Columbo and the room for recording devices, let alone listeners in the next room. He was so confident in his own position that he neglected to consider the possibility that he could make himself vulnerable. It was more important to him to boast than preserve his safety.

Ironically, Salah feared the influence of Westernization on Suaria, but when faced with the consequences of his actions, he found American prisons far more humane than those of his own country. Had Salah refused to confess, his political cause might have been advanced, but at the risk of his own life. He knew that his treatment in Suaria would not be "justice... [but] barbarism." This is one of only two cases (the other being "Strange Bedfellows") where Columbo uses an implied threat of physical violence to provoke a confession (the supposed bomb in "Short Fuse" was a harmless and unspoken trap that was only unnerving to someone with guilty knowledge). Here, Salah, by his own loose tongue, has set himself up for punishment under Suarian law, and it's obvious he fears torture, imprisonment under harsh conditions, and a painful death. The offer of American justice is, in some ways, an offer of mercy, but Salah would not have faced the prospect of a brutal Suarian punishment had Columbo not stage-managed the situation to put him in danger. This is a moral gray zone for the lieutenant, though once again, the prospect of violent revolution ought to serve as a counter-point in any ethical reckoning.

Salah was initially immune to legal prosecution, but he was not immune to the downfall resulting from his own pride.

Chapter Thirty-Four: Identity Crisis

Nelson Brenner (Patrick McGoohan)

Patrick McGoohan's second of four *Columbo* killer roles is a tale of espionage, disguise, and intimidation. As the episode opens, a pair of secret agents meet at an amusement park due to the reasoning that a public place is somehow more secure, even though a park employee snaps a picture of them. Nelson Brenner and A.J. Henderson (Leslie Nielsen) are longtime CIA men, and Henderson accuses Brenner of being a double agent and wants his share of a profitable past endeavor. Brenner is amenable and recruits Henderson for his services regarding an upcoming project connected to a mysterious figure named Steinmetz. Brenner asks Henderson to wait under a pier that night for further instructions, but instead of embarking on a new mission, Henderson meets his death when Brenner bludgeons him and tries to make it look like a mugging gone wrong.

Columbo enters thirteen minutes into the episode and quickly doubts the mugging theory. A little digging leads him to a photograph of the pair, and some questioning brings him to Brenner, who has written a speech for a local businessman as part of his "official" business and is now watching it being delivered. Faced with the photograph, Brenner is forced to admit to knowing Henderson and claims that he wanted to hire him for a job at his company. Columbo later interviews Brenner at his lavish home and learns that Brenner's alibi at the time of the crime is that he was dictating a speech for a commodity brokers luncheon. Brenner set his clock to chime a false time in order to create this alibi on the tape.

A man named Lawrence Melville (Otis Young) becomes a suspect after being seen following Henderson out of a restaurant. Planning to frame him, Brenner sets up a meeting, wearing a convincing disguise. As it turns out, Brenner and Steinmetz are the same person. Steinmetz asks Melville to drive a car away for him, but before Melville can get very far, Steinmetz detonates a small bomb. Melville survives, but due to Henderson's possessions being planted in the car, Melville's now in the crosshairs for the crime.

Columbo's willing to believe in Melville's innocence and gets the injured man to provide him with a description of Steinmetz. During a run-in with some cloak-and-dagger types, the lieutenant learns that Brenner is a valuable covert operator. When Columbo next sees Brenner, he tells him point blank he thinks he's involved in the crime, leading to a polite threat from Brenner. Later, though, Brenner's much more amiable, offering Columbo money to pay for gas and a drink at his house.

At his mansion, Brenner demonstrates that he's had Columbo's house bugged and provides further evidence of his power, trying to both charm and frighten the lieutenant. But Columbo isn't fazed, and he's convinced that Brenner is a dishonest spy who uses his position to enrich himself.

In the final confrontation, Columbo reveals through an altered photograph of Brenner that he believes that Steinmetz is simply Brenner with his toupee removed and glasses and a fake beard on his face. Brenner repeats his alibi, but Columbo points out that the lecture couldn't have been recorded at night, only in the morning. He observes the sound of the blinds being drawn, indicating that it was bright outside, but Brenner deflects this with a claim that this was a privacy issue. Less explainable is the fact that Brenner slipped a mention of the Chinese boycotting the Olympics into the speech, but that information wasn't made public until the A.M. hours. Additionally, Henderson's jacket was removed, indicating that a fellow agent, searching for a gun, went over the body. With Brenner's alibi is shattered, the crooked spy admits that the presence of witnesses prevented him from properly setting up the crime scene. There's no trace of remorse, but there's still a bit of amusement in his voice.

The relationship between Columbo and Brenner is driven by a series of power plays, and for the vast majority of "Identity Crisis," Brenner is in the position of dominance. He has wealth and influence and even has the backing of the CIA. It's not until the final seconds of the episode that Columbo manages to flip the situation around to his advantage. Even before Brenner learns that Columbo is a police detective, he tries to dismiss Columbo, coldly hissing that Columbo has the wrong room when he walks into the lecture. Columbo's presentation of his credentials swiftly provides him with some respect, but this evaporates the moment that he indicates that Brenner is a suspect.

When Columbo comes to question Brenner at a Sunday pool party at his mansion, he explains his presence with a standard "I was in the neighborhood" before observing in the very next sentence just how isolated the area is. These contradictory comments may be deliberate, or they may be an inadvertent revelation of the truth, but the fact remains that an alert man like Brenner will realize at once that this is a pretext, and if Columbo made a special trip out here, his suspicions must be directed squarely towards Brenner. Brenner swiftly turns to threats, saying, "I have powerful and important friends," and he must "respectfully request that you do not harass me," describing the investigation as a "ridiculous predicament with you." Brenner hisses, "Don't harass me," again later on when Columbo makes it clear he thinks he was involved in the crime.

After the CIA agents explain the situation, Brenner feels sufficiently confident in his position that he can deign to be nicer to Columbo, though his graciousness is consistently tainted by his constant assertions of dominance. When Columbo needs money to pay for refilling his gas tank, Brenner arrives and offers him ten dollars, a show of both his current amicable mood and his wealth. The invitation to his mansion for a cocktail comes with the slightly ominous compliment, "You rather fascinate me."

It's not just a social occasion. Brenner's invitation is very much a power play. His mansion, servant, and home furnishings all indicate his considerable wealth. Columbo's observes the gambling games on display, indicating that Brenner's the sort of man who enjoys taking risks for potential profit. Brenner illustrates the sort of power he holds by playing some of Mrs. Columbo's favorite opera (a nice bit of continuity to "Étude in Black," where we learn she loves classical music), and Columbo deduces without indignation that Brenner has bugged his house. Brenner admits this with plenty of glee, but he explains he's had the bugs removed. He just wanted to show what he *could* do, with the unspoken implication that the situation could get much, much worse. There's a bit of snobbery as well when Columbo sees some awards on the wall, and Brenner patronizingly tells him that they're written in Latin and he wouldn't understand them. But why would Brenner be so sure about this? Columbo's Italian—he could have gone to Catholic school or had a similar religious education. It's quite possible that he learned some Latin along the way. This little quip seems to reflect that Brenner can't miss the opportunity to show his perceived intellectual superiority, though, in the final scene, Columbo's understated triumph indicates that he loves to show off his own cleverness as well.

Columbo has effectively shattered Brenner's alibi, but has he really captured Brenner? Brenner seems supremely unworried by the closing net around him. It's probably that he thinks that his perceived value to the CIA will mean that they'll pull the necessary strings to get him to get him out of trouble. Will this optimistic plan work? It's certainly possible, though any evidence of Brenner's duplicity might make the double agent effectively *persona non grata*, and the publicity of the arrest may also taint any potential value he might have as a spy. The ending leaves Brenner's fate open to debate, but the final note shows that Columbo has triumphed in their duel. Columbo refused to be intimidated by a powerful opponent, and that doggedness certainly earned a substantial measure of respect from Brenner.

The viewer knows very little about what made Brenner the man he is. How did he enter the world of the CIA? When did he realize he could enrich himself from unscrupulous behavior? Was there a political motive for his subversion of the CIA, or was it just greed? How did he come up with the persona of Steinmetz? There are no answers to these questions. Viewers don't know if he was a good spy who went bad, or if he was always crooked. Whatever his character arc, it is known that he is willing to kill and maim in order to keep his secrets hidden and probably maintain the cash flow that keeps him in luxury as well. But is there some other motive besides money that drives his perfidy?

The title "Identity Crisis" is more than just the fact that Brenner has created the parallel persona of Steinmetz. It reflects how Brenner's character is, in some ways, more of a cipher than most *Columbo* murderers. There are plenty of gaps in the information available, preventing viewers from gaining a full picture of how Brenner went from a duplicitous CIA agent to a cold-blooded killer. What is known is how Brenner loved both the thrill of gambling for high stakes and the rush of demonstrating his power and influence. The picture of Brenner's background may be incomplete, but his vices and ruthlessness are made clear through his actions.

Brenner was a man who loved to show just how clever he was, and ironically, by showing off his knowledge of current events, he wound up incriminating himself through an unnecessary rhetorical flourish.

Chapter Thirty-Five: A Matter of Honor

Luis Montoya (Ricardo Montalban)

Columbo can't even take a vacation without getting caught up in a murder. A visit to Mexico soon becomes a homicide investigation with an unusual motive. Luis Montoya is renowned for his triumphs as a bullfighter, though it's been a long time since he was in the ring due to a leg injury. Curro Rangel (A Martinez), a young man working with Montoya's bulls, has been seriously injured by the animals. Hector Rangel (Robert Carricart), Curro's father, is a longtime employee of Montoya's who is about to leave his job. Before he leaves, however, Hector agrees to help Montoya put down a particularly violent bull. While in the arena, Montoya fires a tranquilizer dart into Hector, sets the bull loose, and allows Hector to be attacked by the aggressive bovine.

Nine and a half minutes in, Columbo appears. He's visiting Mexico and accidentally rear-ends another car. The situation spirals out of control quickly, especially given Columbo's limited fluency in Spanish. Thankfully, police officer Commandante Sanchez (Pedro Armendáriz, Jr.) comes to Columbo's rescue. The Commandante has followed Columbo's career with great interest, mentioning the "Troubled Waters" case specifically, and now he wants a chance to get to know the legendary detective over the course of the few days it will take to handle the bureaucratic nightmare caused by Columbo's car accident.

Sanchez asks for Columbo's help investigating Hector's death, and

Columbo agrees. Montoya pushes the theory that Hector foolishly sought to kill the bull for what it did to his son and explains how he rescued Curro before the bull could fatally wound the youth. After examining the crime scene, Columbo is suspicious, and as an American, he's the only one who can even look at Montoya cross-eyed. Montoya is a local legend and a bullfighter acclaimed as the bravest of the brave. He's highly respected as a pillar of strength and toughness, and Sanchez isn't comfortable treating him as a suspect. Though he has no official status, Columbo starts his usual routine of hanging around Montoya and asking questions. It starts out cordially enough, but as Columbo uncovers more inconsistencies, Montoya eventually snaps and bans him from his property.

Not deterred, Columbo sets up a trap and lures Montoya to the arena. When a bull is released, Montoya freezes, and other men have to stabilize the bull. Montoya was once a fearless matador, but at some point, he lost his nerve, and now the sight of a charging bull paralyzes him. Hector saved his son, not Montoya. The exceedingly vain retired matador couldn't bear for anybody to know he was no longer the dashing figure of bravery he once was, and to protect his reputation, he killed his friend. Now, everybody knows about Montoya's shame, and he quietly allows himself to be arrested.

The title of the episode is "A Matter of Honor," though "A Matter of Pride" or "A Matter of Ego" might be equally descriptive titles. For Montoya, preserving his public image of a man who is strong to the point of invulnerability is essential, even if it no longer accurately reflects the truth of his mental state. From a contemporary American viewpoint, there is no shame in suffering from a condition such as post-traumatic stress disorder, which could very likely have been the cause of Montoya's mental condition. His being injured by a bull left a wound that went far beyond physical pain and scarred his psyche as well.

But, as several characters mention throughout the episode, there are cultural factors at work here. A man of Montoya's background has to live up to the ideals of machismo. Bullfighting is called "a way of life." Showing weakness or cowardice is unacceptable. Essentially, Montoya had to maintain the image of the fearless matador with nerves of steel, because losing face would be more than just a temporary embarrassment. It would mean the permanent annihilation of his reputation, the destruction of his personal legend, and the desecration of his memory. A moment of cowardice would overshadow a career filled with heroism.

Montoya put his personal legend not just above the truth, but over another human being's life. Hector was a longtime employee and friend, and when Hector's son Curro was attacked by the bull, Montoya was unable to help him. There is no indication that Hector intended to tell anybody the truth. Hector wasn't going to blackmail him or sue him. There was simply no reason for Montoya to kill him…aside from the fact that Hector knew Montoya's secret, and Montoya couldn't bear for anybody to be aware of that. Perhaps there was a bit of displacement here—Montoya couldn't face bulls anymore, but he could manage deadly force against a human opponent who didn't threaten him physically.

Lethal violence isn't an option for Montoya as he deals with his other human opponent, Columbo. At first, Montoya is warm towards the lieutenant, explaining the differences in their cultures and accepting his questions, saying, "So inquisitive… I find him amusing." Columbo takes Montoya's measure early on, noting he's quite vain and obsessed with maintaining his public image. Columbo's poking around his estate initially makes Montoya suspicious, but after Columbo politely listens to Montoya expound upon his past glories, the retired matador tells the detective, "You're welcome here any time." When Columbo brings up the evidence that the dead man was tranquilized and points out something unusual with the account books, Montoya's pleasantness evaporates, saying, "I don't appreciate this little war of nerves you are conducting," and raves in Spanish, attacks Columbo for his ignorance of bullfighting, and insists that the death was an accident. As Columbo points out more glaring errors in Montoya's preferred story, Montoya snaps, saying, "My courtesy has been rewarded with accusation…I must ask you to leave my house and not return."

Montoya is all smiles and graciousness until Columbo tries to look behind his polished veneer. For Montoya, there is only one acceptable way for other people to regard him: with admiring deference. Montoya's self-worth comes from more than being an alpha male—he has to be seen as a god among men. Being seen as a "god that bleeds" is unthinkable. By this point, Montoya's identity is inextricably intertwined with his past triumphs. It's not enough that he can't see himself as he really is. He demands that others view him in the way that he wants them to: with awe. The bravado masking insecurity is tragic, even pathetic.

Montoya can't form a real relationship with Columbo in part because the ex-matador's not really a genuine person himself. He's a fictionalized superhero, who flies above hoi polloi and only deigns to brighten their lives with his brilliance. How could a humble little policeman be a threat to the great and glorious Luis Montoya? It was actually easy to track the crime to him, as Montoya made a great many errors and overlooked plenty of details, thinking that the Mexican police would never dare to question him. At the end, when Montoya has been unmasked, he gives the tools of the matador's trade to Columbo, a sign of surrender and a tribute to the lieutenant's detecting skills. This is his first and only show of humility, and it's a sincere one. Montoya believed in his own legend, thinking that his career as a bullfighter was the cornerstone of his identity, and couldn't imagine living without the world worshiping his famous courage.

But it was all a load of bull.

Chapter Thirty-Six: Now You See Him

Stefan Mueller aka "The Great Santini" (Jack Cassidy)

Legendary *Columbo* killer Jack Cassidy makes his third and final appearance in "Now You See Him," and the results are magical. "The Great Santini" is a stage magician currently working at a club, but he earned $100,000 on a recent tour. Now, Jesse Jerome (Nehemiah Persoff), the club's owner, wants half of that in order to buy his silence. Santini's real name is Stefan Mueller, and during WWII he was an SS Officer. But blackmailing is tantamount to suicide on *Columbo*, and Santini has a deadly plan.

During his nightly performance, Santini performs his showstopper trick of stepping into a small box, which is then lifted up and immersed in water. The trick works because Santini slips out of a panel at the bottom of the box before it's placed in the water. While the audience thinks that Santini's onstage, he's actually dressing up as a waiter and making his way to Jerome's office. Using a microphone, he creates the impression that he's still in his dressing room by supposedly talking through the closed door when a waiter leaves him a glass of brandy. Santini picks the lock on Jerome's door and shoots him, taking the letter Jerome was in the middle of typing, accusing Santini/Mueller of war crimes.

Twenty-three minutes and forty-five seconds into the episode, Columbo enters, looking rather different with a haircut and a new coat—a gift from his wife that he doesn't like, but he can't admit his antipathy towards the garment. Bob Dishy returns as Sgt. Wilson (his first name is John J. here, but it was Frederic in his earlier appearance in "The Greenhouse Jungle."). Wilson notes that Santini has an alibi, but Columbo's suspicions bring him straight to the illusionist, who's being quite coy about his location at the time of the crime, all under the pretense of a magician never revealing his secrets.

Columbo keeps pursuing Santini, even joining his act as a guest assistant and compelling him to prove his lockpicking skills by giving him a pair of police handcuffs and watching him escape. Meanwhile, Columbo figures out how Santini set up his alibi and performed a trick where he supposedly knew what number his waiter was thinking of when he dropped off the brandy glass. Santini laughs off Columbo's suspicions, telling the lieutenant that he won't use his magical powers to disappear.

Columbo's ease with the investigation improves the moment he switches back to his trademark coat. Despite struggling to keep up with Columbo, it's Sgt. Wilson who helps Columbo crack the case by observing that Jerome's typewriter had a special tape on it that kept track of every key typed. The typewriter kept a record of Jerome's incriminating letter, and Columbo produces the proof with a little of his own sleight of hand. Santini burns a copy of the letter with a magical flourish, but Columbo and the other policemen have plenty more. Santini admits his guilt, mourning, "And I thought I'd performed the perfect murder." Columbo informs him there's no such thing as a flawless crime…such a concept is "just an illusion."

A magician's relationship with the audience has to be one where the performer deceives the viewers, and they are aware that they're being fooled. Part of the enjoyment comes from trying to figure out how something inexplicable was done, and if a magician's secrets are revealed, that destroys the mystique, and the performance loses all of its charm and excitement. It's this principle that drives Santini's connection to Columbo. Santini uses card tricks in an attempt to impress Columbo and uses a fairly sound psychological tactic of making Columbo work to find out the details behind his alibi. Simply showing Columbo how the trick onstage was done would have been too obvious. Making Columbo have to struggle and investigate makes the alibi seem more solid, as it wasn't simply dropped in his lap. Given the reluctance with which Santini parted with the information behind his alibi, saying that he'd rather confess to a murder than make his secrets public, makes it sound like he's unconcerned about being arrested. This is magician's misdirection, attempting to use clever psychology to provoke a false conclusion: if a man isn't worried about a police investigation, he must be innocent.

The successful magician must always maintain a level of superiority towards his audience. The magician has to be cleverer than the audience so they don't figure out the trick, and the magician's hands have to be swifter than the audience's eyes. Normally, the audience doesn't get to engage or challenge the magician, but Columbo gives himself that opportunity by forcing himself on Santini as his assistant, even though Santini would obviously much rather have "a beautiful young woman" on stage with him. Columbo flips the power dynamic on Santini by challenging him to a trick—producing a pair of police handcuffs and testing Santini to free himself from them. Of course, Santini succeeds in less than thirty seconds, and he unlocks the cuffs with plenty of showmanship as well. It's a fleeting moment of triumph, as once Columbo winks and says, "I knew you could do it," Santini realizes that this was a lose-lose situation. When he unlocked the cuffs, he proved that he could have unlocked the victim's office door. If he'd failed to do it, he would lose face to the audience. Santini attempts to regain a level of control by asking for "a round of applause for the lieutenant who tried to outwit the master" and pickpockets Columbo's badge as well as another way to reestablish dominance in the relationship.

Later, once Santini thinks Columbo's been forced to accept his alibi, he's politely dismissive of the lieutenant, saying, "Oh no...someone I thought I'd seen the last of." He's not trying to win over Columbo or befriend him. He's tried to treat Columbo just like the standard audience member to be dazzled and duped. But you can't fool someone who knows how the trick works.

At the end, when Columbo is armed with the crucial evidence, Santini utilizes a tactic that few murderers attempt—a blunt attempt to destroy the proof against him by using a magic trick to set the letter on fire, though it's thwarted by the fact that Columbo made plenty of copies. It's a bold move, and it shows just how brazen Santini is when he believes that he needs to take action. Another man might have tried to eat the letter, but Santini used the opportunity to use his magic trick skills and demonstrate his showmanship. Even when he was in a crisis situation, Santini couldn't resist an opportunity to show off his abilities.

Given Santini's background as a Nazi, he certainly had a history of cruelty and a disregard for human life. He demonstrates no remorse for his crimes, past or present, but there is one point that bears further consideration. Santini has an adult daughter Della (Cynthia Sikes), who appears briefly in the episode, working as his onstage assistant. Certainly, Santini wants to protect himself from being charged with war crimes, but he also has a viable motive in protecting his daughter from the fallout from his own exposure and disgrace. At least, he has this motive on paper. In the actual episode, he expresses no concern for her public reputation or psychological well-being in the wake of the revelations, and given the ease with which he admits his guilt, he's not thinking about the broader repercussions of his confession. Even at the moment of his arrest, he maintains his dignity, glaring at the officer leading him away, silently glaring at the handcuffs as if to say, "Really? Don't you realize that I could free myself from those in mere seconds?"

Most murderers try to commit their crimes in the shadows, but as a performer, Santini had to exercise his flair for the dramatic. He used his skills in designing illusions, lockpicking, and disguises in order to commit the crime. In many ways, his plan signed his own name to the shooting. It was a murder committed in a way that only he could have done it.

Chapter Thirty-Seven: Last Salute to the Commodore

Charles Clay (Robert Vaughn) and Swanny Swanson (Fred Draper)

Of all of *Columbo*'s episodes, "Last Salute to the Commodore" provokes the strongest negative reactions from fans. It's quite different from every other entry in the series, both tonally and in terms of the reveal of the killer.

Commodore Otis Swanson (John Dehner) has made a fortune through his shipbuilding business. Despite his wealth, he's not a happy man, as he's severely disappointed in his hard-drinking daughter Joanna (Diane Baker), her husband Charles, and his other relative "Swanny" Swanson (Fred Draper). Furious with how they've been running his business, he threatens that major changes are coming… and soon winds up dead.

Charles Clay is shown standing over the Commodore's corpse, cleaning up the crime scene, and dropping the body into the ocean. The implication to the unsuspicious viewer is that Charles is the killer, even though the actual murder is not shown on-screen.

Columbo appears fourteen minutes into the episode, and it's immediately apparent that he's a little off, acting as if he's having a bad reaction to a prescription medication that's making him rather slow and loopy. Many of his mannerisms are exaggerated as well. Columbo brings Charles along on the investigations, taking him to the boat in an overcrowded car. Charles generally stands off to the side, looking uncomfortable. Later, the Commodore's body is recovered. Columbo clearly suspects Charles, but his theories are shot down when Charles winds up dead, and afterwards Columbo discovers his alibi.

Columbo continues his investigation and realizes that the alibis are based on people seeing the Commodore sailing his boat from a distance. He also discovers that the Commodore was planning to marry a much younger woman. Asking Swanny to dress up like the Commodore, Columbo suggests that any of the suspects could have impersonated the Commodore to create an alibi. All the suspects are gathered together in one room, and in traditional whodunit fashion, Columbo explains the clues, clasps the Commodore's pocket watch between his hands, and holds the ticking timepiece to each suspect's ear, identifying it as "the Commodore's watch." All the suspects respond differently, but Swanny quips that "it isn't." Columbo reveals that the killer broke the Commodore's pocket watch and reset it to create a false time of death. Columbo has since had the watch repaired, and the only reason why Swanny would think it wasn't the Commodore's watch his because he smashed it himself.

Swanny is arrested on this scanty evidence, and Columbo triumphantly sails across the marina to have lunch with his wife.

The traditional analysis of the killer's actions and connections to Columbo can't really be applied to this episode, as "Last Salute to the Commodore" is so different from most entries in the series.

Charles Clay is *not* a killer, but for the purposes of this analysis, he is considered one because he covered up the crime under the false assumption that his wife was responsible for her father's death, and he wanted to protect her inheritance. He *believes* that he is making himself an accessory to murder, not realizing that his wife is completely innocent. Technically and legally, Clay is innocent of murder, but *morally*, he is an accessory after the fact, aside from definitely being guilty of illegal disposal of a body. His motives are simple. If Joanna is convicted of her father's murder, she doesn't inherit, and Charles loses a lot of money. Charles isn't particularly fond of his wife and wouldn't care if she were arrested, but losing out on the inheritance is unthinkable to him, so he has to take steps to protect the woman he despises.

It's hazardous to explore Columbo's personal feelings towards Charles or any of the other characters, as he behaves so differently from normal. The lazy, slurred way he collapses on the couch and throws his arm around Charles, for example, is unlike anything else in the series. Is he being friendly, manipulative, or has he had a stroke? Charles clearly doesn't care much for Columbo, though few specific reasons are given other than annoyance at the detective's digging into the crime. Mostly, he looks at the lieutenant as if he's a repulsive imposition upon him, but little verbal depth is given to his feelings.

As for Swanny, he has precious little screen time with Columbo, so they fail to develop anything even remotely resembling the relationship that the lieutenant forms with most murderers. They only have a few brief conversations, but apparently, Swanny was sufficiently amicable towards Columbo to help him by dressing as the Commodore, destroying his own alibi along with everybody else's. It's not the most logical decision for Swanny to make, but nothing about this episode matches traditional *Columbo* character development and plot structure. In any case, Swanny seems to enjoy the attention that comes with a dramatic reveal and probably couldn't resist the chance to stand in the spotlight, even when it had the potential to destroy his plans.

It is clear that Swanny has a ruthless streak to him, what with murdering both the Commodore and Charles and framing his relative Joanna for the crimes. Joanna was the principal beneficiary of the will, but if she was convicted of her father's murder, the massive inheritance would pass to Swanny. Swanny was willing to wipe out his entire family in order to become rich. The desire for wealth at the expense of others, including close family, is common in the *Columbo* series, but few other killers maintain such a jolly demeanor throughout the entire episode.

"Last Salute to the Commodore" does not lend itself to an in-depth analysis of characterization in the same way that most of the other episodes in the series do, but completeness requires its inclusion. The episode breaks the standard "inverted mystery" trope and skips over the traditional bond between detective and killer. Everything about "Last Salute to the Commodore" is an exception to the general rules regarding *Columbo*, and as such, it needs to be treated as an anomaly.

VI

SEASON SIX

Chapter Thirty-Eight: Fade in to Murder

Ward Fowler (William Shatner)

Detective Lucerne is rich, dapper, and cultured, and the central character on a television crime show. He's also played by a murderer.

Ward Fowler plays Lucerne in a hit series. He's won an Emmy for the role, but he's not happy. His producer, Clare Daley (Lola Albright), helped make him a star, but she's siphoning most of his earnings from the show away from him through blackmail, as she knows he deserted his duties during the Korean War. Tired of being under her thumb, Fowler sets up an alibi by watching television at a friend's home and then drugging his pal. Fowler disguises himself as a mugger and then finds his producer at a sandwich shop and shoots her, making it look like a holdup gone wrong. After disposing of the evidence, Fowler returns to his friend's home, and by using a recording of the television show and resetting his friend's watch (not realizing that his pal habitually keeps his watch five minutes fast), he awakens his buddy to create an alibi.

Columbo arrives fifteen and a quarter minutes into the episode and, after examining the crime scene, goes to interview Fowler on the set of his show. Fowler's initially angered when Columbo knocks over some equipment, but the moment he learns Columbo's from the police, he's a lot nicer. After Fowler pretends he doesn't remember where he was the previous night, his friend comes to his rescue with the alibi. Columbo professes to be a great fan of the show, and when Fowler offers to help the investigation, the lieutenant happily accepts.

Over the course of the episode, Columbo works alongside Fowler as he uncovers clues, and the two become quite chummy, though Columbo never loses sight of the fact that the actor is his chief suspect. The lieutenant steadily uncovers evidence linking Fowler to the crime, and when confronted with it, Fowler's usually more amused than threatened. Columbo confronts Fowler with trace evidence from his clothing on the gun and reveals that Fowler neglected to wipe his fingerprints off the bullets. Fowler's stunned but not repentant, saying, "Damn! I always forget something. That's always how the third act ends. You see, I've had no rehearsal as a murderer."

After Columbo's prompt, he confesses, saying, "She was a blackmailer. And up to now, I've been glad I killed her." Showing no remorse, he declares that he thinks he had the sympathetic role in this little drama.

This episode has a lot of screen time between detective and killer, and unusual stress is placed upon the developing friendship between the two men. The summary of the episode is a bit shorter than usual because so much of the episode is about the conversations held between the two men, which will be addressed in more detail here. Notwithstanding the initial annoyance at Columbo when the lieutenant causes a ruckus on set, there are few detective/killer relationships as cordial as in "Fade into Murder." By the end of their first meeting, Fowler offers his services to help with the investigation. Perhaps it's a poor strategy for Fowler to draw attention to himself, but like other killers, Fowler wanted to keep track of Columbo's progress. Additionally, Fowler seems to relish the opportunity to play detective in real life, even if it's his own crime he's investigating.

When reconstructing the crime, Fowler, like many other killers, tries to push his preferred narrative of a holdup gone wrong, but Columbo notes how the positions of the wound indicate that the victim had her arms down when she was shot, indicating deliberate murder. When Columbo contradicts Fowler's suggestions, instead of sulking and doubling down like most killers, Fowler amiably declares, "I suppose if that's your instinct, it must be right." Fowler can't resist the opportunity to present his deductions on the crime, declaring that due to the positioning, the murderer must have been an "expert marksman," a declaration that rebounds back at him later when Columbo realizes that decades earlier, Fowler's military training made him a skilled shooter.

Fowler gives himself away at times when he wants to encourage Columbo to go down the wrong path. Columbo notes that there's makeup on the inside of the recovered ski mask worn by the killer, and when Columbo suggests that the killer was a woman, Fowler leaps with excitement, glossing over the surviving witness, stating the shooter had a man's voice. The delighted grin at this scene is really a giveaway, though Fowler has no idea his glee is disproportionate to the situation.

For his part, Columbo enjoys the opportunity to rub shoulders with a television actor whose work he enjoys. In a telling scene in Fowler's trailer, he tries on Lieutenant Lucerne's hat and mugs in the mirror. It indicates that at least some of his declarations to famous killers that he and his wife are big aficionados of their work aren't merely conversational gambits. Columbo really is a fan of Fowler, and as the investigation progresses, the viewer gets a sense that Columbo's saddened at the impending loss of his favorite show, but no TV series is so great that the lead actor can get away with murder. When Fowler walks in on Columbo, he's surprisingly good-humored about the intrusion. Soon afterwards, Fowler catches Columbo setting a trap for him about where the murder weapon might have come from, and Fowler takes no umbrage to the revelation that Columbo sees him as a suspect. It's certainly expected, and it in no way sours his attitude towards Columbo.

Almost unsettlingly, Fowler slips into the persona of Lieutenant Lucerne on multiple occasions and notes that Ward Fowler really ought to be Columbo's chief suspect. It's not clear if Fowler's even aware of what he's doing, but it seems as if Fowler can't help falling into character. Is he really so certain of the strength of his alibi that he feels he can't shine the light of suspicion on himself? Or is his grip on reality cracking, and is he starting to see "Fowler" and "Lucerne" as distinct individuals, separate from himself, depending on his current perspective? Or is it some misguided double bluff? It's unclear, but in the final scenes, Fowler professes to have interviewed himself and acts surprised to learn that he is an expert marksman. In what might be the "Lucerne" characterization, the actor declares that "Fowler" never told him about his skills with a gun. Actor/killers often have fragile mental states on *Columbo*, as "Dagger of the Mind" showed two thespians crumbling psychologically; "Forgotten Lady" had a physiological cause for an actress's fading mind; and "Requiem for a Falling Star" had the murderous actress sane but emotionally and mentally exhausted by the episode's end. As Fowler seems unable to tell where his persona ends and Lucerne begins, it seems as if the actor has suffered a psychotic break. Or is he simply acting up a storm?

How should the discerning viewer evaluate Fowler's state of mind? If one is inclined to be charitable, one could argue that due to mental illness, he is not wholly responsible for his actions. It is known that he deserted from the Korean War, but it is possible that his experiences in combat caused him severe psychological strain, leading to his desertion. It's arguable that he turned to acting in order to deal with his traumas. Given the skepticism with which dissociative identity disorder, more popularly known as multiple personality disorder, is held in the psychiatric community, Fowler's condition should not be given that name, but it's possible that Fowler utilized different personas as a means of processing his invisible scars inflicted by the horrors of war.

Viewed from this perspective, the man who will be referred to as Fowler has lived under at least four different names and possibly has created as many personas. There's Ward Fowler, the urbane, sophisticated actor. There's Lieutenant Lucerne, the brilliant detective. Then there's John Snelling, Fowler's presumed birth name and the name under which he fought in the Korean War. After deserting, he adopted the name of Charles Kipling and began acting in Canada under that name. It's hazardous to call each of these four names personas, as one cannot be certain whether or not the man who will be referred to as "Fowler" for purposes of convenience could really differentiate between the four or whether mental illness affected his ability to tell the difference between reality and affectation. If his descent into insanity is real, it's possible that he really did see the figures of Lieutenant Lucerne and Ward Fowler as individuals somehow separate from himself with which he could interact.

In contrast, if one views Ward Fowler with a particularly suspicious mind, one might argue that a skillful performer is simply playing a long game, realizing that if he is arrested, he might have a fair shot of escaping severe punishment by feigning (or at least exaggerating) serious mental illness. This interpretation would explain some of the seemingly over-the-top statements he makes, such as saying that he talked to himself to find out if he was being blackmailed or not. The affectations and unconventional reactions may have been exaggerated due to his overplaying his role. Certainly, the care and attention with which he planned his crime indicate that he had solid mental capacities, though it's possible the act of committing the murder, followed by the strain of the investigation, led to his unraveling.

As Fowler cannot be properly interviewed and examined, the ambiguity remains at the episode's end. Perhaps Fowler really did suffer a mental break from reality, or perhaps he hoped to be sentenced to a comfortable stay in a mental hospital, followed by a miraculous recovery and release, possibly even a resumption of his career.

But if one looks at his four known names, it's indicated that he played four different parts over the course of his lifetime, and it may have been hard to ignore and deny his past as John Snelling. It may have been more convenient and pleasurable to live life as the big television star Ward Fowler, and it may have been fun to play a skillful sleuth onscreen, but it's notable that when he tells Columbo about his pre-Fowler life, he makes it sound like Charles Kipling was his only past persona. Kipling may have had a mildly shady background, but in "Fowler's" telling, Kipling was a generally honorable man living an obscure actor's life. His true origins as John Snelling, a man who deserted from the Korean War, was the one persona that he actively denied and repressed. What childhood influences, youthful relationships, and psychological damage he might have incurred as Snelling are unknown. This does, however, mean that Snelling, the original and most genuine of the personas, is the one the viewer knows the least about, and one can only theorize whether or not glimpses of Snelling pop up inadvertently over the course of the episode.

It should also be remembered that Fowler seemingly cannot pass up an opportunity to put on a performance. In his first moments with Columbo, he makes a great show of pretending that he has no clue where he was the previous night and then gets to act relieved once his friend is able to come to his rescue with an alibi. When Columbo hams it up when filming a video with Ward for fun, Fowler seems to delight in being able to play pretend with a friend. Acting is more than just a job or a craft to him; it's a pure delight in his life, and it's reasonable to postulate that he might have seized every opportunity to play a part, and certainly, many actors would relish the chance to sink their teeth into the role of a madman.

In the end, it's up to viewer interpretation to decide whether Fowler was truly a sick man or if he was a skillful trickster who tried to use his acting abilities to game the system. What's less debatable is the fact that he seems to genuinely enjoy Columbo's company and to respect him as a detective. Certainly, any amount of deception is possible, but based on the interactions between the two, there's a strong indication that the warmth and friendliness really are genuine.

It cannot be known definitively if Ward Fowler was delusional or scheming, but whatever his true mental state might have been, he did respect Columbo as a detective and as a man. Perhaps his final statement is an invitation for Columbo to view him as a friend and equal, saying it would be "an enormous favor…[to] stop calling [him] "sir."

Chapter Thirty-Nine: Old Fashioned Murder

Ruth Lytton (Joyce Van Patten)

A dysfunctional family, a tiny museum, and some decades-old secrets boil up into a multiple murder case. Ruth Lytton is one of a trio of siblings who run a small gallery filled with antiquities, but as one might imagine, such an enterprise is not particularly profitable. Patrons are scarce, and revenue is far below where it needs to be to keep the enterprise solvent. Ruth's brother Edward (Tim O'Connor) believes that the smartest plan is to sell the contents of the museum, and split the profits three ways. Ruth is having none of that, so she decides to commit fratricide.

She recruits security guard Milton Shaeffer (Peter S. Feibleman) to break into the museum for a little robbery, claiming she needs the insurance money. Down on his luck and desperate for funds, Shaeffer agrees. Following Ruth's plan, Shaeffer fakes his own death by pretending to be shot while making a telephone call to his brother. A bit later, while Shaeffer's robbing the museum, Ruth shoots him for real. When Edward, who has been working late into the night on an inventory, comes to investigate, Ruth shoots her brother with a second gun, then places the weapons in the dead men's hands to create the impression that the two men killed each other, switching off the light as she leaves.

Columbo enters a little under eighteen minutes into the episode, following up on a concerned call made by Shaeffer's brother. Suffering from allergies, Columbo doesn't know whether or not there's been a murder, only that Shaeffer's brother is worried. As Columbo drinks tea with the Lyttons, he learns that Ruth was once engaged, but her fiancé ran off with her sister Phyllis (Celeste Holm) and had a daughter Janie (Jeannie Berlin). Ruth views her niece as the daughter she might have had, but clearly, she doesn't care about her enough to protect her from a terrible shock. Ruth allows Janie to discover the bodies.

Columbo's suspicious of the murderous tableau, noting that the light was off, and since dead men can't flip switches, a third person was there. Schaeffer was also dressed as if he was heading for a warm climate, so the lieutenant suspects the truth isn't as obvious as the killer wants it to appear. Columbo investigates and realizes that Schaeffer was anticipating a financial windfall and was planning to leave the country.

As the episode progresses, Columbo converses with Ruth, but she's very coy about revealing details from her past, especially her love life. Columbo learns her ex-fiancé turned brother-in-law died suddenly years earlier and immediately suspects that she killed him. As Columbo reveals he suspects the surviving members of the Lytton family, Ruth tucks a gold antique from the museum's collection (ostensibly stolen sometime earlier) amongst Janie's possessions, causing her niece to be arrested. Columbo knows Janie's innocent, however, and he brings her a cheeseburger and watches as she uses the golden item she supposedly stole as an ashtray, all while he tells Janie he thinks Ruth poisoned her father and framed her.

In the final confrontation, Columbo explains that the stolen object was a gold belt buckle, but Janie didn't know what it was—she thought it was an ashtray. Edward's inventory proves that the buckle was there at the time of his death, meaning it was stolen after the murder. Janie tells Ruth that Columbo thinks she committed both murders and her former fiancé as well and insists that her aunt never would do such a thing. Realizing that Columbo is prepared to make all of the Lyttons' family secrets public, Ruth, using nothing but telling gazes, makes a deal with Columbo. If he decides to treat her ex-fiancé's death as natural, she'll confess to both of the more recent murders. Columbo silently accepts her terms, and Ruth quietly leaves with him.

This final moment is one of the rare cases where Columbo makes anything approximating a deal with a killer. On many crime shows, the villain makes some sort of deal– a confession for a reduced sentence, or implicating someone else for a similar consideration. Usually, Columbo has no need to negotiate—he has sufficient proof, whether it's forensic evidence, useful testimony, or a fatal slip by the killer—to make an arrest. But here, the lieutenant lacks a metaphorical smoking gun to make his case. Columbo knows that if Ruth poisoned her ex-fiancé, the odds of finding proof of foul play through an exhumation are unlikely, though it depends on the toxin used. He's not about to send an innocent girl to prison, and he didn't put Janie in that position anyway—Ruth did. Columbo often uses a clever trick to make his case, but in this case, he's trying something quite different: an emotional appeal.

Ruth's motivations here are confusing and open to interpretation. How does she really feel about her family? Certainly she wasn't particularly fond of her brother, as she puts the continuation of the museum above his life. She bears a grudge against her sister for running off with her fiancé, changing the course of her life. But does she really care about her niece? Does she really see her as the daughter she never had, or is Janie a painful reminder of a double betrayal? Viewers can come to different conclusions here, but based on Ruth's conflicting treatment of Janie, it seems as if Ruth is driven by interlinked feelings of both love and hate. When she calls Janie the daughter she might have had, there seems to be some genuine affection in her tone and eyes. When Ruth gives her niece a break from inventory duties, she's definitely doing so to clear the museum for the murder she plans, but she also seems to be happy to allow Janie to go out and have fun. Still, she sets Janie up for the potentially traumatizing shock of discovering two bodies, and Ruth plants the gold belt buckle in her niece's room in order to incriminate her, causing her to spend several hours in a cell. Yet in the final scene, when Janie looks at her aunt with dewy eyes, telling

Ruth that she knows how much her aunt loves the whole family and would never do anything to harm them, the niece's plea strikes a chord in the murderous aunt. Clearly, she doesn't want Janie to go to jail for a crime she didn't commit, but at the same time, she knows that her confession will have a devastating effect on her surviving relatives. Janie's belief in the sort of woman her aunt is will be shattered, and both Janie and Phyllis will be publicly humiliated by people learning of Ruth's crimes. By confessing, Ruth will gain a level of revenge against her surviving family members, though her imprisonment will very likely lead to the closing of her beloved museum and the sale of the collection, a point which she may or may not have considered. By taking Columbo's arm as they leave, Ruth takes a last shot at Phyllis, who once bragged about always leaving a room on a man's arm.

Ultimately, Ruth's contradictory feelings towards Janie, as both surrogate daughter and symbol of betrayal, may have caused Ruth to develop an abusive relationship towards her niece, where she's maternal and loving to Janie's face, but she harms Janie in ways that can't obviously be traced back to her. From the way Janie speaks about her aunt, she may have been trained to be emotionally dependent upon Ruth. It's open to debate, but Janie may unknowingly have become the victim of psychological manipulation. Phyllis is mostly concerned about herself, often commenting on how men routinely pay attention to her and always striving to be the center of attention. Janie likely only had Ruth to turn to for support and attention when growing up, so Ruth certainly had a strong impact on her. The question lies in how much of this was negative.

In any event, Columbo uses the affection Ruth has for Janie to his advantage. Throughout their interactions, Ruth and Columbo have been polite, even cordial. Perhaps the defining feature of their relationship is that Ruth consistently makes it clear that she is aware of Columbo's tactics and how he's trying to assess her and her capabilities. Often, murderers try to assert their intellectual superiority from the outset, emphasizing that they're smarter than Columbo. Ruth's approach is different. Ruth subtly acknowledges that Columbo is an intelligent man, but she wants to make it clear that she is also a clever woman and she is not going to be a pushover for him. After Columbo sets up a rudimentary trap to test her story about the guard, she asks him if tripping up people is a part of his job and warns him to "never underestimate me." She understands that Columbo's ploys are a critical part of his investigation, but she'd appreciate it if he was "a little cleverer" with his suspicions. When Columbo says "I wouldn't say that I was suspicious," Ruth responds by saying "Your delicacy does you credit."

This exchange is emblematic of the relationship between the pair. Columbo suspects her of the murders, and Ruth is fully aware of this. But their conversations are always marked by respect and politeness. There are no attempts on Ruth's part to threaten the lieutenant's job, nor is there the coldly furious condemnation that Columbo displays towards the worst offenders. Ruth is a complex character whose motivations are open to debate, but what can be determined is that the elopement of her fiancé and her sister wounded her in a way that never truly healed, and her relationship with her niece is filled with contradictory emotions. As Ruth's appreciation for Columbo accepting her deal and taking her arm as they leave the room in the final moments illustrates, she truly desires to be treated with respect, especially after being treated so disrespectfully in the past.

Chapter Forty: The Bye-Bye Sky High I.Q. Murder Case

Oliver Brandt (Theodore Bikel)

Just because someone's very intelligent, that doesn't mean that those considerable brains can create the perfect murder. Oliver Brandt spends his spare time in an elegant mansion that serves as a base for the Sigma Club, a group of people with genius-level intellects. Brandt is an accountant whose wife, Vivian (Samantha Eggar), has a taste for the finer things in life, and the bills for her desires far exceed Brandt's modest income. Therefore, Brandt has been siphoning cash from his clients, and his dear friend Bertie Hastings (Sorrel Booke) has uncovered the truth. After a brief attempt to convince Hastings not to report his findings, Brandt tickles his friend in order to put him in a better mood, and when that fails, Brandt shoots his pal twice, mournfully declaring, "I really did love you, Bertie." Brandt then arranges to have the sound of shots heard while he's with his fellow high-I.Q. pals, giving him an alibi.

Columbo enters seventeen minutes into the episode. Brandt's quite friendly to him and even suggests that Columbo could be a potential member of the club. Columbo focuses on the case, poking holes in the theory that a burglar broke into the house, shot Hastings, and stole his wallet. Columbo questions Brandt at a local park and quickly uncovers Brandt's embezzlement. Meanwhile, Brandt's composure is crumbling. He snaps at subordinates, perspires and squirms in obvious discomfort, and is clearly losing control of his nerves.

At the episode's climax, Columbo meets a badly frayed Brandt at the scene of the crime and reveals that he thinks he knows how the murder was committed with a gun and silencer, showing how the sound of a couple of shots could have been replicated using ordinary objects found in the room, including a record player and a thick dictionary, plus a pair of squibs. Columbo deliberately leaves part of the recreation of the crime sloppy, leaving the triggering of the squibs up to chance. Enraged, Brandt demonstrates how they could have been set to explode with far more certainty, realizing a moment later that he's given himself away. Resigned to his fate, Brandt offers Columbo another brain teaser. After Columbo unravels the solution with a modicum of effort, Brandt suggests that Columbo's brains might be put to better use in another field, but Columbo insists that detective work is where he's meant to be.

Traditionally, murderers underestimate Columbo's intelligence when they are first introduced, only gradually realizing that the detective poses a threat as time passes and they see him at work. In contrast, Brandt instantly recognizes the lieutenant's brainpower, giving him logic puzzles. Some of this may be due to his innate desire to seek out other clever people, but some of this may also be a gambit to get on Columbo's good side by flattery. In the normal episode template, the killers are firmly convinced of their innate intellectual superiority and do not fear the investigator because they believe that their murder plan is impervious to scrutiny. Brandt is one of the few murderers who not only appreciates Columbo's intelligence but also takes a genuine interest in it.

There's a very good characterization scene where Columbo explains how he developed his skills, explaining that he's always been surrounded by smart people, and he knew that he couldn't outthink them, but if he tried hard enough, he might be able to succeed through pure tenacity. Columbo may sell his own cranial capacity short, but what is certain is the fact that he embodies the old axiom about genius being one percent inspiration and ninety-nine percent perspiration.

Brandt, in contrast, has plenty of brainpower, but he doesn't put in the effort to make his murder plan absolutely watertight. It should be noted that for all of Brandt's cleverness, his plan for getting away with murder isn't as ingenious as he imagines. Not only does Columbo figure out how the sound of the shots was faked, but Caroline Treynor (Carol Jones), a young girl, also figures out how the trick was worked, though she doesn't accuse Brandt of the crime. This illustrates a critical point—intelligence and creativity are not necessarily synonymous. A very smart person can figure out a way to replicate the sounds of shots and a body falling, but it's much more difficult to figure out a way so complex that someone else of comparable intelligence cannot figure out how it was done.

The relationship between Columbo and Brandt is cordial, as Brandt seems to take a genuine liking to Columbo. Perhaps it's based on his appreciation for intelligence, but Brandt consistently treats Columbo with respect, though as the episode progresses, Brandt's composure steadily and thoroughly frays. In "Swan Song," Tommy Brown may have realized that his guilt would eventually lead to a confession, but Brandt is the first killer in the series to be completely battered by the strain of committing the crime, exhibiting guilt to the point of mental collapse. Shortly after the murder, Brandt is calm, good-humored, and natural. With each subsequent scene, he frays a little more. As Columbo questions him in the park, he fails at hiding all of his jitters. Later, he snaps at an employee and attacks that person verbally, far beyond any reasonable show of temper. He takes out his pent-up emotion in a public manner, and his lack of control is telling as to how much the situation has sapped his self-control. His spirit is utterly drained when he confesses his embezzlement (though not the murder) to his wife. She's blasé, and offers him no compassion. It's at that moment when Brandt realizes that his wife doesn't really care about him, but only about the comfortable lifestyle he provides her with, allowing her to purchase whatever she desires. As distraught as he is, Brandt can still see that all that his misappropriation of funds has done is buy the company of a woman who is concerned about material things, but not him as a man. Despite all of his smarts, Brandt failed to see that one cannot buy love, and his embezzlement was an empty, meaningless waste of effort. The theft, and therefore the murder, were all for nothing, and this realization crushes Brandt's spirit even further.

In his final conversation with Columbo, Brandt is obviously crumbling, suffering from the guilt of murdering his beloved friend and hating himself for being such a fool as to commit criminal acts for a woman who was at best indifferent to him. He mourns how his intelligence has been as much a curse to him as a blessing, noting that he never really had a proper childhood as he was an "imitation adult" who often had to disguise his cleverness. Even with people of similar intelligence, he wasn't comfortable, calling his fellow club members "eccentric bores." When he gives himself away as a result of Columbo's trap, it's possible that he was so beaten down that he couldn't see the danger he was heading into, but it's arguably more likely that subconsciously, he knew what he was doing, and desired to reveal the truth so he could surrender and rid himself of the mental and spiritual burdens that were pulverizing him.

Brandt always defined himself by his intelligence, but his true defining characteristic was his conscience. No other *Columbo* killer is so thoroughly laid low by the power of guilt, and "The Bye-Bye Sky High I.Q. Murder Case" is perhaps the one time in the entire series that Columbo's presence is arguably superfluous. Columbo didn't really need to trick Brandt into giving himself away. Brandt was radiating contrition, and one way or another, he would have faced justice within a very short time.

VII

SEASON SEVEN

Chapter Forty-One: Try and Catch Me

Abigail Mitchell (Ruth Gordon)

Of all of the *Columbo* killers, Abigail Mitchell is one of, if not *the* most sympathetic characters. Not only is she genuinely friendly and affectionate towards Columbo, but her motive is unique. While most murderers kill for money, lust, or power, Mitchell takes a life in order to avenge the death of her beloved niece. At least, she *believed* that her niece had been murdered and that she knew who'd done it.

Mitchell is a respected and successful mystery writer, but she was devastated when her niece Phyllis died in a boating "accident." She's convinced that her nephew-in-law Edmund Galvin (Charles Frank) killed her, and after completing her own investigation, realizes that if she wants justice for Phyllis, she'll have to take matters into her own hands. To Galvin's face, she plays the role of the doting aunt, setting up a will where if one dies, the other will inherit everything the deceased owns. Galvin thinks he's in line to receive the profits from Mitchell's copious literary output, while Mitchell plans to recover her niece's money. She asks Galvin to place some boxes in her huge walk-in safe, but once he's inside, she snaps at him, saying, "You murdered my Phyllis. Did you really think I didn't know?" Before he can respond, she slams the safe door in his face and locks it.

Mitchell has made sure that Galvin wasn't seen coming inside her house, and when she sees Galvin's keys, she buries them in a sand pot ashtray before hurrying out to catch a cross-country flight. While she's in New York a few days later, her secretary opens the safe and finds Galvin's body. He suffocated in the airtight safe.

When Mitchell returns, she arrives to see Columbo emerging from the safe nineteen minutes into the episode. He observes that the safe is completely soundproof and states his excitement at meeting such a famous author. He wonders how the deceased got into the safe while the alarm was on, and Mitchell, not having a ready answer, acts old and confused, a ruse that doesn't fool Columbo for a second, and he tells her as much.

As the investigation proceeds, Mitchell and Columbo build a very friendly relationship as they talk over tea about both her writing habits and the case. There's a level of casualness in their conversation, as she considers it improper to bring a lawyer. Few *Columbo* suspects ever bring up the need for a lawyer, and when they do, they wield the possibility of legal representation almost as a threat rather than as a breach of etiquette. Mitchell makes a number of suggestions about what happened, such as the possibility that Galvin, having the combination to the safe, broke in to help himself to "an advance against his inheritance." Columbo points out a couple of contradictions, including the fact that the burglar alarm was on and that the safe dial had been turned, so it's unlikely to have been simply pulled shut.

Without clear answers to Columbo's questions, Mitchell does a little bit of obfuscation with the evidence, "accidentally" covering a hidden house key with her own fingerprints so Columbo can't prove that Galvin didn't let himself in with the key himself. But it's Galvin's keys that prove to be the central piece of evidence to the case, as they've vanished from the sand pot. As it turns out, Mitchell's secretary Veronica (Mariette Hartley) found them and is using them to negotiate a much higher salary and a voyage on a luxury cruise alongside her employer. Unlike nearly every other *Columbo* killer who's being blackmailed, Mitchell decides to acquiesce to these requests rather than permanently silence her extorting employee. Later, Columbo meets her at a pier right before she can toss the keys into the water, and Mitchell decides to change her tactics, claiming she found the keys in the garden.

Mitchell and Columbo have several other notable moments, such as when Columbo crashes a women's club meeting, and she ropes him into giving an impromptu speech. She slyly informs the guests that the lieutenant is an expert on chemicals in detection, but Columbo quickly recovers his poise and turns the speech into a commentary on murderers he has liked over the course of his career, not because of their crimes, but because no one's all evil. He gently makes a couple of veiled remarks towards Mitchell, indicating his suspicions of her. Later, when the pair head for a visit to the dead man's apartment, they take her luxury car. When he tells her that his own car is very rare, Mitchell responds, "I can see why." She initially flatters Columbo at the apartment, declaring, "What a treat to watch a consummate professional at work!" She follows him, mirroring his movements. The first and only real moment of tension between the two comes when Columbo asks her not to go on a planned cruise to the Far East, and with the first sign of temper, Mitchell tells him to speak to her lawyer. Columbo then contradicts Mitchell's statement that her niece and nephew-in-law had a happy relationship, as there are no pictures of Phyllis at her widower's apartment, concluding by saying, "And I'll be very glad to talk to your attorney, ma'am."

Right before Mitchell sails off on her cruise, Columbo arrives with a warrant, bringing her back to the scene of the crime. He shows a photograph of the crime scene, proving the keys weren't where she said they were when she found them. He then shows her something hidden inside the lightbulb socket in the safe. Galvin tore off part of the title page of her latest manuscript, *The Night I was Murdered*, and reveals that Galvin used a burnt match to black out two words, creating the dying message "*I was Murdered*... by Abigail Mitchell." After Columbo gently declines Mitchell's request for clemency, she goes away with him amicably.

Any analysis of Mitchell's character has to consider the two possible and equally valid answers to this question: *Was she correct about Galvin murdering her niece?* If she's right, then she punished a man who the law couldn't touch, based mainly upon her own instincts. If she's wrong, then she killed an innocent man because the situation fits her worldview based on a career built upon fictional murders. She must have been certain, but how could she be without the kind of evidence that she could give to the police? It's likely that she believed her knowledge of human nature and her nephew's character allowed her to see the culpability in his words and expressions that most people couldn't detect. The viewer never knows for sure what happened, and the episode must be viewed as potentially a tale of vigilante justice and possibly as a tragedy based upon unfounded suspicions.

Still, the theory that Mitchell's mind was warped from all of her years of writing mysteries has to bear another possibility in mind, based on the fact that her niece's body was never found. Every mystery writer knows that one should never assume that someone is dead until their corpse has been recovered and positively identified. What does it mean that Mitchell didn't cling to some sort of hope that her niece might still be alive? Why didn't she pursue the possibility that the supposed boating accident was all just a trick played by the husband and wife together, possibly for life insurance reasons? Phyllis could have disappeared and changed her appearance, planning for the two to reconnect later with her using an assumed identity. All of her pictures could have been removed so no one would notice the physical similarities between Galvin's first and second wives. Perhaps Mitchell never seriously considered this possibility because she believed that her bond with her niece was so strong that Phyllis would never cause her beloved aunt the heartbreak of believing she was dead. Yet, it's the kind of twist a mystery writer ought to think of instinctively.

Certainly, Galvin's death is, if not physically painful, the most psychologically crushing of any victim's death, as he had nothing to do but sit in the dark for a lengthy stretch of time as his oxygen depleted, hoping against hope that he could survive long enough for someone to open the safe for him. For arguably the most endearing and defensible killer in the series, she inflicted the most trauma upon her target. When another fan-favorite killer, Adrian Carsini, left his victim to suffocate in a small room, he at least left that man unconscious.

It's also notable that Mitchell really doesn't fool anybody with her murder plan. Columbo, of course, suspects her at once. Her secretary, Veronica, swiftly figures out what happened, and Mitchell shows that she's morally above most of the series' other killers by choosing placation over homicide to keep her quiet. Additionally, a pointed comment by her lawyer indicates that he believes she's responsible for her nephew-in-law's death, though he couches his words in careful, legal ambiguity. The reason for this is she committed a crime that's straight out of one of her novels. Anybody could plan a murder, including shooting or stabbing, but a mysterious asphyxiation in a safe while she's across the country? Metaphorically, the death of her nephew has her fingerprints all over it. It's larger than life, dramatic, and colorful. It's exactly the sort of crime that would feature in one of her books, and though the physical absence is scanty, in a stylistic sense, she signed her name to the murder. Not only that, but the little holes in her plot make one wonder if she was fortunate enough to have a good editor who could catch any similar shortcomings in her novels.

More than any other killer, Mitchell seems to be having the time of her life during the investigation. No one else is nearly has happy to be watching Columbo work, no one else seems to derive so much joy from sparring with him. Indeed, sometimes the happiness is a giveaway, as Mitchell can't keep the delight out of her voice as she thinks about Galvin lighting matches in the safe, trading a little bit of light for precious oxygen. The title of the episode reflects that, in many ways, this is a game for her, a battle of wits that, unlike most killers, she doesn't want to avoid. She hopes to win, but she's thrilled to have such a superb sparring partner in Columbo, and being able to live out a real-life investigation and testing her own resourcefulness is a positive thrill for her. When the two meet on the pier, Mitchell says, "I'm beginning to be very fond of you, Lieutenant. I think you're a very kind man." Columbo replies, "Don't count on it, Miss Mitchell. Don't count on it." This exchange illustrates how, for Mitchell, this investigation is an amusing challenge, but for Columbo, despite his liking for her personally, the case is part of his job, and he can't stop his search for the truth.

In the last minutes of the episode, Mitchell tries a tactic used by no other killer– pleading for a free pass, asking, "I don't suppose you would consider making an exception in my case," describing herself as "an old woman" who is "generally harmless." Columbo shows slight reluctance, but observes that they're both professionals, and he can't just let her go. She's not upset and concludes the episode with a respectful tribute to his abilities, saying, "If you had investigated my niece's death, all this need never have happened."

Therein lies a deep irony. Had the police been able to prove Phyllis's murder, Mitchell would never have taken the law into her own hands. But they couldn't convict or exonerate Galvin, and no one else could be as sure as Mitchell what really happened. The police can, however, charge her. It shows that if he was guilty—and that's by no means certain—Galvin was actually a more skillful murderer than his aunt-in-law, though, in the end, justice caught up with both of them in very different forms.

Chapter Forty-Two: Murder Under Glass

Paul Gerard (Louis Jourdan)

Paul Gerard is a food critic who charges money for positive reviews. His shoddy ethics don't stop at cash for raves—when Italian restauranteur Vittorio Rossi (Michael V. Gazzo) refuses to keep paying and plans to expose Gerard's dirty dealings to the world, Gerard turns to murder. In order to prevent exposure, Gerard poisons Rossi, though the specific method isn't made immediately apparent.

Columbo arrives at the crime scene ten minutes and fifteen seconds into the episode, sampling the food before he hears the word "poison." The cook at the restaurant starts eating everything in sight to prove his food is safe, but Gerard is quite calm.

As the investigation continues, Columbo learns that there's been a change in location for an upcoming awards dinner and determines that the poison was in the wine, but they can't determine the specific kind of poison that was used. Columbo starts interviewing numerous other restauranteurs, getting plenty of free food along the way, including a Japanese dinner made by Gerard himself, where he learns about fugu, the Japanese seafood delicacy that can poison the eater if it's improperly prepared.

At the climax, Columbo invites Gerard to Rossi's restaurant for a meal he cooked himself. It starts out friendly enough, but Columbo makes it clear he knows how the food review extortion scheme works, and Gerard decides the lieutenant is too dangerous to him to live. He tries to poison Columbo the same he killed Rossi, but Columbo's ready for him. Gerard rigged a corkscrew to inject the fugu poison into the wine. Columbo anticipated the attack, and he switched the glasses. The fugu-laced wine and the corkscrew are enough to convict Gerard, who sullenly expresses his dislike for Columbo at the episode's end.

The relationship between Gerard and Columbo is polite and professional at first, with Gerard calmly answering questions at their first meeting, and when Columbo meets Gerard again at a restaurant, Gerard, at least outwardly, is very cordial and says, "I'm beginning to regard you as an old acquaintance, Lieutenant." It's worth noting that Gerard uses the word "acquaintance" rather than "friend." Columbo uses the tried-and-true tactic of drawing his chief suspect into the investigation, running questions by him, and taking note of the answers. When Columbo explains that a witness confirms that the poisoned bottle of wine wasn't opened until after he left, Gerard disingenuously claims that he didn't realize he was on the list of suspects. It's a bit too precious a claim, as anybody with an average I.Q. would know immediately that being at the scene of the crime would automatically place someone under suspicion. Gerard tries to turn the homicide into an accident, suggesting that the poison in the wine was the result of a farming accident caused by insecticide-tainted grapes. It's not a silly suggestion, but the tests didn't detect any popular insecticides or pesticides, and it's unlikely that only one bottle would have been contaminated rather than dozens. Columbo provides an alternative theory that Gerard was the intended victim, and Gerard embraces it immediately, as it points all suspicion away from him.

This proves to be a vital psychological error. Just the prospect of being the intended victim ought to send Gerard into a panic, demanding police protection until an arrest has been made. But, instead, Gerard can't help but show some delight at the fact that the lieutenant's looking into a scenario that absolves him of all blame, and he's crestfallen when Columbo points out how nonsensical the theory is, rather than being relieved that he doesn't have a target on his back. It's the same basic mistake he made earlier at their first meeting. As Columbo points out, the moment an innocent man learned that he had shared a meal with a man who died of poisoning, he ought to have panicked, demanding a doctor and a stomach pump. Instead, there wasn't a hint of worry, and that was a dead giveaway that Gerard knew he wasn't in danger, a fact he could only have known if he was aware of the source of the poison. Gerard simply didn't realize that he should've acted differently if he was to come across as an innocent man.

Gerard was a corrupt critic, seeking not just money, but power as well, wanting the influence that came with being to shape popularity. As his pleasure in the spotlight at an awards banquet proves, Gerard likes attention and shapes careers for better or worse. When restauranteurs wanted his help to grow their businesses, they put themselves in Gerard's power. When Rossi sought to destroy Gerard's scheme, the balance of power shifted, and it was more than just a threat to Gerard's reputation, but to his ego as well. Gerard was a vain man, believing that his charm could persuade his clearly uneasy assistant to continue with the unethical business, but he didn't give her the full attention necessary to secure the loyalty of a partner in crime. He treated her somewhat disinterestedly, and she eventually realizes his lack of commitment to her and quits in a cathartic manner. From the surprise on his face, it's evidence that he never believed that he could be rejected like that. Columbo recognizes Gerard's pride and tries to puncture it, looking him directly in the eye when he explains that he has a suspect and unnerving him with a public announcement that the killer will be arrested in twenty-four hours, a gambit meant to make Gerard anxious. With the arrogance of a killer who thinks he's too clever to be caught, Gerard is foolish enough to think that he can utilize the same murder method twice and get away with it.

The final conversation between Gerard and Columbo sees Gerard defeated, realizing that he's been captured due to his own attempt to kill Columbo. He's not happy about it, saying, "You're a very able man, Lieutenant. I respect that. But I really don't care for you very much." Columbo isn't visibly offended and responds with the politest possible denigration, saying, "I respect your talent, but I don't like anything else about you."

Gerard gave himself away because of his inability to consider how an innocent man might behave, believing that acting in what he thought was a charming manner was more important than considering the psychology of a man who didn't know what was happening. The final confrontation with Columbo left a sour taste in his mouth, leaving him unable to appreciate fully the final quality meal he would eat before a lifetime of prison food.

Chapter Forty-Three: Make Me a Perfect Murder

Kay Freestone (Trish Van Devere)

The so-called "ratings game" can be lethal, especially when someone believes that murder is her only way to climb the corporate ladder. Kay Freestone is a television producer. Her boyfriend Marc McAndrews (Laurence Luckinbill) also works for the network, and when he gets a promotion to New York, and she doesn't get the job as his replacement, she decides to use a gun to get what she wants.

Freestone's alibi is to pretend she's in the projection room and then to rush from a preview showing of her latest TV movie to McAndrews' office and back between reels. She has a very narrow time window, and she times herself carefully, hurries out of the projection room, tracks down McAndrews and shoots him, hides the murder weapon atop an elevator, and manages to get back just before the end of the reel, deliberately dropping one of the white gloves she used during the shooting upon the floor in order to be rid of it.

Columbo actually appears in the first seconds of the episode, singing in his car, but he doesn't meet Freestone until a little over twenty-four minutes into the episode. He's lying on the sofa, reading a script, recreating the victim's final moments. At first, Freestone's bemused by his antics, but then she's amused by his eccentricities. Columbo rejects the theory that the killing was committed by a bloodthirsty activist against television violence, saying that from the way the victim positioned his reading glasses, he recognized the killer. Freestone tries to push her preferred narrative of the crime, but Columbo doesn't accept it. Their conversation is amicable, but her face clouds as the lieutenant leaves.

Meanwhile, Freestone's taking over McAndrews' job on a trial basis, but things don't go well. She tries to cast an actress with an addiction problem in a live show designed for a family audience, but when the actress proves incapable of performing, Freestone substitutes her dark crime drama in the time slot, leading to a ratings disaster and angry viewers, and her boss blames her and fires her. Now she committed the murder for nothing save revenge, and she can't even claim the luxury car her former lover bought her as a "Dear Jane" present, for fear of exposing their relationship.

Columbo and Freestone have a surprisingly friendly connection. The two have several conversations at Freestone's workplace and at her dilapidated childhood home. After some digging on Columbo's part, he uncovers proof of their affair, and she's forced to admit it. At one point, they ride in an elevator, and she sees that the murder weapon has fallen and is illuminated by the ceiling lights. She retrieves it at the first opportunity, but it's all been a trap. Columbo and his team found the weapon earlier and placed a look-alike gun where its shadow would be seen, and then made sure she saw it.

Columbo goes through the case with her, explaining her taking the gun has been caught on video and that he found a white glove with powder burns on the projection room floor. Freestone's caught, but she notes that contrary to popular belief that caught murderers find peace, she doesn't feel any relief. Though she goes away quietly, she declares her plans to "fight" and "survive," declaring that she "might even win."

Freestone and Columbo have a remarkably affable repartee, as their conversations frequently straddle the boundary between interrogation and friendly conversation. There are no threats or attacks on Freestone's part, and Columbo's final moments aren't flushed with the triumph he feels when he brings down a particularly abhorrent killer. Certainly, Freestone is charmed by Columbo's mannerisms and demeanor, but some of this may be built on relief because her actions indicate that she doesn't consider the lieutenant to be a serious threat to her. She isn't the first killer to underestimate Columbo, of course. For his part, Columbo shows her respect by listening to her arguments for why the killer might have been a radical protesting the content of television programming, though he skillfully points out the flaws in her observations.

While their initial conversation at the office is fairly standard by *Columbo* standards, a later interaction takes an unusual turn. Columbo meets Freestone at a dilapidated house and soon learns it's where she was raised. The location gives her a chance to show him how far she's come, and Columbo shares details of his own upbringing with five brothers and one sister. It's a bonding moment, as Columbo displays a genuine love for his family, a trait that Freestone appreciates. At one point, Freestone starts rubbing Columbo's shoulders, ostensibly to help him relax. This rather intimate and unasked-for touching comes across as a bit of flirting, based not on physical attraction, but as an attempt to convince Columbo to stop pursuing her as a suspect. Columbo is having none of this, and he politely yet bluntly asks her if she'd have gotten the job if the victim hadn't been murdered. This causes her to stop massaging him immediately, and her tone cools as she smokes and asks him if he thinks she killed McAndrews. Columbo demurs by saying she has an alibi and notes that she's not the sort of person who would commit murder simply to gain a job. It's a telling observation, as through his ability to read people, Columbo realizes that Freestone's murder had to feature a personal aspect beyond mere gain.

At one point in their conversation, she declares, "You're a very special man, Lieutenant. You accept things as they are. I try to change them." That's an important point driving her character. Freestone wants everything to suit her desires and goals, from her career trajectory to the behavior of the performers working on her projects. When her career stalled, she was willing to commit murder in order to get it back on her preferred track. When an actress's addictions made her nearly unemployable, Freestone tried to keep her sober and offered her an incredible opportunity.

Freestone's compassion for the actress Valerie Kirk (Lainie Kazan), who suffers from substance abuse problems, illustrates a softer side of her character. Even though her colleagues believe that Kirk cannot be counted on to perform in a live television show, Freestone believes in Kirk, thinking that she can help her conquer her addiction and give a great performance. But why is this? What is it about Kirk that makes Freestone bet her career on the actress, a bet she loses? This is total conjecture, but based upon some oblique hints at her broken-down former home, it's possible that during her youth, someone she loved might have had a problem with addiction. An addiction might have been part of the reason for the poverty of her early years, and it might explain her attempts to protect Kirk. Freestone might have conflated her loved one with Kirk, causing her to obsess over saving the actress as a substitute for a family member that she couldn't rescue from the crushing grip of addiction. To reiterate, this is a theory based on vague clues, but it explains why she would go through so much trouble for Kirk.

Indeed, Freestone's obsession with rescuing Kirk's career is one of the reasons why she doesn't get the job she desires. Most executives would have avoided Kirk as an unacceptable risk, but at the very least, Freestone ought to have been prudent enough to train an understudy in her place. Her male colleagues, including her victim, accuse her of being excessively emotional and relying too much on instinct instead of sound business decisions. Is this fair? Or is it sexism? Certainly, there may be a substantial amount of misogyny at play here. McAndrews was an unquestionable heel towards her, giving her an expensive car as a "going-away" present rather than a job, which had the effect of treating her like a prostitute. McAndrews was definitely a cad in the way he handled his breakup, though with Freestone's obsession with the job, she may have been with him primarily to advance her career, and McAndrews might have realized her central motivation for their affair and despised her for it, though not enough to stop sleeping with her. McAndrews was using Freestone for sex, but she was also using him to climb the corporate ladder. The emotional component that led Freestone to kill him may not have been spurned love, but rather wounded pride based upon his callous words towards her.

The other man at the network who hurts her career is her boss. When he fires her for the Kirk debacle, one might argue that he would have been more understanding towards a man, but at the same time, she cost the network a lot of money with the jettisoned live show and the poorly timed TV movie, so strictly as a matter of dollars and cents, her firing is justified. It's also possible that her boss is aware of Columbo's investigation and is letting her go due to suspected complicity in the crimes.

Freestone was an intelligent woman who made poor decisions at times. She certainly had talent as a television executive, as evidenced by her many awards, and she also had dedication and passion for her craft. However, her style of management caused her to make impulsive or poorly thought-out choices at times, which backfired badly in her career. Little mistakes, such as her thoughtless disposal of a gunpowder-stained glove, were easily avoidable, but she lacked the focus to notice and fix her mistakes. She was not a wholly evil person, as she had copious amounts of empathy, but she also had large reserves of vengefulness, which proved central to her downfall. What harmed her as a television executive and a killer was the fact that she could become so focused on her goals that she became blinded to some of the problems and details that could prevent her achievement of them, and she often acted as if her mere belief in her eventual success would actually translate to victory, triumphing purely through luck and positive thinking rather than taking the care and scrupulousness necessary to achieve the desired result. She planned her crime according to a rigid schedule, but mentally glossing over some aspects of her scheme blinded her to her plot's shortcomings.

Kay Freestone optimistically thought she might wind up winning in court, but given the strength of the case against her, it's highly unlikely that she enjoyed a Hollywood ending.

Chapter Forty-Four: How to Dial a Murder

Eric Mason (Nichol Williamson)

Eric Mason is a behavioral psychologist and motivational speaker with a taste for manipulating not just people, but animals as well. Mason's first murder took place long before the episode opens when he realized that his wife was having an affair with Dr. Charles Hunter (Joel Fabiani). Furious and desiring revenge, Mason arranged for his wife to have a fatal car crash and is now planning an even gorier death for Hunter. The bad doctor pretends not to know about the affair and treats Hunter like his dearest friend. Mason, a classic film fan and collector of movie props, trains a pair of Doberman Pinchers named Laurel and Hardy to rush into the house when they hear a phone ring and rip a target to shreds after hearing the code word "Rosebud."

Mason invites Hunter to his home while he's crafting an alibi at the hospital, having his heart checked with an electrocardiogram. When he's alone in the room, he phones Hunter and asks him the name of the sled in *Citizen Kane*. After the unsuspicious Hunter says the word Laurel and Hardy attack, Mason celebrates at the hospital.

Columbo arrives ten and three-quarter minutes into the episode, happily playing with Laurel and Hardy. They appear to be sweet-natured dogs, and he's upset at the prospect of them being put down for killing a human.

Columbo suspects something's amiss, as the dial tone on the disconnected telephone indicates that someone had called Hunter at the time of the attack. So why didn't the person on the other end call the police?

Columbo has dual challenges with this investigation. Not only does he have to prove Mason's involvement in the crime, but he also has to demonstrate that the dogs were not responsible for their actions. He soon realizes that the two goals are connected. As a dog trainer (Tricia O'Neil) informs him, if he can identify the code word that was used to weaponize the Dobermans, she can retrain the dogs and prevent them from being euthanized.

Through a mixture of perseverance and luck, Columbo stumbles across "Rosebud," and the dog trainer is able to reprogram Laurel and Hardy. Soon afterwards, Columbo demonstrates that he knows exactly how the crime was committed, having found the dummy used to train the dogs and the electrocardiogram results demonstrating Mason's elevated heart rate at the time of the crime. In an attempt to silence the lieutenant, Mason calls out "Rosebud" to get them to attack Columbo. Fortunately for the detective, the retrained dogs pounce on him in the friendliest manner possible, but the attack attempt is enough proof for an arrest. Beaten, Mason quietly admits that Columbo has done a very strong job with his investigation, and Columbo declares, "I just enjoy the pleasure of the game."

This isn't the friendliest or most complex of the Columbo-killer relationships. Mason falls into the mold of killers who like to assert their own intellectual dominance. While traditionally murderers begin by treating the lieutenant in a friendly manner and grow more hostile with time, Mason begins by acting cold and superior towards Columbo, although later he becomes not exactly friendly, but more willing to spend time talking with Columbo. Possibly, he views his conversations as a necessary form of reconnaissance, vital to figuring out how far the lieutenant has come in his investigation. Mason does tell the lieutenant that he recognizes the sharpness behind his seeming amiability, saying, "You're a fascinating man... [you] pass yourself off as a puppy in a raincoat...[but you're] laying a minefield." Initially, Mason falls into the standard trope of expecting

Columbo to accept his preferred narrative without further inquiry, testily asking, "It's not that I haven't been impressed with your company, but what is there to settle?" Mason seems genuinely stunned to learn that there are some dangling threads that a conscientious investigator is compelled to tie up before closing the case.

Later, the two play a psychological word association game in front of the fire, with Columbo freely admitting that "murder" is the word that drives his life. First, Mason offers Columbo words, asking for the first word to pop intoColumbo's head. After the round, the doctor concludes that Columbo had a happy and normal childhood. The words Columbo chooses to ask Mason are meant to reveal hints about the murder and the code word, and it's indicated that Mason is shaping his responses so as not to reveal anything incriminating, especially in his final response, when he makes it known that he's seen the word association game as a trap the whole time. From his comments to Columbo and other characters, Mason is happiest when he's in total control of the situation, but he can't always be assured of his own power.

As usual, Columbo relishes the chance to show his true cleverness to the killer. Part of this may be due to his fondness for dogs, and he's especially motivated to save the lives of two canines he believes are mere pawns in a twisted man's game. The climax is centered around a pool table belonging to W.C. Fields, and there's a sense that Columbo is getting a kick out of playing with a piece of classic Hollywood memorabilia. As they play, Columbo reveals the various clues with a touch of showmanship, revealing one clue after another in the pockets of the pool table. Which each clue, Columbo points out how foolish it was to leave this evidence around, such as scraps of fabric from the dummy where the dogs were initially trained to kill, the electrocardiogram report showing his elevated heart rate, and a photograph of Mason's victims posed romantically, an item that Mason really should have taken from Hunter's desk and destroyed as soon as he knew Hunter wouldn't miss it. Knowing that the only way to prove Mason's guilt is to prove that he knows the code word that makes the dog attack, Columbo baits him, trying to not-to-blatantly provoke Mason into trying to murder him with Laurel and Hardy. It works, and it shows just how easy it is for Mason to be manipulated, which is ironic due to Mason's self-confidence in his own knowledge of how to control the minds of other people, as well as dogs.

What makes Mason a particularly unsettling villain is just how macabre a murder method he chooses. With the possible exception of bombs and setting fire to cars, no other means of dispatching victims in the series are as gruesome as being mauled by dogs. It demonstrates an extreme level of sadism, a desire to not simply kill a man, but to fill his final moments with indescribable terror and pain.

Mason was also prepared to sacrifice the lives of two dogs who were guilty of nothing other than being abusively trained to be killers. When he tries to kill Columbo, Mason should be aware that if he kills Columbo with the dogs, not only would it be very suspicious, but it would also ruin his valuable pool table. It's not a well-thought-out plan, but it seems as if Mason's desire to actually see death by the canine in front of him outweighs prudence.

Mason was clearly an intelligent man, as he was well-educated and successful in his career. So why, as Columbo observed, did he commit such a clumsy murder? The murder of his wife was more skillful– the lieutenant admits he can't prove that crime. But Columbo correctly remarks that "you left enough clues to sink a ship," and these mistakes were coupled with "stupid lies." Of all the *Columbo* killers, Mason leaves more incriminating evidence around than almost anyone else. It's almost as if, subconsciously, Mason wanted to be caught. Perhaps Mason felt incredible guilt over the death of his wife, but couldn't express it knowingly, so his unconscious led him to make mistakes that would lead to his own downfall.

Chapter Forty-Five: The Conspirators

Joe Devlin (Clive Revill)

In "The Conspirators," *Columbo* takes on a case with a strong political angle, as the murder is connected to "The Troubles." Joe Devlin is an Irish poet and musician and the author of the book *Up from Ignorance*. He presents himself as a man of peace, having abandoned the radicalism of his teenage years, and is now fundraising for the victims of political violence in Northern Ireland. The reality is quite different. He's funneling money to arms dealers to promote the cause of Irish reunification through force, though most of his donors don't know about his true goals.

Devlin visits the arms dealer Vincent Pauley (Albert Paulsen), who asks for a lot more money and time before giving him the guns he wants. After a quick investigation shows that Pauley means to abscond with the cash, Devlin proves that he's not as nonviolent as his public persona claims and shoots Pauley. Devlin, who had recently been drinking his favorite whiskey with Pauley, kicks the bottle over to the body.

Columbo appears nearly twenty and a half minutes into the episode, playing a pinball machine and commenting on 'the way I keep steering and pushing and pulling at things," which is not just a description of the game, but a metaphor for his investigative style as well. Columbo declares that he and Mrs. Columbo recently caught Devlin's one-man show. With this, Columbo begins one of the more amiable interactions with a killer in his career, as the pair play pinball together, though internally, Devlin starts some powerful self-recriminations when Columbo reveals that he's discovered an autographed copy of Devlin's book amongst the deceased's possessions, along with the political slogan "Ourselves Alone." Devlin claims the book must been signed during a busy public gathering and that the political message was added by Pauley later. The discomfort is obvious in Devlin's demeanor, and Columbo picks up on it.

Over the course of the investigation, Columbo and Devlin play darts together, swap limericks, and even drink whiskey together. A barmaid, knowing that Devlin's a regular, brings him his favorite "Irish Dew" whiskey, despite his clumsy attempts to wave her away. It's too late, and Columbo recognizes the bottle as the same kind as the one found at the crime scene. Just as he did while drinking with his victim, Devlin scratches a little mark on the whiskey bottle, declaring "this far and no further," noting ahead of time how much he'll drink on a given night.

Columbo meets the O'Connells (Jeanette Nolan and Bernard Behrens), a prosperous and seemingly respectable mother-and-son duo who are behind the fundraising and gunrunning. The lieutenant also figures out that a note stating "LAP 213" refers to Pier 213 at Los Angeles Harbor and searches an Ireland-bound boat for weapons but finds nothing. Just in time, Columbo realizes that the weapons are actually on the tugboat guiding the larger ship and prevents the weapons from crossing the Atlantic.

Next, Columbo has a final meeting with Devlin and explains that every diamond is cut slightly differently, so when Devlin scratched the bottle found at the crime scene to limit his drinking, it left a distinct pattern on the glass that can be traced back to him. Realizing that his unique drinking habits have incriminated him, Devlin says he has "no regrets," even when Columbo confronts him on his own hypocrisy in raising money for war while claiming to be a man of peace, and the two have one last drink together.

The remarkably civil final moments are reflective of the general tone of the detective/killer relationship in this episode. Other than his slightly terse response after the almost obligatory "one more thing," there's usually a smile on Devlin's face and a humorous twinkle in his eye. While most murderers turn hostile towards Columbo when he catches them in a lie or a contradiction, Devlin is one of the few to vent any frustration towards himself, waiting until he's alone to self-recriminate with an emotional "you bloody fool!" once he realizes the autographed book leads back to him. Devlin has carefully created a laid-back persona, but this casualness extends into his murder plans. Had he put a little more care and thought into his crime, he would have remembered to take away not just the book, but the scratched bottle as well. Even if he hadn't been aware of the fact that the scratches could be traced back to the gemstone on his ring, he ought to have considered that his signature drinking habit of marking bottles would have linked him to the crime scene, though he could have argued that the bottle had been taken from somewhere else and left as a frame-up. Devlin's a man who overlooks critical details simply because he doesn't bother to focus on them. He's a storyteller, but he never gained the knack of scrutinizing his narratives for plot holes.

But Columbo has based his career on picking up on the minute points that most people miss, and he also knows how to interact with people to get the information he needs. At one point, Devlin references an early interaction with a policeman challenging him, using his authority as a weapon and relying on intimidation. Columbo's approach is very different, as his style is to attempt to befriend his chief suspect, calling him "a creative person" and flattering his intelligence. For his part, Devlin actively courts Columbo's company by inviting him to lunch, though his motives certainly aren't social. He's insinuating himself into the investigation to find out more about how much the lieutenant has uncovered. He doesn't anticipate that Columbo will wind up finding out much more about him and what kind of man he is.

Much of what shaped Devlin's psyche is open to speculation. Unlike most murderers, who are concerned with purely selfish motives, Devlin has devoted his life to the political cause of Northern Ireland. This chapter will not delve into the complex history of The Troubles, because the focus of this study is based upon a fictional character's psyche. Many people have gotten involved in activism regarding this particularly thorny and long-lasting conflict over the decades, but there is a sharp moral difference between violent and non-violent means of promoting societal and political change. When this episode was filmed in the 1970s, the conflict was exceptionally turbulent, and a young man who had grown up during earlier decades would have been exposed to a volatile situation filled with passionate opinions, and a youth filled with idealism would have been particularly susceptible to a political movement that offered him a chance to make a difference. Devlin was arrested for carrying dynamite when he was fourteen, so it's known that from early adolescence, he was prepared to do serious damage to property and potentially harm other people and even himself. It's not certain how he concluded that violence was the best way to achieve his goals, but this approach became the driving force of his life.

While these reasons for embracing violence are not fully known, his reasons for publicly presenting himself as a nonviolent activist seem to be pragmatic in nature. Most people will be far happier to donate money to a man who eschews bloodshed, and in any case, professing peacefulness is the only way to raise money legally. Taking the stance he does may allow him to raise the cash he needs, but it adds a dark layer of hypocrisy to his actions, and it should be noted that once his true actions become public knowledge, potential donors will become far more suspicious of legitimately nonviolent protesters in the future, and worthy causes might miss out on donations due to this. Why didn't Devlin decide that the best way he could help the people of Northern Ireland would be to actually embrace nonviolent means? It will never be known for sure, but based on his attitudes throughout the episode, Devlin had a deep-seated sense of anger connected to his political goals, and he did not know how to relieve that fury except through violent means.

Columbo notes that the killer must have had a sense of humor due to his leaving the whiskey bottle with the slogan "let each man be paid in full" behind as a final comment justifying the murder. Joe Devlin did not have to become a murderer. With his charm and people skills, he could have genuinely become the force for peace and reconciliation he professed to be. However, he made a choice to pursue violence, and he was willing to sacrifice not just Pauley's life for his goals, but the lives of everybody who would fall victim to the guns he was running as well. Devlin did not practice what he preached, and as a result, he not only threw away his own life, but harmed the reputation of his cause, as well.

VIII

SEASON EIGHT

Chapter Forty-Six: Columbo Goes to the Guillotine

Elliott Blake (Anthony Andrews)

Following a hiatus lasting over a decade, *Columbo* returned to television in 1989. Most of the episodes were a bit longer than the average previous entries, lasting around a hundred minutes each, but Columbo was still Columbo, and the murderers were still certain they could charm and outsmart the lieutenant (one would have thought Columbo would have received a well-deserved promotion by this point, but apparently his bosses weren't in a hurry to reward a career full of jobs well done).

Columbo Goes to the Guillotine opens with Elliott Blake, a self-proclaimed psychic, attempting to dazzle the government with his prowess in the hopes that he'll be hired to do some consulting work for them. Max Dyson (Anthony Zerbe) is a professional magician who, like Houdini before him, sidelines in debunking those who fraudulently claim to have supernatural powers. The government has asked Dyson to run one final test for them, and some government operatives are each given books of maps, told to pick a page randomly, and without looking, draw a spot on the map with a marker. After driving to the location they picked, they are supposed to take a photograph of their location. From a considerable distance away, Blake manages to duplicate the locations in a series of sketches, and the government accepts that Blake has psychic powers.

But there's more to Blake and Dyson's relationship than previously thought. Dyson was once a magical mentor to Blake, and the pair somehow wound up in an African prison together. Despite a mutual escape plan, Dyson betrayed Blake and left him stewing in jail until Blake managed to get released years later. Dyson rigged the test as a means of making amends, but Blake is not in a forgiving mood. Blake visits Dyson at his loft filled with magic tricks and illusion equipment, and points a gun at Dyson, though he unloads it after a bit of conversation, seemingly forgiving Dyson. However, when Dyson is tinkering with a guillotine set, Blake throws the switch and decapitates Dyson.

Columbo is called in to investigate about twenty-five and a half minutes into the episode, uncovering the grisly scene. The lieutenant acts excited around a "real" psychic, and Blake tries to impress him by guessing the shapes of some ESP cards Columbo selects. After the funeral (attended by many practitioners of the magical arts), Columbo requests that Blake join him at the crime scene to see if he can "sense" anything connected to the crime. Blake makes a grand show of picking up psychic vibrations around the murder scene, claiming to sense suicidal thoughts. As he strolls around the room, he surreptitiously retrieves a cartridge he left behind earlier when he unloaded his gun. At the end of the performance, Columbo expresses his appreciation, but declares it couldn't have been a suicide, as Dyson bought a lot of corned beef and cabbage right before he died, and a suicidal man wouldn't have done that and left it uneaten. Not only that, but due to the type of screwdriver found by the dead man's hand (the planted tool didn't match the screws, as Blake didn't consider the difference between flathead and Phillips when he tried to make it look like Dyson was tinkering with the guillotine), it's unlikely to be an accident, either. That just leaves murder.

Right before Blake flies off to his new job as a government consultant, Columbo produces a court order to bring him back. Columbo already illustrated he knows how Blake worked the ESP card shape trick (he saw the movement of Columbo's pencil), and now, with the help of a kid with an interest in illusions, Columbo repeats the map vision demonstration. All the pages in the map book were the same, and there was no ink in the marker. Every map was marked in the same spot, and so the agents all drove to predetermined places to see predetermined sites, which Blake already knew so he could draw them while feigning mental strain. Disgusted, the government agents realize Blake is a fraud.

Columbo invites Blake back to the murder scene, walking him through how he figured out he was guilty, telling Blake he knew he picked up the cartridge and pointing out other little mistakes Blake made. Finally, Columbo lies down on the guillotine, asking him to throw the switch as a demonstration. The guillotine is marked with two different labels, and one switch will send down a harmless trick blade, while the other sends down a razor-sharp instrument of death. A quietly furious Blake tries to decapitate Columbo, but Columbo makes a very big gamble in his estimation of his suspect and switches the labels. Using what he thought was the "kill" blade proves Blake's homicidal tendencies. As he makes the arrest, Columbo pulls the trigger of a gun for the first time in the series, but it's a trick pistol, releasing only a little flag with the word "BANG" on it. It's Columbo's little joke in retaliation against one of a very small number of murderers who have tried to kill him.

There are only five other *Columbo* murders who try to kill the lieutenant (or at least seriously consider it), and that's an arguable number as two of those five only consider shooting him in a fleeting moment, only to be dissuaded almost instantaneously by the lieutenant's words or the circumstances. How did Columbo and Blake get to that point? When the vast majority of killers end the episode on friendly or at least respectful terms with Columbo, what caused so much rancor in their relationship that Blake decided to attack the lieutenant? The two of them began their acquaintance on relatively amicable terms. Columbo played up his "clueless" persona, which both amused and disarmed Blake. When Blake identifies Columbo by name before the sleuth can introduce himself, a surprised Columbo declares that Blake "knew who I was right away! That's incredible!" Forcing himself to swallow his contempt for a man he believes is so easily fooled and hiding his delight that such a gullible man is in charge of the investigation, Blake gently points out that "Your ID badge helped." Columbo plays the part of a curious fan, subtly playing to Blake's vanity while keeping Blake's opinion of him unjustly low. When Columbo asks if Blake can read his mind, and Blake successfully pulls off the ESP card trick, Columbo has set the false power dynamic between them. Blake is convinced that Columbo is a man who is easily amused and fooled, though the truth about who the true psychological manipulator is and who the patsy is remains obscured to the ersatz psychic until the end of the episode. By the end of the conversation, Blake permits himself an additional pat on the back by suggesting he could be better at Columbo's job rather than Columbo himself, not-so-modestly declaring that with his mind-reading ability, "I could make some wonderful detective."

As the episode progresses, Columbo gradually makes it clear that he knows that Blake possesses no more power to see into the future than a Magic 8 Ball. Blake couldn't resist the opportunity to play up his abilities when he pretended to read the room for psychic vibrations and wound up failing in both his attempts to promote both suicide and accident. (He might have regained a bit of face if he'd thought to say that Dyson had fallen victim to a killer with a tendency to self-harm, who possibly killed by accident, and that he'd picked up those emotions.) As it stands, Blake has to admit that he's picked up the "wrong vibrations," admitting to failure with as much dignity as possible.

But, the hits Columbo delivers on Blake continue over the final half-hour of the episode, as he shows how Blake's seemingly dazzling feats of ESP were simply tricks. Columbo's pulling back the curtain and exposing the humbug who proclaimed he had powers he didn't actually possess stripped Blake of his public persona, and with the collapse of his deal with the government, Blake could be reduced to performing at children's birthday parties to make ends meet. Many *Columbo* killers would still have their lucrative professions if they escaped the reach of the law, but Blake's reputation is in tatters after Columbo's investigation. To be fair to Columbo, Blake was a fraud who sought to profit from the injudicious use of taxpayer money. All Columbo did was alert the government to Blake's swindle. By the end, Blake has nothing to lose except his freedom, and due to his petty desire to avenge a perceived injury, he loses even that.

Blake destroyed himself due to his desire for revenge. He had everything he wanted– thanks to Dyson, he had a lucrative opportunity to work with the government, pretending to use his powers to help the country. All he had to do was walk away and profit. Instead, he chose to vent his wrath, and it wound up costing him everything. Perhaps there was more to it than that. Blake might have theorized that in the future, Dyson could have blackmailed him, though this is not entirely likely, as Dyson could have destroyed his own reputation and possibly faced repercussions from the government as well with such revelations.

Blake considered himself a skilled deceiver, as his career depended on being able to make people believe he had powers he didn't actually possess. But one can't fool all of the people all of the time, and when Columbo showed that he knew that Blake was nothing more than a particularly smooth illusionist, Blake's pride was wounded. He loved fooling people, reveling in being able to deceive otherwise intelligent individuals. Having a disheveled policeman see right through him, treating his deceptions as cheap parlor tricks, was a painful blow to his ego. After Columbo walked through his assessment of the crime, Blake knew that the lieutenant didn't have enough evidence for an arrest. But he was so angry at Columbo for ruining his shot at a consultancy that he lost all sense of proportion and tried to kill Columbo. Rather than walking away with a blemished career but also his freedom, Blake gave into a violent impulse just as he had earlier, thereby writing his own ticket to prison.

Chapter Forty-Seven: Murder, Smoke and Shadows

Alex Brady (Fisher Stevens)

Alex Brady is a big-budget director with a God complex. With multiple hits on his résumé despite his youth, Brady is not only obsessed with making brilliant movies, but he's also addicted to manipulating the people around him, not just to add authenticity to his films, but for the thrill of pushing human beings around like pawns on a chessboard. Arrogant as well as controlling, Brady may have developed difficulties telling the difference between fantasy and reality, and when he thinks that he can remove a person from the world as easily as he could delete a scene from a film, it leads him to a terrible fall from grace.

Brady is in the process of making another movie, and he's so confident in his position as a director that he believes that he can brush aside the studio executive Mr. Marosco's (Steven Hill) request for him to rush production on his movie for an Easter release. Brady spends much of his off time in his office, filled with the kinds of entertainments and luxuries with which an adolescent boy dreams of surrounding himself, ranging from an ice cream soda fountain to toy trains to a waterbed. The young director's comfort is shattered, however, when his old pal Leonard Fisher (Jeff Perry) stops by with revenge in his heart. For years, Fisher has believed that his beloved sister Jenny was killed in a run-of-the-mill vehicle accident, but with the death of their mutual friend Buddy, Fisher's come into some information that changes his previous beliefs. Buddy kept an incriminating outtake from an amateur film Brady made as a teenager, and it reveals that Jenny was actually killed in a stunt gone wrong. Brady covered up the true circumstances of Jenny's death, and now Fisher wants to turn Brady into the authorities.

If only Fisher had watched more crime television shows like *Columbo*, he would know that when a person you plan to send to jail begs you to wait for a few hours so he can prove his innocence, that person is plotting your murder. Brady's claim that the footage has been faked is pure nonsense, but Fisher unwisely waits in Brady's office while Brady plans a very cinematic death for his friend. After it gets dark, Brady lures Fisher to an alleyway in the studio, having previously arranged for the machine that sprays water upon the pavement (wet roads glisten and are more visually appealing on-screen during nighttime shoots) to arrive. Fisher is forced towards a fence that Brady has electrified, and with high voltage rushing through his body and water at his feet, Brady's fatally electrocuted. Offscreen, Brady then disfigures his dead friend's face and removes all the identification he can on the body. The corpse is left on a beach in the hopes that the authorities will write it off as the result of a random lightning strike.

Just over twenty-two minutes into the episode, Brady walks in on Columbo in his office, playing with Brady's toy trains. When the detective introduces himself, Brady knows that something has gone wrong, for if his plans had proceeded as hoped, the police would never have made any connection between him and the electrocuted John Doe on the beach. Brady immediately launches into a completely insincere charm offensive, declaring, "How did you know? You are the answer to a filmmaker's prayers." Many people, even those who don't work anywhere close to the entertainment industry, harbor secret dreams of getting a big break in the movies after some powerful person sees them and wants to put them in their production. The possibility of appearing in a major movie might make some detectives reluctant to investigate the director, but Columbo isn't fazed, though he does declare, "That is as fine a greeting as I've ever received."

Columbo explains that a copy of the book *The Films of Alex Brady* was found near the body, and there were some phone numbers written inside that led him to Brady. Columbo also observes a pair of unfinished ice cream sodas off to one side that Brady had prepared for himself and Fisher before Fisher dropped his bombshell. Noting how full they are, Columbo deduces that two people were there, and something made them too upset to consume the ice cream sodas—possibly an argument. Brady admits Columbo's right without providing details, and as soon as the detective leaves, he angrily throws the glasses in the sink, upset at himself for not cleaning them up and furious at Columbo for seeing through him.

When Columbo next sees Brady, his arrival interrupts a big kiss between the director and his actress girlfriend, Ruth Jernigan (Molly Hagan). The Lieutenant informs him there was a traveler's cheque tucked away in a money belt, helping him identify the body. This is an example of Brady's propensity to get so involved in the broader narrative he's trying to create that he overlooks little details that destroy his intended illusion. Brady forgets that his best work is behind the camera and falls into the common mistake amongst *Columbo* murderers of overplaying his grief and distress. Perhaps Columbo sees right through this, for though he doesn't say anything to call Brady out, he offers minimal sympathy and asks if he can make himself an ice cream soda.

It's likely that Brady senses that Columbo suspects him, because he no longer tries to sway the detective with dreams of Tinseltown fame. When Columbo arrives at the studio, viewers are delighted and relieved to see that even after a decade since the first run of the show ended, Dog is still alive! As Columbo wanders onto a live set, Brady decides to discombobulate him to avoid the questions, so Brady tells Columbo to sit on a seat on a rising director's crane and proceeds to spin the seats around, leaving Columbo so dizzy he can't investigate. It's a power play that other murderers have used in the past, and as always, it's only temporarily effective.

Columbo returns and finds his way onto another film set featuring a rapidly changing projected background. As Brady changes the display from a desert to a *Star Wars*-esque shot of a ship, a bit of megalomania seeps through as he marvels over the control moviemaking allows him. Tipsy with his creative power, he declares, "You've left the world of your own reality" and entered mine. You lost your substance. What's real?... I'm the substance, and you're the shadow. I created you, and I can destroy you." This is a real hint that Brady may not be very tightly tethered to reality. Brady's egomania, such as in his refusal to show respect to the studio executive who bankrolls his creative projects, is more than just a lack of humility. It's a lack of ability to recognize the fact that he can't direct the world around him like he can a film.

This moment marks a watershed moment for Brady, as from this point onwards, his personal and professional lives enter a downward spiral. Columbo has observed the damage done to the victim's shoes, including a blown-off heel found by the gate, so he knows how the electrocution was committed. Brady's worried about the progress the lieutenant's investigation will make, but he's not panicking just yet.

Later, when Brady is enjoying a private moment with Jernigan, she reveals her concerns over a previous incident that led to their earlier breakup. Brady was directing her, and she began an affair with her co-star. Upon reflection, she now realizes that Brady cared so little about their relationship that he subtly placed the two actors in such a way that they would become intimate in real life, leading to more convincing love scenes on-screen. As she breaks up with him for good, Jernigan rages at him, calling him "Alex the director...the master manipulator." Jernigan understandably feels used and disrespected and knows that she could never mean as much to Brady as one of his movies. Still, Brady didn't put a gun to her head and force her to sleep with her co-star. He merely led her into temptation, and part of her anger may come from her own self-recriminations over being unfaithful.

When Columbo shows up soon afterwards, Brady explodes with an angry greeting, and Columbo points out he's found some cab drivers who can prove that the victim visited Brady at his office, giving the lie to Brady's claim he never saw him. This leads Brady to plan a clumsy gambit. During

Columbo's lunch at the studio commissary, he overhears two extras, a bridesmaid and a nurse, talking about narcotics use on the sets and implying that Fisher was involved in the drug trade, and that's why he was killed. Before Columbo can question the pair, the two slip away, and Columbo is blocked from following them by a security guard who doesn't believe he's a detective. Columbo informs Brady that he's leaving the studio to concentrate on the new narcotics lead, and the line "A real detective doesn't belong in the movies" brings a triumphant smile to Brady's face as Columbo drives away.

But Brady's luck is fading fast. His attempt to fire his secretary, an older woman named Rose Walker (Nan Martin) who disapproves of him, backfires when she reveals at lunch she knows the truth, so he changes tactics and bribes her with a trip around the world. Soon afterwards, Marosco tells Brady he's pulling funding on the movie and taking steps to scuttle Brady's career, as he's very upset at how Brady disrespected him. This certainly sounds like a business decision based on vengeance rather than cold economics, as a lot of money has clearly gone into the movie. Though it isn't spelled out, it makes more sense to presume that Columbo has told Marosco his suspicions and asked the studio head to hit Brady with this devastating news, suggesting that some other director could be hired to salvage the investment.

Brady wanders into an indoor set, grappling with the realization that he may have lost the creative outlet that has given his life purpose. Columbo appears, putting up a retrieved copy of the film of the death of Jenny Fisher. He goes through the evidence, including Fisher's ticket used as a bookmark in Brady's office and the damaged shoes. Columbo wasn't fooled for long by the two extras who so conveniently sat next to him and talked about narcotics being the motive for the murder, noting that there was no reason for a nurse and a bridesmaid to be there when a little investigation revealed that no wedding or hospital scenes were being filmed that day. The extras and the security guard were all part of a ploy to distract Columbo. Brady responds with characteristic hubris, asking, "Do you really think some underpaid policeman is going to arrest me with all of that circumstantial claptrap?"

Columbo pulls his trump card, revealing that Brady's secretary has been very helpful to the investigation all along and will testify that Brady tried to bribe her with a round-the-world trip. Brady's declaration that it's her word against his, but Columbo reveals that the busboy and waitress were actually detectives, and Jernigan has gotten her revenge by disguising herself as a cocktail waitress and becoming a witness to the bribery as well. Each witness is introduced with a drumroll and a spotlight, and in the face of this mounting evidence against him, Brady doesn't confess, but he does hallucinate that Columbo is wearing a ringmaster's costume.

Columbo ends the episode with a parting shot, saying, "The only thing that's given me any pleasure in this case has been charging you with murder, and I must say, that's been a very great pleasure, sir." This may not be entirely true, as surely the ice cream soda gave him pleasure. In any case, if Columbo is the ringmaster in Brady's fantasy, then though it isn't shown, Brady is very likely the clown. A very sad clown.

The final comments illustrate how Columbo and Brady have failed to form any sort of amicable relationship. While most killers develop a measure of genuine respect for Columbo, Brady never sees him as anything more than a lesser being to be manipulated, condescended to, and patronized. As for Columbo, he doesn't even seem to have much respect for Brady as a director. He passes on the patter he gives most celebrities, failing to rave about how much he and Mrs. Columbo loves Brady's movies. The two of them never bond or share any genuine moments, and Brady is particularly frustrated by Columbo's refusal to go down the paths set for him. Columbo was a particularly vexing problem for Brady. The lieutenant simply wouldn't take direction.

The final scene is ambiguous. Has Brady descended into madness? Has the shock of losing his movie and his career caused a psychotic break? It's unclear, but it makes one wonder after one ponders the legal definition of insanity, and that is the inability to tell the difference between right and wrong. This adds a new twist to Brady's "smoke and shadows" speeches, as he meditated on what was real and what was just a moviemaking illusion. If

Brady believes that moviemaking blurs the line between reality and fantasy, and he has repeatedly demonstrated his problems treating actual human beings differently from characters in his films, it's quite possible that he really is delusional, though this does not necessarily mean that he is not legally responsible for his actions.

What is certain is that Brady had an oversized ego and an undersized conscience. His great passion in life was making movies, but it became insufficient merely to control fictional worlds. He had to control the real world as well. Had the tape of the accident been released to the authorities, it's even doubtful if Brady would have suffered serious legal repercussions, as the death was indeed an accident, and as negligence was unlikely to be proven, he might have faced only minor legal consequences for altering the scene of an accident. As he was a teenager at the time, the public and Hollywood might even have forgiven him, and his career might not have suffered, though this best-case scenario would not have been guaranteed. Such a revelation, however, was more than just a reminder that he once had acted as a foolish and frightened adolescent. The film of the fatal accident was a case of cold, shocking reality imposing its way into Brady's world of make-believe. Brady could create all sorts of illusions on-screen, but real life proved more powerful than any fiction he could create, and he could not bring a dead girl back to life. When he murdered Fisher, he thought that he could direct a safe and respectable future for himself, but thanks to Columbo, Brady's last project was a flop.

Chapter Forty-Eight: Sex and the Married Detective

Dr. Joan Allenby (Lindsay Crouse)

Most of the episodes of the eighth season of *Columbo* feature the recurring theme of illusion and deception. In the previous episodes, a fake psychic and a director tried to use their abilities to persuade and dupe in order to get away with murder. In "Sex and the Married Detective," Dr. Joan Allenby loses her idealized self-image, and she embraces a fantasy persona that becomes everything she hadn't realized she wanted to be. Unfortunately for her and her unfaithful lover, her journey into fantasy involves a very real murder.

Dr. Allenby is a therapist who specializes in helping her patients with their sex lives. Unfortunately, the doctor is in a "physician, heal thyself" situation. Allenby is in a relationship with her associate David Kincaid (Stephen Macht), but when she comes back unexpectedly after her flight to Chicago is canceled and discovers Kincaid in the middle of a passionate tryst with her assistant, Cindy (Julia Montgomery), she's enraged. As if the betrayal wasn't bad enough, she overhears the pair mocking her, with Kincaid comparing her physical amorousness to rice pudding. This shatters Allenby's self-image as an expert in healthy and passionate relationships, and she decides to murder Kincaid as revenge for his disrespect.

Allenby disguises herself in a black dress, black hat, and a long black wig, creating the persona of "Lisa." She approaches Kincaid in a bar, and he's intrigued by her new persona. They go back to the office, where there's a bedroom for therapy-seeking couples to use. She shoots him, messes up the scene to suggest a struggle, sprinkles a little vial of blood on the floor, and plants some evidence to create the impression that the mysterious "Lisa" is the killer.

Columbo appears on the scene twenty-three-and-a-half minutes into the episode with coffee and a cigar. Allenby, not knowing who he is, informs him that smoking isn't allowed in the elevator and puts out his cigar in his coffee. He notices a tag dangling from her coat, a point that will become important later as the retrieval of the tag will help him break down her supposed alibi in Chicago. As they approach her office, she swoons into Columbo's arms as she sees the body carried away, and acts stunned when Columbo says he was shot by an unknown woman.

Much of the humor from the episode comes from Columbo's discomfort over Allenby's frank discussion of sexual matters. He's much more comfortable with the criminal investigation, as he notices the victim had no keys and suggests the mystery woman took them, an idea with which Allenby quickly concurs. Allenby insists that her relationship with the deceased was very strong, and they had wonderful sex, but only with each other. When she demands equal candor from Columbo from his relationship with his wife, an embarrassed Columbo hurries away. He later informs her that Mrs. Columbo read Allenby's book *The Courtesan Complex* and found it so enthralling she made him read it. Just talking about the subject makes Columbo uneasy.

Columbo interviews the bartender and learns that the mysterious woman in black's name is Lisa. After he traces the keys back to the valet parker, he wonders how the deceased unlocked the clinic door. This is Allenby's first big mistake, as she unlocked the door with her own keys. Unnerved, Allenby starts talking into the mirror, Gollum-like, slipping into Lisa's persona. She knows she should destroy the costume, but instead goes out dressed up as Lisa, acting far more uninhibited than usual.

Columbo continues to unravel Allenby's false clues, as the false blood from another woman, the black hairs from the wig, and the saliva on the cigarette Allenby smoked as "Lisa" indicate that *three* women, not one, were in the room at the time of the crime. This is before the television public was fully aware of DNA testing, but the essence of this information is that Allenby has left behind plenty of trace evidence connected to her, and the use of the wig only muddles the issue.

Allenby continues to go out in the Lisa persona, acting as the life of the party in bars, playing pool, and getting someone to call Columbo about her. Columbo's already figured out the truth, and he invites Allenby back to the office, where a police detective dressed as Lisa appears and vanishes, freaking out Allenby, but as she says nothing about it to Columbo, he considers that evidence of guilt. The two sit and talk, and Allenby quickly confesses to everything, explaining why she did it and complementing Columbo on his investigative skills. Their conversation is quite civil, even friendly, and Allenby seems relieved to admit the truth to a particularly caring and understanding Columbo, who serves as *her* therapist in that final scene.

This closing scene represents the culmination of a particularly cordial relationship between detective and killer. This friendliness is based on Allenby's growing respect for Columbo, as well as by Columbo's particularly sympathetic treatment of her. Perhaps this is due to his realization that this was not a cold-blooded murder for profit, but a premeditated crime of passion, which are fairly rare amongst Columbo's investigations.

While some killers seek to unnerve Columbo by placing him in an uncomfortable situation, such as exposing him to heights, Allenby utilizes a psychological approach. A slight smile indicates that she was amused by how flustered Columbo became by her questions about his sexual life, though it's possible that her questions were asked out of genuine professional curiosity and not out of a calculated desire to unnerve the detective. At one point, Allenby demonstrates her full control over a situation. For example, when Columbo walks into a group therapy session and asks to stay, she replies with a sharp "absolutely not!" This is an absolutely correct position to take, as Columbo is not a patient, and her real patients deserve privacy as they talk about their most sensitive issues. It's a rare instance where Columbo crosses a line when he tries to integrate himself into his suspect's life at inconvenient opportunities. Ironically, this moment marks the high point in Allenby's position of strength, as from this point onwards, her own understanding of the lines between fantasy and reality starts to blur, and her resilience against the pressure of an investigation begins to crumble.

When Columbo informs her that the police have retrieved the murder weapon, Allenby is visibly nervous, providing a clear indication of her guilty conscience. As Allenby tries to calm her nerves, she slips into Lisa's persona, becoming bolder and more relaxed in a way that her natural persona is not. Back as herself, Allenby reassures herself that Columbo's gone as far as he can go in his investigation and that she's safe, a bit of false optimism that reflects how she underestimates him.

It's notable that instead of confronting Allenby with hard evidence, Columbo feels that his best approach is to wear her down psychologically. He arranges for a phone call to unnerve her, a ruse that she finds insulting and one instance where Columbo's apology seems genuine. But the appearance of "Lisa' as played by a policewoman, coupled with a steady barrage of evidence, is enough to wear Allenby down, and by the end, she confesses, like the need to unburden her soul was overwhelming. She appreciates his grasp of her psychological state, saying he's "very intuitive…you would have made a splendid therapist." Columbo's theory about Kincaid having an affair with Cindy is based on guesswork and intuition, but when confronted with this accurate statement, Allenby confirms it. At any point in this conversation, Allenby could simply have said she had nothing more to say without a lawyer, and she would have had a fighting chance at trial. But instead, she allows herself to confess, behaving as if getting caught is really a relief.

Once the truth about Kincaid's unfaithfulness is revealed, Allenby becomes able to confront the issue directly. It was his laughing at her that made her snap, realizing that "I was his joke." There is a quote often attributed to Margaret Atwood that is frequently cited in gender studies courses, stating that "Men are afraid that women will laugh at them. Women are afraid that men will kill them." The line argues that men are primarily concerned about their pride and that women can deliver humiliating blows to their egos, whereas women face threats to their physical safety from the males in their lives. "Sex and the Married Detective" provides a total reversal and rebuttal to this oft-repeated line, illustrating that murder is not merely a crime committed by men, but more pointedly, that women are just as susceptible to attacks on their vanity as men.

It was this attack on her self-worth and public persona that led Allenby to become a murderess. With her image of herself destroyed, there was only one place for her to turn, and that was into the realm of her imagination, where she embraced Lisa as the embodiment of the sexually confident, mysterious, and desirable woman that she wished she was. As she confesses, when Allenby fired the fatal shot, "I went beyond the fantasy, and I wasn't even frightened." However, she was frightened by the fact that she was so happy becoming someone other than herself in Lisa. She realizes that while she encouraged her patients to explore their fantasies, she never realized before just how powerful and all-consuming they could become when nursed and left unchecked. Admitting to her chagrin that she preferred being Lisa to being herself, she declares that this truth is scarier to her than being charged with murder.

The difference between the Allenby of the opening scene and the Allenby who walked in on Kincaid cheating on her is night and day. In her opening moments, Allenby sees herself as a healer, a smart, courageous therapist who helps people break down their inhibitions and liberate them into a world of carnal pleasure and fulfillment. It's implied that much of this was due to her relationship with Kincaid. When she overhears Kincaid and Cindy, not just her self-image, but her entire worldview is challenged. Sexual freedom was supposed to bring fulfillment, but as Allenby realizes, in that moment, unfaithfulness is often founded in contempt and cruelty, and it's all fun and games until someone has her heart broken. It's at that moment that the so-called "sexpert" realizes that she doesn't know as much about the consequences of passion as she thought she did. Allenby's approach to sex didn't actually liberate her, it merely led to an annihilation of her self-image when she realized her partner in romance and business didn't see her as the vibrant and strong force fueled by the freeing power of ardor she believed herself to be.

When the person closest to her declared he found her bland and boring, and she realized that Kincaid's primary motive for being in their relationship was probably based on financial concerns rather than affection, Allenby was forced to ask a critical question. If she wasn't the life-affirming mistress of sex that she thought she was, then who was she? As she didn't have a comforting answer to this question, she instead asked herself who she wanted to be. The response to this was that she wished to be a woman like Lisa, but whether or not this was a mostly healthy or largely destructive desire is left unanswered.

The final moments have Allenby ask Columbo a surprising question: "Do you think less of me?" *Columbo's* villains often want the lieutenant to admire how clever and resourceful they are, but few of them actually worry about looking pathetic in his eyes. Notably, Allenby's concern isn't about him despising her as a killer, but about the possibility of him looking down on her as a woman finding fulfillment in playing pretend. Columbo responds with kindness, saying that he's a policeman and judging is for others, but that "I've enjoyed our talks very much, and I think I do understand."

Chapter Forty-Nine: Grand Deceptions

Colonel Frank Brailie (Robert Foxworth)

There are some professions that seem to produce more *Columbo* killers than others. The medical profession produces many murderers, as do the creative arts. The military has also produced a substantial number of opponents for the lieutenant, and in every case, the soldiers gone wrong have surrendered peacefully. Colonel Frank Brailie is the latest *Columbo* killer to be unworthy of his uniform. Brailie works for a charitable foundation and think tank run by the celebrated military hero General Jack Padget (Stephen Elliott), a decent and honorable man who is a wheelchair user married to a much younger wife, Jenny (Janet Eilber). Brailie is embezzling funds from the foundation and using them to promote illegal arms sales around the world, pocketing the profits. Not only that, but he's having an affair with Jenny Padget.

But shady misdeeds have a habit of moving into the light, and General Padget asks Sergeant Major Lester Keegan (Andy Romano) to do a little forensic accounting on the foundation's finances. Rather than report the missing money, Keegan engages in gross dereliction of duty and blackmails Brailie. Alas for Keegan, blackmailers tend to have a very brief life span on this series unless they're working alongside Columbo or for "generally harmless" elderly mystery writers.

Brailie plans to commit his crime during an evening party in honor of the General. Jenny Padget asks her boyfriend to help her set up a lovely gift for her husband– a refurbished study lined with books with a table filled with soldier miniatures in the center of the room, perfect for reenacting historical battles. Brailie's alibi consists of loading up the miniatures in cardboard boxes labeled "Books" and the books in boxes marked "Miniatures." The plan is to have the boxes delivered at different times, so when Brailie needs the alibi later in the day, he's supposedly putting together the miniatures into an elaborate diorama that requires hours of careful placement. Placing the books on the shelves will only take a small fraction of the time. So Brailie sets up the miniatures earlier in the day while telling others he's shelving the books, and he only needs a few minutes to shove the books on the shelves in the evening when Jenny Padget believes him to be hard at work setting up the miniatures. While Keegan and some other soldiers are in the woods, acting out some war games with actual explosions, Brailie sneaks out into the night, dons a dark costume, stabs Keegan, and places his body over an explosive device, which goes off soon afterwards.

Columbo arrives twenty-three minutes into the episode, crawling around the ground at the scene of the death. He meets Brailie soon afterwards and tells him that it's probable that this was an accident. But Brailie's actions soon make Columbo suspicious, especially when he sees Brailie cleaning up mud on the floor of Keegan's cabin, where he changed his clothes right after the murder.

After digging around and finding some more suspicious items, like dirt and twigs in unusual places on the dead man's body, and the fact that Keegan abruptly stopped looking for a new job, Columbo requests a second autopsy, and this more thorough examination proves the cause of death was a stab wound and was therefore a homicide. Amiably, he declares "Nobody wanted it to be an accident more than me," as murder requires so much additional paperwork.

The investigation continues, and Columbo eventually uncovers both the embezzlement and the affair. He presents both findings to the General, who's enraged and out for vengeance until Brailie points out that if he's arrested, Jenny Padget's name will be dragged through the mud. The

General knew his wife was cheating on him but didn't realize who her lover was until then, and accepted it due to their age difference. As he still loves her and wants to protect his wife, the General retreats. After speaking with Columbo, Jenny Padget is willing to face whatever comes, and so right after Brailie is flushed with triumph after supposedly checkmating the General, Columbo meets him at the house, accuses him of the murder, and rips apart his alibi, illustrating how the books wouldn't fit into the boxes marked "Books," but they would fit into the "Miniatures" boxes. With the Padgets unwilling to shield him, Brailie informs Columbo, "I seem to have misjudged myself…and you," and admits that he has lost the battle before being arrested.

The relationship between Brailie and Columbo is one of the weaker detective/killer connections in the series. The interaction between the two is shallow, as neither man develops any affection or respect for the other over the course of the investigation. The most emotion Brailie demonstrates towards Columbo is some poorly veiled impatience when he wants Columbo to leave, and the lieutenant willfully ignores him and hangs around longer than desired.

Brailie's interactions with Columbo tend to be clipped and dismissive. Brailie notices the detective's doggedness, declaring "I don't think I'd like you on my trail." When Columbo shows up at the foundation's offices to dig a little deeper, the Colonel explains that his job is to develop military plans that can't go wrong, but Columbo tempers this confidence with the veiled remark that all plans can fail. At this time, Columbo has no evidence of murder and admits as much, and when Brailie points out a shrunken head that's meant as a reminder of caution with enemies, it's unclear whether Brailie's making a veiled threat, or if he's simply pointing out a macabre conversation piece.

Notably, Columbo has much warmer and notable connections to the Padgets. He charms the General by explaining his historical theory that Gettysburg only happened because Robert E. Lee needed shoes, and they bond over the miniatures. Likewise, Columbo earns Jenny Padget's trust after confronting her about the affair (he found a toothbrush at the cabin covered in her fingerprints), and convinces her to do the right thing.

What led Colonel Frank Brailie to murder? He was a greedy man who fed his desire for wealth by embezzlement, and his willingness to profit by selling weapons to dangerous groups around the world shows that he had no genuine loyalties to his nation or world peace. As long as his bank account swelled, he didn't care if the world burned. Given his willingness to expose Jenny Padget to public opprobrium, it appears that his affair with her was not fueled by genuine affection, but instead originated as his insurance policy against the General revealing his wrongdoing. It is ironic that although he worked for a think tank promoting military tactics, his own plans were poorly thought out. He was not skilled at hiding his misappropriation of funds, as his theft was quickly detected by Keegan. His murder was not well-planned either, as the stab wound was detectable after a more careful autopsy. It would have been far wiser for him to kill Keegan with a blow on the head, as such a wound could have been attributed to debris falling from the explosion. He also overlooked the critical point that the sizes of the shipping boxes undercut his alibi.

Brailie, therefore, was a shoddy strategist. He suffered from the poor judgment that has affected many aggressive military leaders in the past—he believed that after an attack, victory would fall into place on its own. But, as many invading armies have learned, to their dismay, armed resistance and other unforeseen circumstances may undercut what they thought would be an easy triumph. Not only that, but Brailie's defenses were shockingly weak. Not only did he fail to note a gaping hole in his alibi, but like other *Columbo* killers, he believed that other people were as morally flawed as he was. Brailie was sure that Jenny Padget would encourage her husband to stay silent to protect her own reputation. He failed to realize that she held justice more important than embarrassment.

Columbo identified Brailie's Achilles' heel the first day he met him when he noticed Brailie cleaning up mud in Keegan's quarters. The lieutenant noted that was "peculiar for someone as arrogant as you are," for a man infatuated with his own authority would have ordered someone else to take care of a messy, menial task. It was Brailie's egotism and short-sightedness that led to his total defeat.

IX

SEASON NINE

Chapter Fifty: Murder: A Self Portrait

Max Barsini (Patrick Bauchau)

Max Barsini. Artist. Philanderer. Egoist. Murderer. This is a rough sketch of a man who wanted the women in his life to stay in the positions he posed them in forever. As the episode begins, the acclaimed painter is surrounded by three women. There's Louise (Fionnula Flanagan), Barsini's first wife who still bears his surname, lives next door to him, and cooks elaborate meals for all four members of the group. Vanessa (Shera Danese) is Barsini's second wife, who had an affair with Barsini while he was still married to Louise and now is threatened by history repeating itself. Barsini has made his latest model, Julie (Isabel García Lorca), his mistress.

It's an odd situation, with Barsini luxuriating in his harem, Julie enjoying being a famous artist's muse, Vanessa seething over the betrayal, and Louise seemingly taking the whole situation stoically. But Louise isn't just accepting these unconventional living conditions, for after much therapy, she has decided to leave Barsini's orbit, pursue a relationship with another man, and move away from him. Barsini won't have that, so one day, while Louise sunbathes, he knocks her out with a solvent-dipped painting rag and leaves her in the ocean to drown, having set up an alibi by pretending to paint a picture in a restaurateur friend's loft, a painting he actually completed much earlier.

Columbo starts investigating, and after some interactions, Barsini offers to paint Columbo's portrait. During the sittings, the pair discuss Louise's death and the odd dreams she recounted on audio tape for her therapy sessions. Eventually, Columbo concludes that Barsini not only killed Louise, but he murdered his agent Harry Chudow as well, who had stolen a hefty portion of the profits of Barsini's artwork. It's unclear if Louise was fully aware of what happened and covered for Barsini, if she was only vaguely aware of what happened, or if she repressed the memory of the crime. In any event, Columbo found traces of a unique brand of red paint on Louise's face, left there by the rag Barsini used to render her unconscious. Barsini, with his plot unraveled and Vanessa and Julie both, having left him, surrenders, leaving behind one last masterpiece: a brilliant portrait of Columbo that captures the man's charm, intelligence, and sense of humor.

The interactions between Columbo and Barzini are unique, as they are primarily discussions between the two men as Columbo poses for Barzini's picture. Columbo does not meet Barzini until nearly half an hour into the episode (a scene with Columbo and Dog at a Basset Hound Fair was probably added just to introduce the detective earlier). Columbo doubts that the drowning was an accident from the beginning, noting that one contact lens was in the deceased's eye, and the other was in her beach bag.

Though he doesn't show it in detail, Barzini is clearly threatened by Columbo's question, and it's probable that the offer to paint his portrait is a distraction meant to derail his investigation. It works at first—Columbo forgets the questions he planned to ask after receiving the offer. Barzini doesn't make too much of an effort to win over Columbo– he refuses to include Dog in the picture and says outright, "Don't expect to find your portrait completely flattering."

There's a bit of investigation outside of Barzini's presence as Columbo searches the room where the artist claimed to have been painting at the time of the murder and discovers the sink doesn't work, so he couldn't have washed his brushes. Columbo spends much of his sittings playing the deceased's tapes, discussing her dreams. Columbo theorizes that many of her bizarre dreams include unconscious puns that lead to the truth about the murdered agent. A bowl of berries, for example, suggests that the body was buried. Barzini sneers at Columbo's attempts at dream analysis, but there's a strong indication that Columbo hit his mark. After the second sitting, when Columbo determines the truth about the agent's fate, Barzini ends the session with a mild fit of pique, declaring that he's bored with both the painting and the dream discussion.

By the time Barzini and Columbo meet for the third sitting, Barzini makes it clear that this will be the last time they meet. He declares that it is "time for ending painful relationships" and states that he will not speak to Columbo anymore after finishing the painting. It's a challenge that Columbo excitedly accepts. With just a brief period of time, before Barzini finishes his portrait, Columbo has to make his case and lay out his evidence, hoping to crack Barzini to the point where he's ready to confess, or at least accept that Columbo has a strong case against him. After a blunt accusation that Barzini murdered his first wife, Columbo demolishes his alibi, noting that without running water in the loft, he couldn't possibly have cleaned his paintbrushes, which means that the portrait was completed elsewhere. After going through the other clues, mostly involving paint that was found where it shouldn't have been, Barzini realizes that Columbo has caught him. Though he doesn't break down, Barzini's clearly a beaten man. The loss of all three women in his life, each of whom rejected him, has clearly hurt his ego. Being confronted with the basic errors he made is all that's needed to push Barzini into coming along quietly. It's not the most dramatic ending to an episode. There's no clever trick or twist or slip to serve as an admission of guilt. Columbo doesn't put any additional pressure on Barzini; he simply wears him down with facts, and by the fortunate coincidence of his second wife and mistress leaving him, Barzini is psychologically primed for surrender.

Looking at the title of this episode, one might wonder what the self-portrait of Max Barsini might look like. Would it capture the essential cruelty and selfishness of his nature, exemplified through his desire to possess women's loyalty and obedience without giving any genuine love or respect in return? Would his brushstrokes capture the arrogance of a man who believed himself to be a genius? Certainly, Barsini possessed great artistic talent, though his skill at plotting a murder and his knowledge of human nature was far below what might be termed a "genius" level. Or would his explosive temper, his narcissism, and his implacable thirst for controlling others and situations find form on the canvas?

On reflection, it is most unlikely that Barsini would create a portrait of Dorian Gray. While he told Columbo he wished to capture his "policeman's soul" and later explained he was compelled to paint what he saw, it is unlikely that a man of Barsini's vanity would have the honesty and humility to paint himself metaphorical warts and all. Barsini saw himself as a brilliant artist whose talent set him above lesser mortals, someone whose great gifts needed to be nurtured by other, less exceptional people. Barsini could not abide it when people refused to be as pliant to his whims as paint upon a canvas, and while his artistic vision of the world featured himself upon an exalted plane, worshiped by a trio of enraptured women, the reality was quite different. Love that is unreturned and treated with contempt is unlikely to last, and Barsini's mental self-portrait was actually an idealized caricature of himself that exaggerated his perceived strengths and ignored his many shortcomings.

Chapter Fifty-One: Columbo Cries Wolf

Sean Brantley (Ian Buchanan)

Columbo has never seriously suspected an innocent person of murder and all of the people he concludes are murderers are, in fact, guilty. Sean Brantley is the only Columbo killer to commit his first murder *after* Columbo becomes convinced of his culpability.

Brantley runs the magazine *Bachelor's World*, though his primary interests lie not in writing articles, but in living a glamorous and luxurious lifestyle in a fancy mansion (currently being renovated) surrounded by beautiful women. Most of the magazine's profits go into funding Brantley's culture of excess and hedonism, and when Brantley's business partner and publisher Dian Hunter (Dierdre Hall) quarrels with him, threatens to sell her stock to a British investor and disappears soon afterwards, suspicions arise, and Columbo is called to investigate.

When Columbo arrives sixteen minutes into the episode, there's no proof of foul play. Notably, no killing has been presented on-screen. A woman presumed to be the missing Hunter was seen leaving the mansion, though she was too bundled up to identify positively. A gunshot heard in the night adds to the suspicion of foul play. Columbo's suspicions rise when Brantley shows zero concern over his missing partner, explaining that she's in the habit of disappearing for long stretches of time without warning. Columbo checks the surveillance video at the airport for proof that Hunter went to Europe, and he discovers a woman matching Hunter's description, though her face is obscured with a hat and sunglasses. When the woman takes cream in her coffee, Columbo remembers a loud comment a testy Brantley made earlier about Hunter only drinking black coffee, leading Columbo to believe the woman in the video is a decoy, who flew to London under Hunter's name and disappeared into her true persona immediately after landing.

After explaining his theory to Brantley, the magazine mogul admits Columbo's argument seems logical, but he refuses to believe Hunter is truly dead. Columbo keeps digging, eventually concluding that Hunter was shot in her limo and the body was hidden somewhere in the estate. As Brantley has an alibi, Columbo suspects his young girlfriend killed and impersonated Hunter. Over several days, Columbo scrutinizes the mansion's grounds, becoming a figure of fun for Brantley and the models. A postcard supposedly from Hunter (with inconclusive handwriting) fails to convince the detective that she's alive, and soon, there's a media circus connected to her disappearance. Columbo goes on record with his superiors and the media that he believes she's been murdered, and he's gobsmacked when Hunter arrives, very much alive, and gives a press conference.

It was all a publicity stunt. Hunter and Brantley faked her disappearance, thereby raising the magazine's profile and boosting sales. Columbo realizes that Brantley played him, setting false clues that Columbo gobbled up because he *wanted* there to be a case for him to solve. Disgusted and humiliated, Columbo shuffles away, knowing that he's going to face a terrible fallout from his bosses.

Hunter and Brantley celebrate, but Brantley's jovial mood is crushed when Hunter announces her plan to sell out her stake in the company to the British investor. She'll make a fortune, and the new management will maximize its profits, so Brantley can kiss his lavish lifestyle goodbye. That won't do for him, so Brantley snaps Hunter's neck.

The next day, Hunter has disappeared again, and Columbo defies a direct order and rushes to the mansion to investigate. Columbo is wary that he's being played again, but he digs around and notices that Hunter's fur coat is in the closet, but her fancy pager is missing. Under the terms of their partnership, Brantley maintains full control of the magazine if Hunter disappears. Just as a cranky Brantley orders Columbo to leave, Columbo begs permission to make one phone call. As soon as he hangs up, a buzzing noise emanates from behind the bathroom wall. Columbo called Hunter's pager, betting that Brantley had failed to remove it from her body. Knocking down a portion of a recently renovated wall, Columbo reveals Hunter's dead body, stuffed in a garment bag. Triumphant, Columbo reveals the one-word message he sent to her pager: GOTCHA.

Brantley is the sole *Columbo* killer who has the detective exactly where he wants him for most of the episode. For all of their ingenuity, no murderer manages to deceive Columbo for long, because he can detect the misdirection and point out the inconsistencies in their narratives. In recent years, many arson investigators (though far from all) have been criticized and, in some cases, even discredited for their inadequate training and for concluding there was criminal activity when there was none. Some critics note that "if you look for arson, you will find evidence of arson," even when there is other evidence pointing in a different direction. Comparably, if Columbo looks for murder, he will find evidence of murder, thanks to the fact that every clue has been carefully staged. He's not looking for a fake homicide.

To be fair to Columbo, real murders are common, but the circumstances at the heart of this episode are particularly uncommon. Most *Columbo* killers go out of their way to appear guilty. Brantley was striving to appear guilty before he'd committed the crime. When most *Columbo* suspects would have been calling lawyers and influential friends to stop Columbo's investigation, Brantley had to restrain his glee.

As Columbo was following Brantley's carefully laid trail of bread crumbs, Brantley was developing mixed emotions towards the man he was fooling so thoroughly. There was certainly the contempt that con artists felt towards their marks, but there was also real respect as well. Early on, Brantley makes a snide remark that Colombo has "read too many mystery stories," and Columbo good-naturedly parries this remark with a self-deprecating remark about how he can never figure out fictional crimes. Soon afterwards, Brantley challenges Columbo's public persona, informing him that he's not the "naïve bumbling detective" he presents himself as. While Columbo tries to be subtle about his suspicions, Brantley, who was anticipating this scrutiny, snaps, "Stop playing games. Come out from behind that cigar smoke of yours…. You're not a subtle man." This taunting is almost certainly not real anger, but it is probably careful goading, as Brantley adopts the persona who is afraid of his crimes being uncovered, as opposed to a man using reverse psychology to encourage an investigation into a nonexistent crime. Brantley's a more subtle actor than many of the other murderers, who ham up ersatz grief.

Eventually, Brantley takes on a more openly antagonistic stance, taunting Columbo for his "middle-class morality" in response to Brantley's womanizing. It's at this point that Columbo drops any pretenses regarding his suspicions, telling him that he knows he's guilty, though nothing can be proved without a corpse. When Brantley says, "Columbo, you're the most stubborn man I've ever met," there's real admiration, feigned frustration, and well-hidden delight, as he couldn't possibly have found a perfect detective to send on a wild goose chase. A few more barbs, like calling Columbo's actions "insane behavior," are enough to keep Columbo motivated until Hunter's surprise return.

Columbo bottles up his anger, but the disgust is not just at Brantley for his manipulative plan, but at himself for falling for the scheme. Brantley's triumphant leer shows that he knows that Columbo has deduced the whole plot, and Columbo's grimace illustrates just how much of a blow his reputation will take for this fiasco. When Brantley gloatingly hands Columbo a glass of champagne, Columbo tells him he "made a fool out of me…but I gotta hand it to you, you did it well." With that, Columbo pours out the champagne on the ground, grimacing as he anticipates the fallout, while Brantley mocks him by saying, "You win some, you lose some."

In most cases, Columbo's apprehension of the killer is purely a professional triumph, with no malice or feelings of vengeance towards the perpetrator. This time is different. The speed and recklessness with which

Columbo drives towards the mansion shows that he is driven by more than his usual dedication. All killers have tried to fool him, but none succeeded so spectacularly and destructively. Columbo is a humble man in many ways, but this was a body blow to his ego, made worse by how Brantley reveled in his triumph. Once Brantley becomes an actual murderer, the roles have changed. Brantley is no longer completely safe from legal repercussions, and now Columbo has genuine clues to follow. When Brantley becomes upset by Columbo's investigation, it's from a real fear that the dogged detection will figure out the truth. Columbo, for his part, reverts to his standard aw-shucks, apologetic persona, saying, "I'm sorry, sir. I don't blame you for being angry." This disarms Brantley, allowing Columbo the opportunity to find the body. Brantley took Columbo's dignity and reputation, but with just one word—GOTCHA—Columbo got both of them back.

Brantley is unique amongst the Columbo killers, as most of them believed that they had created the perfect crime. Brantley believed that he had committed the perfect *non-crime*, a profitable publicity stunt that could enrich himself without serious consequence. Unlike every other villain in the series, he could enjoy his interactions with Columbo, who was performing his expected part perfectly. While every other antagonist faked innocence, Brantley faked guilt. Most episodes see the villain of the week suffer from fraying tensions, whereas Brantley had to restrain himself to keep from laughing.

He was undone, however, by the fact that he wasn't as irresistible to women as he thought he was. Brantley planned that his charade would assure his decadent lifestyle for years to come, and when Hunter revealed that her upcoming sale would make her rich and leave him without a mansion or a harem, he felt betrayed and desperate. When he killed Hunter, he thought that the notoriety would prevent an investigation. He forgot his own observations that Columbo was absolutely relentless in his investigations, and by underestimating his opponent's resolve for justice and vengeance, Brantley set himself up for the standard crushing fall faced by *Columbo* murderers.

Sean Brantley was a man entranced by a self-created, glamorous world of luxury, decadence, and beautiful women. His desperation to remain living in this fantasy world led him to take a life, leading him to the ironic fate of being confined to a stark, unpleasant prison where females are rarely seen.

Chapter Fifty-Two: Agenda for Murder

Oscar Finch (Patrick McGoohan)

One of the most acclaimed *Columbo* guest stars returns to act and direct in *Agenda for Murder*, as Patrick McGoohan takes on his third role as a killer, playing Oscar Finch, a prominent lawyer and a handler for Congressman Paul Mackey, a leading candidate to be a vice-presidential nominee. Finch expects that once Mackey is elected, the V.P. will use his influence to get Finch the post of Attorney General.

Unfortunately for Finch, his dreams of glory are threatened when his influential yet unsavory acquaintance Frank Staplin (Louis Zorich) summons him for a late-night consultation. Even though Finch isn't quite sure what the subject of the meeting will be, he's clearly aware that he may need to commit a homicide in the near future as he prepares a quasi-alibi for himself, burning a cigar in his law office and setting fire to the gunpowder from a bullet as well, taking the scorched residue with him. When Finch arrives at Staplin's house after a brisk walk in the rain (he doesn't want his car seen at Staplin's home), Staplin is rather jovial despite his problems. Staplin is an unscrupulous, wealthy man with a habit of skirting the law. Finch helped Staplin out of a jam in the past by destroying evidence. Now Staplin wants another similar favor to avoid a criminal conviction and lengthy prison sentence. When Finch balks, Staplin, still good-humored and snacking on some expensive cheese, which he has shared with Finch, threatens blackmail. Refusing to submit, Finch shoots and kills Staplin, arranging the body and gun to imitate a suicide, leaving traces of the burnt gunpowder he brought with him on Staplin's hand to achieve verisimilitude.

Twenty-one minutes into the episode, Columbo arrives at the scene to investigate. While Columbo professes cluelessness at how the deceased man's fax machine works, his observational skills remain exceptional, and he notices that all the blood is under the gun but not on it, indicating that the gun was placed by the dead man's hand a period of time after the fatal shot, thereby meaning murder, not suicide. While this analysis of the blood evidence is fine police work, the discovery Columbo takes the most pleasure in is the large wedge of Reggiano cheese on the dead man's desk. Columbo believes that it would be a crime to waste such a beautiful piece of cheese and insists that it be wrapped up and properly stored.

After a quick tap of the telephone "redial" button sends him to Finch, Columbo arrives to see Finch's secretary using air freshener to rid the office of the odor of cigar smoke. Columbo starts questioning Finch, and the attorney swiftly becomes the target of his investigation, though Columbo maintains a particularly amicable relationship with Finch for most of the episode. Finch falsely claims he didn't see Staplin, but the late man did call him that evening, seriously distraught and desperate. As the investigation continues, Columbo repeatedly interrupts Finch's busy schedule with questions. Columbo's discovery that Staplin sent his wife ethnic jokes via fax right before his death indicates that Staplin was not in a suicidal mood.

Columbo has a hard time gathering solid evidence over the course of the investigation. He notices the dry patch in Finch's parking spot, illustrating that a car was there at the time of a brief rainstorm, a point that will prove important later, but it's not nearly enough proof for an arrest on its own. Columbo hopes that Finch's suit, damaged from his walk in the rain, will prove Finch was outside for an extended period of time, but the suit is grabbed and laundered before Columbo can have it analyzed. When Columbo talks to Finch about the reasons why he's sure it couldn't be a suicide, the lawyer deftly provides alternative theories, casting reasonable doubt on many of Columbo's major points. Most of Columbo's clues prove inadequate to make a case, but Finch steadily gains respect for the detective's skills and realizes he has to protect himself.

Finch realizes that he'll need a solid alibi, so he confesses to Mackey, knowing that to protect his own reputation, the congressman will claim he was with Finch at the time of the murder. Finch summons Columbo to a meeting, making a big show about how he's never broken an oath before, but he needs to renege on his promise to keep his meeting with the congressman secret in order to prove his whereabouts, and the congressman confirms his story. Mackey, therefore, becomes an accessory after the fact, and though he confirms Finch's fake alibi to Columbo, the congressman doesn't have the stamina for a protracted investigation. Later, when he says he quit smoking, Columbo challenges him about the cigar smoke at Finch's office, leading to a clumsy backtrack from Mackey. Mackey grows increasingly short-tempered and flustered around Columbo, as opposed to the suave and always-collected Finch, and Columbo warns Mackey that it's not wise to perjure himself for Finch's sake.

Columbo finally confronts Finch at a victory party after the primary election, accusing him of the murder. He points out that there was only one dry spot in the parking lot, proving that the congressman couldn't have been there otherwise there would've been two dry spots. This blow to his alibi fails to faze Finch, but another piece of evidence proves Finch's presence at the crime scene. Earlier, Columbo preserved a piece of Finch's chewing gum, thereby obtaining an imprint of Finch's tooth marks. Columbo explains that they matched Finch's distinctive chipped tooth to the nibble on a piece of the cheese found at the scene of the crime. Stunned at the fact that his failure to finish his snack led to his downfall, Finch drops his confident air and defeatedly reflects on how "one bite of cheese" betrayed him.

Recent determinations on the unreliability of bite mark evidence might make some viewers wonder if Finch's conviction might be overturned decades later, but in the context of the episode, it's a major win for Columbo. It's not made clear, though, what happened to the congressman—was he arrested as an accessory? How did this affect his political career? It's not certain, but given the seriousness of the situation, it's reasonable to be pessimistic about Mackey's fate.

Patrick McGoohan reportedly took considerable pleasure in his contributions to the *Columbo* series, and throughout the episode, it seems like the actor is having a great deal of fun. Unlike most wealthy and powerful killers, he never threatens to attack Columbo's career or have him taken off the case. Though Finch is initially annoyed by Columbo parking in his spot (he asks if that "oxidized relic is yours?"), he grants Columbo a five-minute interview and explains that he received a desperate phone call from Staplin. Finch acts as if that brief explanation will be enough to send Columbo on his way, but of course, Columbo continues his questioning soon afterwards. Finch gains an appreciation for Columbo's dedication and demonstrates that he realizes how Columbo uses a persona to disarm suspects, saying, "You're rather subtle for a man who appears to be so overt." Still, Finch tries to exert dominance in the conversation by stressing his busy schedule, brushing away further questions by pompously declaring, "I detest being late, and I also detest having to repeat myself."

Few suspects maintain as tight a control over the length of each questioning session as Finch. Each time they meet, Finch stresses how little time he has to spare, and it's all Columbo can do to coax out an additional question. When Columbo produces the Jewish joke Staplin faxed to his wife as evidence Staplin wasn't suicidal, Finch and Columbo share a belly laugh, and it's an indication Finch has taken a genuine liking to Columbo.

When the congressman worries about Columbo's investigation, Finch dismisses these fears, saying, "He's harmless," describing Columbo as a "jumped-up Boy Scout." When Columbo runs through his reasons for why it couldn't be a suicide, Finch is certain Columbo's bluffing, parrying Columbo's implications with good humor. Throughout it all, Finch carries himself with the assured confidence of a man who believes he's far too clever to be caught.

By their final meeting, there's a slight degree of genuineness when Finch calls Columbo's arrival "an unexpected pleasure." Columbo's surprisingly polite accusation, "I think you did it, sir," provokes no anger nor even a metaphorical ruffling of feathers. When the pair retreat to a private room, Finch simply says, "I'm very disappointed in you, sir. I thought we had a nice relationship going." To this, Columbo replies, "Well, nothing's perfect, sir." Notably, very few killers refer to Columbo as "sir" at any point, preferring a blunt "Columbo" or using his title "Lieutenant." Finch's comment illustrates a level of respect for Columbo while still maintaining his lofty air. Prior to the final reveal of the bitten cheese, Finch makes a great show of dismissing Columbo's case as "a load of unsubstantiated circumstantial poppycock." There's no malice, and instead of telling Columbo to get out, like many killers would have, Finch graciously tells the lieutenant to stay and enjoy the party. Columbo's warrant to bring Finch in for questions provokes a dismissive reply that the whole affair is a farce.

The bite mark evidence proves absolutely crushing for Finch, and it's notable how he goes from a confident and dismissive man to becoming blindsided and conscious that he is checkmated. It's probable that part of the reason he is so stunned by this turn of events is because he realizes that he only has himself to blame for his own downfall. Throughout the episode, he prides himself on his intelligence, careful planning, and attention to detail. Now, he has been undone by a simple mistake. Throughout the episode, Finch takes little bites of food whenever something tasty is handy, and his own often unconscious habit eventually gives him away. Finch was a man who focused on the little details, with the attention of the skilled lawyer who knew that a lack of care could lead to disaster. Popping the rest of a cheese cube into his mouth would've destroyed the evidence. The fact that he had failed to catch his own little mistake was a blow against his own meticulous nature.

Finch didn't have to kill Staplin. He could have acquiesced to the blackmail, though sabotaging a prosecutor's case might have been too risky for him. He could have offered to use his influence to concoct a plea deal for Staplin or have found a connection willing to accept some information, whether genuine or manufactured, to reduce Staplin's sentence. Or he could have told Staplin to do his worst, trying to ride out the scandal as the fever dream of a man desperate to escape just punishment by attacking innocent people. All of these nonviolent options carried risks and probable consequences, yet all were less risky and held fewer negative repercussions than murder. But like many men of intense ambition, Finch was only concerned with achieving his goals. He wanted the respect and power that came with being the Attorney General of the United States, and he wanted a prominent position of influence, and it didn't matter to him that he was not morally worthy of such a title and responsibility. It was the goal and Finch's ego that mattered, not the duty that a public servant owes Americans. Finch's vanity led him to believe that he could commit murder without consequences, and the revelation that he could have been saved by eating just a little bit more shook him to his core.

A famous proverb is analogous here: "For want of a nail the shoe was lost, for want of a shoe the horse was lost, for want of a horse the rider was lost; for want of a rider the message was lost, for want of a message the battle was lost, for want of a battle the kingdom was lost, and all for want of a horseshoe nail." Oscar Finch's actions not only torpedoed his own career goals, but it's very possible that he simultaneously shattered Congressman Mackey's Vice-Presidential bid as well, and perhaps the entire ticket, meaning that Finch getting exposed as a murderer may have decided a presidential election, potentially altering the direction of the nation and even the world for four years, possibly eight. And all because of a nibbled cube of cheese.

Chapter Fifty-Three: Rest in Peace, Mrs. Columbo

Vivian Dimitri (Helen Shaver)

Most murderers just want to outwit Columbo. Vivian Dimitri wants to kill him and his wife.

In the opening scene, a heartbroken Columbo is sobbing at a rainy funeral, and viewers are shocked to learn that the coffin being lowered into the ground is Mrs. Columbo's. Amongst the crowd of mourners, Vivian Dimitri isn't sad. She's triumphant at having succeeded in killing Mrs. Columbo, and she plans to murder the lieutenant next.

The narrative flashes backwards, and it's revealed that Dimitri's husband, Pete Garibaldi, embezzled funds and went to jail for manslaughter after killing one of the clients he defrauded. Garibaldi passed away in jail from heart problems, and rather than recognizing that he deserved to be in prison, Dimitri blames two men for sending the man she loved to jail, believing that incarceration weakened his heart. Charlie Chambers (Edward Winter) blew the whistle on Garibaldi, and Columbo built a case against Garibaldi and arrested him.

Focusing her obsessive hatred on these two men, Dimitri shoots Chambers and takes his ATM card. She goes on a date with a married man, Leland St. John (Ian McShane), slipping out briefly to withdraw some money on Chambers' ATM card, believing this will give her an alibi. Later, when Columbo questions her about the crime, she claims not to have an alibi, saying she went home and had a cold supper and a hot bath all by herself. A little digging leads Columbo to discover she spent the night with St. John, and Dimitri admits she was really with him, which St. John grudgingly corroborates. But Columbo isn't fooled, and when he realizes that the victim had plenty of cash and didn't need to withdraw a little bit more, he knows that the supposedly reluctant alibi is all a sham.

Columbo realizes that Vivian Dimitri is really Annette Garibaldi, and she claims she needed a "clean break" with the past, which is a flimsy excuse considering she worked with the man who sent her husband to jail. The detective and the killer talk about their relationships with their respective spouses. Dimitri pushes to meet Mrs. Columbo and gives him some of her favorite lemon marmalade, which she has poisoned.

Sometime later, Columbo rushes home when an officer tells him his wife has taken ill. Soon, Columbo is heartbroken to learn his wife has died, and after flashing forward to after the funeral, a crushed Columbo goes back to his home with Dimitri, saying that someone who has also lost a beloved spouse will understand his grief. This is supposedly the first time viewers have seen Columbo's house, and there's a picture of his wife on the piano. Claiming to be hungry, Columbo eats some of the lemon marmalade on toast, noting that his wife had consumed some earlier. Shortly after consuming a generous quantity, Columbo starts feeling sick, and Dimitri gloatingly confesses to the murders of Chambers and Mrs. Columbo and delightedly declares that soon he'll be dead on his kitchen floor.

An instantly recovered Columbo disabuses her of this notion. The lemon marmalade he ate isn't from the poisoned jar she gave him. He suspected her from the beginning and had it analyzed. Mrs. Columbo never touched it, and she's alive, though she's battling a cold, at their real home. They are currently in the home of one of Columbo's colleagues, and the real owner of the house arrests Dimitri, though not before she slaps Columbo across the face. Not badly hurt, Columbo calls his wife to let her know he'll be home soon, confirming to viewers that she does indeed exist, but the photograph is of her sister Ruth because Mrs. Columbo doesn't believe she photographs well and has no nice pictures of herself around the house. These last reveals maintain the mystery about Columbo's personal life, as even the most loyal viewer has no idea what Columbo's home or what Mrs. Columbo looks like, other than the fact that she was described as having black hair in "Troubled Waters."

Throughout the episode, Dimitri is firmly convinced that she is in control of the situation, and that she has completely deceived Columbo as to her true intentions. It never crosses her mind that the detective may have seen through her deceptions and realizes that not only is she a killer, but that she may wish him ill as well.

Remarkably, up until the climax of the episode, the two of them treat each other like new friends, at least to each other's faces. When Columbo begins his routine conversational gambit with Dimitri, he visits her at her home while she's gardening. He informs her that his wife loves flowers and that he's been married twenty-eight or twenty-nine years (he's not sure exactly). It's not exactly clear when Mrs. Columbo became a target for Dimitri, but she soon decides that he wants to make Columbo suffer the loss of a beloved spouse before she murders him.

Dimitri makes no attempt to hide her past identity when Columbo realizes that he sent her husband to jail, declaring, "I wondered how long it was gonna take you to recognize me." She says this with no evident malice. For his part, Columbo doesn't seem to have taken any particular pleasure in bringing her spouse to justice. He tells her, "Even though I arrested him, I liked your husband. I think he was a decent guy. He just did some stupid things."

There's a sharp contradiction in Columbo's personal life when Columbo tells Dimitri that he and his wife "never had children, I'm sorry to say, but we had each other." Columbo has mentioned having at least one child in earlier episodes, so that means it's open to interpretation whether his earlier references to his kids were simply conversational patter, and by this point in his life, he has dropped the pretense, or if he's already suspicious of Dimitri's intentions towards himself and his wife, and he's pretending he doesn't have any children simply to keep them safely off her radar. Like so much about Columbo, this point will remain permanently ambiguous.

Over the course of their interactions, Dimitri is warm and friendly to Columbo, constantly pushing to meet Mrs. Columbo, though her insistence on meeting her is an immediate red flag. Through the stiffness in his body language, though not in his face and tone, Columbo seems to sense danger and demurs politely, though he always leaves the possibility open that Mrs. Columbo will meet her. When he accepts poisoned lemon marmalade from her, he shows nothing but gratitude, even though it's later confirmed that he is totally suspicious of the gift.

Unlike most of the other suspects in the series, Columbo doesn't press her over the discrepancies in her story or try to irritate her into revealing herself. In this case, Columbo's strategy is to keep their relationship as cordial as possible in the hopes of her revealing her endgame and thwarting her before she can do any harm. While in most cases, Columbo initially feigns cluelessness as to the culprit's guilt, in this case, Columbo hides the fact that he's wary of the crimes she'll commit in the future.

One of the most pivotal scenes in the episode is when Columbo speaks to Dimitri's ex-therapist, Dr. Steadman (Roscoe Lee Browne). Though Dr. Steadman cannot break confidentiality, he warns Columbo that it's best to stay away from her. It's a well-played scene, as Dr. Steadman strives to convey to Columbo that Dimitri is a dangerous woman without saying so, and Columbo silently understands just how much hate and resentment she bears toward him.

After covering her rage with ersatz pleasantness for most of the episode, Dimitri's façade cracks as she starts to rant, luxuriating in the belief that her revenge is nearly complete. She seethes about the judge who convicted her husband, calling him a "sick, prejudiced old man." She laughs as Columbo exhibits symptoms of poisoning, patting herself on the back for her cleverness and mocking him for his cluelessness. At the end, when Columbo turns the tables and reveals that the entire day was a huge sham to trap her and that he has never been fooled by anything she's done, it's a crushing blow to her ego. All this time, she's been congratulating herself over how clever she was and what a terrific actress she was, and now she's forced to accept the fact that Columbo was smarter than her and deceived her for as long as he's known her. He maintains his composure, saying he's sorry her husband died, but that doesn't justify her trying to kill him and his wife, saying, "I take that very personally." While almost every other *Columbo* killer exits without incident, Dimitri slaps him and calls him a bastard. It's more than just an example of her violent and flammable nature. It's proof of her talent for self-deception. Despite all her crimes, she believes that she and her husband are the real victims.

Vivian Dimitri is an example of love turned toxic, as her loss has caused her to lash out at people who do not deserve her ire. Charlie Chambers and Columbo did send her husband to jail, but her husband did earn his punishment. Little is known about the man he killed, but it's safe to assume there was no real justification for this loss of life. While it's uncertain as to whether Dimitri was always mentally unstable or if she crumbled in the wake of her husband's incarceration and death, it is undeniable that she was so blinded by her love for her husband that she was incapable of accepting that his jail sentence was a just consequence for his crimes, and her desire for revenge was the product of directing her rage towards anybody else she could lash at other than her husband. Had she been able to consider the situation rationally, she would have realized that her husband was a thief and a killer, and that the law was right to lock him away, and his death in prison was a consequence that could not have been anticipated and one for which Columbo should not be blamed. Instead, Dimitri turned her anger outward, seeing to punish those she felt had wronged her, rather than recognizing the responsibility for her pain lay closer to home. The only real justification for her actions is that she may have been suffering from a form of mental illness or a personality disorder, but even that is not a legal defense, as she should still have had the capability to determine right from wrong.

Vivian Dimitri was a woman who not only incorrectly believed that she was mistreated, but that she was also a criminal mastermind and a manipulative genius. Columbo managed to puncture her self-deluded mental bubble for these latter points, but whether she was ever able to admit her misguided mindset regarding her husband's fate is left unknown. Uniquely in *Columbo*, Vivian Dimitri became a murderess out of a desire for revenge stemming from an inability to assign blame properly.

Chapter Fifty-Four: Uneasy Lies the Crown

Wesley Corman (James Read)

Everybody who decides to commit a murder takes a massive gamble with their futures. Wesley Corman was a gambler who pushed his luck to the limits in an elaborate scheme, and if not for Columbo playing his hand skillfully, Corman might have gained access to a fortune.

Corman is a disinterested dentist, working half-heartedly at his father-in-law's practice, racking up huge gambling debts, and also making some shady business deals to keep his betting habit funded. When his father-in-law Horace Sherwin (Paul Burke) announces that he's sick of his shoddy work and frittering away money and has convinced his daughter to divorce him, Corman takes steps to protect his access to his wife's cash. His wife Lydia (Jo Anderson) is having an affair with the prominent actor Adam Evans (Marshall R. Teague), and Corman is fully aware of this.

When Evans comes to Corman's office for a dental appointment, Corman makes sure the office is empty so no one sees Evans arrive. Evans doesn't know that Corman's aware of the affair and doesn't suspect that Corman has tampered with the filling going into his tooth. Later that night, Corman has established an alibi at a poker game attended by celebrities and Lydia's brother David (Mark Arnott), and while Evans and Lydia are having a romantic evening, Evans suddenly gets ill and dies. Not surprisingly, Lydia freaks out, partly because her first husband, Tony, died exactly the same way on their wedding night.

When Lydia tries to call 911, her call is directed to the poker game because Corman switched the number on the speed dial. When Corman and the impressionable David arrive at the house, Corman argues that the public scandal will destroy the mentally fragile Lydia and convinces David that the most humane thing to do is to make the death look like a car accident. This is a self-serving ploy, as Corman slips a monogrammed matchbook into the dead man's shirt pocket to create a link to the Corman house, resets the phone autodial, and sprinkles powdered digitalis pills into Evans' drink. Evans's body is dressed, and his car is pushed off the road, though Corman knows the authorities will quickly realize this is no automobile accident. This supposed care for his wife's mental state convinces his in-laws that Corman's not such a bad guy after all.

As Corman expected, Columbo appears about twenty-five minutes into the episode and realizes right away this isn't a simple accident. Columbo starts digging and finds the clues Corman planted for him, but to Corman's displeasure, Columbo doesn't jump to the intended conclusion, realizing that a man would put matches in his jacket pocket rather than his shirt pocket. Lydia's family tries to protect her, and Columbo has a challenging but ultimately successful time convincing them that her husband is the real threat to Lydia, not him. After Corman confesses to moving the body to protect his wife, Columbo doesn't believe that Lydia poisoned her lover, realizing that Evans drank two margaritas, and with the amount of poison in the residue, he'd barely have had time to finish one before dying. The poison was administered another way, and the crime scene was staged.

Eventually, Lydia and her family accept that Corman has been manipulating them, and Columbo realizes that Corman killed Evans by using a time-sensitive filling, which dissolved after a few hours and released a lethal dose of poison.[1] Columbo takes Corman, Lydia, and Sherwin to a lab, telling them that some simple tests will prove Digitalis was in the tooth, as some chemical treatments will turn the Digitalis blue. Corman confesses before the tests can be run, and after he's led away, the lab technician, smiling, informs Columbo that there is no such test for digitalis. The experienced gambler Corman was bluffed.

Columbo and Corman do not have the same level of interaction that the detective often has with killers. Columbo's first meeting with Corman is friendly enough, but the relationship cools soon afterwards. But while many murderers seek to act as Columbo's helper on the case, Corman simply wishes to point Columbo in the desired direction, and is upset when Columbo doesn't fall for his narrative. The holes Columbo pokes in his narrative cause Corman to show pique, such as the parking ticket that suggests Corman lied about Evans canceling his dental appointment. When Columbo follows Corman to the racetrack and questions him, Corman is very cold to the detective, aside from offering Columbo bagels at the first meeting (an offer the lieutenant happily accepts), Corman never tries a real charm offensive on Columbo.

The failure to build real connections is one of the reasons why Corman is in the situation that led to murder. Corman never really tried to nurture his relationship with his wife and make sure she felt loved and cared for, which is a primary reason for the dissolution of their relationship. It's quite obvious his main interest is in her money. Corman's failure to build an emotional connection with his father-in-law is another reason why Sherwin disliked him and was so quick to turn against him again once Columbo suggested Corman was the murderer.

Essentially, Corman's great character flaw is that he doesn't attempt to connect with people. He's only concerned with his own interests, which mainly center around gambling. He killed to protect his finances, but also out of wounded pride. He wasn't in love with Lydia, but he resented his wife's adultery and bandaged his wounded pride by killing his wife's lover and framing her. Incidentally, the episode indicates that Lydia's first husband died naturally—Corman wasn't involved—and that Corman simply was inspired by the genuine tragedy to shape his own plan, a particularly cruel plan that was meant to cause extra psychological trauma to his wife.

The lackadaisical approach to relationships carried over to his professional life, and his disinterest in his career is another reason why he was so financially dependent on his wife's money. He also fails to put much effort into defending himself. When Columbo confronts him about his suspicions, admitting that he doesn't know how Corman did it, Corman sneers, "It's fortunate I'm so good-natured, Lieutenant. Somebody else might take offense." As Corman leaves, he asks Columbo to either join him in some fun or stay at the office and figure out how he did it. It's a challenge that Corman doesn't expect Columbo to succeed at, but Columbo sticks around and realizes how the poisoning worked. If Corman had put more thought into his crime, he would have realized that an imaginative person would have made the connection to dental work, but again, Corman was self-satisfied and neglected to consider just how flimsy his defenses were. A stronger-willed killer would have resisted Columbo's final trap, or at least would have kept his mouth shut in the hopes of triumphing in court or challenging Columbo's admittedly fraudulent chemistry demonstration. But he didn't. Corman was fundamentally a lazy man whose primary passion was his gambling. Rather than put in the effort to save himself, Corman decided to fold his hand. Once Columbo told Lydia and his in-laws he thought Corman was guilty, thereby turning them permanently against Corman, Corman's knowledge that he had lost his wife's money and had failed to get revenge by humiliating and mentally crushing her made him decide that denial was no longer worth it. Faced with the prospect of finding another place to practice dentistry, working full-time to make a living, and having little left over to gamble with, Corman decided that prison was the preferable option.

[1] * This may have been inspired by the classic crime story "Madame Sara" by L.T. Meade.

Chapter Fifty-Five: Murder in Malibu

Wayne Jennings (Andrew Stevens)

Murder in Malibu is one of a very small number of *Columbo* episodes where there is an actual question as to the identity of the killer. Wayne Jennings is a man who is very attractive to women. As the episode opens, he's in multiple relationships, the most prominent of which is with the romance writer Theresa Goren (Janet Margolin), whose wealth is probably the attribute of hers that Jennings finds most attractive. Goren is deeply enamored with Jennings, even going so far as to announce their engagement on a television talk show. Her sister, Jess McCurdy (Brenda Vaccaro), who is also her literary agent, is no fan of Jennings and is constantly trying to turn Goren against him. Eventually, it seems like the older sibling succeeds, and Goren breaks off the relationship over the phone. Jennings is distraught and is seen firing a gun and running away, with Goren lying on the ground. It seems clear to the viewer that Jennings is the killer, but soon, there's a plot twist.

Columbo arrives at the crime scene a little over nineteen minutes into the episode. The officer at the scene suggests it was a robbery gone wrong, but unsurprisingly, the detective thinks there's more to the story. Jennings arrives at the scene soon afterwards, and Columbo starts questioning him, noticing how distraught he is. After McCurdy explains that her sister broke off the relationship, Jennings cracks and confesses, saying he lost his head and shot her while she was lying down. As he's being Mirandized,

Columbo receives the news that the victim was actually shot multiple times. The first shot was the fatal one, fired from a different gun from the one Jennings used, meaning that Jennings shot a dead woman.

As shooting a corpse is not a serious crime, Jennings is released. As Columbo's investigation continues, he learns that Goren didn't actually break off the relationship, but McCurdy pretended to be her sister on the telephone. After learning this, Jennings pursues McCurdy, and it soon becomes clear that McCurdy's hostility towards Jennings was based in part on her own attraction to him. The two begin a relationship, but it ends before it really gets off the ground, as Columbo realizes that one of them committed the crime, and the guilty one is Jennings. He shoots his fiancée after thinking she broke up with him and tries to set up an alibi with an answering machine message, which is flawed due to the sound of some crows, which gives away his true location. The true giveaway was the fact that the victim was dressed after she died, and the victim's underwear was put on backwards. Only a man would make such a mistake, so Jennings committed the murder after all.

As Columbo always plays his cards close to his chest, it's hard to tell exactly when Columbo started to suspect Jennings and if he ever really stopped. Certainly, Columbo doesn't rush to embrace the officer on the scene's theory that the murder was a robbery gone bad. When Jennings arrives at the crime scene, full of tears, recriminations, a car stuffed with flowers, and his grandmother's wedding ring, the viewer cannot be sure if Columbo immediately senses the fakery. Certainly, Columbo tries to create a bit of a bond with Jennings over their automobiles, advancing the conversational gambit, "You know, I've got kind of a classic car, too," and asking about his mileage. It doesn't work. Unlike most *Columbo* killers, Jennings isn't interested in attempting to befriend or charm or influence the detective.

It's up to interpretation how Columbo responds to the way women fawn over Jennings—some men would be impressed, others jealous, and still others confused. Comparably, it's uncertain how Columbo responds to Jennings' first confession. Is he convinced, or is he suspicious because it comes so easily? The hyper-emotional breakdown with minimal provocation is unlike nearly any other confession Columbo's witnessed, and coupled with McCurdy's barb about Jennings' acting ambitions, it's a fair bet that Columbo sensed that Jennings overplayed his role. There's a physical mistake that gives Jennings's fakery away as well. Jennings "fainted" back and to the side after hearing the pronouncement that he shot a dead body, and usually people who faint fall face forward.

There's not much strong interaction between sleuth and killer. When Columbo checks in on a very worked-up Jennings at the hospital, Columbo tries to draw Jennings to assist him in the investigation, saying, "You're the one person I can count on most to help find the real killer. And we will. Don't worry." When Columbo mentions the million-dollar insurance policy in Jennings' favor, Jennings replies that he doesn't want to profit from her death and that the money will go to charity. It's not clear if this is an investment to disarm McCurdy in his pursuit of getting his hands on the inheritance from her, or if Jennings is all talk and zero actual donation. When Jennings joins Columbo at the crime scene and in a cherry-picker to get an overhead view of the area, Jennings is emotionally uninvolved and largely disinterested. There just isn't the classic level of interplay and gamesmanship that marks the best *Columbo* interactions.

Jennings is one of the shallowest *Columbo* villains. There's no real bond between him and the detective, and his defining character feature (and flaw) is that he is a man determined to coast by on life based on his good looks and charm. There's a lot of unspoken self-confidence, where he seems convinced that he can wrap any woman around his little finger with a little bit of charisma. Indeed, the ease with which McCurdy succumbs to his charms is a bit unconvincing, just as his scheme for getting away with murder is.

The basic premise, where a suspect is supposedly cleared of committing a murder because he tried to kill the victim after the deceased was already dead, is not original to this episode. An episode of *Murder, She Wrote* used exactly the same premise; Erle Stanley Gardner considered a comparable situation from a legal standpoint in multiple novels, and other stories have used it over the years, with many variants, such as in the Oscar-winning movie *Gosford Park*. It's not the most common crime fiction trope for deflecting suspicion, but mystery fans are likely to come across it with mild regularity. In other usages, the killer supposedly attacked the already deceased victim, thinking the target was asleep. Jennings' story falls apart a bit under scrutiny. He was so upset that he just shot the woman he loved while she was lying down fully dressed? It's not quite the same as thinking the victim was lying down in the dark, and it shows that Jennings is not a great plotter. His alibi is easily shattered through background noise, and once someone starts doubting his story and wonders if he fired the first shot, too, he's an obvious target of suspicion.

Wayne Jennings was a womanizer and a gold-digger who believed that he could bend women to his will with minimal effort. While this high opinion of his own manipulative powers was based partly on experience, he ultimately failed due to a lack of attention to detail and an adherence to a clumsy plan that he thought he could pull off through sheer charisma. Unfortunately for him, he couldn't fool Columbo.

X

SEASON TEN

Chapter Fifty-Six: Columbo Goes to College

Justin Rowe (Stephen Caffrey) and Cooper Redman (Gary Hershberger)

Justin Rowe and Cooper Redman are a pair of students at Freemont College who prefer partying to studying, but they can put a lot of effort into a project they're interested in pursuing. Unfortunately, instead of devoting their skills towards genuine scholarship, they turn their attention to murder.

Rowe and Redman are on thin ice with their parents, whose patience regarding their hedonistic lifestyles has been stretched to the breaking point. One of their instructors, Prof. Rusk (James Sutorius), catches them cheating on a test and vows that they will face consequences. As their parents' money can't help them out of this, they decide to murder Rusk. They set up a device in a parking garage, allowing them to shoot and kill the professor by remote control while they sit in a lecture hall. It would be the perfect alibi, but their guest lecturer is none other than Columbo.

Columbo, who first appears about fifteen minutes into the episode, references "Agenda for Murder" and is right at the scene of the crime when the body is discovered. Most of the other students in the class seem genuinely friendly towards Columbo, but Rowe and Redman view the detective with deep contempt, sneering at his intelligence and fashion sense behind his back, though to his face, they are exaggeratedly sycophantic. They actually work as his "helpers" over the course of the investigation, believing that their proximity to Columbo will help them direct the detective's focus in their preferred direction: into the professor's personal life. The pair push the theory that Rusk's womanizing led to his murder, and Columbo pretends to be convinced by them.

Rowe and Redman's belief that they are firmly in control of the situation is disrupted when video of the murder is released on the news—the camera they used to record the scene of the crime so they knew when to press the button to attack Rusk inadvertently broadcast the footage to a nearby home with a powerful satellite dish, where it was recorded on a VCR.

The murderers seek to blame an innocent man, Dominic Doyle (William Lucking), and plant the weapon in their patsy's car, believing that will close the case, but Columbo throws them for a loop when he reenacts the crime, showing he knows exactly how it was done, and informs them that they fell into a trap. The gun was placed in Doyle's wife's car, and only Rowe and Redman had been fed false information about which car belonged to Doyle. Caught, the pair are defiant yet unrepentant, making the incriminating statements "We did it, Lieutenant, because we knew how to do it" and "My father doesn't like to see me fail" as they are led away by the police.

Never before have *Columbo* killers behaved so obsequiously to the Lieutenant's face and so contemptuously behind his back. When they offer their assistance, they act like Columbo's biggest fans. The moment they think he's out of earshot, any semblance of respect evaporates. They failed to pay attention to Columbo's lecture, where he stresses the importance of instinct and withholding how much information you know. He tells the class, "I follow my nose… Don't talk too much. If you know something, keep it to yourself." Perhaps Rowe and Redman were too busy making cracks about Columbo's tailor to hear this sage advice. In any event, they are so convinced of their own cleverness and believability that when they feed Columbo information about their victim's promiscuity, they later sneer, "This guy's gonna swallow anything."

But in reality, the killers aren't the ones who are skilled at deceiving their enemies. It's Columbo who sees right through them and disguises his perception through seeming credulity. While the killers force themselves to keep a straight face while offering insincere compliments about Columbo's classic car, Columbo acts like they're his protégés, telling them, "We're in this together." Minutes later, he catches them a short distance away as they laugh and mock his mannerisms, thinking he's not looking. They didn't even take the precaution of getting out of sight before showing their disrespect. Columbo doesn't get angry; he simply says, "Very funny," to himself, and he quietly watches their imitations. Rowe and Redman genuinely believe Columbo is a fool. At one point, one killer even asks, "Do you think Columbo's parents were related?" Perhaps they inherited their contempt from their parents. Robert Culp returns to the series after three turns as a killer. This time, he's playing Rowe's father, and he treats Columbo with the disdain one might give a particularly blockheaded underling, and his wife (Maree Cheatham) is no better, calling Columbo a "rumpled little dumbbell." Of course, they're wrong, but we never see their reactions when they learn just how mistaken they really were.

This is one of the rare cases where the viewer sees how the killers' minds were shaped to develop the flaws and shortcomings that led them on their journeys to becoming murderers. From what we see of the Rowes (not so much the Redmans), Rowe was raised in a privileged environment where his family's money and influence got them what they wanted when they wanted it. Mr. and Mrs. Rowe view people of lower social status as innately inferior in most ways, and it seems that this contempt and overinflated self-regard was passed onto their son. It's unclear if Rowe influenced Redman for the worse or if they were both innately disposed towards narcissism, and while it's debatable how deeply Rowes' snobbery scarred their son, in the end, Rowe chose to commit murder of his own free will, and he and Redman must bear the full responsibility for their actions, as whatever shortcomings their parents may have demonstrated while raising them, they never advocated homicide as a solution to problems.

Rowe and Redman may remind those viewers with a knowledge of the historical true crime of the Leopold and Loeb case, where two college students murdered a boy for what was later dubbed "an intellectual thrill." While there are some parallels, there are critical differences—there is no gay relationship between Rowe and Redman—part of the reason for their being on thin ice is because of their playboy ways with women. Also, they kill to prevent their expulsion and disgrace, rather than their desire to commit the perfect crime purely for the sake of it, though they do take pleasure in committing what they *think* is a flawless homicide. There is one distinct comparison between the real-life and fictional killers—both pairs have a firm belief in their own superiority.

Rowe and Redman were raised in an environment where hedonism brought no consequences, and their bubbles of self-esteem were never burst. One is an inveterate womanizer who got three girlfriends pregnant, all of whom had abortions. When Rowe and Redman were finally faced with an opportunity to accept the consequences for their shortcomings, they instead decided that murder to preserve the status quo was the preferable option. Not only were they willing to take the life of a man who was prepared to reveal their cheating to the world, but they also were willing to send an innocent man that they barely knew and had done them no harm to prison, an additional, unnecessary, and cruel extra step. In their final moments on-screen, they not only show no remorse, but they also fail to demonstrate the simple good sense of keeping their mouths shut to avoid incriminating themselves further. The final comment, where one implies that his father will fund their defense, is probably prescient. A man of such wealth and prominence is unlikely to wish to bear the social stigma of a homicidal son, and it's probable that both Rowe and Redman, analogous to Leopold and Loeb in real life, will benefit from the best legal counsel money can buy. Whether this will lead to reduced consequences is unknown, but it is made manifest that neither Rowe nor Redman has learned any lasting moral lessons during their time at college.

Chapter Fifty-Seven: Caution: Murder Can Be Hazardous to Your Health

Wade Anders (George Hamilton)

Smoking kills…and so does Wade Anders. Anders is the host of a popular television true crime show, but when Budd Clarke (Peter Haskell), a rival who believes that the hosting position should be rightfully his, decides to push Anders out the door with a little blackmail, Anders decides that he needs to commit a crime worthy of an episode of his show. Clarke discovered that years earlier, Anders starred in a dirty movie, and realizes that this bit of information will cost Anders his prominent job. And so, like many *Columbo* guest stars before him, Anders decides to eliminate his problem with murder, poisoning a cigarette and slipping it to Clarke when he visits Clarke's home.

Columbo appears nearly twenty-eight minutes into the episode as he arrives at the crime scene. Dog is confirmed to be alive and well when Columbo mentions his own pet to a friendly dog living close to the crime scene. Once Columbo realizes how the victim died, he comments "I gotta quit smoking." The detective performs his usual brilliant observations, noting that the cigarettes on the desk (planted by Anders) weren't actually smoked, as there are no nicotine stains on the filters. Columbo also realizes that someone other than the dead man printed an article at the scene of the crime due to various discrepancies and physical impossibilities, leading to the conclusion that someone else was there, possibly Clarke's killer.

Columbo and Anders do not meet until nearly halfway through the episode, and Columbo tests Anders frequently, pointing out the little mistakes he made in setting the scene and pressuring Anders to admit the fact that several details in the scene do not make sense. Anders steadily grows increasingly frustrated at Columbo as the investigation proceeds, but believes that he is protected by a security camera video that gives him an alibi for the time of Clarke's death. Unfortunately for Anders, Columbo's diligence and attention to detail lead him to prove that the video was altered– the hedges in the video are trimmed in one scene but not in a later one, proving that the video does not cover the events of a single day in order. Not only that, but the friendly dog living next to the crime scene has a habit of putting his paws on the cars of people who visit, leaving behind distinctive scratches on the paint due to his missing claw, proving Anders lied when he said he'd never visited Clarke's home. Caught, Anders surrenders with bitter grace, saying, "A dog? Man's best friend? Well, at least you got a good story for our show." Columbo replies, "No, I don't think so, but it will be a good story for the 11:00 news."

Anders' attitude towards Columbo can best be described as polite yet condescending. When they meet thirty-eight-and-a-half minutes into the episode, Anders is very calm and civil, and when Columbo explains why he's suspicious about the circumstances of Clarke's death, he says, "I think you're onto something, Lieutenant… That's good work…" A bit of undisguised contempt seeps into his voice when Columbo suggests using one of his own cases on the television show. Anders disgustedly sneers, "Everyone's out to make a buck." There's a real current of arrogance in Anders' manner, as he seems to feel that his prominent television job makes him somehow superior to men like Columbo. When Columbo visits Anders while he's getting his hair trimmed, and proves through the differently crushed cigarette butts that someone else besides Clarke was at the scene of the crime. This produces Anders' cold remark, "Maybe you should host the show." Columbo isn't visibly hurt by this, remarking, "He's got a great sense of humor, hasn't he?"

Anders never builds a genuine connection with Columbo, and Columbo seems to have decided a policy of attrition and annoyance is the best way to approach Anders. Like most celebrities who cross Columbo's path, Columbo asks for a signed photograph for his wife's collection. After repeated visits, Anders asks Columbo why he doesn't simply ask for his alibi for the time of the crime. It's an important point– Columbo is using his longtime gambit of not accusing the suspect directly, but subtly making the target aware that he is under suspicion, making the suspect the one to address the fact Columbo believes him to be a murderer. Columbo seems to be treating Anders like one of his own hard-boiled eggs, gently tapping him from different directions until he finally cracks. This culminates in a scene where Columbo's car bumps into Anders' vehicle, and it's not clear if the collision was deliberate or accidental. In any event, the damage to Anders' car causes him to fly into a frenzy, ranting about the expense of the repairs and the difficulty in fixing a specialty car. Another conversation at an awards show leads to Anders snapping at a colleague after Columbo casually brings up blackmail.

Throughout the episode, Columbo's tactic is to scrape away Anders' polished veneer. A television presenter has to maintain a certain level of authority and believability to earn the respect of his audience, and Anders has molded himself into a respectable public figure. Columbo intends to reveal the true man behind the façade, and what he finds is a short-tempered and supercilious man who places an exceptionally high value upon his personal status symbols and who continually tries to tear others down in order to stay on the pedestal on which he has placed himself. The final exchange between the pair reflects Columbo delivering a final puncture to Anders' ego. Anders believed he had created a flawless scheme for homicide, only for Columbo to dismiss his creation as a pedestrian and fatally flawed murder plan.

Wade Anders wanted to keep his profitable and prominent television job. This is understandable, and whatever one feels about the morality of appearing in sexually explicit films, Anders was leading a respectable career at that point. Admittedly, if Clarke was correct and not just wallowing in sour grapes, the means by which Anders obtained the job may not have been entirely just, but similar frustrations over who comes up triumphant are universal in show business and many other fields. Lots of people, like Clarke, feel that they are more deserving of a position than the person who actually got the job. Very few of them turn to blackmail in order to overturn the hiring committee's decision. While blackmail itself may be evidence of a moral failing, it is not a capital offense. Blackmailers, aside from the ones working with Columbo to bring killers to justice rather than profit, rarely prosper on the show. Anders' defense counsel could certainly argue that Anders was acting to protect a lapse in judgment of his past from ruining his future. In any event, Anders could have fought Clarke, pointing out that they were in a situation of mutually assured destruction. If Clarke revealed Anders' embarrassing secret, Anders could have told the world about Clarke's blackmail attempt, and such a revelation would probably have convinced the network that an extortionist was not the sort of person they wanted hosting their crime show. By pointing out that Clarke would gain nothing and possibly have his own career derailed by his blackmail being revealed, Anders could have avoided committing murder and potentially could have saved his position as well. Offering to share hosting duties on the show could have also defused the situation.

While Anders' desire to salvage his public image is understandable, the fact remains that Anders placed his own reputation and lucrative career above another human being's life. A threat to his social status rather than his life does not justify the use of lethal force. Anders valued prestige and prominence over Clarke's life, and he chose to become a murderer.

Chapter Fifty-Eight: Columbo and the Murder of a Rock Star

Hugh Creighton (Dabney Coleman) and Trish Fairbanks (Shera Danese)

A handful of the *Columbo* killers work with a partner. Sometimes, the murdering pair have genuine affection for each other; occasionally, one of the killers is only using the other until the inconvenient partner can be killed. Hugh Creighton is perhaps the only *Columbo* killer to be stuck with an accomplice he doesn't want, didn't expect, and cannot eliminate.

Creighton is a man who hates to fail. He's a defense lawyer who has a reputation for never losing a case. He's in a relationship with a much younger singer, Marcy Edwards (Cheryl Paris), and she's cheating on him. Furious, Creighton locks her out of the house and throws out her belongings. Creighton believes that she's entitled to nothing, but due to the length of their relationship, Edwards insists that she should receive $5 million in "palimony" upon the dissolution of their relationship and believes she has a good chance of prevailing in court. Like many killers before him, Creighton decides that murder is the more economical option.

Creighton doses a bottle of champagne, but this doesn't go to plan— Edwards only takes a sip of the sparkling wine after detecting the adulterant, though she doesn't realize what affected the flavor. Her boyfriend Neddy

Malcolm (Julian Stone) consumes much more of it, and he's unconscious when Creighton enters. The actual killing isn't shown onscreen, but there's no doubt that it was Creighton who strangled Edwards to death and left evidence implicating the boyfriend. When he awakens, Malcolm sprints away into the night.

Columbo appears just over twenty minutes into the episode, immediately finding suspicious clues, such as the number of corks and their location (caused by Creighton disposing of the drugged champagne in the kitchen). Columbo conducts his investigation with the expected focus on Creighton, uses his connections to track down Malcolm and clear him, and eventually accuses Creighton of the crime.

Trish Fairbanks realizes right away that Creighton used her to set up an alibi for him, and blackmails Creighton into making her not only a full partner in the law firm, but his fiancée as well, making sure that her death would do him no good because of documents that would be made public after her demise. Creighton's appalled by this turn of events, but he's powerless to stop her takeover of his life. Before she knew he planned murder, Fairbanks set up an alibi for Creighton by driving his car while wearing a mask made out of a photograph of him. While wearing the mask, Fairbanks triggered a speeding ticket after being caught by an automated speed trap. Creighton and Fairbanks revel in their perceived victory, with Creighton snarking that the parking ticket may be the only case he's ever lost.

Columbo isn't daunted, and he realizes that the lack of shadows in the traffic cam photograph prove that the driver of the car was wearing a mask and some rare berries that got stuck on the hood of the car Creighton used to travel to the scene of the crime complete the case. Satisfied that he's checkmated Creighton, Columbo takes great pleasure in reading him his rights to make sure that he can't escape due to a technicality.

The relationship between Columbo and Creighton is a strained one, as Creighton loves to flaunt his wealth and influence, but also frequently attempts to discredit Columbo just as he would if the detective was a witness in court. In a parallel manner, Columbo first meets Creighton in a courtroom, as Creighton is using all sorts of tactics to distract his opponent during an address to the jury. Turnabout is fair play, however, and Columbo interrupts Creighton's final statement when he first meets him thirty-two minutes into the episode. Creighton is quite upset, even showing Columbo the disrespect of getting his name wrong ("Columbus") before Columbo justifies the disruption by informing him of the murder.

From that point onwards, Creighton treats Columbo more civilly, though he does treat him like an underling at his beck and call. Despite having no official authority, Creighton acts as if he believes that his orders will be obeyed without question. After they arrive at the morgue, Creighton demands to see the autopsy reports. When Columbo says that's not possible, Creighton throws his weight around until he gets his way. This is Creighton's attempt to maintain a level of control over the investigation, keeping an eye on how much has been uncovered and potentially directing the inquiries in his preferred directions. Additionally, by acting as if he's anxious to see a resolution to the case, he believes he is making himself look innocent.

Creighton clearly does have influence over law enforcement, as he soon informs Columbo that he expects him for dinner and his boss has granted permission for him to bring the case files with him. Columbo meets Creighton at a fancy restaurant, and though there's an invitation for Columbo to order whatever he wants, Creighton orders only soup, an action that would subtly pressure most guests to order a similarly light and inexpensive meal. Columbo is having none of this, however, and regains a certain level of control over the situation by ordering enough food to fill a buffet. Creighton may be able to influence Columbo's bosses, but Columbo uses the meal to show that Creighton can't control him.

Creighton has trouble controlling his own emotions, getting furious at the suggestion of his girlfriend being unfaithful and rudely stating that he doesn't want "a stupid mistake" to lead to the killer going free. He becomes unreasonably incredulous when Columbo explains why he thinks Creighton's preferred suspect is innocent. As the episode progresses, it becomes very clear to Creighton that he hasn't fooled Columbo, and in response to a direct question as to whether Columbo thinks he's guilty, Columbo bluntly replies, "Yes sir, I think it's a real possibility." This leads to Creighton unceremoniously kicking Columbo out of his office. After a quick scene with a higher-up that illustrates just how much trouble Columbo must have had with the police bureaucracy over the course of his career when he investigated the rich and influential, Creighton realizes that he's squarely in Columbo's crosshairs. He attempts to publicly ridicule Columbo by calling him a "lunatic" and hews to the old maxim about a man who serves as his own attorney having a fool for a client, hiring another capable lawyer who won't let him answer questions.

Throughout the episode, Creighton treats Columbo as not just an opponent, but as a lesser being who deserves condescension at best and outright ridicule at worst. There's no scenes of grudging affection or respect, just ordering about and bullying. Columbo's face is understandably particularly triumphant when he takes Creighton away from his planned fancy evening with Fairbanks and arrests him. This is one of the cases where Columbo derives powerful pleasure from seeing a killer get his comeuppance.

Should Trish Fairbanks be counted as one of the *Columbo* killers? The answer is yes. She didn't plan the killing, but she did deduce what happened and seek to profit from it. By wearing a photograph mask of Creighton, she *must* have known that there was some shady reason for the deception, as this is not a normal duty. Fairbanks almost certainly figured that she was being used to create an alibi and realized that she might be able to utilize the opportunity to her advantage, even though she didn't know for certain what Creighton would be doing that could provide an opportunity for extortion later. In fact, this is a confusing action on Creighton's part, as it's unclear what sort of excuse he gave for this action. Did he really expect his subordinate to obey orders without question and that she would never deduce that he was using her to pretend he was somewhere else at an important time? It's a gaping hole in Creighton's plan.

Fairbanks' actions make her an accessory after the fact and a blackmailer who seeks both a partnership in the firm and complete security by marrying him. It seems like she's thrilled by this power trip, reveling in making over her workspace and showing absolutely no fear in linking her lot with a murderer. Fairbanks puts a lot of trust in the incriminatory statement she has arranged to have delivered to the authorities after she dies, and it's unclear whether Creighton's increasing displeasure with the unexpected turn of events is the prelude to another act of violence, or if he is attempting to resign himself to an unpleasant fate. His sudden engagement to Fairbanks also serves to harm his narrative that he's heartbroken over his girlfriend's demise. In any event, Fairbanks was willing to exploit Edwards' death for wealth, prestige, and power.

Though Columbo finds the new relationship between Creighton and Fairbanks suspicious, it's not certain whether or not Columbo really believed that he had a case against her. At the end, Fairbanks is not seen being arrested, and Columbo gives no hint that he will be coming for her at a later time. This does not necessarily mean that she got away with it. Creighton might have fought the murder charges in court, but if he decided the case was hopeless or if he decided to negotiate a plea bargain in exchange for a reduced sentence, he might have implicated Fairbanks as a means of getting revenge against her and preventing her from thriving as the head of the law firm. The uncorroborated testimony of an accomplice is often not enough for a conviction, but if the authorities were to gain access to the accusatory letter Fairbanks tucked away as insurance, the document she thought would keep her alive might wind up sending her to jail.

Like most of the *Columbo* murderers, Creighton could have avoided his downfall had he simply overcome some of his basic character flaws. Creighton is a man with immense pride. He is immensely proud of his record as an unbeaten lawyer, and he took pleasure in having a famous musician girlfriend who was a fraction of his age. When she cheated on him, it was a massive blow to his ego. Initially, he simply sought to cut her from his life, but when she decided that she wanted and deserved substantial compensation at the end of their relationship, Creighton decided that nothing would do but kill her.

It's unclear exactly how wealthy Creighton was, but if he really wanted to get rid of her, he could probably have either paid her what she wanted or negotiated a deal for a lesser amount. If she insisted on full payment, given his legal connections and resources, it's possible that he could have either triumphed over her in court or reduced her palimony to a pittance. But the critical issue facing him wasn't money (though he certainly cared about it), but his pride. Had this matter gone to court, the details of Edwards' extra-relationship activities would have been made public knowledge, and if it was widely known that he was cuckolded, humiliation would follow. Late in the episode, when Creighton proclaims how much his late girlfriend meant to him and how he doesn't want her name "smeared in the newspapers," he's really worried about how having an unfaithful girlfriend will affect how others think of *him*. In addition, had Edwards been able to substantiate her allegations of unethical behavior, Creighton could have lost his career and reputation. This threat led Creighton to decide that the woman who dealt a body blow to his pride must pay with her life, and the man she had cheated with would be framed for her death. It was a risky scheme, but Creighton's high self-regard led him to convince himself that he simply couldn't lose.

XI

SEASON ELEVEN

Chapter Fifty-Nine: Death Hits the Jackpot

Leon Lamarr (Rip Torn) and Nancy Brower (Jamie Rose)

"Death Hits the Jackpot" is a story of how two people steeped in betrayal and greed are undone by their own character flaws. Rip Torn's Leon Lamarr is one of the most exuberantly slimy of the *Columbo* killers, a man who takes what he wants and finds himself stunned when the bill comes due.

This is another case where two people collaborate on a crime, though the fact that they are in cahoots is held back until a dramatic moment and then revealed as a surprise. The second villain of this story is Nancy Brower, the wife of the victim.

As the story opens, Freddy Brower (Gary Kroeger), a photographer, is trying to wrap up a contentious divorce with Nancy. He wants her to sign the decree and end the marriage while she is holding out for a more advantageous financial settlement. Freddy's frustration evaporates when he catches the lottery drawing on television and checks his ticket, discovering that he won thirty million dollars. He's thrilled, but as he is reluctant to share his windfall with a woman he clearly has no lingering affection for, he turns to his uncle for advice on how to avoid being compelled to hand over half the money to his soon-to-be ex. This proves to be a fatal mistake.

His uncle, Leon Lamarr, is a jeweler whose poor investments have wiped out his finances. Just as he's reeling from the shock, Freddy comes to ask for help. It's clear that Freddy is far too trusting, as anybody with a trace of perception can tell from the wicked glint in Leon's eye that he's plotting to pocket the lottery winnings for himself. Leon immediately proposes that Freddy give him the ticket, and he'll cash it himself and give Freddy the money, leaving Nancy out in the cold. Freddy signs his own death warrant and agrees.

After a bit of publicity, Leon suggests to his wife (it's unclear if she's always been affectionate towards him, or if the lottery winnings have rekindled a new passion for him) that they throw a Halloween costume party with the theme "Dress as Your Favorite Millionaire." To no viewer's surprise, shortly before the guests arrive, Leon hurries over to Freddy's apartment (wearing his King George III costume), where he knocks his nephew out before drowning him in a bathtub, making it look like a slip-and-fall accident. Viewers may be more surprised by the twist that Leon is actually having an affair with Nancy, who calls Leon after he returns home in order to create an alibi, creating the impression that Freddy is still alive and using the phone.

Columbo appears thirty-two and a half minutes into the narrative, examining the crime scene and comforting a pet monkey who's distraught by the sudden death. When he arrives at Leon's party to break the news, the detective's rumpled raincoat is mistaken as a costume depicting an eccentric millionaire. Leon acts heartbroken, making a dramatic show of tears over his nephew's demise. The next day, when Columbo visits the dress shop where Nancy works, Nancy is less emotional, displaying no signs of being upset.

As Columbo continues his investigation, he discovers that Freddy was acting like a man living far beyond his means, buying a case of champagne (the brand is the same one that plays a prominent role in "Columbo and the Murder of a Rock Star") and ordering a $175,000 luxury car. Increasingly suspicious, Columbo discovers that the lottery numbers match a series of numbers on the settings dial on one of Freddy's cameras, solidifying his belief that it was Freddy who bought the ticket. Columbo keeps digging, finding inconsistencies in the killers' stories, and eventually confronts Leon with the critical evidence. The pet monkey, who is attracted to shiny objects, handled the medallion Leon wore as part of his George III costume, leaving behind a simian fingerprint. This disproves Leon's assertion that he wasn't at the scene of the crime. There is, however, no forensic evidence to prove Nancy's guilt, so Columbo switches to psychological tactics to capture her. Columbo explains how Leon appropriated Freddy's lottery winnings, and now Nancy is set to inherit the entire $30 million. Nancy can't hide her glee, which enrages Leon, leading him to confess her involvement, thereby solidifying the case against himself, all out of uncontrollable rage and spite. Nancy has a meltdown as she is arrested.

With a little more self-control and finesse, Nancy might have been able to save herself. If she'd said something along the lines of "I simply can't believe it, Lieutenant. I don't believe that dear Uncle Leon could have done such a horrible thing. Don't you worry, Uncle Leon. I'm going to make sure you get the finest defense lawyer money can buy. You just sit tight and I'll look after you." That might've placated Leon, leaving him quiet.

Then again, it's possible that Leon would have wanted to make absolutely certain that as an accessory to the murder, Nancy couldn't possibly inherit the money. The provisions of Freddy's will aren't clear, but if Columbo was able to prove Freddie bought the ticket, with both Leon and Nancy charged with the crime, the lottery winnings would probably pass on to Freddy's next of kin, which, as far as is revealed in the episode, would be Leon's son and daughter. There are a number of "ifs" involved, but it's possible that a few quick calculations led Leon to conclude that if he couldn't enjoy the money himself, he could ensure the futures of his children. Then again, that may be giving Leon too much credit, and he could have simply cut his own throat to spite his face. Indeed, throughout the episode, Leon and Nancy are proven to be less skilled at understanding other people than they think they are, and their skills at understanding human nature are weaker than they believe.

For much of the episode, Leon and Nancy seem amused by Columbo, though following the classic pattern, Leon, who has far more screen time with the detective, grows increasingly frustrated by Columbo's constant questions and appearances. While the pair are having a tryst, Nancy says she found Columbo "kind of cute" and liked him. Once again, villains find Columbo amusing as long as they do not consider him a threat. The moment Columbo starts casting suspicions, he becomes far less charming to them.

Nancy does not express the same level of exasperation that Leon does. When Columbo questions her as to why she never signed the divorce papers, she presents him with a sob story about not really wanting to end the marriage, all well-salted with copious amounts of crocodile tears. This illustrates a combination of arrogance and overconfidence, as Columbo isn't fooled for a moment by her histrionics, while Nancy is convinced that she's wrapped the detective around her middle finger. Until the last moment, Nancy's wrapped up in the delusion that she has the upper hand, and her misplaced self-confidence is crucial to her downfall.

Meanwhile, Columbo's questioning quickly leads to Leon becoming exasperated. In their second meeting, Columbo is quite friendly to Leon, wishing to shake the hand of the man who bought the $30 million lottery ticket. Their relationship doesn't stay cordial for long, as Leon takes offense to Columbo's observation that Freddy's watch was a cheap knockoff, as Leon gave the timepiece to his nephew as a gift. Columbo's theory that Freddy pawned the watch due to his precarious financial situation and wore an imitation to hide his actions immediately placates Leon, who apologizes in an apparently sincere way. It's a nice moment, as the seemingly genuine regret humanizes a man who is largely a moustache-twirling villain, albeit one who's quite fun to watch.

Leon's temper frays quickly, though, as Columbo casts doubt upon his assertion Freddy was coming to the party, as Freddy had no costume. Columbo's discovery that the lottery numbers were far more likely to come from Freddy, as they're settings on a camera, further unnerve Leon, and when Columbo stumbles into a jewelry auction and accidentally drives up the bidding, he responds to the detective with a barely veiled expression of frustration. At the end, when Columbo declares Freddie was murdered and asks for Leon's alibi, Leon's grip on his temper frays completely. Clearly, Leon is not a man who responds to pressure well. His consternation is not the result of a guilty conscience burning with shame, but rather the anxiety of a man who is seeing his carefully laid plans starting to unravel, and his blustering is clearly the reaction of a guilty man, and it all helps Columbo gauge just how close Leon is to the breaking point.

After scrutinizing the relationship between Leon and Nancy, it becomes very clear that it is not a love affair, so much as it is a lust affair. We rarely see the two converse or express any shared interests save for a passion for money—a widespread interest, but not one that is known to form the basis of a healthy and lasting relationship. At no point does Nancy bring up the possibility of Leon divorcing his wife and marrying her, so while her affair with Leon certainly didn't help her relationship with Freddy, it wasn't the primary cause of the divorce? It is never made clear when their affair began, but while they never psychologically scrutinize their reasons for their adultery, it's highly implied that the taboo nature of the relationship, that of an uncle and a niece by marriage, fuels their passion, with it becoming all the more scandalous because it is incestuous by law, though not blood.

Indeed, by the last third of the episode, even the most observant viewer would be hard-pressed to find any semblance of affection between the pair. Nancy's primary interest is the money, and at one point, Leon's facial expressions imply that he's trying to think of a way to kill her so he can keep all the cash for himself and tie up a loose end. With no genuine affection between the pair, it's no wonder that their alliance crumbles so spectacularly.

Ultimately, Leon and Nancy are an unholy pair who thought that they could have it all, but wound up losing everything. Certainly, Freddy created the chain of circumstances that led to his own death by his unwillingness to report his winnings, though wanting to keep as much as one can is a pretty common emotion during a bitter divorce. Leon's actions were a terrible betrayal, as Freddy truly loved his uncle. If Leon had explained just how precarious his own finances were, certainly Freddy would have given Leon some money, or at least loaned him enough to keep him solvent. There was no need for murder, but it happened due to the destructive nature of greed.

Chapter Sixty: No Time to Die

Rudolph Arnold Strassa (Daniel McDonald)

Not to be confused with the James Bond movie of the same name, "No Time to Die" is an aberration in the *Columbo* series. This episode is doubly unique. First, it does not contain a murder. Secondly, the primary villain, Rudolph Arnold Strassa, has no interaction with Columbo. The two do not meet or converse, and Columbo never even gets a chance to look at Strassa before Strassa's death.

The discrepancy is due to the fact that this is not an original script, like the overwhelming majority of *Columbo* episodes. Instead, it is an adaptation of one of Ed McBain's 87th Precinct novels, *So Long As You Both Shall Live*, a police procedural, just like "Undercover," a few episodes later. The narrative opens with Columbo having a grand old time at his nephew's wedding. This is the first and only time viewers see one of Columbo's oft-mentioned relatives in the flesh. The woman seen next to Columbo at one point is not the ever-absent Mrs. Columbo, but is instead a random guest he just happens to be talking to at that moment. The real Mrs. Columbo is in Chicago, looking after her mother. The groom is Detective Andy Parma, the son of Columbo's sister. A throwaway line refers to Columbo's sister Abby and her husband Dan, who are "no longer with us." The bride, Melissa, is a fashion model who has a dangerous, obsessed stalker after her.

This stalker is Rudolph Arnold Strassa, who kidnaps Melissa on her wedding night, leaving Andy, who left her alone for a few minutes in the honeymoon suite while he was taking a shower, to wonder what has happened to his new bride. Naturally, Andy turns to his uncle for help, and over the course of the episode, Columbo leads the investigation, talking to guests and hotel employees, looking for clues. Columbo's investigation is different from most of his others, as he doesn't need to use the same level of psychological tactics to speak to villains. Aside from utilizing a bit of diplomatic tact by promising Melissa's father that his wife will be kept in the dark about the kidnapping so she won't be distraught, Columbo doesn't need to use his people skills as much as he just need to utilize a law enforcement professional's dogged determination to chase down every lead he can find. Given the unusual format of this episode, Columbo never has the chance to get into Strassa's head and form a connection with him.

Strassa is different from all of the other *Columbo* villains, chiefly because he is so obviously villainous. Every other one of the killers could easily fit into polite society, being intelligent, cultured, and generally possessing a certain level of charm. Not so Strassa, the only one to be distinctly, incontrovertibly...*creepy*. All of the other antagonists could pass themselves off as decent, friendly individuals, and most of them actually could have been pillars of society if they'd only had the moral fiber to suppress their homicidal tendencies. But Strassa clearly cannot ever be a fully functional member of society. He's unquestionably mentally ill, an obsessed stalker with a purring, rancidly oily demeanor. It's impossible to spend more than a few moments with him without breaking out into goosebumps all over, and it's ironic that the most clearly antisocial of all the *Columbo* villains is the only one never to actually kill anybody.

Even though he's not a murderer, Strassa is still guilty of the crime of kidnapping. After developing an obsessive crush on the gorgeous model Melissa, Strassa built up a disturbingly large collection of photographs of her. After he kidnaps her and brings her to his home, he speaks to her in an ominous tone, telling her that screaming will do her no good, and declares that he will make her his bride. Her protestation that she already has a husband is countered by his assertion that Andy is not truly her spouse because the marriage has not yet been consummated.

Any sane person would know that, barring the most extreme case of Stockholm syndrome, there is no way that Melissa would ever reciprocate his feelings. Does he realize believe that he can find happiness with her? Is he even planning to live happily ever after with her? There's a hint that he's planning a murder-suicide immediately after the wedding, but it's ambiguous. Strassa ought to know there is no way that his kidnapping can bring true love, and that the abduction of an intelligent, resourceful woman cannot be a long-term situation, but he doesn't seem to care. He is, quite simply, overwhelmed by his own obsession, and the fetters of reality have no hold over him.

Why is Strassa the way he is? The episode provides a brief explanation for how his mind became irretrievably warped. During his formative years, Strassa's surgeon father slit the throat of his wife before committing suicide. Understandably, Strassa's psyche never healed from that trauma. It's enough to illustrate a central reason why there's something wrong with him, but hardly any additional time is devoted to explaining what made him so broken, and Strassa remains little more than a character defined largely by his general psychopathy and obsession with Melissa. As a person, he lacks the humanity and personality that define the great *Columbo* antagonists.

On balance, Strassa, as a character, is not the sort of fellow who could have the standard relationship with Columbo. Columbo simply couldn't develop the same level of rapport with a man who was clearly deranged. There certainly could have been a scene where Columbo, finding some sort of link to Strassa, came to question him at his workplace, quickly realizing that there was something very wrong with the guy. The back and forth between the two, however, would have been quite different, as Strassa is not the sort who could have adopted the falsely friendly, ersatz helpful persona that the vast majority of *Columbo* villains utilize upon their first meeting.

Strassa further diverges from many standard *Columbo* villains by not being a wealthy person, nor does he have a direct connection to money or power or fame. His only connection to the glamorous world of

Southern California is his fanatical infatuation with Melissa. He lives in a fairly simple house, where the most prominent adornments are the soundproofing and blacked-out windows he uses to imprison his captive. As his early return thwarting Melissa's escape illustrates, he's not a particularly valued or respected worker, as he was fired from his job for reasons that are not made clear. Ultimately, Strassa is a mentally ill, twisted man who lives an unremarkable life of little benefit to society. The only bright spot in his life is his twisted fantasies. He's not even a brilliant criminal. While most of the *Columbo* murderers devise a clever plan to shield themselves from the consequences of their crimes, Strassa's main concern is the abduction, and it is a relatively easy matter for the authorities to track him down in just under fourteen hours. Perhaps Strassa did indeed intend to die soon after "marrying" Melissa. Perhaps he was so wrapped up in his fantasies that he never managed to consider the risks of getting caught. In any event, Strassa is brought down by solid, efficient police work, though it never matches the intuitive brilliance of Columbo's best investigations. That reflects the source material, as McBain made much of the "realism" and "accuracy" of his police procedurals.

There is an interesting character moment for Columbo at the end. Columbo famously never uses his firearm and rarely carries one. In the final scene, he's compelled to carry a gun in the raid on Strassa's home. After his nephew fatally shoots Strassa and embraces his rescued bride, Columbo simply looks at his gun as if he doesn't know what to do with it.

In a way, Columbo's perplexity reflects the feelings that fans might have as they view this aberration of an episode. Leaving aside the actual quality of the episode, which is open to debate, "No Time to Die" certainly lacks the standard attribute that makes the show so beloved: the interaction between detective and killer. Aside from Falk himself, "No Time to Die" is largely indistinguishable from most other cop shows, with a team of dedicated professionals, none of which are especially distinctive characters save for Columbo and an unsettlingly sinister criminal.

Chapter Sixty-One: A Bird in the Hand…

Harold McCain (Greg Evigan) and Dolores McCain (Tyne Daly)

"A Bird in the Hand" is one of the few *Columbo* mysteries where there are actual questions as to the identity of the killer, and the only one where two killers commit crimes independently of each other (not counting the brief scene at the start of "Undercover" where an unlucky pair commit simultaneous mutual homicide, which is the catalyst to the mystery, not the central crime at the heart of the mystery). In this episode, two people independently plan to kill the same person, and when one succeeds first, the consequences lead to two additional homicides.

Dolores McCain is Harold McCain's aunt by marriage. As the episode begins, they have a very amicable relationship. Both of their public personas hide darker aspects. Harold acts like a friendly fellow with a cowboy's sense of style, but is really a gambling addict who will stop at nothing to protect himself from the fallout of his losses. Dolores presents herself as a warm and nurturing maternal sort when, in fact, she has a ruthless homicidal streak.

Harold's evil side is revealed earlier than Dolores's. His obsession with games of chance has left him deeply in debt to the kind of people who demand payment in either cash or blood. As his uncle, "Big" Fred McCain, the owner of a football team, is not willing to subsidize his nephew's gambling habit, Harold decides that a pipe bomb is the best solution to his problems. It's unclear whether Harold believes that he'll be provided for in the will, or if Dolores can be easily persuaded to bail him out financially.

Harold expects that the pipe bomb under the Rolls will kill his uncle, but exercise proves to be more dangerous to Big Fred than driving. While he's out for a jog, Big Fred becomes the victim of a hit-and-run. Harold is stunned by this turn of events, but he realizes that the pipe bomb is now a dangerous liability. Unfortunately, Columbo's presence at the scene (eighteen minutes into the episode) prevents him from disconnecting the explosives, and Harold is unable to stop the gardener from moving the booby-trapped car, and the innocent man is killed in a fiery blast, making this a rare case of a murder that Columbo actually witnesses. With the gardener's death, Harold becomes an actual killer, though his victim is not the one he intended.

As usual, Columbo has a sense for identifying a killer, and he initiates his usual tactic of drawing his main suspect into his investigation. Columbo asks Harold to think of people who might have wished Big Fred ill and draws Harold into a reenactment of the crime. As Columbo demonstrates, the bomb was almost certainly installed by a left-handed person and casually notes Harold's left-handedness. Any chance of a friendly relationship between the two is shattered in that moment, as one reason for Harold being a terrible gambler is immediately made clear. The man has no poker face. The moment Columbo matter-of-factly points out that his left-handedness is an attribute shared by the killer, Harold loses his composure and immediately starts blustering about how he could be ambidextrous. It's an obvious sign of panic, and it makes one wonder how Harold planned to get away with the murder if it had gone according to plan. It's almost as if he never bothered to consider the obvious possibility that he'd be a suspect and, therefore, spent no time rehearsing his reactions to an accusation or even a suggestion of guilt. Harold is flustered and angry, and he storms away, insisting that Columbo has nothing against him. It's a miserable performance (for the character, not the actor), and one that screams culpability. When Columbo casually asks him "You won't go far, will you?" it's apparent that the detective believes he has his bomber squarely within his sights.

Columbo and Harold don't have much screen time together, and therefore don't build anything approximating the complexity or rapport of the best relationships between sleuth and slayer. Their arc is a very brief one, as their first major scene revolves around Harold trying and failing to not become a murderer, and their second scene depicts Harold quickly unravelling as Columbo uncovers clue after clue pointing in his direction. The arc between the two moves far faster than comparable examples in most other episodes, which is a necessity because of the plot.

While the murders of Big Fred and Harold are not shown on-screen, the identity of the killer is pretty easy to deduce simply by logical thinking outside of the clues inserted into the episode. After all, there's only one other person with a clear motive to kill Big Fred, and she's played by the only other prominent performer in the cast. Dolores is the obvious killer, and the last act of the episode focuses on Columbo's redirection of his investigation.

Harold is certainly not the brightest of the *Columbo* murderers, but he is not a total fool, as he correctly deduces that Big Fred was not the victim of a random careless driver, but instead was murdered by Dolores. He attempts to wheedle money from her, and his informing Dolores of his suspicions indicates that even if he is not completely stupid, his brains are still fairly weak. Shortly after a mildly acrimonious confrontation between the two, Harold is shot and killed, though, unlike most *Columbo* murders, the death is not shown on-screen, and the killer is not shown.

But the capable viewer and Columbo both know where to direct their suspicions, and Columbo quickly interviews Dolores, who is acting highly distraught. He shows her a video recording of the death of the gardener, noting that Harold flinched *before* the explosion occurred, and Dolores happily embraces the theory that Harold was guilty. When Columbo points out some holes in her story that put her under suspicion, her personality changes. The gregarious façade drops, and she quickly snaps and directs him to address all future questions to her lawyer. This is not the first indication that Dolores isn't as fluffy and dotty as she appears, as earlier she indicates that she has some shrewd business sense and is not as soft a touch as her nephew supposed she was.

After a brief time of further investigation, Columbo obeys and confronts her by crashing a football party with her lawyer present. She stares coldly at him, and the lawyer insists he's here to make sure he doesn't "take advantage" of her. As it happens, the lawyer is both wrong about Columbo's personality and his own legal skills. Columbo quickly makes short work of Dolores' attempt at an alibi and provides proof of her killing Harold, before asserting he's quite certain she's responsible for Big Fred's death. Whatever Dolores is paying her lawyer is too much, as he freaks out at the realization his client is a double murderess.

Columbo tells Dolores that Harold would have killed Big Fred, "but you got there first," silently pressing home the point that if she'd only waited a few hours, she could have been legally and morally in the clear. He may not be able to prove she murdered her husband (which means that she may still inherit his fortune), but he has enough evidence to arrest her for her nephew's murder. Citing the title of the episode, Columbo wraps up his case, and it's enough to convince Dolores, who all but confesses before toasting Columbo with champagne before going away quietly.

Harold was a weak and foolish man who sought to feed his gambling habit. He planned poorly, acted impulsively, and failed to think ahead. Afterwards, his actions attracted suspicion. He was a clumsy criminal focused on his personal appetites. Dolores, in contrast, is a cool-headed killer, who planned cleverly, acted without conscience, and though she wasn't quite shrewd enough to avoid suspicion, she did enough to minimize the evidence against her in her first crime, and she was undone by some little details she could not have anticipated. Harold built no real connection with Columbo, but while Dolores did not really come to like him, the detective at least earned her respect. Both aunt and nephew were gamblers who bet everything and lost, with a central difference between them being that Dolores was at least able to accept her defeat with dignity.

XII

SEASON TWELVE

Chapter Sixty-Two: It's All in the Game

Lauren Staton (Faye Dunaway) and Lisa Martin (Claudia Christian)

Columbo has had a wide spectrum of relationships with the people he investigates. Some have treated him like a friend, others have despised him, a few have made him their confidant, and most have appreciated his skills as a detective to varying extents. Only Lauren Staton, however, has expressed a genuine romantic attraction to the detective. As the episode progresses, Staton may have begun by using flirtation as a means of distracting Columbo and putting him off his game during his investigation, but as the story unfolds, she finds herself connecting to the man in a way that simultaneously surprises and pleases her. On Columbo's side, the extent of his feelings for Staton is debatable. Clearly Columbo feels a certain level of temptation towards Staton, but the degree to which he is battling his emotions is up to interpretation.

Columbo has very limited screen time with Martin, and there is no development of any sort of connection to her. His feelings towards Martin are developed second-hand through his relationship with Staton. Ultimately, Columbo's final actions towards Martin are subject to a good deal of moral scrutiny, and in the end, viewers can be justified in viewing this episode as one of Columbo's most morally questionable moments, possibly as one of his most human actions where he put morality and sympathy above the letter of the law, but also potentially as one of his most pragmatic decisions where an imperfect though largely positive result was chosen as opposed to a wholly negative ending.

As the episode begins, the slimy Nick Franco (Armando Pucci) is romancing both Staton and Lisa Martin, and the two decide he has to die. The relationship between the two women is kept deliberately ambiguous for most of the episode, as it could be interpreted as both platonic friendship and romantic, as well as the true answer, confirmed at the end, that of a mother-daughter bond. Likewise, the motive for the crime is also unstated until the episode's finale. Are they upset over Nick for dating them both, or is there something more to their disgust towards him?

Whatever their reasons, one night, Martin goes with Nick to his apartment, where Staton fatally shoots him. Staton returns to a party to establish an alibi, and Martin keeps the body warm with an electric blanket before firing a shot to create the impression Nick has just been killed and running out of the apartment with the blanket. When Columbo arrives nearly twenty minutes into the episode, he's sleepy, disheveled, and wearing pajamas under his coat. He's got one of his trademark hard-boiled eggs for sustenance, and he needs coffee and juice to awaken him. Meeting Staton is a sharper shock to his system than any beverage, and their relationship is immediately cordial. When she talks to Martin later, she notes how "considerate" Columbo was to her. The detective made a point of saying he'd try to keep her name out of the press. Later, she says to Martin, "I'm not always sure what he's thinking," and "I think he kind of likes me." While many suspects complain about Columbo's cigar, Staton says she likes it.

Soon afterwards, Columbo "accidentally" runs into Staton at a clothing store. When he tries his usual routine of challenging her story (she suggested Nick planned to play poker, but Columbo can find no evidence of cardplaying), Staton informs him she dislikes his tie, saying it makes him look old. Buying him a new one, she tells him with a smile that perhaps someday, if they get to know each other better, she'll give him a new suit as a present. The ensuing questioning is unlike any of Columbo's others, as there's a level of flirtation that's completely new to Columbo. He muses on this point, saying, "If a beautiful woman plays her cards right, she usually gets what she wants." Her coming on to him makes him feel suspicious rather than flattered, saying, "I'm not even sure if she did anything," but he wonders why she would make a play for him. Columbo has always embraced his persona of a working-class schlub, and when a beautiful and sophisticated woman smiles at him as she tries on hats and tells him with all apparent sincerity that he "has a nice head of hair," it seems to have a powerful effect on him.

The first two times in the store she kisses Columbo on the lips, he seems so stunned that it's possible he's not quite sure that what just happened is real and not just some lightly erotic dream. Later on, the third and last time they kiss, he seems to be a bit more aware of his situation. It does seem as if Columbo's holding back in many ways, both because he's married and because Staton's a person of interest in a murder. At one point, when Staton asks what his first name is, he says, "Lieutenant." Not only is that a running gag, but it's a quiet reference to folktales where certain individuals or creatures were careful never to reveal their true names, lest the person learning their name gain a kind of magical power over them. By keeping back such a piece of information, Columbo manages to keep a significant level of emotional distance between himself and Staton.

As the episode unfolds, it's difficult to tell which character is manipulating the other, or if they're both genuinely being drawn closer. Whenever he tries to bring up holes in her story, like how she might've known Nick wasn't home, she immediately distracts him with her feminine wiles. In one phone conversation between Staton and Martin, Staton declares, "I'll do anything. Charm him. Seduce him... Even run off for a weekend in Mexico." These don't appear to be unpleasant prospects to her, as she admits, "I really like him." Her chief goal is to make herself more interesting than the investigation.

The two exchange gifts. Columbo presents her with a bouquet of roses in a violin case, which delights her. It's unknown whether he paid for them himself (how would he explain the missing money to Mrs. Columbo?) or if he was able to charge them as an expense for the investigation. Soon afterwards, she buys a luxury bed for Dog, and he declares that even if she went around the world three times, she couldn't possibly find a nicer gift.

While the pair are having a special steak in Barney's kitchen, they have the first frosty moment in their relationship. Columbo insists on talking about the case and about Nick's poor character. She immediately becomes hostile and insists that anything regarding the long-term plans for their relationship is "a private matter." It's not certain how much of this coldness is genuine and how much is a calculated ploy to put off Columbo. This is a continuation of Staton's confidence that she can emotionally manipulate and distract Columbo, so he won't focus properly on the case.

Staton, as much as she likes Columbo, doesn't really believe his detecting powers are sufficient to bring her down, saying, "he's just pecking at the edges… he can never find out what really happened." She doesn't realize just how dogged he is, as we learn in another conversation that the longest Columbo has ever worked on a case is nine years and four months, and he'll keep investigating as long as he's making progress. Staton clearly underestimated him, as Columbo figured out the basics of the plan fairly early on, and after some solid police work, he tracked down Martin.

Columbo invites Staton to the precinct and shows her that Martin is being questioned. He explains how he found Martin—Nick called her twelve times over ten days, which was a link Staton did not anticipate. As Staton learns that Columbo could potentially arrest Martin, she asks him, "Can you solve this case without a confession?" After he replies in the negative, she asks, "Would you do anything to hurt me?" When he doesn't respond, she asks, "If you could solve this case, would you do anything to keep from hurting me?" When Columbo says "Yes," she adds, "Let that girl go."

All it took to destroy Staton's resistance was the prospect of Martin going to jail. Staton writes a full confession, all true aside from the fact she says she had an unnamed male accomplice. Staton reveals that Martin is her daughter, a revelation that seems to stun Columbo. Nick brutalized Martin, even going so far as to slash her throat with a razor, threatening her life. Columbo makes the decision not to charge Martin, and Staton acknowledges this by saying, "Thanks for the flowers." Martin flees to Europe, and Staton goes to prison.

In the final scene, the viewer can apply several different interpretations to Columbo's downbeat demeanor. Normally, Columbo ends the episode on a note of quiet triumph, for regardless of his personal opinion of the killer, he knows that justice has been done and he has succeeded in a challenging task. The final moments of this episode show Columbo at Barney's Beanery, where the proprietor asks, "How do you lock up a lady, how you feel about her?" Columbo responds, "Who said I felt anything for her?" and leaves, saying, "It's Thursday night. I'm taking the wife bowling." The ending is a reaffirmation of who Columbo truly is: a man who is committed to his relationship with his longtime wife and a man who is most comfortable in blue-collar settings and activities.

After a critical look at Columbo's actions and reactions over the course of the episode, there are multiple ways of evaluating his mindset. The standard interpretation is to suppose that Columbo indeed became infatuated with Staton and enjoyed a very brief emotional fling with her before realizing that his true loyalties were to his wife and the law. Another way to judge Columbo's actions is to embrace Columbo's question, "Who said I felt anything for her?" Many undercover agents pursue relationships with people connected to crimes, with varying degrees of intensity. The events of this episode may have been mentally (if not necessarily morally) justified as a necessary police tactic rather than cheating. It is possible that Columbo spent time with Staton as a slightly different way of getting to know her and understanding her as a suspect. Often, he treats a suspect as someone he's trying to befriend, and the interactions with Staton, mirroring the early stages of a romantic relationship, could have been a means of better understanding his chief suspect. As is often the case, genuine attraction and affection might have affected him to an uncertain extent. Whether Columbo's connection with Staton began out of a desire to pursue an attraction, or was based on a strategic plan to catch a killer is open to debate, but it is fair to conclude that no matter what his original intentions were, his time with Staton affected him in unexpected and powerful ways.

This may add another twist to the title of the episode. "The Game" may, in part, refer to the process of trying to build some sort of relationship with the suspect in order to get evidence against them or a confession. Columbo's time spent with Staton was "all in the game." Until, perhaps, it wasn't anymore.

In the episode's closing moments, Columbo could be reacting to the end of his relationship with Staton. Perhaps he's wondering what might have been, or perhaps he's feeling remorse over even thinking about what might have happened to his marriage and the destructive fallout in the wake of a full-fledged affair. Certainly, Catholic guilt might be a factor. Perhaps the guilt isn't just about his feelings for Staton, but about his decision to let Martin go. He might have done it as a favor to Staton, but it was also a potentially strategic decision to get a confession. The case could essentially be closed, and as the accomplice who helped Staton build her alibi didn't actually pull the trigger, it is easier to justify letting the confederate go.

Was it right, or at least morally justifiable, for Columbo to let Martin go? Certainly, as a survivor of domestic abuse, Martin can be seen as a victim as well as a perpetrator. As she was not in immediate fear for her life or safety at the time of the killing, she was legally unable to assert self-defense. This is a difficult situation, as anybody who has ever been trapped in a violent and abusive relationship can attest. As much as one wants to escape such a situation, often the law is incapable of stopping an abuser unless that person is caught in the act of violence, and even then, stay-away and restraining orders are easily violated, and abusers can often be let out of prison angrier than when they entered.

Ultimately, this episode leaves plenty of dangling questions, which actually enhance any discussions of the plot. The extent of Staton and Columbo's feelings for each other and how far they might pursue those feelings are open to debate. Likewise, the moral and practical issues connected to allowing Martin to go free are similarly contentious. Perhaps Peter Falk wanted to add some more facets to his character here, as this was the sole script he wrote for the series. The relationship between Staton and Columbo is the most powerful, emotionally complex, and ambiguous connection of the series.

Chapter Sixty-Three: Butterfly in Shades of Grey

Fielding Chase (William Shatner)

William Shatner's second *Columbo* murderer has a very different relationship with the detective than in his first appearance. Shatner's first turn in "Fade in to Murder" was as an actor whose grasp of reality was a little bit blurred, and he formed an unlikely friendship with Columbo. In contrast, Fielding Chase is an arrogant talk radio host who treats Columbo with all the warmth and respect one might show to a pebble caught in one's shoe.

From the opening scene, Chase is portrayed as opinionated and condescending, and a few quick comments indicate that his politics have a conservative bent. One of the investigators for his show, Gerry Winters (Jack Laufer), believes that Chase's adopted daughter Victoria (Molly Hagan) is being stifled both emotionally and professionally by Fielding, as Fielding keeps Molly on a short leash, preferring that her career remain intertwined with his. Gerry believes that Vicky is a talented writer and wants her to move away to pursue her dreams of being a novelist.

Fielding can't have that and decides to launch a dual-pronged attack to preserve the status quo. He decides to shoot Gerry, setting up a phone call that, by using an extension in Gerry's home and recording it all on his answering machine, will provide him with an alibi. Later, he uses his influence with publishers to block Vicky's book and reject it in such a crushing manner that Vicky will lose all confidence in her ability to create fiction and continue to devote her life to his radio show and media empire. One can wonder just how long Fielding intends to dominate her life. Will his intended hold over Vicky end with his retirement or his death, or does he have plans for her to continue his legacy after his death? It isn't clear, but Fielding clearly enjoys the power he exerts as an opinion influencer and is aware of the effects he has upon the political sphere. This power is intoxicant to him, and perhaps the power he exerts over Molly is similarly stimulating to him.

How should Fielding's relationship with Molly be interpreted? Gerry hints that Fielding may have amorous intentions towards Molly, which enrages Fielding. Perhaps there is some level of truth to this. After all, Vicky is the daughter of Fielding's lost love, and it's possible that he sees his former paramour in Vicky. It's ambiguous, so one could make a solid case that Fielding's feelings towards his adopted daughter could be purely paternal, but a carnal aspect is also a possibility. It's conceivable that Fielding doesn't even realize the extent and nature of his emotions. Certainly, Vicky doesn't act as if she's aware that her adopted father's love for her may not be entirely pure.

Whether or not incestuous lust is present, it is justifiable to diagnose Fielding as a narcissistic parent. Certainly Fielding cares about his daughter, but he believes that they both would be happier if Vicky were to live out her existence in the manner preferred by Fielding. Fielding wants Vicky to work alongside him, promoting his show and continuing to live in his mansion. There's a level of protectiveness here, both towards Vicky as a person and towards Fielding himself, who wants his daughter to devote her life to building up his career, perpetuating his goals, and preserving his legacy. As long as Vicky plays that role, he's happy. When she seeks to carve out her own niche in life, he responds negatively. Perhaps he doesn't see it as a full-fledged betrayal, as he hardly ever responds to Vicky angrily (though he does lose his temper with most of the other people who cross him).

He does, at the very least, consider Vicky's cravings for independence to be the height of foolishness. Fielding is willing to hurt Vicky by crushing her dreams, all so he can force her to continue living the life he considers to be mutually ideal. Notably, he could have found a way to try to keep Vicky close to him while allowing her to pursue her career as a writer. Had he tried, he might have found an L.A.-based publisher willing to accept Vicky's work and perhaps proposed a new work schedule to Vicky. Noting that a writer's life rarely brings a steady and lucrative income, he could have given her time off from his radio show, allowing her to continue with him and keeping her close while still making decent money from a steady job, and allowing her to save money on housing. Fielding does not do that, partly because he dislikes Vicky having her own life and opinions differing from his own. When Vicky objects to Fielding's smear tactics against a political enemy on his show, he treats her legitimate, ethical objections as one would the complaints of a petulant child. Ultimately, Fielding's good relationship with his daughter is contingent upon her remaining in his shadow, which is increasingly stifling for Vicky, leading to her leaving him to begin an independent chapter of her own life. This is a major ego blow for Fielding.

As devastating as Vicky walking away from him is for Fielding, Columbo defeating him is even worse. From the beginning, when Columbo appears twenty-three minutes into the narrative, Fielding underestimates him. Columbo's attempt to speak to him at the crime scene is met with a curt "I'm sorry, I don't have time right now," though Fielding becomes apologetic as soon as Columbo identifies himself as a detective. Fielding's attempts at helpfulness are bolstered by an empty declaration that "What matters most is bringing Gerry's killer to justice." He attempts to point suspicion elsewhere by pointing out that Gerry was gay and hints that a boyfriend is the most likely suspect. Like many *Columbo* killers, Fielding seems to run out of geniality midway through their first meeting. Columbo, unfazed by Fielding's attempts at misdirection, latches onto Fielding's statement that Gerry was shot in the back. This knowledge contradicts Fielding's assertions that he hadn't entered the house, and this obvious slip marks the start of Fielding's undisguised hostility towards Columbo.

When they arrive at Fielding's mansion, Fielding denigrates Columbo's car, pointing out that his mansion took four years to build and that he hopes Columbo's car doesn't have an oil leak. Fielding plays the answering machine tape of the murder in front of Columbo and his daughter and then makes a great show of his contrition for thoughtlessly playing the distressing recording in front of Columbo and his distraught daughter while simultaneously stressing his alibi. As he berates himself for upsetting Vicky, he calls himself an idiot. Of course, he doesn't mean it. Fielding's entire self-persona revolves around the assumption that he is the cleverest person in any room he walks into, and he doesn't take kindly to a shabby little homicide detective trying to pick apart the plot that he considers a masterpiece of murder.

When Columbo visits Fielding at a restaurant, Fielding welcomes him over with a tolerant finger-wag. Columbo asks for an autograph for his cousin Dominic, and after complying, Fielding tartly asks, "And now, can we get to the point, if there is one?" From this point onwards, Fielding treats every second with Columbo as a gross imposition on his precious time. He'd forgotten that not long ago, he'd expressed a desire to help catch Gerry's killer. Now, he can scarcely be bothered to spare a few minutes with the lead detective.

In response to Columbo's question about the angry outburst Fielding spat out at the deceased, Fielding dismisses it by admitting he has a "short temper" and smears the witnesses as "a gaggle of tourists." Later on, at Chase's office complex, Fielding jovially mocks Columbo's cigar, asking, "Are you burning ragweed here, or did somebody die?" He peppers Columbo with one insult after another. After Columbo's classic "one more thing…" Fielding mockingly asks if there's a "Problem with your short-term memory. Perhaps you should consult a physician." In this case, Columbo's catchphrase provokes his target to reveal his own sneering true colors. Chidingly, Fielding says, "You waste more time worrying about minutia" as Columbo pokes hole after hole in his story.

Many killers are dismissive towards Columbo, but few match Fielding for unveiled contempt. Later, Columbo's arrival at Fielding's mansion is met with, "Well, well, well... the ubiquitous Lieutenant Columbo..." Fielding tells a household employee that "a funny little man from the police department. is going to make an appearance." Columbo's "I hope I'm not intruding" is met with a sharp "As a matter of fact, you are." Columbo, almost certainly as a test and not out of genuine suspicion, floats the possibility that Vicky was involved in the crime and is slapped with the retort, "Lieutenant, you're a fool..." adding that if he continues along these lines, "You will be a very unhappy policeman." With that, he tells Columbo to stay away from him and his daughter.

Fielding threw his weight about with his influential friends. He spoke to the mayor, who talked to the commissioner, who called Columbo's captain, leading to Columbo being "called on the carpet for an hour." This doesn't deter the lieutenant at all. Soon afterwards, Columbo's greeting is met with "Go away, Columbo," and a threat to call security. Vicky is placating and apologetic. This is just the start of Vicky's sharp break from her father, and right after she leaves Fielding's mansion to strike out on her own, Columbo arrives and flat-out accuses him. When the detective asks him to come downtown to meet with a witness, Fielding rages, calling Columbo's routine "tiresome' and threatening to "destroy" not just Columbo, but the entire police department. Clearly, he doesn't wield this level of power, but it's quite possible he believes he does.

On the way downtown, some undercover police officers disguised as cyclists stage an accident and disable Fielding's car. As Fielding can't get cell phone reception from that point in the mountainous road, Columbo proves that his alibi is false and that Fielding couldn't possibly have taken the victim's phone call in the location. Fielding grips a rifle in his trunk, implying that he's considering murdering Columbo, but the police revealing themselves stops him. In any event, he couldn't possibly have gotten away with such a clumsy slaying. Truly caught, Fielding admits, "Columbo... I may have misread you."

This statement isn't an admission of guilt, but it is something different yet deep. It is the start of his pride starting to crack. The prospect that someone, especially a man who Fielding considers his social inferior, could outwit him is anathema to Fielding. Columbo's frequent and perceptive questioning was a constant series of assaults against his own believed cleverness, and his confidence in himself has taken a major body blow. Viewers never see what happens to the killers after their arrests, but it is likely that a man like Fielding, with such a high opinion of himself, would recover and potentially revel in crafting a very public defense of himself. As it stands, Fielding is forced to admit his own mistakes, at least to himself, and seeing his cultivated veneer of superiority being stripped away is bound to be a humiliating experience for him.

Fielding Chase was a man who was obsessed with his own brilliance and importance, a raging egoist who sought to crush his political enemies and control his daughter. Fielding was a bully and a petty tyrant, a man who always believed himself to be right, which blinded him to the flaws in his plan and his unhealthy relationships with others. By failing to grasp the limits of his own intelligence and influence in his attempts to exert power, he wound up losing everything.

Chapter Sixty-Four: Undercover

Irving Krutch (Ed Begley, Jr.)

"Undercover" is another *Columbo* episode that doesn't fit the traditional "inverted mystery" format. After "No Time to Die," it's the second of two novels based on an Ed McBain novel, in this case, *Jigsaw*. Given its source material, it's not surprising that this storyline feels a lot more like a standard police procedural than it does a typical *Columbo* outing.

This is the last of the episodes where there is any doubt about the identity of the killer, or at least the person responsible for one of the murders. The opening scene features a simultaneous homicide—two men manage to take each other's lives in a fight—one with a gun, the other with a knife. Columbo appears rather earlier in the episode than usual, about four minutes into the narrative. A search of the crime scene reveals a cut piece of a photograph, and Columbo's puzzled (pun completely intended) until insurance investigator Irving Krutch stops by the precinct to tell them a story of a heist gone wrong. A group of robbers stole $4 million in cash, carefully hid it, marked its location on a photograph, and then cut the photograph into pieces, giving each piece to a different trusted person. Before they could retrieve the money, they were all killed after being chased by the authorities. Krutch—who has a habit of referring to himself in the third person—works for the company that insured the stolen cash. His years-long investigation has stalled, and he asks Columbo to help him retrieve the money by tracking down the other missing photo pieces, along with half of a torn list of the people who are the keepers of the pieces. The simultaneous homicide was connected to the hunt for the remaining parts of the photograph.

And so, Columbo begins an unconventional means of investigation—going undercover. Over the course of the episode, he assumes the identities of a petty criminal, a homeless man, and a Mafia don. His new personas are convincing to those he meets, but the nature of the mystery means that instead of focusing his energies primarily on one person, he's trying to extract information from a wide variety of characters.

Just as the mystery is unconventional, so is Columbo himself. Under pressure from his boss, this is one of the rare times he's forced to carry a gun, though he never fires it. He has to indulge in some self-defensive tactics to save himself from physical harm, and he's not successful in protecting himself all the time, as he's given a nasty head wound at one point. When he identifies his assailant, Columbo doesn't use his standard measures of psychological exploration and manipulation, but instead hammers away at the perpetrator verbally with the help of a colleague until the guilty man confesses. Columbo also relies more heavily on his colleagues than usual, working as part of a team. Mrs. Columbo is scarcely mentioned, though it would be interesting to see what she had to say about her husband being away from home, doing dangerous work. Dog does get a shout-out at the very end, but overall, the Columbo depicted in this episode is not quite the same man viewers are used to seeing.

Over the course of the episode, both a potential witness and an art gallery employee are murdered. During the closing stretch of the story, Columbo identifies his assailant, but after a brief interview, he discovers that the man who knocked him out is not the killer, and is mildly forgiving when the assailant's confession leads to a break in the case, offering the man a light sentence (which it's unclear he has the authority to offer) in return for the information. Columbo suspects Krutch, but the insurance investigator has alibis for both crimes, thanks to his girlfriend. Once Columbo proves Krutch was at the scene of a crime due to a fingerprint on a coin in a parking meter, Krutch's girlfriend rescinds the alibi. Faced with the evidence against him, Krutch cracks and confesses, stating the killings weren't premeditated. Rather than expressing contrition, he voices anger at his female victim for hindering his attempts at retrieving the photo piece and also mourns that he came so close to retrieving the money, only to be undone by Columbo's investigation. Krutch managed to get ahold of the final puzzle piece showing where "X" marks the spot (what a dramatic coincidence that it was that piece which was the last to be discovered!), but it's the police who find the money, though, by the time the box with the cash is retrieved, Columbo declares "I saw enough of this case" and leaves for some quality time with Dog.

Columbo and Krutch have one of the briefest relationships in the series' canon. After their initial meeting, Columbo and Krutch have a short phone call where Krutch expresses his delight with the progress made in the investigation. Columbo questions Krutch at his apartment, initially accepting his alibi before demolishing it under scrutiny. Krutch is not one of the criminal masterminds of the *Columbo* universe. While many of the *Columbo* killers plotted out elaborate crimes with inventive alibis, Krutch's homicides were strictly second-degree, possibly even manslaughter, due to lack of premeditation and minimal desire to kill. His alibi is simple—convincing someone to lie for him. It is also easy to break. Though not directly stated, it's pretty certain that his girlfriend Susan Endicott (Kristin Bauer) has no deep affection for him, given how coldly she gave him up once her own freedom was threatened. Perhaps he bought his alibi by promising her a share of the money.

Viewers are not provided with an in-depth glimpse of Krutch's moral downfall, though one can theorize based on the available dialogue. It's impossible to tell whether Krutch began his career as an insurance investigator as a basically honest man or if he always had a crooked streak, but he clearly developed an obsession with the stolen money, hoping that he'd retrieve the $4 million and live comfortably ever after. There's no indication he had a plan for laundering the money to explain his sudden windfall. Whether a longing for money corrupted him or whether his character was always looking for the opportunity to seize easy wealth is open to speculation.

Ultimately, Irving Krutch was a man with no real malice towards his victims, only a passionate love for large sums of money. Lacking the investigative skills to track down the photo pieces himself, he thought that he could exploit the police into doing his work for him, though he was not prepared for the authorities' investigation to be his own undoing. The relationship between detective and killer is one of the shallowest in the series, with Krutch not only failing to be particularly charmed by the Lieutenant, but also not feeling any real annoyance, either. Other than a mild respect for Columbo's efficiency, Krutch holds little emotional connection with the detective. Likewise, Krutch is unlikely to rank very high on the list of killers Columbo "likes and even respects," as they have little dialogue beyond the bare minimum needed to advance the investigation, and Krutch's actions were fueled by greed. Essentially, Irving Krutch's covetousness for a hidden treasure and his decisions to prioritize the pursuit of that treasure over the lives of other human beings proved to be his undoing, and his investigation that overwhelmed his life for several years turned out to be nothing more than a futile and bloody quest for fool's gold.

XIII

SEASON THIRTEEN

Chapter Sixty-Five: Strange Bedfellows

Graham McVeigh (George Wendt)

Graham McVeigh was a man with a problem threatening his business and his dreams, and he came up with a seriously flawed plan to solve it. By failing to think through the ramifications of his actions and the unintended consequences of his crimes, Graham managed to doom himself. In essence, Graham's murders were poorly planned and executed because he was sloppy. He was drawn into homicide due to his brother's gambling addiction and was caught because he was a different kind of gambler, a man who bet his freedom on his own cleverness and lost.

As the episode opens, Graham enters a pawn shop in order to buy an untraceable gun. It is immediately apparent that he is not a master criminal. Graham wished to disguise himself so as not to be recognized, but he went overboard by wearing a trench coat, hat, and sunglasses. While such a getup might prevent a positive witness identification, an unintended consequence was that it is the kind of outfit that attracts attention and sticks in people's memories.

Graham is a horse breeder and racer who has put great time and care into raising a horse named Fiddling Bull. Unfortunately for Graham, his horse breeding company is a family business, and his brother Teddy (Jeff Yagher) inherited half of it. Teddy is a compulsive gambler, and his mounting debts imperil Graham's finances as well. Graham has allowed his horse to run slower than it could in order to help Teddy win bets in the past, but now Graham is no longer willing to allow his prized horse to remain an also-ran. After deliberately setting Teddy up for a big loss, he prepares to kill his brother.

In order to divert suspicion, Graham decides to make Teddy's bookie, Bruno Romano (Jay Acovone), the patsy. Graham disguises himself with a fake beard and sunglasses (a far better disguise than the trench coat ensemble) and slips into the restaurant where Bruno has an office. Unfortunately, though he changes his appearance, he doesn't change his drink, and ordering a "scotch and soda, easy on the soda" proves to be a giveaway later. After releasing some mice in the bathroom, when a female patron screams at the sight of the infestation, Graham sneaks into Bruno's office and makes a telephone call to Teddy, knowing that the phone record will implicate Bruno. Later that night, Graham drives Teddy to an isolated area, shoots him, and bicycles away from the scene.

Columbo's first encounter with Graham is fairly cordial. Making his entrance twenty minutes into the episode, Columbo reaches the crime scene in a sorry state. He's met with the running gag of the uniformed officer at the scene not recognizing him as a detective, and he's even more disheveled than usual after eating some spoiled clams, making no attempt to hide the bottle of Pepto Bismol he's carrying. When Columbo arrives at Graham's farm, Graham yells at him to get off his private property, though his attitude does a one-eighty once Columbo identifies himself. Graham acts upset when he hears the news about his brother, though in a rare exception for *Columbo* killers, he doesn't overplay his supposed grief. Graham carefully acts like a man who knows nothing about the crime, asking if it was an accident. When Columbo informs him it was murder, Graham swiftly mentions his brother's gambling debts. The first moment when Columbo starts suspecting Graham is very subtle, for when Graham lights a cigarette, Columbo asks for one as well, and Graham amiably obliges. At first glance, it seems like another example of Columbo's nicotine habit, but it's actually evidence-gathering, as Graham left cigarette ash at the scene of the crime.

Soon afterwards, Graham calls Bruno to his house to pay off the debt. When Bruno arrives, Graham shoots him, places the gun from Teddy's murder in Bruno's hand after firing it again, and presents the homicide tableau to the police as a case of self-defense.

Notably, Graham's plan has a distinct resemblance to two previous *Columbo* episodes. The tension between two brothers over a family business, coupled with the use of a bicycle to escape a crime scene, is reminiscent of "Any Old Port in a Storm." In the second murder, making it look like the shooting was in self-defense, a response to the victim firing first, is straight out of "Negative Reaction." Perhaps Columbo's suspicions are stirred by a case of déjà vu. Graham's plan proves no more infallible than either of the other earlier cases.

Columbo is suspicious of Graham's self-defense story from the very beginning. When he hears Graham's story, Columbo replies by saying, "Yes sir, you sure were lucky," in a way that, when coupled with the expression on his face, makes it immediately apparent to regular viewers that Columbo isn't buying one little mite of what Graham is selling.

The standard *Columbo* interactions ensue, as Columbo questions an increasingly irritated Graham, but the big difference in this episode's narrative comes from Columbo being brought to the home of Vincenzo Fortelli (Rod Steiger), a "retired" Mafia don, for a discussion over lunch. The bookie Graham killed was a pal of the former mobster, and Columbo is told quite clearly that he'll get the first chance to bring Graham to justice, but if he doesn't do it quickly, then Fortelli will go outside the law to see the dead man's killer punished.

Soon, Fortelli starts threatening Graham, accusing him of murder, demanding he turn over the horse farm to him as recompense, followed by an attempt on his life. Increasingly frazzled, Graham turns to Columbo for help, but there's only so much the police can do. The episode climaxes with Fortelli capturing Graham and preparing to execute him. A little pressure sends Columbo running away in fear, and in desperation, Graham makes a full confession, preferring to live in prison rather than die that evening.

As the savvy viewer will have predicted, this confrontation is all a piece of theater. Columbo and Fortelli are working together, and the odd partnership between the police officer and the organized crime boss forms the impetus behind the episode's title. Fortelli's supposed goons are actually undercover police officers and had Graham decided to stick to his guns and refuse to confess or even try to fight his way out of the situation, he would not have been arrested, and any physical harm he might have caused to Fortelli or the undercover officers could have been easily defended as self-preservation. Fortelli does hint afterwards that had the scheme hadn't worked, he would have gone outside the law to get revenge, in which case, the police might have been compelled to provide Graham with protection.

This is not Columbo's finest moment in terms of capturing a criminal. There's none of his classic ingenious brilliance or dogged determination, just psychological pressure and threats. It's also the sort of tactic that would get a case thrown out of court—a confession made in fear of one's life is not valid. Instead of skillfully surgically dissecting a murderer's plot, it's brute force—a psychological third degree followed by a threat—admit your guilt or die. With the right lawyer, a coda to this episode could see Graham getting off scot-free. As it stands, it's not a case of a killer's plans being cleverly undone so much a murderer being forced into prison. Justice is done, but corners have been cut, and it's not a clean solution.

In the earlier cases where fear was used to provoke a confession, "Short Fuse" had the killer in no real danger, and Columbo never said anything to suggest the murderer's life was threatened. It was the killer's guilty knowledge that made him afraid, so this was a clever psychological trap. "A Case of Immunity" saw a guilty man confessing, believing he was safe from consequences, only to retract his own diplomatic privileges when he feared the brutal justice system of his home country. Certainly, there was some pressure there, but this was actual international law, and Columbo manipulated the murderer (who had already admitted guilt through his own volition) to offer him a preferable option of life in prison in a comparably humane American prison.

Though he was threatened more than any other *Columbo* killer, Graham actually had a fairly amicable relationship with Columbo, at least at first.

He was quite friendly with the detective until Columbo started voicing his suspicions of him. One meeting at the racetrack is particularly genial until Columbo begins pointing out points that didn't make sense. Graham is able to plug an early hole in his narrative by suggesting a parking valet left the cigarette ash in the car, but later, when Columbo notes that the mice that caused a useful distraction were country mice, the kind that might be found at the horse ranch, Graham gets upset, missing an opportunity to calmly explain that the mice might've hitched a ride on some car that took a drive through the countryside.

Towards the end, when Graham's plans are unraveling and so is his composure, Graham tries to shoo Columbo away, but before he does, he asks, "Are we still friends?... I just don't want you to feel insulted when I tell you to leave." When Columbo begins his trademark line, Graham snaps, "No Lieutenant, there is no "just one more thing...Goodbye." It's a harsh response, spoken by a man who's on the end of his tether and cannot withstand further questioning.

In order to realize how Graham became a double murderer, it's important to realize that it was a long process. Addiction in all of its forms takes a terrible toll, not just on the addict, but everybody close to that person. Gambling addiction, where there's no limit to how much money can be lost, can destroy the financial stability of many people around the addict. This in no way excuses Graham's crimes, but it explains how a generally amiable man could think that his only way out of losing his beloved farm was with bullets. It also raises the question: is there a non-violent path Graham could've taken? Was there a legal way he could've kept his brother from destroying his horse breeding business and losing the farm? Was it possible to treat his brother's gambling addiction? Unlike most of the other *Columbo* murderers, where one can righteously state that the killer should've given up the dreams for the inheritance or the plans to marry a lover or whatever, there's no ready, moral path to dictate to the killer either than "just accept your brother gambling away your life and destroying everything you've struggled to create." Again, this is not to say the homicide is justified, but this is one of the cases where the killer's descent is due in part to his being victimized by the victim.

Notably, had Graham not decided to frame the bookie for his brother's murder, Fortelli wouldn't have gotten involved. Perhaps if Graham had somehow managed to make his brother's death look like an accident, possibly by getting thrown from a horse, he might have avoided the confrontation that led to his undoing. It still would have been an abhorrent fratricide, but it would have put him in a safer position, and he might have even been able to plead justification in court.

It's ironic that one of the killers with the sloppiest plans was unable to be captured through clever police work and instead had to be brought down by threats. Graham became a killer because he loved his farm and horses more than his brother, and he also murdered a bookie who did him no harm as part of a misguided attempt to protect himself. While many of the *Columbo* killers seem to have always had a flaw in their moral make-up, Graham comes across as one of the individuals who could've been a solid citizen if he hadn't endured an extended threat to his business. And so, in an attempt to save his business through murder, Graham, like so many killers before him, wound up busted after a poorly executed gamble.

Chapter Sixty-Six: A Trace of Murder

Patrick Kinsley (David Rasche) and Cathleen Calvert (Shera Danese)

The killers, Patrick Kinsley and Cathleen Calvert, share a unique motive in the *Columbo* canon. Most of the murderers seek to gain something directly from someone's death, and in the occasional instances where they frame someone else for the murder, it's either an impersonal smearing out of convenience (as in "Strange Bedfellows") or for eventual gain (à la "Suitable for Framing"). In this episode, the killers take the life of a man solely for the purpose of putting Cathleen's husband in prison.

Clifford Calvert (Barry Corbin) is a bit of a bully, a wealthy man whose financial position is threatened by a lawsuit and SEC violations. Howard Seltzer (Raye Birk) is suing him, and this litigation could destroy Clifford's finances. Due to the complex legal situation, divorcing Clifford or killing him would leave Cathleen broke, but if Clifford were thrown into prison, she'd still have access to all of his funds. Therefore, Cathleen and her lover Kinsley decide to murder Howard and frame Clifford for the crime.

Kinsley goes to Howard's home and shoots him, leaving behind trace evidence to implicate Clifford. Soon afterwards, the police arrive (Columbo arrives eighteen and a half minutes into the episode), and when Kinsley shows up again, it's revealed he's a crime scene investigator for LAPD's forensics unit. Though Kinsley is experienced in the field and in the classroom, this is the first time he and Columbo have worked together.

Columbo and Kinsley seemingly make an effective investigating duo. Over the course of the investigation, Columbo gathers up all of the physical clues pointing in Clifford's direction, with a little subtle guidance from Kinsley here and there. Yet despite the mountain of evidence against Clifford, Columbo can't help but suspect his chief suspect is innocent and that there's something shady about Cathleen. He can't explain away the forensic clues until his observational skills lead to the realization that Kinsley and Cathleen are much better acquainted than they've led him to believe, as Kinsley knows more about Cathleen's coffee-drinking and automobile riding habits than a very casual acquaintance should. Realizing the truth, Columbo plays the pair off each other, driving them both to implicate the other in confessions, thereby clearing Clifford.

Kinsley and Cathleen spend less time in Columbo's crosshairs than almost any other killer. With Clifford as the primary suspect and Cathleen having an alibi for the murder, it's not until quite late in in the episode that Columbo first starts looking at her with suspicion. Cathleen feigns cluelessness about the crime when Columbo first meets her and later acts defensive and angry when Columbo begins investigating her husband in earnest. It's not exactly clear if Columbo's nose for phonies alerts him to the fact that something's up with her, though at one point, Cathleen can't hide a triumphant leer when Columbo discovers the incriminating material she planted on the back of her husband's jacket. It's possible that Columbo caught a glimpse of this revelation of her true feelings, and it started leading him in the right direction. Still, Columbo's time with her is limited, though he tries to present himself as an ally to her late in the episode, presenting himself as being open to the possibility of her husband's innocence. Columbo's abrupt realization that Cathleen and Kinsley are well acquainted with each other is so sudden it's implied he never seriously viewed her as a viable suspect until that point.

Comparatively, Kinsley is one of the few *Columbo* killers to have a genuinely amicable relationship with Columbo with absolutely no guile or suspicion on the lieutenant's part, at least until the final act of the episode.

Kinsley and Columbo have a far more detailed relationship. Columbo recognizes Kinsley's skill at the crime scene early on, and while he rarely works in close partnership with his fellow members of law enforcement, he seems to take an immediate liking to Kinsley, happily accepting the CSI's help. At one point, Columbo makes his sole reference to Peter Falk's real-life glass eye, saying, "Three eyes are better than one." Like most murderers initially, Kinsley is amused by Columbo and sees him as nonthreatening, going so far as to say "I think the guy's a little goofy." When Columbo tells Kinsley he always eats every bit of an apple, Kinsley chidingly tells him the seeds contain cyanide, but when Columbo flinches, he slightly patronizingly tells him there's not nearly enough poison in one apple's seeds to cause any harm. Kinsley does show some respect for Columbo's tenacity, calling him a "tiger," and he never expresses the frustration most killers do with Columbo until the very end, when Columbo deliberately keeps him waiting in order to get Kinsley anxious and more willing to confess. Columbo doesn't express any rage or betrayal at Kinsley's deception, merely being astounded at the effrontery of the pair. It's a very lucky point that Kinsley hasn't been working in the field too long, as once the news of his crimes is made public, every case he ever worked on is now subject to being thrown out of court.

And so, how did Kinsley and Cathleen become the killers they were? Given the ease with which they turned on each other, it's not accurate to call them "lovers." "Lusters" is more appropriate. Their relationship was based on strong physical attraction and a shared desire for Clifford's money. While the initial plan to frame Clifford for murder so they could maintain access to his wealth was Cathleen's idea, it's implied that the actual frame-up was based entirely on Kinsley's plan and his knowledge of forensics. Most of the *Columbo* killers were content to simply murder their victims, but Cathleen and Kinsley were not only prepared to take a life, but they were also willing to send an innocent man to prison for the remainder of his days, a crueler fate than almost any other killer, aside from the others who tried to frame blameless people. Between that particularly heartless plan, the betrayal of Columbo's trust, and the fact every case Kinsley ever worked on is now vulnerable to being overturned due to his presence as a corrupt agent of the law, the pair must rank as two of the more malicious murderers in the series.

Chapter Sixty-Seven: Ashes to Ashes

Eric Prince (Patrick McGoohan)

A murderous turn by Patrick McGoohan is always a treat for *Columbo* fans, and in his fourth and final appearance playing a killer, he takes on the character of the mortician Eric Prince, who has one more body in his funeral home than there ought to be.

When Verity Chandler (Rue McClanahan), a prominent Hollywood gossip columnist, meets Prince at his lavish place of business, she threatens to reveal his unsavory practices, including blackmailing the living with incriminating evidence found on the dead. Her desire to bring him down is fueled by the shabby way he treated her sometime earlier, and when she smirks at his coming downfall, he clubs her to death with a trocar– a long, thin metal implement used to extract combustible gases from the departed.

Unlike most murderers, Prince has an easy and effective means of disposing of a body: the crematorium. As two fully grown bodies might be too much for the oven, he sets the corpse of Mr. Houston (the deceased Hollywood star who was supposed to be cremated) aside and instead incinerates Verity's body, and the cremains are scattered over the ocean. Later that night, Prince breaks into Verity's home, deletes the files regarding his malfeasance, plants a story on her computer that she was investigating a cocaine ring, and adjusts the clock on her computer when saving a file before setting it back in order to create an alibi. He stages a struggle and leaves, hoping to create the impression that the gossip columnist was abducted by drug dealers.

When Columbo arrives twenty-one minutes into the movie with Dog in tow, he isn't fooled. When he first meets Prince half an hour into the episode, Prince coldly chastises him for smoking a cigar in the coffin display room, though his demeanor alters dramatically once Columbo reveals his profession and mission, as is the case for most suspects. Their initial relationship is very polite, with Columbo declaring that Prince's funeral parlor is really "a lovely place to go."

At Verity's house, Columbo explains in Prince's presence why Verity's abduction was faked, picking apart all of Prince's red herrings as Prince quietly accepts the demolishing of his deceptions. Meanwhile, the temporary breakdown of the cremation oven causes Prince some anxiety, but it's quickly repaired, and Prince soon has an opportunity to cremate the body of the late Hollywood star along with the already charred remains of a man killed in an explosion.

Columbo continues to investigate, eventually discovering an unsolved case regarding the missing necklace of film legend Dorothea Page. Her diamond jewelry disappeared after Prince picked up her body, and though Prince was suspected, no one ever proved what happened to it. Prince's workplace was searched, but no diamonds were ever found. Eventually, Columbo tracks down the man who fenced the diamonds for Prince and continues to question Prince at an awards dinner and at the funeral parlor.

Eventually, Columbo and Prince have a civilized discussion, as Columbo explains how he knows that Prince hid the necklace inside Dorothea Page's body and then extracted the gems after they survived the cremation. He then used the money to fund his successful business. After some quiet banter, Prince is convinced that Columbo has no proof until Columbo retrieves the urn containing the cremains of Mr. Houston and the explosion victim. Houston was a war veteran who carried a piece of shrapnel in his body for the rest of his life, and the bit of metal's presence in the urn was enough to cause Prince to concede defeat.

The relationship between Columbo and Prince is one of the more cordial in the series. Part of this is certainly due to McGoohan's enthusiasm and obvious love for working on the show alongside his real-life friend Falk. In their first couple of meetings, both are polite to each other, and Prince plays up the traditional killer's helpfulness, though he does a rather poor job of masking his disappointment when Columbo sees through his simplistic attempt at an alibi, as it's quite easy to change a computer clock and create a fake time stamp.

Later, when Columbo questions Prince at a dinner honoring him for his work as an undertaker, Prince silkily greets him, saying, "Always a pleasure to see you. You intrigue me." The conversation continues in a hearse for privacy, and Prince seems stunned by how effectively Columbo has uncovered his secrets. After a few minutes, Prince's demeanor chills, and he ends the conversation. A moment later, when Prince buys a round of drinks for his peers, Columbo asks with a smile if he is included. After Prince stiffens and walks away, Columbo follows him with an amiable "just kidding." Prince's attitude becomes quite terse as he explains that this is his "night of honor" and he'd "like to enjoy it."

Perhaps Prince is worried about being exposed at first, but after reflection, he realizes that his position is much more secure than he'd realized, and when Columbo comes by the funeral home later, he all but walks Columbo through his crime, handing him the weapon and happily explaining how the cremation oven works. When Columbo correctly elaborates upon his theory of the crime, Prince cheerfully fills in the blanks and says that he is the only one who could have committed the murder, but without a body, there's no way to prove it. With a cackle, Prince tells Columbo, "That's the tricky thing about burning questions. Once they're burned, they're just ashes." Prince's villainous laugh shows how he has let his guard down, as he's totally confident in his own security.

In the final minutes, Columbo interrupts a funeral, asking for another chat, and with a hiss, Prince makes an appointment for them to talk later. It's an almost-overly civilized conversation in Prince's office, as Prince serves tea from a fancy set. Columbo lulls and flatters Prince. Earlier, he complimented him on his sense of style, and over tea, Columbo explains how he's been pursuing murderers for a quarter of a century, and Prince is the first one he hasn't been able to catch. It's not clear if Columbo's track record is really that good or if he's playing up to Prince's vanity. Perhaps there was some added twist that led to an arrest after "Forgotten Lady" or "It's All in the Game." Columbo explains he's talking about his track record because it pleases him, especially because he can't "lay a finger" on Prince. Prince discreetly preens, convinced of his own safety. He even gives Columbo a set of sugar tongs as a gift, which Columbo uses to extract Houston's shrapnel from the cremains.

Ultimately, Prince gives up much too easily, saying, "Very good. Very, very good." There's no malice, frustration, or threats, just a request for Columbo to join him in the police car. Columbo happily replies he will if Prince wants, saying, "It's your funeral." It's another case where Columbo's detection is met with respect, and the end relationship is practically friendly. Yet Prince should not assume he's been checkmated. After all, Prince could claim that the shrapnel got caught in the machine, and came out after the next cremation. There's only evidence to indicate that Houston may have been cremated after he supposedly was, and no definitive proof that Verity was in that earlier urn.

Indeed, there's no proof of murder, either. Even if some DNA evidence could possibly be found in some lingering cremains that proved Verity was burned, Columbo can't prove murder. If Prince had put forward the story that Verity had simply died of a heart attack or had a dizzy spell and fatally hit her head on the table and that he'd burned her body out of fear that he'd be wrongly blamed, he could potentially be acquitted due to reasonable doubt, though he might be found guilty of wrongful disposal of a body. He would even escape punishment for stealing the diamonds due to the statute of limitations. He could potentially even walk away without prison time, given skillful legal counsel. His reputation, and therefore his business, might take a hit, but having to sell the funeral home would be preferable to a prison sentence.

So, why did Prince surrender so easily? Perhaps, as in the way he set up his alibi, he was simply not that imaginative and didn't see the options open to him. If one wishes to be more charitable, perhaps one could argue that

Prince was feeling guilty, though there's not much evidence of that. Prince giving up is not the action of a master criminal, but of a man who doesn't want to keep fighting, assuming, of course, that he's simply biding his time until he makes a call to his attorney. After all, he doesn't say anything that counts as a full confession. In the end, Columbo has clearly earned Prince's respect due to his investigative skills, but has Columbo really secured a conviction? It's an open question, and Prince's crime, committed on the spur of the moment, shows that he's not a cold-blooded murderer. Yet even if he won an acquittal, the revelations of his shady dealings might make him a pariah, as the rich and famous would balk at turning their loved ones over to a man who just might give them someone else's cremains. Prince wanted to make a comfortable living by going outside the law, but it all turned to ashes in the end.

Chapter Sixty-Eight: Murder with Too Many Notes

Findlay Crawford (Billy Connolly)

How far would one go to protect your unearned reputation? If that someone is the movie composer, Findlay Crawford, the solution is to murder the young protégé who helped him gain a reputation as a brilliant musical scorer. Crawford is widely regarded as one of the great talents in his field, but this is all because he appropriated the work of his apprentice, Gabriel McEnery (Chad Willet). It's hard to get a shot in Hollywood, and McEnery believed that by working with a famous name and creating work that would be passed off as Crawford's, he could improve his own chances of a successful career. The last several film scores that were released under Crawford's name were either entirely or almost completely McEnery's creations, and McEnery received no credit for his music. This is especially galling to McEnery because one of his most recent scores for a crime movie won "Hollywood's major award" (for legal reasons, the show can't use the terms "Oscar" or "Academy Award," even though the statuette shown in one photograph looks just like an Oscar).

Finally fed up, McEnery demands recognition, threatening to tell the world the truth unless he gets the acclaim he believes he deserves. Initially, Crawford is very warm, contrite, and supportive, and he declares that henceforth, McEnery will get all the kudos that's coming to him, starting with an opportunity to conduct at an upcoming concert. The moment an excited McEnery leaves, however, Crawford's demeanor changes, and he plots his protégé's murder.

Soon afterward, McEnery is ready for the concert, and Crawford proposes a champagne toast. Of course, he's spiked the drink, and an unconscious McEnery is quickly dressed in a tuxedo and dragged to the roof of the building where the concert is being held. A timer activates a trapdoor on the roof, which tilts and sends McEnery falling to his death.

Columbo appears twenty-eight minutes into the episode, and when he questions witnesses, he's immediately struck by the fact that the witnesses to the fall heard no screaming and realizes McEnery was either dead or drugged when he fell. When Columbo and Crawford first meet, Crawford has plied himself heavily with alcohol, mourning that McEnery was like a son to him and saying it must have been some tragic accident. Columbo sees the intoxicated Crawford home, making a point of going infuriatingly slowly and stopping often to ask questions, such as what happened to McEnery's missing conducing baton, all as part of a plan to take Crawford's measure.

Columbo continues to bother Crawford at a recording session and continues to investigate the scene of the crime to figure out how the fall was arranged, eventually realizing that an elevator was timed to rise, push open the trapdoor, and send McEnery falling off the roof. Along the way, Columbo expresses sympathy to McEnery's girlfriend, Becca, winning her trust and assistance. Meanwhile, Crawford tries to remove any evidence of his plagiarism by breaking into McEnery's home and stealing his original notes.

However, these notes prove unnecessary to unraveling Crawford's plan, and in the climactic scene, Columbo reenacts the crime, demonstrating that McEnery's conducting baton was found at the bottom of the elevator shaft, and could only have fallen there if the trapdoor was open. Additionally, McEnery had a habit of "signing" his scores with the musical letters G-A-B-E and communicating with his girlfriend B-E-C-C-A the same way. Faced with this evidence, Crawford takes his arrest in good spirits, signing an autograph and wondering if there's a penitentiary with "a decent music program." There's no guilt expressed, just amiable humor.

While Columbo's ability to annoy a suspect is legendary, for most of the series' run, the irritation he causes comes from appearing frequently and asking questions, and it's continually implied by comparing the reactions of the guilty to the innocent that the hostile reactions and anxiety are based on either a troubled conscience or anxiety over getting caught. The annoyance comes from Columbo's mere presence. As Columbo makes a great show of driving slowly, stopping, and peppering Crawford with questions, this is one of the rare cases where he's going to dramatic lengths in order to provoke frustration and impatience in Crawford. It's more than just being a constant but polite and reasonable non-threatening presence. It's about making sure that his suspect is pushed to what might potentially be the breaking point. It's unlikely that Columbo expected Crawford to crack and confess, but it does demonstrate how Crawford responds when his patience is sorely tried. Would Crawford lash out and scream? Threaten to call Columbo's superiors? Instead, when Columbo declares that his car is out of gas (it isn't) and he'll have to drive Crawford's car for him, Crawford laughs and declares that he's "resigned to his fate." This tells Columbo that Crawford has a sense of humor and control over his temper. The correct approach is not to try to pressure him until he snaps, but to apply a gentler approach to study Crawford's façade for cracks.

Columbo employs a different tactic when he comes to a recording session. His presence causes a disruption, causing Crawford to snap at him, saying, "Good morning. You just ruined a perfectly good take." Crawford was more upset over the harm caused to his music than he was about being inconvenienced getting home. Coupled with Crawford sneering at Columbo's taste in music, Columbo realizes Crawford's connection to his music is his Achilles' heel. The scene where Columbo acts like he can't come up with the titles *Jaws* and *Psycho* when he hears snippets of their themes may seem a bit jarring (assuming it is a feint), as Columbo is overplaying his role a bit, but upon further consideration, it's all deliberate. How can pretending he knows less about movie music than he actually does affect Crawford? Columbo might have expected angry snapping, but instead, Crawford takes it all as a joke. This scene illustrates how Columbo has to adjust his strategy. Goading Crawford into making a mistake is unlikely to work. Crawford's control over his emotions means that he might detect a trap. Simply by presenting him with the facts, however, may lead to calm acceptance of the strength of Columbo's case, and indeed, that's the approach that ultimately brings down Crawford.

Once again, all of the Columbo killers are ultimately brought down by a critical character flaw, or a combination of character defects. Crawford's central weaknesses are sloth and pride. Either he's unwilling to put the effort into crafting his own scores, or for whatever reason, he's run out of creative energy. He must've had the talent and ability to create decent scores in the past. That's how he's made his name unless he's been plagiarizing people who can't complain the whole time. Yet now, he's not even bothering to revise his apprentice's work. Did he really believe he could exploit McEnery forever? Couldn't he have made some effort to contribute to the scores and give himself plausible deniability that he did at least some of the work? In any event, Crawford must have been so enamored with his own reputation that he was unwilling for McEnery to cast any aspersion about his abilities.

Crawford's plot had fatal flaws in it, as a simple blood test would have found the drugs in McEnery's system, and an analysis of the stomach contents would indicate that it was administered in champagne. Given that the dose would've taken effect very swiftly and there was no champagne class handy, it's an obvious giveaway that the death was staged. Bottom line, a little thought and a very basic knowledge of what autopsies can do would have told Crawford that there was no way he'd get away with the "accidental fall" narrative. Aside from missing little points about Gabe never wearing dress shoes and the sound of the elevator creaking making its way onto an audio recording, there was no need for Crawford to steal McEnery's original copy of the score. All Crawford had to do was claim that McEnery simply copied his work after it had been written or taken notes from something Crawford had played contemporaneously. It would've been his word against a dead man. It's a sloppy murder plan with awkward follow-through, and it shows that Crawford puts insufficient effort into both his scores and his crimes.

Really, if Crawford had only done what he had told McEnery he would do at the beginning, everything might have worked out well for everybody. Had Crawford essentially bought McEnery's silence by making a full-fledged push to advance McEnery's career and get him more opportunities and credit, all could have been well. Crawford could have kept his reputation as a mentor and perhaps even found another young talent to exploit. Crawford would've had to find a replacement for McEnery anyway, if he wanted to keep getting scoring jobs. Hollywood screenwriters often have people radically rework their scripts for no credit, and plenty of academics slap their names on their graduate students' articles while contributing nothing to the research. This kind of exploitation of subordinates is considered part of the game in many circles, as unethical as it may be. All Crawford had to do was say that he'd worked heavily with McEnery, and there's no way to prove he wasn't responsible for much of the work. Bottom line, murder was an option where the risks far outweighed the rewards. Crawford was a man who was willing to base his career on the work of someone else, and he couldn't even put the necessary effort into protecting himself after resorting to lethal force.

In the end, Crawford could have put up more of a fight, or at least stated that he was going to mount a defense. He could have argued that he'd dictated much of his work to McEnery, and asked him to polish his music, and McEnery must have sprinkled his own personal touches on the score. The "G-A-B-E" motif could be glossed over as a bit of vandalism by an underling trying to insert himself into something prominent. (Just think— if McEnery's parents had named him "Rollo" or "Tully" or "Jim," his killer might have walked away scot-free!) As for the baton... there's no proof when it was placed where it was, and Crawford could argue at trial that someone (perhaps Becca, who bore a grudge against him) planted the baton and wiped the dust from the controls. This version of events wouldn't have answered every question, but it only takes one credulous and stubborn juror to cause a mistrial.

Columbo has done his usual diligence, but it's not one of his strongest cases. Crawford could have struggled, but his closing lines indicate he's thrown in his hand. It's a fitting epitaph for a character who took credit for another person's work and whose own crime creation was no masterpiece. Crawford put a minimal amount of effort into his career and his murder plot, and the shoddiness showed. He didn't even put that much effort into charming or antagonizing Columbo, and as a result, the two have one of the weaker relationships in the series. Crawford was a mediocre criminal, but a good loser.

Chapter Sixty-Nine: Columbo Likes the Nightlife

Justin Price (Matthew Rhys) and Vanessa Farrow (Jennifer Sky)

The final episode of *Columbo* begins very differently in a tonal sense from the previous seasons. The font for the introductory credits is radically dissimilar from the earlier episodes. The techno party music is at odds with the traditional introductory tunes and Henry Mancini's "NBC Mystery Movie Theme." But the heart of the narrative remains the same. Justin Price and Vanessa Farrow don't start out with the intention of being murderers. They fall into homicide through a twist of fate.

Price is quietly dating Farrow, though their relationship is kept a secret due to the fact that Farrow has a contentious relationship with Tony Galper (Carmine Giovinazzo), her ex-husband, who just happens to be providing much of the funding for Price's new nightclub. When Tony comes to Farrow's house, he discovers a photograph leading him to realize her relationship with Price, leading to a physical altercation. Tony falls onto a coffee table and is killed (much like in "Death Lends a Hand" from the first season). At this point, Farrow has a strong case for self-defense. But Tony has connections to organized crime, and the mob won't be pleased with her, no matter how justified she is. When Price answers her call and arrives at the scene, he brings up a further complication. If Tony's death is announced, the funds he planned to transfer to the nightclub will be canceled, and Price's new business will fail. Tony's demise has to be kept quiet for at least thirty-six hours when the money will be safely deposited into Price's accounts.

And so, the pair clean up the crime scene, and Tony's body is disposed of in a location not disclosed to the viewer at this point. A day and a half later, all seems well until Farrow gets an unsettling call, asking, "Did you really think you were going to get away with it? Where did you put the body, Vanessa?" A tabloid photographer, Linwood Coben (Douglas Roberts) happened to be following Tony, and took pictures of the altercation. Like most *Columbo* blackmailers, Linwood signed his own death warrant. Until this point, though Price and Farrow were in a sticky situation, their actions were at least morally defensible. Now, in order to rid himself of the threat, Price decides to kill Linwood, attempting to strangle him instead of paying him. A struggle ensues, and eventually, Price shoves Linwood out the window to his death.

Columbo appears a little over twenty-two minutes into the episode. After a quick look through the crime scene (including finding a disgusting clue in an even worse place, and not washing his hands afterwards), he's pretty sure it isn't suicide. He meets Price at the club, and Price, like most killers, is initially helpful. Farrow is much more apprehensive around Columbo. The detective keeps asking questions while his suspects grow antsier, and soon Freddie (Steven R. Schirripa), an emissary from an organized crime family, informs Columbo about their concerns over the missing Tony.

By the end, the killers' nerves are badly frayed, and Columbo stopping the party at the nightclub's opening doesn't help matters. Columbo had been impressed by the koi fish swimming in tanks built into the floor, but he realized that one tank had fewer fish than the others, causing him to suspect that the tank was a bit smaller than the others. A ground-penetrating radar device reveals that Tony's body was hidden underneath that tank, proving that Tony sleeps with the fishes. The killers are silently arrested, and Columbo has successfully solved his last case.

The deaths in "Columbo Likes the Nightlife" aren't the cleverly planned "perfect" crimes of murders past. As stressed earlier, Tony's death is arguably self-defense, and Linwood's faked suicide is rather clumsily done, with little attention to detail and some heavy-handed pushing of the suicide theory by Price. Price comes across as a man who chooses a path and follows it, failing to think more than a move or two ahead. When he decides to hide the body on the club's floor, it's a convenient hiding location, which is in a place he can watch over, but not a place he can totally control. After all, fish tanks can leak, and if anything ever went wrong with the tank atop Tony's body, it's quite possible the necessary repairs would lead to the discovery of the corpse. By hiding the corpse on his own property, he's as good as signed his own confession should the remains be found, as indeed they were. Additionally, the suicide was so awkwardly done that a skilled forensic investigator was bound to find some obvious problems, which is exactly what happened. It's not made clear if Linwood really did attempt suicide a year earlier, as Price suggests, but if this isn't true, it would be an easy matter for Columbo to prove that Linwood had no medical history of self-harm. Ultimately, Price acts rashly and hopes for the best, and it's his failure to look ahead and scrutinize his plans for problems that prove to be his undoing.

Price and Columbo's relationship follows the traditional pattern. After an introduction, Price acts friendly and helpful, hoping to steer Columbo in his preferred direction. Upon Columbo's return, the detective's question "Is this a bad time?" is met with an amiable "Couldn't be worse!," though Columbo's request for "Two minutes!" is accepted graciously. Price is all smiles until the moment Columbo leaves. Later, Price sends Columbo a wacky-colored shirt as an example of stylish clubwear, and his motive in doing so is debatable. Perhaps Price can't resist a little joke, or perhaps he thinks it's a good distraction, as what murderer would think to send the investigating officer a shirt? In any case, Price can't keep up his pleasant façade, as at his next meeting with Columbo, he fails to keep all of the annoyance out of his voice when he says, "I was wondering when I'd see you again." Soon afterward, the testiness is palpable when he says, "My day wouldn't be complete without one of your little visits." As Columbo keeps peppering him with questions, Price eventually walks away, folding his head in his hands and muttering, "You really are something else, Lieutenant." He does shield himself with a strong point—as Tony was an enthusiastic investor in the club, why would Price kill him? That's a convincing argument, though Columbo's realization of what really happened punctures that defense. Price's crumbling temper is a classic case of the pressure wearing away at a suspect. In this case, it's more likely that that this is fear over getting caught than it is guilt.

Even if Price had been able to keep his anxiety and annoyance in check, he would more likely than not have been unable to escape justice, thanks to the flaws in his plan. At the end, when he threatens Columbo with a lawsuit for temporarily halting the opening night party, Columbo isn't the least bit fazed, even though he can't be completely certain that he's right. Price's last, desperate lashing out, shouting, "This is ridiculous, Columbo, even for you!" is the exclamation of a beaten man knowing the punch he throws won't hit his target, a final and pointless release by a man who realizes he's a move away from checkmate. A moment later, once Columbo has revealed the corpse under the fish tank, Price doesn't confess, and he doesn't need to, as his defeat is obvious.

Likewise, Farrow never really had the mental makeup to get away with murder. With the right legal counsel, she would have escaped prison, but it's likely that the strain of worrying about her ex-husband's criminal associates seeking vengeance would have drained any joy from her freedom. It's possible that a marriage to a violent and controlling man left lasting psychological scars on Farrow. If Price wanted to protect her, she could potentially walk if her lawyers, with Price's help, argued that she was unaware of Price's role in Linwood's death. Still, it wouldn't guarantee her safety from the forces of organized crime, especially since she was unlikely to have enough information to enter the Witness Protection Program, as she never attempted to use any knowledge she might have as a weapon against her ex-husband.

In any case, having to go into hiding would destroy Farrow's dreams of acting stardom. At the risk of sounding uncharitable, her lack of control over her reactions towards Columbo illustrates that her acting skills aren't that strong. In their first meeting, she mistakes him for a salesman, and when she realizes he's a policeman (Columbo eventually shows his badge, saying, "Sometimes I'm a little slow with this thing"), her anxiety is obvious. She practically freaks out when Columbo realizes she just got a new coffee table due to the indentations on the carpet. Later, her stress is even stronger when Columbo "runs into" her at a clothing store and tells her that her ex is missing. When she admits she doesn't have an alibi for the night of Linwood's death, it's further proof of how poorly Price planned the murder. Price could have handled everything himself and told her to spend the night with friends. By the end, Farrow's a nervous wreck, desperate to see Price for comfort even though self-preservation would require them to stay apart.

Price and Farrow were less skillful at handling the pressure of an investigation than most of the series' murderers. Price was short-sighted, planning shallowly and thinking only of achieving his immediate goals. Farrow was too flustered and frightened to handle herself properly under questioning. A clumsy murder plan, coupled with anxious suspects, made their defeat nearly inevitable. Indeed, a viewer would be justified in thinking that a detective far less skillful than Columbo could have caught the pair. While there are many entertaining portions of this episode, fans could wish that Columbo's final case had him battling a killer far worthier of his steel.

CONCLUSION

Creating a Better Killer

I wanted to write a book about murderers. Fictional murderers, not real ones. Part of this stemmed from reading hundreds of recent crime novels during the pandemic and being disappointed by nearly all of the villains of the stories. I was a judge for a mystery novel contest, and in a dishearteningly large percentage of the books, the characterizations of the killers were simplistic, one-dimensional, and just plain lazy.

In these poorly written mysteries, the killer was often just plain evil or insane, or was simply the embodiment of political opinions the author didn't like, or was a complete non-entity, a bland and forgettable charisma vacuum who appeared in maybe eight pages of the book, had no distinctive characteristics, and had zero memorable scenes with the detective. There was no discernible character arc, and often the primary motivation for becoming a killer was simply being a bad person. Worse still was the frequent appearance of Sudden Onset Murderous Psychopath Syndrome, where a previously milquetoast character turned on a dime into a monster with an unquenchable blood lust.

In at least twenty of the novels I read over the course of just three months, the climax of the book went something like this. Twenty pages from the end of the novel, the writer seemed to decide that the book was long enough and needed to be wrapped up immediately, and they'd choose to make the killer the seemingly harmless character who the protagonist had never bothered to suspect. Almost every climactic scene read something like this:

Sheriff Bob thanked Joe for his help. Joe sure was a great guy. You could totally trust good old Joe.

"Well, I'm going to keep looking for the missing suspect, Joe. Thanks for all your help."

"No problem, Bob. Have a good night," Joe said in a totally non-suspicious manner.

As Bob walked back to his car, he chuckled to himself. Joe was the nicest guy in the world. Suddenly, he remembered he'd forgotten to tell Joe about the potluck at the town hall on Friday. He doubled back inside, but Joe was nowhere to be found. To his surprise, Bob heard the sound of a chainsaw from the basement, and forgetting that he'd left his gun in the glove compartment of his car, he hurried down the stairs, and to his shock, he saw Joe holding a chainsaw, spattered with gore, and standing above the remains of the missing suspect. Joe looked up with an expression Bob had never seen before.

"You shouldn't have come back in the house, Bob..."

And then there'd be a scuffle, and Bad Joe would wind up dead or at least arrested. The above passage is a parody, but it's based on an awful lot of poor writing. Too many authors take no time to figure out what makes a killer commit the crimes he does. They simply paint the character as a madman, or assume that holding certain political opinions or religious beliefs rots someone's soul. After plowing through scores of these novels, I realized that someone needed to write a guide not just showing people how to create a nuanced, unique antagonist, but also how to build that character's connection to the hero of the story.

After a bit of thought, I realized that I didn't want to write a book about great murderers in detective fiction only to fill the book with spoiler warnings. And then it came to me. Write about the one major franchise where the identity of the murderer isn't a spoiler (most of the time): *Columbo*.

So that's why I decided to write this book. I wanted to explore examples of strong characterization, interaction between antagonists, and study the many roads that characters could take on their journey to villainy. I hope that this book has a positive impact on both creators and consumers of culture.

There are several points that writers need to remember when crafting fictional murderers. These are some of the lessons that *Columbo* teaches about crafting quality villains.

1) Every murderer must have more than a motive. A catalyst is necessary.

It's a well-established maxim that you can't have murder without a motive. But there are far more motives than murders. Nearly everybody needs or wants more money, but only a fraction of the population steals to get richer, and even fewer individuals kill to increase their incomes. What makes those people kill? Is it something inherently broken in their characters? Is it possible that they were pushed beyond their limits?

On *Columbo*, most of the killers act because *they believe they have planned the perfect murder*. First, they believe that they are intelligent and creative enough to come up with an unassailable plan. Second, given the opportunity to kill, they have no moral compunction holding them back when they are convinced they can get away with it. Third, they lack the analytical ability to foresee how another person could find and explore the flaws in their plans, leading to conclusive evidence proving their guilt. It's a case of tunnel vision, as they grow so enamored with their plans that they can't conceive of them not working. And when they realize that their deadly creation is inherently flawed, it's a blow to both their ego and their sense of self-preservation. *Columbo* villains, therefore, must have a considerable amount of self-confidence, even arrogance, to believe that the law cannot touch them.

When crafting a cold-blooded murderer (those who kill on impulse or by accident are different), one must ask: what sort of person would take advantage of a perceived opportunity to get away with homicide? Once a writer has the answer to that question, they have the core of their villain's psyche.

2) The perpetrator must behave in a psychologically consistent manner.

Some *Columbo* killers expect to be suspected and revel in the anticipated questioning, and delight in their supposed revelations of their innocence. Often, there's a lack of foresight. The killers believe that revealing the evidence they believe will clear them is the final chapter. They never expect that it's only the end of Act One and that they didn't write all of the following scenes themselves.

In a *Columbo*-style-inverted mystery, the viewer knows exactly who the killer is (most of the time). But in a traditional whodunit, the reader should be guessing up through the very end. How does the killer disguise guilt? Do the murderer's nerves fray a bit? Can the killer remain calm? When I say "a psychologically consistent manner," I do not mean that the killer must respond in the same way throughout the mystery. If the murderer is calm and pleasant, then what is going on in that person's head to ensure that tranquility? If the killer loses his or her temper, then what causes that rupture? *Columbo* is full of instances where the detective finds the little pressure points that crack the veneer, whether it's messiness, persistence, personal questions, or just asking "one more thing," wearing down patience to see what happens when the mask slips. Clues are essential to a great whodunit, but some of the best clues are psychological. The fictional murderer is a battle of wits, and the prize is freedom. What will that character do to escape capture? Every individual behaves differently, so it's imperative for the killer to decide just what steps to take.

3) Very few murderers are completely evil.

All too often in crime fiction today, the killer is a one-dimensional psychopath. But as Columbo notes, "there's a little niceness in everybody." Mad monsters are not nearly as compelling—or unsettling—as essentially ordinary people who just crossed the line most people would never dare to approach. The line between "basically good person" and murderer often comes down to a single, deadly choice, one from which there's no turning back. A clumsy writer fills a villain with every repulsive trait imaginable. Skilled writers never forget the humanity of their antagonists, because unless one's writing dabbles in the supernatural, they're all just human beings, exercising their free will. Becoming a murderer is a choice, and when crafting a fictional killer, the writer must explore what leads to the wrong choice. And that leads to the closely related next point...

4) Weak villains embody the characteristics their creators hate. Strong villains feature characteristics audience members wish they had.

I have lost count of all of the terrible books, television episodes, and movies where the villain is nothing more than a walking amalgam of political opinions, religious beliefs, or attitudes loathed by the writer. How many police procedurals have been switched off at the fifteen-minute mark because it's clear to even the most disinterested viewer that the character who is clearly a reference to a controversial real-life figure is the villain? There's a huge difference between a symbol and a fully-formed human being.

While the *Columbo* villains have many points of similarity, they almost all begin their character arcs from a place of perceived strength. They've killed, and they believe themselves to be untouchable. Most of these characters live the lives that the viewers wish they had—rich, successful, comfortable. Yet they want more, something that they think will make their lives complete, and they're willing to kill to get it, and they believe they can take a life to get it. But pride comes before destruction and a haughty spirit before a fall, and most audiences love seeing a disliked figure being humbled. There's precious little satisfaction in seeing the downfall of someone the audience has always viewed with derision. Strong villains often have impressive characteristics. In many cases, if they'd only had a strong conscience, they might have been the hero of the story.

5) Characters are only as strong as their relationships with other characters.

Yes, there's an element of exaggeration to this statement, but aside from the plotting, the best moments on *Columbo* happen when Peter Falk has great chemistry with that episode's villain. Columbo begins each case as an underdog, but he triumphs through insight and tenacity. Just what sort of detective does it take to catch a certain type of villain? In almost every case, murderers have to hide their guilt from those around them. How does that affect their everyday interactions? How do they take on the persona of an innocent person? How well do they handle the pressure of questioning? What lies do they tell to hide their guilt? What mistakes might they make in their cover-ups? In *Columbo,* most villains only have a set amount of patience in their dealings with the lieutenant. Once it's gone, they start to snap. How should the villain handle the battle of wits? How can strain and deception be presented in a way that isn't immediately obvious? There are infinite ways for a fictional murderer to interact with innocent people and the detective. How do people who are aware of their guilt respond to people who don't know that fact? When the writer knows how the killer acts around other people, the writer then has the structure for the murderer's character arc.

Of course, there is no reason why writers absolutely have to follow these rules. Many real-life crimes are totally unpremeditated, practically random events. Plenty of actual criminals have personalities that are like stale toast. But these are some of the lessons that *Columbo* teaches about characterization, and their lessons of connecting the antagonist to the protagonist have applications far beyond the mystery genre. These are steps to creating great characters and strong character relationships. I would encourage all aspiring writers who wish to create strong antagonists to watch *Columbo* episodes and take note of what interactions and reactions interest them most strongly. I also hope that this book encourages viewers to use their entertainment as more than just a passive experience, allowing them to analyze and understand rather than merely consume.

And just one more thing...
This book is meant as an enthusiastic fan tribute to Peter Falk, Richard

Levinson, William Link, and all the other actors, writers, and directors who made the show possible. This critical analysis will hopefully enrich other fans' understanding of their work.

–*Chris Chan*

Acknowledgements

Special thanks to the Dames of Detection: Verena Rose, Harriette Sackler, and Shawn Reilly Simmons of Level Best Books for their belief in this book. As always, none of this would be possible without my parents Drs. Carlyle and Patricia Chan.

About the Author

Chris Chan is a writer, educator and historian. He works as a researcher and "International Goodwill Ambassador" for Agatha Christie Ltd. His true crime articles, reviews, and short fiction have appeared in *The Strand, The Wisconsin Magazine of History, Mystery Weekly, Gilbert!,* Nerd HQ, Akashic Books' *Mondays are Murder* webseries, *The Baker Street Journal, The MX Book of New Sherlock Holmes Stories, Masthead: The Best New England Crime Stories, Sherlock Holmes Mystery Magazine,* and multiple Belanger Books anthologies. He is the creator of the Funderburke and Kaiming mysteries, a series featuring private investigators who work for a school and help students during times of crisis. Funderburke and Kaiming are featured in the novels *Ghosting My Friend* and *She Ruined Our Lives.* The Funderburke short story "The Six-Year- Old Serial Killer" was nominated for a Derringer Award. His first book, *Sherlock & Irene: The Secret Truth Behind "A Scandal in Bohemia,"* was published in 2020 by MX Publishing, and he is also the author of the comedic novels *Sherlock's Secretary* and *Nessie's Nemesis,* and the anthology *Of Course He Pushed Him and other Sherlock Holmes Stories.* His book *Murder Most Grotesque: The Comedic Crime Fiction of Joyce Porter* (Level Best Books) was nominated for the 2022 Agatha Award for Best Non-Fiction.

SOCIAL MEDIA HANDLES:
Twitter: @GKCfan
Facebook: https://www.facebook.com/chrischanauthorpage

Instagram: https://www.instagram.com/chan3589/

AUTHOR WEBSITE:

Blog: https://chrischancrimeandcriticism.blogspot.com

Also by Chris Chan

Non-fiction literary criticism:

Sherlock & Irene: The Secret Truth Behind "A Scandal in Bohemia" (2020, MX Publishing)

Murder Most Grotesque: The Comedic Crime Fiction of Joyce Porter (2021, Level Best Books)

The Autistic Sleuth: Screen Portrayals of Detectives on the Spectrum in Sherlock Holmes Adaptations, The Millennium Trilogy, The Bridge, Death Note, The Curious Incident of the Dog in the Night-Time, and Other Productions (2024, MX Publishing)

Novels:

Sherlock's Secretary (2021, MX Publishing)

Ghosting My Friend (2023, Level Best Books)

Nessie's Nemesis (2023, MX Publishing)

She Ruined Our Lives (2024, Level Best Books)

Short Story Collections:

Of Course He Pushed Him (2022, MX Publishing)